PORKIES

John Henry Bennett

PORKIES is the second book in the trilogy comprising PIGS, PORKIES, and LIES DAMN LIES

Cambridge Dictionary
Porkies; Noun.UK. (Also Pork Pies). UK humorous slang: Lies.

Secret Intelligence Service SIS (MI6).
Collects Britain's foreign intelligence and provides a global covert capability to protect and defend national security of the UK.

Security Service (MI5)
Britain's intelligence agency protecting the UK's national security against threats such as terrorism and espionage.

DGSE (Direction Générale de la Sécurité Extérieure)
French Government equivalent of MI6

CIA (Central Intelligence Agency)
United States Government equivalent of MI6

Mossad (Institute for Intelligence and Special Operations) Israel's National Intelligence Agency

---

International Time:
Time of the day is always local time. Readers should remember that Europe and Gulf countries can be 1, 2, 3 or 4 hours ahead of the UK.

Previous book in the trilogy:
PIGS by John Henry Bennett

Personae

SIS (MI6) Deputy Director - Norman Spencer; looking forward to his retirement in a few years.

Harry Baxter - Middle rank SIS operative, ex-Intelligence Corps, Army, divorced, years of Gulf and Middle East experience.

Tom Denman - colleague of Harry, one level down.

Anna Harrison [Anne Hardy] - Mossad agent

Saif - A physicist.

Tahir - A water engineer in London.

Tariq Hashmi - Owner with Atif Masood of a London engineering company.

Atif Masood - The other related owner of the London engineering company.

Philippe Roberge - London Head of DGSE (*Direction Générale de la Sécurité Extérieure*)

Alain Dubois - DGSE operative Europe and the Gulf.

Jack DeCosta - CIA, Head of Station, London

Sir James Bollington - UK High Commissioner Islamabad Pakistan
Charles Urwin - First Secretary UK High Commission, Islamabad Pakistan

Zahira Urwin - Pakistani wife of Charles Urwin

Nadeem Kirmani - Father of Zahira. Very successful international businessman and Pakistan Government Minister in two separate administrations.
Kamran Kirmani - elder brother of Zahira
Azmat Kirmani - younger brother of Zahira

James Readman - New Director General SIS (MI6)

Gilles Deniaud - DGSE Section Head of Alain Dubois

Jeremy Hollingworth - Third Secretary UK High Commission Islamabad Pakistan
Marion Simpson - Secretariat High Commission

Inspector Irfan Chaudry-FIA (Federal Investigation Agency) Islamabad Pakistan

Frank Stansfield - Previous SIS colleague of the Deputy

Georges Gagnier - Mossad Lebanon, embedded in AFD

Jonathan Peters - UK Ambassador to Lebanon

Major Mike Thompson RA - Military Attaché, British Embassy Damascus Syria

Stepan Volkov - FSB (Russian Secret Service), Head of Station, Islamabad.

Omar Najjar - Syrian member of Jihad Committee.

Eran Lang - Mossad Head of Station Paris

Nabil Selmi - Algerian Paris
Salim Matoub - Algerian Paris

Amri Behar - Algerian London

Deputy Director General Aatif Durrani - ISI (Inter-Services Intelligence) Pakistan
Director Tariq Kassar - FIA (Federal Investigation Agency) Pakistan

Quentin Horncastle – Foreign Office

****

PROLOGUE

Houses of Parliament Westminster London

At 3.00pm, Tuesday 14th March 2006, the Speaker called for the Prime Minister.
He stood up to a packed and muted House.
He cleared his throat, delaying his start for maximum theatrical effect.
'Yesterday, a great many of you will have seen, and heard in the media, details of the thwarted attack on Sunday on this House, which, if it had been successful, would have resulted in a major loss of life, both of the public and of members of this Chamber.
Let me pay tribute to the members of the Security Services who have prevented a major terrorist assault on the heart of British democracy.
After months of observation and liaison work with our overseas partners the terrorist's plan was determined, and the network infiltrated.
An attempt was made to penetrate the Palace of Westminster in broad daylight, and thankfully, due to the quick-witted, trained response by CO19 of the Metropolitan Police, a major tragedy has been avoided. Regretfully, the vehicle exploded when hit, preventing us bringing the perpetrators to trial.
At the same time two pedestrians were slightly injured, but I can report they are recovering well, and their injuries are not described as serious.
I ask this House to bear such facts in mind when considering the very necessary extensions to the current Terrorism Bill before Parliament, which I am sure will enable us to combat, more effectively, the very real threats that face us today.'

A general murmur of approval ran round the House as the Prime Minister sat down, as the Leader of Her Majesty's Opposition rose to concur with the tribute and the proposal.
Below London, at a depth between 10 -15 feet, the self-propelled pig travelled slowly and silently along the pipe at about 50 yards per hour. It had been calculated that it should arrive close to the Houses of Parliament at about 1515hrs.

--

London Evening Standard Office
A Press Release, contained in a sealed envelope, sat on a junior editor's desk at the London Evening Standard.
The envelope had a large label on the front stating; **'Not to be opened until 1530hrs Tuesday the 14th March 2006'**.

The 'dirty' bomb would cause considerable damage both physical, and by contamination. Public fear would be contagious.
Inside the slowly moving pig the timing device glowed in the dark.

0 hours, 12 minutes, 59…58…57…56…55secs…

I

Sunday, 12th March – Tuesday 14th March 2006

Two days earlier, Sunday 12th March 2006
1745hrs Factory Hounslow West London
The car pulled up quietly in front of the factory and the driver and passenger walked quickly inside. Saif, the physicist, and Tahir, the water engineer, were greeted nervously by Atif and Tariq as they entered the small office.
Tariq spoke first, 'Well, did you get it done?'
'Yes', Tahir replied, looking to Saif for support and corroboration.
'It went well, my brothers, exactly as planned,' said Saif.
As he finished speaking the office door was smashed open, and two balaclava wearing SO19 specialists entered with weapons at their shoulders, shouting instructions for everybody to get down on the floor.
Paralyzed initially by the onslaught, they froze, before being pushed roughly to the ground, with both barrels being pointed at them.
A third SO19 officer entered, handcuffing each in turn, before lifting them up and shepherding them quickly outside to a black windowless van, the rear doors of which were open.
They were quickly bundled in, accompanied by the SO19 officer, the doors shut, and driven away, followed by a smaller van carrying the other two SO19 officers.
Inside the van the four men looked at each other bleakly before Atif, speaking in Urdu, said,

'We know nothing. Deny everything.'

'Shut up. No talking,' shouted the officer.

Atif had said enough for now.

Following the abduction of Tom Denman, Harry had decided to increase surveillance, and also to have a unit of SO19 on standby.

Now that the two Pakistanis had returned to the factory for a meeting with Tariq and Atif, the senior SO19 officer had decided to pull them all in. Nothing substantive, but reasonable suspicion, under the circumstances, would do.

They were taken to a Police Holding Centre near Heathrow Airport, where they were then placed in a single cell, given food and drink, and told they would be questioned shortly. They exchanged a few words, quietly in Urdu, but were mostly quiet.

Not one of the four had responded in any way, and were following Atif's instruction to the letter!

1930hrs Room C10 SIS (MI6) London

Harry was drafting and redrafting the outline of his report when his telephone rang.

It was SO19 advising of the arrest of the four Pakistanis, now currently being held near Heathrow.

Harry thanked the officer, and immediately arranged, internally, for the pickup and delivery of them to the safe house in West Square.

He was hoping, that if they were essentially second string within their operation, it would be relatively quick and easy to break their resistance, and determine what had been done and where.

As he was wondering which particular line to take when questioning, his telephone rang again.

It was the Deputy, calling on a secure line from his weekend home.

‘What the hell is going on Harry? I’ve just seen the evening news on TV, and they are reporting a car exploding on Westminster Bridge very early this morning. Is this in any way connected with your op?’

‘Yes it is. I’m just putting my report together, as we speak, to brief you in the morning.’

‘Harry, it better be a damn good briefing, because I can think of one Minister who will want to have both our sets of ‘cojones’ if it isn’t! See me at 0830hrs.’

‘This is going to be a long balls aching night,’ Harry thought to himself, as he completed his list of bullet points for his brief tomorrow.

There was going to be a lot of verbal reinforcement to the briefing which would not appear in the official report. He hoped the Deputy would agree.

He added a few more items to his list, perhaps to be included tomorrow, perhaps not. He would review later after questioning the four at the safe house in West Square.

He grabbed a sandwich in the internal cafeteria which he was certain had been made on Friday, plus a mug of dubious coffee which he drank. Caffeine would be very necessary tonight.

2115hrs SIS (MI6) Safe House West Square London

Harry entered the house and enquired how the four had been split up.

The Duty Officer had put Saif, the physicist, with Atif, in one room and Tahir, from the water company, with Tariq, in another.

From the intercepted phone calls and listening devices, identities and functions had been identified, so the pairing was a good mix, initially.

Harry arranged for Tariq to be put in one 'interview' room alone.
After about half an hour of solitude, Harry entered.
Tariq looked up nervously.
'Tariq Hasmi?'
Tariq said nothing.
'Tariq Hasmi?' This time louder.
Harry smashed his fist down onto the table. Tariq jumped.
'I know your name is Tariq Hasmi, so your lack of response doesn't bother me. I am going to be telling you what we know about you, what you are up to, and the very long prison sentence that you will get after your trial.
You are the owner of the factory in Hounslow and you have been under surveillance for a long time. Your telephone discussions have been recorded and your conversations in your office listened to and recorded. Do you understand what I am saying?'
Tariq nodded.
'You are married, with a family, and I think you want to retire to Pakistan.
At the moment, absolutely no chance whatsoever. If you cooperate, then there might be a chance after a number of years. Without cooperation then you will probably die in jail.
Do you understand?'
Tariq nodded again, his head bowed, sunk into his shoulders.
'Right. We know there was to be an explosive device positioned in a sewer, somewhere in London. Where?'
'Tariq spoke falteringly, 'I don't know, I just provided space at my factory.'

'Well, that alone will earn you at least a 12 to14 year sentence. I suggest you start thinking very carefully about your replies to my questions.
Remember this. If you cooperate I can provide some level of protection against your colleagues. If not, then I can tell them 'everything' you have told me. I am quite sure they would then want to question you very thoroughly, given the chance!'
Harry could see Tariq turning pale. He got up from the table and turned to go.
'Think about what I have said. We will talk again.'
Tariq was left to think.
Harry moved down the corridor to another interview room, this one housing Tahir from the water company.
Tahir jumped to his feet as Harry entered, trying to put on an indignant face.
Harry looked at him without expression, staring him out until Tahir dropped his gaze.
'Sit down Tahir Hosni.'
Tahir sat down quickly.
'I've just had a short conversation with Tariq Hashmi, the owner of the factory where the bomb was made.'
Tahir looked very surprised.
'Yes, we know what has been going on. Our surveillance has had the place and all of you, well covered and documented, these last few weeks, Discussions, telephone taps, all the usual, and for you personally, in the fairly near future a very long jail sentence.'
'We know you've planted a bomb in a London sewer. Where?'
'Don't know anything about that. What are you talking about?

'Ah, the innocent one. I'm sure the others will be interested to hear how cooperative you've been. I wonder if they will extend brotherly love to you when they hear what you've told us! I suggest you think about cooperation.'

Harry rose quickly and left before Tahir could comment.

He told the duty officer to place all four in separate cells and to keep lights on throughout the night to disrupt their sleep.

After Saif, the physicist, and Atif had been placed in separate cells, he visited them. Atif first.

Atif was nervous but aggressive.

'Why have I been arrested? Why am I here? I want to see a lawyer immediately! I know my rights!'

Harry said nothing for a few seconds and then spoke, hardly more than a whisper.

'Atif Masood, you are a member of a group that has made and planted a bomb designed to kill and murder innocent people. Don't talk to me about your fucking rights. You are in a sound proof location where I could, if I wanted to, kick the shit out of you all night long, and nobody would be the wiser.

But I don't need to do that, because when I tell your brothers what you have told me, they will do it for me the next time you all meet!'

Atif sat, looking sullenly at Harry in a defensive posture, but well aware that what he was saying was probably true.

Harry spoke again.

'I hope, that when your case comes to trial, they put you away for a very, very long time, and, assuming you are released, eventually, they kick your arse straight back to Pakistan. Take your bloody Jihad somewhere else.'

With that Harry left Atif to his thoughts, and no doubt personal concerns.

His last stop was the cell holding Saif Jarwar.

Saif was sitting nervously on the chair as Harry entered.

He rose as Harry crossed the room and slapped him hard across the face.

'Self-defence is what will go in my report. I was attacked by Saif Jarwar as I started to question him about the bomb he had made and planted.

His plan was an unprovoked attack on innocent civilians designed to kill, maim or severely injure anybody in the bomb blast area.'

Saif cringed on his chair, holding his already reddening cheek.

Harry put his face very close to Saif and repeated, very quietly, what he had said to Atif, merely modifying it to assure Saif that he would never leave prison for such a crime, and would therefore in all probability die in jail.

He assured Atif that questioning and 'thorough' interrogation would start the next day, so have some answers ready.

Harry turned and left quickly, repeating his instruction to the duty officer and his team to make the quartet's night as uncomfortable as possible. Noise and light treatment to be carried out.

He returned to Vauxhall Cross to continue with his report that he would discuss with the Deputy in the morning. He had a change of clothes at the office, plus his futon for nights like this. Christ, it was going to be a hell of a week, that's for sure!

--

Monday 13th March 2006

0900hrs Deputy's Office SIS (MI6) London

Harry knocked and entered.

The Deputy looked up and gestured Harry to a chair.

'Before we start Harry, you should be aware that I have been given the Police reports covering the incident on Westminster Bridge early on Sunday morning that I believe you were involved in.'

Harry nodded and the Deputy continued.

'Additionally, SO19 have confirmed the arrest of four suspects, their initial standby instruction coming from you. The four suspects were then handed over to us, and I would assume they are in one of our safe establishments?'

Harry nodded, 'Yes, West Square, I saw them all briefly last night.'

'I want a thorough briefing Harry, for a variety of reasons, so wind the clock back a little and fill me in, in some detail. I'm sure the Minister will want that at some point,' he said grimly.

Harry then explained what had happened during the previous week, including the arrest of Fayez and the abduction of Tom Denman.

He skated lightly over the contact and cooperation of Alain Dubois of DGSE (*Direction Générale de la Sécurité Extérieure)*, not avoiding it, but being somewhat economical with the detail.

The Deputy listened intently as Harry brought his verbal report up to the Sunday morning and the exchange of Fayez for Tom.

He interrupted when Harry explained that Ahmed Al-Marri had demanded his Volvo instead of using his Toyota.

'Did you have any idea he was going to do this?'

'None at all. I thought he would bundle Fayez into his Toyota and just clear off.'
'So he then drove off in your Volvo, with Fayez in the back, down Whitehall to the traffic lights, turned left onto Westminster Bridge and then the car exploded?'
'Yes.'
'How the hell did that happen Harry?'
Harry was silent for a few seconds.
When he replied he spoke slowly.
'I have reported directly to you now for a number of years, and you know that I have always told you 'as it is', with no prevarication, or half-truths.
I don't want to lie to you on this occasion, so am going to refuse to answer that question.
There is no conjecture in my report, purely a statement which includes the explosion.
I believe my report covers all the main points necessary for any subsequent investigation, but if you want an official response from me, which can only be verbal, and which therefore cannot be confirmed, I would say the following
My assumption must be that explosives were being carried by Ahmed and that, somehow, they were detonated.'
The Deputy frowned and said, 'But we know that's probably BS Harry.'
'Your opinion, but that is my response.'
'Harry, listen to me, very carefully.
The Minister and others will want answers and a credible story for the press and media.
If this is your position and response I am suspending you immediately for an initial period of four weeks. I have no other choice. Do you understand?'
Harry nodded.

The Deputy continued, 'I am delighted that Tom was retrieved safely, and personally don't give a damn if a few Jihadists lose their lives, but, and it's a big but, you know what our press are like, let alone Ministers, in wanting to get the real story!'

Harry interjected, 'I can understand your reaction, but if I am suspended let it be effective 48hrs from now. I've got to get the location of the bomb out of our detainees. I'm sure they'll cough by tonight.'

The Deputy paused.

'Right, suspension starts 0900hrs, Wednesday morning.

One further thing Harry. I suggest you take some leave and get abroad and find some sun. Your last vacation was disrupted in December so you have a valid reason. It would make life somewhat easier for both of us if there is a post op investigation.'

'Yes, I agree obviously. I appreciate your action. I'll get on with the questioning if that's all?'

'For the time being Harry. As one politician previously said 'A week in politics is a long time!' Don't forget. 0900hrs Wednesday. I don't want you in the building.'

Harry left, grateful that no questioning had arisen concerning DGSE. He knew they would deny any involvement if the matter was raised.

He went back to his office, Room C10, to telephone Tom to see how he was, and was surprised to find him waiting in Room C10.

'What are you doing in? I thought you'd have a few days off to recover?'

'I thought you might be a bit thin on the ground, plus I can assist in the interrogation of the detainees, which Jane has just briefed me on.'

'Why not?'

Harry then debriefed Tom on his abduction and treatment, and then updated him on his meeting with the Deputy, carefully omitting the questions of the car explosion, and his suspension starting the following day.
At about 1130hrs they left to go to the safe house.

1200hrs.Safe House. West Square, London SE.
Harry and Tom discussed with the Duty Officer what had happened overnight.
The routine had been the same, sleep deprivation, lights on/off, repeatedly linked with noise. He advised them that the four were all in a very exhausted and nervous state, only basic food and water had been provided.
It was agreed that Tom would interrogate Tahir, the water engineer and Tariq the owner of the factory, whilst Harry would handle Saif the physicist and Atif the nephew of Tariq.
After initial 'interviews' Tom and Harry would compare findings and exchange pairs, working on a 'bad cop/good cop' scenario.
Threatening interrogation followed by considerate conversation can often be very effective particularly when the subject is very tired, emotionally distraught, and looking at long jail sentences.
The interrogation by Harry and Tom was spread over the next eight hours, hot and cold in delivery, wearing down the detainees until one was bound to crack.
Each of the four was questioned alternately by Harry and Tom, interspersed with periods of isolation for nervous reflection, continued light deprivation, limited amount of food and water, the

atmosphere laced with threats and cajoling to save their respective skins.

Tariq, the factory owner, was the first to crack.

His reasoning was simple. If he cooperated then he might be let off, or only receive a short jail term, after which he could retire to Pakistan.

He was no idealist like his nephew; his interest was money pure and simple. Let the Jihadists do their thing; no concern of his.

Tariq was closely followed by Tahir, the water engineer.

An almost identical profile, money being the driver. If he had been successful then it would enhance his reputation, and therefore increase his monetary returns in the future.

However in both their cases, self-preservation, to the exclusion of others, kicked in.

Harry and Tom now knew how the bomb had been planted, but where it was on its' journey they had no idea. Neither were they aware of its 'dirty' content.

Saif, the physicist, had been careful, even though worn down and exhausted, to omit this detail when questioned.

By 2100hrs, Harry and Tom had enough to base their assumptions on a general area where the bomb might be.

They alerted staff back at Vauxhall Cross to put together appropriate recovery teams, manned by engineers trained in the recovery and defusing of most types of terrorist bombs.

Purely, as a matter of course, the teams were fitted with nuclear, biological and chemical protection suits, this being standard drill, not from any particular Intel.

Precise knowledge of the timing and detonation devices was sketchy to say the least. Saif was reluctant, even under severe physical and psychological pressure, to divulge this information. In fact, under pressure from Fayez, he had lied about his capability in this area, doing this to safeguard his payments, nothing else.
Harry explained to Tom that it would not be possible to get the teams in place before the morning, and even after that it would still be like looking for a fish in a river.
They both stood down leaving the Duty officer to maintain detention status and an unfriendly environment.

Tuesday 14th March 2006

1030hrs SIS (MI6) Vauxhall Cross London
The Deputy put down his telephone with a slight smile playing across his lips.
From a non-attributable source he had been advised that the Minister was resigning with effect from today, and would be replaced by a 'younger' face.
The source had told him that the PM was having a reshuffle, clearing out some of the old guard, and bringing in some of the 'new boys' who would be both grateful, and certainly more pliant.
The PM did not have to rely so heavily on former 'comrades' now, the cull was swift, with no argument or discussion.
Harry was sitting in his office C10 re-writing his report for the Deputy when the phone rang.
It was the Deputy calling Harry to his office immediately.

Harry went up a floor and entered the Deputy's office.

'Some potentially good news Harry', he said, before proceeding to give him the content of his recent telephone discussion.

'As the new boy is taking over from tomorrow that will no doubt ease the pressure on any investigation concerning your car incident. There is no way he will want to get embroiled in that sort of detail on day one!

I am currently writing a few lines that will be passed through the Home Office Permanent Secretary to the PM who can use them at PMQ this afternoon. That should ensure that a number of backsides will be covered, including yours!

Notwithstanding the change in our political master, your current suspension still stands, and I want you out of here tomorrow as we agreed.

Any questions as to your whereabouts will be covered by 'Following up on certain lines of enquiry and Intel verification'.

Now, any positive leads as to where this bomb is located?'

'All we know, after interrogation, is that it was placed in a London West End sewer on a self-propelled pig. The sewer, we think, is too small to get a man down, so we are having to try and read the line from water company maps and several access points.

We have the crews checking with radiography equipment but it's a very slow job. God knows how long it will take.'

'Can we put any more pressure on our detainees, within reason, to put the fear of God up them?

You're away tomorrow, but Tom could take the lead in your absence.'

‘Leave that with me, I’ll discuss with Tom, and see if we can give these beggars some low grade grief.’

Harry left the Deputy, putting his re-drafting to one side and made his way to the safe house in West Square.

Tom was there having been continuing a line of interrogation on all four detainees, with some new responses and indications of cooperation, specifically from Tariq.

What had been uncovered, on the promise of a more favourable judgement by turning partial Queen’s Evidence, was that there was a ‘dirty’ component in the bomb. This Tariq had overheard, although possessing no real technical understanding, so he said.

He had also heard that it was designed to strike ‘at the heart of British democracy’, and assumed this meant the House of Commons.

Harry contacted the engineer teams and advised them to review all sewers leading to, around, and from the House. Timing was completely unknown as yet.

Harry then decided to give Saif the physicist one last chance.

He entered the detention cell and spoke slowly and carefully.

‘You have one last chance to give me the timing and passage of this bomb; otherwise I personally will give you a thorough work-over.

Innocent people will die unless we can stop it, and if I have to break one of your arms to get the truth, I will.

Alternatively, I will have one of our medics’ give you an injection which will make you tell us all we want.

Lastly, and understand this. You can disappear. No one will know where you've gone. There will be no official acknowledgement that you were in custody. You will just have disappeared off the face of the earth.
Now which option would you like?'

Saif was, by now, completely exhausted, drained physically and mentally, hovering in that surreal state where dreaming and actuality overlap.

He was not trained for this, and had reached the end of his resistance.

He looked with blank and vacant eyes at Harry and muttered something.

'What was that?' Harry shouted, causing Saif to wince.

'It will be in the sewer down Whitehall to the Parliament.'

'Yes, and what about the timing, you bastard?' Harry shouted, smashing his fist onto the table again.

'About three o'clock Tuesday' he replied, just above a whisper.

'You mean today?'

'If it's Tuesday today, yes.'

Harry left the room, meeting up with Tom and giving him the update as he called the engineer teams.

He advised them as to projected time and also the possibility of a 'dirty' element which would require careful handling.

As he finished his phone call Harry glanced at his watch. It was just before midday.

Calling the Deputy he requested Red Alert 1 in Whitehall. Clear the area, divert traffic, in fact lockdown. Public reason to be issued advising

accidental chemical contamination in one of the main sewers. Hence clearance and diversion.
The Deputy immediately called the Police Commissioner on the Crisis line ensuring immediate lockdown. He then called Harry to advise that the PM would be making a statement at PMQ that afternoon.

--

At 1500hrs the PM rose to his feet after being called by the Speaker.

--

Harry, at the same time, had crossed the river from Vauxhall Cross, and was on Millbank, between Lambeth and Westminster Bridges, when he received a call on his mobile.
It was one of the engineer teams, who had picked up with scanners and other equipment, an object in the sewer running down Whitehall, which was currently located roughly level with Whitehall Place, itself about one third of the way down Whitehall.
Additionally the object was not, repeat not, moving at all. Also, there did not appear to be any radio signals emanating from the device. The team was trying to get access as close as they could, and would be checking for any radioactivity as a matter of course.
Harry made his way across Parliament Square and entered Whitehall, now cordoned off, towards Whitehall Place, where he could see the engineer team had their vans and equipment.
In about fifteen minutes the whole Whitehall area had been secured, any questions from curious pedestrians being dealt with by police at each end,

explaining that there had been a severe chemical spillage into the sewer that required fairly drastic treatment, and as a consequence full Health and Safety considerations had to be applied to the public.

Harry asked the Team Leader as to current status to be advised that although the object had been located it would be some time before they could gain access. Harry checked his watch. It was 1.45pm. An hour and a quarter until possible ignition. He discussed this with the Chief Engineer, who advised that although there was no indication of any electrical source the triggering device could be purely mechanical. He advised the Deputy by mobile phone of the current status and warned him of the possible consequences, also, despite protestations from the Deputy that he would stay with the Engineer teams until resolution.

At this point the Chief Engineer had identified a manhole in Whitehall Place that, on available drawings, showed a small service access into the main sewer down which a slim man could crawl.

A volunteer was found within the team who, with minimum protective clothing, but with closed circuit oxygen supply and radio comms, was lowered carefully down the access from road level.

Harry saw by his watch that the time was 2.20 pm and it was 2.40pm before they heard, by radio, that the volunteer had reached the junction with the main sewer.

The engineer, wearing a helmet with an incorporated light, could see the self-propelled pig stuck at a slight angle against the wall, stopped where part of the old Victorian sewer had fallen in, creating a barrier over which the pig could not travel. Inching his way toward it he could see no activity indicated until his head was adjacent to the unit and he saw a timing indicator glowing in the dark. A small self-contained timer mounted on the top of the unit.

The engineer radioed up his finding requesting instructions.

Harry and the Chief Engineer decided that with the information as to ignition timing the instruction was simple. Disable the timer.

Inside his protective clothing and under his oxygen mask the engineer was sweating heavily, waiting for his instructions, and wondering if the timer was booby trapped or not.

The instruction came over the radio which he acknowledged.

He pulled out his cutters from his breast pocket and leaned across the unit to the timer. It looked like a simple connection to the main casing comprising two wires. However in the limited space it was not possible to see if there was another junction box between the timer and the casing. The risk of booby-trapping remained. He realised from the instruction he had received that there was no further time available.

He cut the first cable.

The sweat was running down his forehead into his eyes giving him semi-blurred vision. Nothing could be done as his full head mask could not be removed.

He squinted at the second cable, briefly thought of his family and cut the second cable, closing his eyes at the same time.

Nothing happened. Opening his eyes all he could see now in the gloom was the residual glow of the timer, showing a stationary 3 minutes and 23 seconds, before it faded from view.

He radioed up that the timer had been disabled and started his slow inching back to the access shaft.
Harry and the Chief Engineer breathed a sigh of relief as it was clear that the first level of risk had passed. Now recovery of the bomb would be relatively straightforward. However concern still existed concerning the 'dirty' element.
Calling the Deputy on his mobile Harry updated him as to status and that Whitehall would be closed for probably at least a further 24 hours.
Harry was well aware that he had sailed very close to the wind during this operation, but he rationalised it on a 'needs must' basis and would argue his case, if it came to that, on the strengths of his convictions and the moral rightness in this hidden, but persistent 'war'.
He made his way back to Vauxhall Cross.

--

At about 1815hrs the Deputy called on the internal phone.
'Harry, you know what I told you earlier about the Minister, and the fact he was being replaced.'
'Yes.'
'I've just been advised he dropped dead in his office from a massive heart attack as he was writing his resignation letter.'
Harry was silent, not really knowing how to reply.
The Deputy continued, 'I couldn't stand the man, but you don't wish that on anybody, do you?'
Harry agreed.
'Harry, your temporary suspension effective tomorrow 0900hrs still stands, you understand?'
Harry didn't argue. He needed to unwind, get away for a time. See Anna perhaps. Who knows?
Tom could handle the tidying up. The prosecution of the four detainees. A deal struck behind closed

doors linked to a quiet extradition to Pakistan. Who knows?
He telephoned the Chief Engineer as to progress.
Some small radiation was evident, but suitable casing was on its way to further cover the 'dirty' elements incorporated in the bomb along with plastic explosives.
The area would be sealed off for a further 24 hours, whilst all components of the bomb were extracted, and it was clear there was no risk to the public from any radiation exposure.
'A damn near run thing', Harry thought, as he thanked the Team Leader for his update.

He advised the Deputy of the Sitrep on a closed line, briefed Tom on his new responsibilities in his absence, finished his report, cleared his desk, thanked Jane for her assistance in clearing up the admin after him, and went home to his apartment in Clapham.

II

Wed 15th Mar - Mon 20th Mar 2006 London

For a weekday Harry had slept in late. It was about 0900hrs.

Last night he'd come home, via the Indian takeaway, bought some lager at the local food store, ate and drank whilst watching boring TV, and climbed into bed at about 2300hrs.

Sleep had been fitful, but from 0400hrs he had slept the sleep of the just, and woke with a start at 0900hrs.

He padded around the apartment, eating breakfast on the hoof, wondering where he should go for a holiday. Not Cyprus. Not after the last experience! That would be tempting fate!

He wondered if Anna could get away for a time. He recalled their last break together. Good to repeat something like that if they could. But a bit warmer climate would be good.

A little later that morning he dialled her mobile number, expecting it to transfer him to her messaging service so that he could leave a message.

It didn't. All that happened was an unobtainable signal which surprised him.

Network failure, I'll try again later, he thought.

After about an hour he tried again, but with the same result.

Later that afternoon he called again but was disappointed to get the same signal response.

He called Tom to see if he could find out if Anna was still working at the Ministry, and/or if his contact David Hadar at the Israeli Embassy had any idea as to why her mobile was now inoperative.

Tom called back within the hour. Anna had not gone into the Ministry the day before, having called in sick, had not appeared today, had not called in, and would therefore not know about the Minister's fatal heart attack.

His contact with David Hadar had raised more questions than answers.

David had responded to his question by stalling. He had said he could not comment on Anna's whereabouts at present, but would, once clarification had been obtained and authorised. He was not prepared to say anything further at the present time.

Harry put down the phone, very perplexed with what he had heard. It didn't really make sense, but did it?

He sat down with a cup of coffee, and his thoughts.

Was there something he was not aware of that would explain her disappearance?

Was Mossad covering for her on an operational issue?

Was there a family problem? He discarded that thought as she had no surviving parents or relatives, or so she had said.

Conjecture was no good. He would have to wait until somebody, including Anna, revealed what was happening.

Harry took this opportunity of allowing his mind to dwell on his own particular set of circumstances.

He had been very fortunate, if not very lucky, that there had been a Cabinet reshuffle; otherwise the previous Ministerial incumbent could have made life very difficult for the Department, the Director

General, and more importantly, the Deputy, and therefore ultimately to him.
He felt tired, he knew he was tired, and he needed to recharge those ageing batteries.
At the same time, he had to admit, to a growing level of cynicism aimed at the 'ruling' parties, no matter of which particular hue, leaning, or inclination.
Rather like the old maxim, 'statistics, more statistics, and damn lies', it was now, 'spin, more spin, and weasel words' that defined the sound bite politics and policies of today.
Just one great big Porky after another.
Everything is now instant; 'long term strategy and planning' is about a week next Tuesday, he thought wryly. Statesmanship was totally absent in the major parties, and individual differentiation was hard to find between them, as they all scrambled to fill the middle ground.
A habit, that appeared almost to be of contagious proportion, was that of a number of politicians who appeared to think that because they had said 'something', that the 'something' had therefore happened! In reality a wish list, not a 'happening'!
He sat flicking idly through some old travel brochures, smiling couples with beatific children, not like his last experience in Cyprus!
Bearing in mind it was March he still wanted some guaranteed sunshine and his eyes fell on the page describing Hurghada, on the Red Sea coast, Egypt.
Direct flights and good hotels appealed so he rang his travel agent. Thirty minutes later he was booked to fly out on Saturday, the 25th March from London Gatwick for a week.
Harry still felt somewhat perplexed and decided to telephone the Deputy on a secure line.

'Yes Harry. What is it?'
Harry explained his concern and the extent to which he and Tom had drawn a blank, plus advising where he would be taking his week's holiday.
'Harry, listen. You are officially under suspension and I have told you to take some vacation. Do that. Plus, you should know that the 'Boy Scouts' across the river are screaming for somebody's head for what happened last Sunday, and I am trying to ensure it is neither mine, nor yours!
So do me a favour. Just clear off and get some rest, and you I will speak when you're back. Alright?'
Harry was in no mood to argue and wished the Deputy 'good luck' before finishing the call.
He sat for a while thinking about recent events, the loose ends, the complexities and unanswered questions, until, with a sense of anger and frustration, he dismissed them from his mind, rose and went down into Clapham to enjoy a meal at his favourite local Indian restaurant.

--

Tel Aviv Israel
Meanwhile, about five hours flying time away, someone was lying on a bed, wondering what her meeting with her direct Mossad boss the next day would bring.
Having returned to Israel without permission and clearly having broken a number of operational and service rules and regulations the meeting would, no doubt, be fairly aggressive. Demonstrating one's 'initiative' in this way is not the way to gain the support of superior officers, neither are personal considerations, or feelings, given much credence or official approval.

Anna did not get much sleep that night. Her reasons were clear to her. The problem was she had decided on her actions arbitrarily, and without recourse to London Mossad Control.

--

Syria

In Damascus several members of the Committee had met and with subdued tones discussed the apparent failure of the operation against the Kuffar in London and the deaths of two of their brothers.

The interim leader said that they would be looking at new strategies in the coming months, joining hands with similar minded groups across the region and beyond, in order to pursue the Jihad against any, and all perceived threats to Islam and Muslims, linked with the ultimate goal of a world Caliphate.

London

At the safe house in West Square four detainees were taken out under cover of darkness to a detention centre outside London to await their trial which would not take place for at least three months. This would provide them with a suitable period for reflection, and whether any further Intel might be forthcoming to the authorities in order to mitigate, and possibly reduce their sentences, but, in any case, would certainly not delay their deportation.

--

Thursday 16th March 2006.

Mossad HQ, Tel Aviv, Israel.

Anna sat in an outer office waiting to be called in to the Interview Room.

She could hear the murmur of voices from within, and realized this would be more than a one to one enquiry.

Suddenly the door opened and a woman gestured for her to enter.

Anna walked in, and saw that an oblong table was set up across the room with a single seat this side.

Two men, who she did not recognize, were seated on the far side, and the woman was obviously there to take notes.

One of the men told her to sit down as he opened the file in front of him.

'I shall call you by your operational name throughout, namely, Anna Harrison. Do you accept that?'

Anna nodded.

'It is stated, that on Monday the 13th March 2006, without communicating with, or receiving permission from your direct London Control, you flew from London Heathrow to Tel Aviv.

As soon as this was discovered by London, and by us here at Mossad HQ, you were immediately suspended from all duties and responsibilities, and instructed to report here today for this Disciplinary Hearing.

Is that correct, and is that also your understanding?'

Anna nodded again.

'Please answer Yes, or No.'

'Yes' she replied, aware now that the proceedings were probably being recorded.

‘In order for us,’ at this point he gestured to include his colleague, ‘to try to understand what triggered this action by you, we would like you, in your own words and in your own time, to explain your reasons behind your complete disregard for normal operational protocols.’

Anna collected her thoughts, and began.

‘I have been operational on this assignment for a long time, in fact, almost seven years.

I have, in my opinion, carried out my task in a thoroughly professional way, providing all available Intel that fell within my orbit, plus some that didn’t.

As you are aware my position as PA to a UK Government Minister for the last few years has obviously put me under closer scrutiny by the UK intelligence services who are always looking for potential conduits for any type of leak, whether specific Intel, or anything of a personal nature that could be exploited adversely.

You will also be aware through London Control that my relationship with the Minister, developed to assist my operation, had cooled, and was creating additional pressure on me with his bullying style.

A combination of circumstances over a long period of time was causing me considerable anxiety, and the pressure was building up to the point of being unbearable.’

At this point in her explanation Anna could feel emotions building; she did not want to appear weepy, but they needed to understand the effects of long term pressures.

She paused to collect her thoughts again, and asked if she could have a glass of water, which the woman note taker provided.

Anna continued,

'To put it bluntly I had reached, in my opinion, a breaking point. I needed to get away and what happened was my reaction to an untenable situation.

I accept that it was irresponsible to return to Tel Aviv without informing London Control, but, frankly, I had what could be called a panic attack.

When that happens rational response tends to go out the window.'

She then fell silent.

The two men looked at each other before one posed a question.

'Are you aware that your Minister died of a heart attack the afternoon you took a flight from London to Tel Aviv?'

Anna stared at him with shocked surprise on her face.

'I had no knowledge of that at all. I have not seen any newspapers since I have been in Tel Aviv.'

'We believe it is only now being released to the news and media channels as the UK Prime Minister has now completed his Government reshuffle, and the Minister's family wanted the announcement to be made after that had been completed.'

Anna sat there in stunned silence, her mind racing as to possible consequences.

The other officer posed another question.

'To what extent did your relationship with Harry Baxter affect your relationship with the Minister, and your performance under your operational brief?'

Coming immediately after the news of the Ministers demise Anna had to ask for the question to be repeated.

She listened to it carefully and then responded, quietly and firmly, keeping her rising anger in check.

'As you will have seen from my overall performance, reports, comms with London Control, Intel collection and analysis, etcetera, any external relationships that have occurred have had no impact whatsoever on my operational brief.

In fact, the contact with Harry Baxter was supported by London Control, as his official function is within Procurement in the UK Ministry of Defence.'

The two men looked at each other, sensing that this would not be the best line of enquiry to address.

The other then confined his comments to the evident breaking of operational protocols, and whether this was an indication that she wished to leave the service.

Anna explained that she wished to serve her country, did not wish to leave the service, wanted the opportunity to recharge her batteries, and to be reassigned to another theatre of operation. Or, be based in Tel Aviv to be deployed on an ad hoc basis, wherever her particular training and skills could be employed.

The two officers looked at each other before the first one spoke.

'We will require a further meeting with you, and your suspension will continue until otherwise advised.

You are ordered not to enter into any form of communication with any colleagues or contacts in the UK, and to confine yourself to the hotel where you are currently staying. You will only make any visits to shops that are absolutely necessary, and you will not travel outside of Tel Aviv, unless special authority has been given. Is that understood?'

Anna replied, 'Clearly understood.'

'We anticipate the further meeting will take place in approximately 72hrs time. Please be available at short notice to attend in this building.'

'Understood.'

Anna left and made her way back to the small hotel where she was staying. It was convenient for the Mossad HQ and was not expensive.

She thought about the line of questioning and realised she had not been completely open about Harry, but open enough to push the threat away.

The death of the Minister, she realised could be of benefit to her.

If she had remained in London her assignment would effectively have been over. The new Minister would want his own PA, and beyond a quick handover she would no longer be required. There might have been an outside chance of picking up a position somewhere else in Whitehall, but remote.

Therefore by the coincidence of her departure and the death of the minister this would mean that her superiors would not be able to impose severe disciplinary measures against her; only sufficient to make an example.

Whether this would extend to permanent or limited suspension only the further meeting would expose, and the final decision would rest with the Director.

There was certainly no point in worrying about conjecture, so Anna took a bath and early dinner before retiring to her room and bed.

The weekend of Friday and Saturday followed, which gave her plenty of time for reflection and thought.

She sat on a balcony for long periods, wondering how the interviews and questioning would go. What would be their comments when she gave her reasons? Would they raise doubts as to her loyalty? Would they want to quickly dismiss her from the service? Her mental equilibrium was not in a good place, and her constructed answers to her posed questions did nothing to inspire her self-confidence.

Finally, on Saturday, she thought that plain honesty in description of her present attitude, and reason for returning to Israel was the only sensible route to take in the impending discussions.

Arising on the Sunday, the 19th March, she received a telephone call at 0830hrs advising that there would be a meeting at 1100hrs with her reporting officers, followed by a short one with the Director.

Whilst dressing Anna ran through the various permutations in her mind as to the likely format of the planned meetings.

Not to second guess the outcome, but to consider what would be the line of questioning in both cases.

She presented herself at HQ at the stated time, and was taken to the same interview room, this time being led directly into it, and waved to the chair.

The manner this morning was brusque, and quicker in tempo.

The questions came faster and were more personal in nature.

'Did the Minister ever indicate that he would leave his wife for you?'

'No.'

'Anything further to add?'

'No.'

'Was your attachment to Harry Baxter deliberate or was emotion involved?'

'It was approved and encouraged by Mossad Control London. After a time 'emotion' was involved, but restricted.'
'What does that mean?'
'It means that natural affection grew out of the relationship. No security issues were compromised, hence the description 'restricted'.'
'Was Mossad London Control aware of your emotional attachment?'
'Yes, I think so, although it was not discussed specifically.'
'Why not?'
'Because, as I have said, no security issues were compromised.'
'Can you be sure? Did Harry Baxter ever suspect your operational role?'
'Yes. But it was never discussed as I knew what his operational role was.'
'What was that?'
'His public position is that he works in procurement in the Ministry of Defence. However, operationally, he is an officer in the UK SIS (MI6). This was known to Mossad Control London and the only comment Harry Baxter ever made to me, indicating our areas of work, was to say 'We're both on the same side'.'
A number of questions followed covering various items of Intel that she had passed on to Control with her analysis. Was the analysis always hers, or did anybody else contribute? Always her sole analysis. What were her feelings when told about the death of the Minister? Neutral, he could be abusive and very unpleasant. She was happy that the relationship was finished. Did she want to see Harry Baxter again? She paused before replying. Yes, if it did not compromise her continued role in

Mossad, if that is what was ultimately decided by the Director.

The officers fell silent for a moment as they reflected on her responses.

One stood up, and said,

'Follow me.'

Anna followed the officer out of the room, down the corridor to the lift which they took to the third floor.

She was led down the corridor to the Director's office and into the ante room.

They waited there for a few minutes until the first interview officer was taken in by the Director's assistant.

Approximately ten minutes later Anna was called in.

The Director spoke slowly and a little wearily,

'Anna Harrison, I shall use your operational name. You have broken most of the standing rules and regulations governing performance issues whilst on operation in the UK.

You did not seek permission or authority from Mossad Control London to withdraw from your operation and return to Israel.

There has been, fortunately for you, an extenuating circumstance which arose at the time you abandoned your post, concerning your employment as PA to a UK Minister.

This circumstance would have required an immediate review of your operational status, and as a result, the possibility of your return to Israel.

The coincidence of what took place at that time mitigates against what would otherwise be your likely dismissal from this Service.

You will be suspended without pay for the next month, during which time your position and

operational status will be reviewed, leading to a reassignment on your return, not necessarily at your current level of service.
Is that understood, and is there anything you wish to say?'
Anna decided that discretion would be sensible in the current climate, so reiterated her loyalty to her country and to Mossad, and said that she looked forward to continued service in the future, at whatever level was decided by the organisation.
She was then dismissed and escorted back to the initial interview room.
There the first officer said,
'Go and have a good think as to what you want to do in the future and at what level. You were fortunate in that you had no black marks against you previously, so no dismissal.
If Admin is your thing, then say so. If you want Ops, then you'll have to demonstrate why you should be given a second chance. Second chances happen very infrequently, if not at all.
The general pace of activities is increasing, the spread and proliferation of terrorist groups is almost exponential, all hostile to the State of Israel.'
Anna said she would think about all the points that had been raised over the next month and agreed to report at Mossad HQ on Sunday the 16th April 2006.
She left the HQ building and went back to the hotel to try and organise a short term furnished apartment rental for at least the next month. She mentioned her search to the hotel owner who, coincidentally, had a relative owning and renting a number of small apartments, whom she was able to contact and strike a satisfactory renewable lease for the

next month or thereafter, dependent on what eventuated.

Moving in was agreed for Thursday, The 23rd March, giving Anna the chance to get organised over the following weekend.

Sitting in her room that evening Anna thought about the events of the last few days and weeks, and naturally Harry featured in those thoughts.

She had acquired a mobile as soon as she had landed in Israel, so, on a whim, she decided to text him.

It was short message apologising for no communication, but saying she was back in Israel, deciding what she was going to do, remembering him with much affection, and wishing him good luck for the future.

Back in London on that Sunday evening Harry was astonished, when his mobile pinged, indicating a text, to see who had sent it.

Having read the text he sat there thinking.

At least he had some point of contact with Anna, however slim.

He suddenly thought of an idea. Why not invite Anna to Hurghada to stay whilst he was there? Israelis have easy access into Egypt for tourism so he would ask her. She could only say No, or hopefully, Yes!

He composed his text, trying to indicate by its mix, his pleasure in hearing from her, plus disappointed surprise that she was now back in Israel, having left London without telling him.

He also mentioned that he was taking some leave and going to Hurghada for a week for some sun and sand, and wondered whether she would like to come.

Her reply text was almost immediate, saying that it would be impossible for her to leave Israel at the present time.
Harry replied, half joking, that in that case he would have to come to Tel Aviv.
It was a little while before Anna replied, texting, in a cautious tone, that if he wanted to make the trip, she would be happy to see him.
At this response Harry was a little nonplussed.
He had initially been disappointed and somewhat hurt that she had left London so abruptly without telling him, but, bearing in mind their chosen professions nothing should come as a surprise.
He thought carefully of his response before texting that he would look at the possibility of flying to Tel Aviv, and see if it could be arranged during his stay in Hurghada.
A short text reply said she looked forward to his news.
Harry looked up what was the most direct route from Hurghada to Tel Aviv and discovered he would have to fly from his resort to Larnaca in Cyprus, and then from there to Tel Aviv.
Complicated, but if he organised it, towards the end of his week, he could then fly direct from Tel Aviv to London.
Question. Should he raise this with the Deputy? Should he even consider going to Israel? Was that clever bearing in mind the sensitivity of his position, and the cautionary advice from the Deputy?
Harry thought he would sleep on that. Tomorrow might provide more clarity.
Waking on the Monday morning Harry sent a text to Anna indicating it would be a very complicated trip for him to travel from Hurghada to Tel Aviv,

so, although he wanted to see her again that would have to be at a more convenient time and place in the future.

Anna replied, indicating that she was sorry he wasn't coming to Tel Aviv, but understanding the reasons and hoping it would be not too long until they met again.

Harry was happy with the response, the language indicating continued warmth and affection between them. Having some time to kill, Harry settled down to read some background briefing on current associations between terrorist groups and the global spread that would pose current and future threats to Western democracies.

'Background: International dimension of terrorism; links between groups; common interests; aims; methods of operation; funding and finance.

Al-Qaeda is the one name that is imprinted in the Western public consciousness forever associated with international terrorism.

- What is less well appreciated is the spread of this organisation across several continents, its relationships with other terrorist groups (both passive and aggressive), and its loose/flexible strategy in pursuit of its aims.

- In South East Asia ties to Al-Qaeda exist in the Philippines, Indonesia, Malaysia, Thailand and Singapore.

- Various groups in all the countries have been arrested and imprisoned for planned attacks on Western embassies and interests.

Divisions within Islam should be understood.

- Al-Qaeda is Sunni, whereas, for example, Lebanese Hezbollah is Shia.

- Sunnis are very anti Shias considering them as heretics and issuing fatwas against senior figures.
- Muslim terrorist groups and factions exist in many countries including, China, Turkey, Syria, Afghanistan, Lebanon, Somalia, in addition to those mentioned above.
- Funding is provided from many sources, including Saudi Arabia, the Turkish and Afghanistan drug trade, plus certain unacknowledged Government sources.
To date in 2006, acknowledged terrorist attacks in January comprised, five in Afghanistan, and five in Spain.
In February there were eight in Spain, one in the Philippines, two in Denmark, one in Iraq, and one in Serbia.
In March, to date, one each in Pakistan, Lebanon, USA, India, Israel, and two in Spain.'

Harry was aware of most of the background briefing, but found the wide spread proliferation depressing reading, bearing in mind financial constraints in Western Governments, which automatically restricted the extent of surveillance and counter terrorist operations. Additionally the army of 'ambulance chasing' lawyers eager to ride on the back of the European Convention of Human Rights, whilst collecting significant fees from the public purse, all in order to protect a small army of immigrant clerics and terrorists, determined to undermine and destroy the very fabric of the society that had allowed them entry, often under the guise of asylum seekers.
He sat back in his chair wondering where his career would be going, when would he meet up with Anna again, how would the Deputy handle the situation

in his absence, what would be his role in the future?
No good second guessing, he thought; enjoy the holiday. At least he would be fresh and ready to face most things on his return.

III

Sunday 16th April – Monday 1st May 2006

1030hrs Mossad HQ Tel Aviv

Anna sat, somewhat nervously, in an ante room of one of the senior Directors.

She was called in promptly at 1030hrs, and took the empty chair at a conference table, where the Director was sitting on one side, flanked by two officers.

The Director opened the interview.

'Anna, I hope the past month has given you the opportunity to reflect on your previous operation and conduct which was contrary to all your training and undertakings to this Service.'

He continued without giving her an opportunity of reply.

'Up to that point your record had been exemplary, with excellent appraisals of intelligence that you were able to collect and distill from large volumes of official communications.

We are assuming that your aberration in returning to Israel without reference to London Mossad Control is a one off. However it has been noted on your records.'

He paused at this time, half expecting Anna to respond. She didn't, feeling that silence, and therefore apparent acceptance of his comments was the best political and practical response under the circumstances.

The Director continued.

'We are proposing that for the next two months you will work with our Intel Analysis Group, reviewing recent intelligence gathered from a number of stations, determining in the usual way to see if there are common links and possible joint strategies.

Following this period, which will enable you to bring yourself up to date, we will then decide if you are ready for assignment on an operational basis, location to be determined and agreed, assuming satisfactory performance and approval by your immediate superiors.

Is that clearly understood?'

Anna nodded, and responded quietly but professionally, thanking the Director for giving her this opportunity, and assuring him that she was keenly looking forward to contributing to the Service again.

A general conversation then followed, including the two officers, one of whom would be her direct supervisor at Intel Analysis, the other, potentially, her supervisor, if she went operational at the end of two months.

It was also agreed that she would start promptly at 0800hrs the following day, Monday, the 17th April.

Various questions were posed, one concerning her recent move into an apartment, the other, out of the blue, whether she had heard from Harry.

She said they had exchanged texts about a month ago; no further contact had been made from either side since then. This seemed to satisfy them, and the meeting terminated after about forty minutes.

Anna went back to her apartment and wrote up her confidential diary, which she locked away securely.

--

London

It was 0915hrs, on Monday the 17th April, and Harry was sitting at his desk in Vauxhall Cross

feeling considerably frustrated at what was happening, or not happening.
Since his holiday in Hurghada he felt as though he had been side-lined.
Let's face it, he thought, that's pretty much what's happened!
He knew the Deputy had been trying to protect him, certainly whilst all the flack was flying after the Westminster Bridge incident.
The Deputy had also told him of a conversation he had had with his opposite number in the French DGSE, saying they had been very happy to be of assistance on that particular op.
That had been a little indelicate; bearing in mind he did not wish to share certain information with the Deputy, in order to protect the Deputy's back, and his own! However the Deputy had not pursued the matter, nor had DGSE proffered further information.
Harry picked up the telephone and called the Deputy's PA, asking for an early meeting, which was agreed for 1100hrs.
Harry was clear in his own mind.
He needed to get away, and a request for an overseas posting was one that he thought the Deputy would agree to.
He had been stationed in London for a reasonable time, about two years, so hoped that would carry some weight.
At 1100hrs he presented himself in The Deputy's office, who waved him in.
'Take a seat Harry. What do want to discuss?'
'Me. In a nutshell. Can I expand?'
'Go ahead.'
'Since the last op, on your advice and recommendation, I have taken some leave to

recharge the batteries, and have been keeping a low profile, concentrating essentially on some background analysis and current Intel.
I've been doing some thinking as to where I am, where my career is, and what I want to do.
I wanted to discuss this informally with you, before I put in an official request, in the hope it would carry your support and recommendation.'
'What exactly do you want, Harry.'
'I would like your approval and support for an overseas posting, location not really a problem, but somewhere where I can make a genuine contribution and get properly stuck in.'
'A bit out of left field Harry, but I can understand, bearing in mind the various threads and complexities of your recent activities.
Leave it with me to mull it over, particularly where the posting would be most effective.
Give me 72 hours and we will discuss again. OK?'
'Fine with me. I look forward to Thursday.'
Harry returned to his office to give some further thought to which overseas stations the Deputy might consider, and which ones he would prefer!

*

Tel Aviv

Anna was poring over recent Intel received from a number of stations and covert sources, including, Beirut, Moscow, Paris, Ankara, New Delhi, and Beijing. Mossad had excellent IT systems, state of the art, with highly sophisticated algorithms, able to scan thousands of words, phrases, patois, and show connections, links, and timelines, which greatly reduced analyst fatigue, but significantly increased total volume, which required to be handled and reviewed.

She realised that the coming month was really a probationary period, where her application and dedication would be noted, linked with her professional capability, which, in total, would convince or otherwise, her superiors as to her suitability for field assignment.
She would apply herself and show them their trust would not be misplaced.
But some of this analysis can be incredibly boring!
She sighed and looked up to see her immediate boss looking at her through the glass window of his office. Neither acknowledged the other, as they both applied themselves to the screens in front of them.
The programmes weren't throwing up anything of note at present, but she realised such work requires a load of stamina and dedication, which one day will throw up a valuable nugget, or the missing piece in a complicated jigsaw.
Show them what you can do, she thought, scrolling down the screen to review Moscow station's reports and analysis.
The day was passing quite quickly until they received the tragic news that came in shortly after 2pm.
It appeared a suicide bomber had targeted a fast food restaurant in Tel Aviv, at about 1.30pm, killing himself and 11 diners. In addition 70 others had been injured.
Later in the day Islamic Jihad claimed responsibility.

--

London
On the Wednesday afternoon Harry telephoned the Deputy's PA to check on the time of his meeting

the following day. It was confirmed as first thing, 0845hrs.

He had been thinking about the various overseas stations, and where the Deputy would place him.

Harry wasn't too concerned as to 'where'; he was more concerned as to 'the what'.

He needed a new challenge, a new environment, something to get the adrenalin flowing again. He was looking forward to the meeting, whatever it may bring.

Thursday the 20th April dawned fair as Harry made his way from Clapham to Vauxhall Cross. He even smiled at one of the Security staff at the main entrance, who was completely surprised at this acknowledgement, and didn't really know how to respond.

He went straight to the Deputy's office where the PA said,

'Go straight in. He's expecting you.'

The Deputy rose from behind his desk and moved forward to shake Harry's hand.

'Good morning Harry. Come and sit down.'

They went over to a small table and chairs, sitting down, as the PA brought in a jug of coffee and two mugs.

The Deputy smiled, 'I always prefer mugs. It means I get the caffeine shot I need!'

'Snap' said Harry. 'That's one thing we won't argue over!'

The Deputy drank from his mug and then said,

'Right Harry. I've given your request some considerable thought. Whether you like my summation is another matter, but hear me out. We can then discuss.

I believe you have read some of the review docs on the various international links of some of the Islamic terrorist groups?'

Harry nodded, as the Deputy continued,

'Part of our current problem is rather like weeds on a paving stone patio. You don't know where the next one is going to spring up!

We have been trying to see some sort of pattern in the attacks that have taken place in the last few months/year, but they are completely random as far as we can see.

This surprises us, because we know that that there have been some joint discussions between disparate terrorist groups, and we thought that the likely outcome would be some sort of co-ordination.

That hasn't happened.

Therefore Harry, I want you to go to Pakistan, based either in Karachi or Islamabad, but probably moving frequently between the two.'

Harry didn't register surprise, but sat, just listening carefully to what the Deputy was saying.

'The reasoning is as follows.

We know that there are a number of groups operating in and from Pakistan, and we have had frequent confirmation that there is tacit approval, or accommodation from the authorities, notwithstanding their public statements from time to time.

We are also aware that Pakistan is turning a blind eye to the logistical and materiel support of insurgent and Taliban groups in Afghanistan. This is hindering NATO operations, and the US is trying to exert counter pressure on the Pakistani leadership to curtail this. We believe financial inducements will be the route. It's worked before.

Having said all that, there are also some clear connections to Indian terrorist attacks and undoubtedly some support for Gulf groups. The relationships are hazy and ill-defined. As part of the bigger picture there are increasing contacts between various terrorist groups in the Middle East, Gulf, Indian sub-continent, and South East Asia, possibly including elements in China.

What I want you to do Harry, is get some more solid definition in this theatre, which will include not only Pakistan, but other Middle East and Gulf countries.

Your role, as Defence Advisor, will be based either in the Trade Mission located in the British Consulate in Karachi, or a similar position in the British High Commission in Islamabad.

That's it, briefly. Is that something that interests you, and that you can get your teeth into?'

Harry responded quickly.

'Yes, in a word.

Challenging, with a wide brief and remit. That is something that can get the grey matter working.

If you sign off the posting when could I start?'

'Probably within a couple of weeks, allowing for Admin to catch up and arrange the necessary diplomatic clearances.

'However, Harry, there is one further element I should explain before you agree. It must remain completely confidential between us at this stage. Understood?'

'Of course.'

'Somewhere within the UK operations in Pakistan we have a leak. As I have said before the Embassy and the High Commission are well known for their porosity. GCHQ have picked up a certain amount of chatter, some local dialect, some base coded

English. Difficult to pin down as to precise content and location but certainly not aiding and abetting World peace!

That will be an additional factor within your posting. It will also require you to keep your eyes open in the back of your head! Unfortunately no one is above scrutiny.'

'From what you are saying then, a fairly toxic mix?'

'Indeed. I suggest you start your own briefing and updates soonest, there's a mountain of background to identify and assimilate.'

'A small request, but could I be based in Islamabad? One, It's the Pakistan Government centre, and two, HQ of ISI, their Inter-Services Intelligence.'

'I'll see what can be arranged, Harry. It will all depend on establishment numbers in the two locations. You know what the Diplomatic Service is like. Everything in their world depends on grades. One of these must have two of those! Otherwise the pyramid might collapse!'

Harry smiled.

'I appreciate that, but are we so very different? Excuse me, a slip of the tongue!'

The Deputy smiled back.

'I think you have a considerable amount of 'homework' to do, before abstract and, may I say, cynical commentary, on our establishment!

I will advise you once diplomatic protocols have been established and confirmed.'

Harry thanked the Deputy and returned to his office to start his 'revision', at the same time energised by the thought of his new assignment.

On the top of a pile of reports sitting on his desk Harry noticed one item that caught his eye. It

described a suicide bomber's attack on the 11th April, just over a week ago, against a large gathering of Sunni worshippers in a park in Karachi.
57 Sunnis had been killed, and over 80 injured. No group had claimed responsibility.
Anywhere, at any time, and no real indication of reason. Certainly no justification.
Harry thought about the number of people that would be affected by such a senseless attack. Many thousands, families and friends.
He shook his head to clear his thoughts and started organising the reports, by country, by month, by proximity to Pakistan, etc. He tended to start by building an outline, and then develop the matrix from there. Is there any sense to be made of it when you join the dots?
In this instance he took Pakistan as the centre, and then located the terrorist attacks by country, date, and declared responsibility (if available).
Although substantial in number no clear pattern emerged from the first three months, January to March, of 2006.
In January, in separate attacks, 5 suicide bombers killed 39 people and injured 101 in Afghanistan, whilst ETA in Spain carried out 5 bomb attacks.
In February, ETA carried out 8 bomb attacks, whilst in Iraq 5 Christians were killed by Muslim extremists.
In March, in Karachi Pakistan, a bomb kills 4 including a US diplomat. In India, 28 Hindus are killed and over 100 injured in a bomb attack. Two ETA attributed bomb attacks are carried out in Spain, whilst in Israel a Palestinian suicide bomber kills himself and 4 Israelis.

Already on April 11th in Pakistan, a suicide bomber kills 57 Sunni worshippers, whilst in Israel on the 17th a suicide bomber kills 11, and injures 70, in a restaurant attack in Tel Aviv.

Whilst reading the details of that last incident Harry's mind immediately swung to Anna, trusting she was safe.

Certainly, from the brief details covering January through mid-April, there was no common thread, other than random indiscriminate bombing, resulting in fatalities and significant injury.

When conducting analysis of the various incidents it was clear that Shia versus Sunni, and vice versa, was the major driver. When dealing with two sects within the same religion, Islam, it is difficult, without recourse to history, to understand the antipathy and hatred extended from one branch to the other.

Over the next few days Harry brought himself up to date with current activities in the region, personnel in the High Commission in Islamabad, and, in particular, classified reports concerning political in-fighting between ruling and opposition groups in Pakistan. GCHQ provided some sketchy background on intercepted traffic, but there was nothing solid to go on.

Pakistan politics, at best, is like a very large muddy pond, or morass.

Feuding, corruption and physical violence is endemic at all levels, without venturing into those areas of duplicity concerning backing and support of terrorist groups, in both internal and external theatres of operation.

For a considerable period of time it had been recognised, but unproven, that tacit support had been extended from the highest level, to Al-Qaeda and Osama Bin Laden.

This decision 'to run with the hare and the hounds' placed considerable pressure on attempts by Her Majesty's Government to create a working environment at High Commissioner level with the Government of Pakistan against the threat of international terrorism. In particular low credence could be given to any shared Intel, knowing the double game that was being played by numerous factions both within, and outside Pakistan's Government Departments.

On Monday the 1st May 2006 Harry sat at his desk and reflected on his review of Pakistan and neighbouring countries over the last ten days.

Whilst lost in thought his telephone rang.

It was the Deputy's PA asking him to come to see the Deputy in half an hour.

Harry agreed, and tidied up his notes and files in case there were specifics to discuss.

At 1030hrs he walked into the Deputy's office, who was talking on the telephone, but who waved him over to the conference table by the window.

Harry could hear the conversation but gave no indication that he was listening.

'I'm about to give him a briefing, so can we leave it like that? If there are any concerns I will revert. Yes, of course I understand the sensitivity. It's always sensitive, isn't it, if it involves Pakistan?'

The last sentence was said with a certain amount of ironic sarcasm.

The Deputy replaced the handset and walked over from his desk to the conference table.

Sitting down he turned to Harry and said,

'You heard that?'

'Sort of. I wasn't sure if I was included, or whether it referred to me.'

'Let me fill you in on a number of factors which will affect you in your new posting to Islamabad.'

Harry nodded and the Deputy continued.

'I'm stating the bloody obvious when I tell you that you can hardly believe anything you read or hear in Pakistan, whether in the High Commission or elsewhere.

Everything leaks like a sieve, the left hand does, or doesn't know, what the right hand is doing, but doesn't know if it should, and is it true or false? What leverage is any particular political party trying to achieve, does it fit in with the 'known' scenario and declared intent, and finally, can we recognize a common thread running through all of this? Answer, unlikely, and probably, No!

I'm just pointing out to you the acute frustration that you will feel in fairly short order, the problem of trust that exists across the board, and the fact that you will feel you are pushing treacle uphill!

I'm being quite serious when I refer to institutional apathy that currently exists at various levels in the High Commission, time servers, jobsworths, etc., plus one particular sensitivity which I will now explain.'

Harry had been listening intently to the Deputy, but had felt his enthusiasm declining as the commentary progressed.

Harry made no comment and the Deputy continued.

'Some years ago an application was made by a career diplomat in the Foreign Office to transfer to SIS. His application after interviews, background research including university, friends, family, political affiliations, etc., finished up on my desk for final appraisal and review.

He was a classic Oxbridge candidate, ticking the majority of boxes, with a clean, if not outstanding record to date. I turned him down.'

Harry's expression posed the question.

'There was something not quite right that was hard for me to put my finger on. During the long interview I realised at one particular point that he thought the process was a formality. That he had already been accepted, and that this was the last tick in the box. There was an underlying arrogance, which was not too hard to detect, and was the reason for my rejection of his application and transfer.'

The Deputy paused but Harry made no comment.

'I've given you this background as the man concerned is First Secretary in the High Commission in Islamabad and will be aware of your real role under the guise of Defence Advisor. It is therefore possible that you may not receive the sort of support that you could expect in normal circumstances, particularly if the individual concerned is holding any sort of grudge against SIS.

Simply Harry, in these circumstances do you wish to continue?'

Harry sat there, his thoughts racing.

If he said NO would that be a mark against him? If he said he was happy to go would that be piling another debit on top of an already difficult operational deployment? Perhaps the challenge was worth it.

'I'm prepared to continue,' he replied. He thought to say he would be '*happy*' to continue might be stretching the point.

‘OK,’ said the Deputy, ‘Let me continue to the meat of what you’ll be up against, or in politico speak, what your ‘challenges’ will be!’

Over the next ninety minutes the Deputy explained, in some depth, a number of the ‘challenges’ that Harry would be party to, and the scenarios and relationships that impacted on this particular theatre and neighbouring countries, particularly India and Afghanistan.

‘Well Harry, I’ve talked long enough. Electronic file and data covering what I have outlined will be made available to you.

I heard today that the necessary clearances, Foreign Office protocols etc., will be in place this week covering your appointment. Your PIA flight to Islamabad is booked for Sunday 14th May, leaving at 2000hrs, arriving Islamabad Monday at 0740hrs.

Finally Harry, the very best of luck. Do not take unnecessary risks, and keep me in the loop, particularly with anything that’s reckoned to be UK negative! Understood?’

Harry nodded his head and murmured agreement.

‘I think I’ve plenty to work on now you’ve briefed me, plus the files and background will give me further reading to complete between now and the 14th.

I can check the files but what is the name of the First Secretary?’

‘Sorry Harry. The most important detail! His name is Charles Urwin. He will obviously be aware that you have received a full briefing, and that past history will have been given to you. He’s clever, quite smooth, some useful friends in high places. Not a man to be trifled with. I would hope he operates in a thoroughly professional way.

However, he's a careerist, and the K beckons ultimately! Therefore, watch your back. There may be still some latent bitterness. Not against you, but possibly against me. We will just have to see.

One last thing. I'd like a final meeting with you on Thursday the 11th, let's say 0900hrs. General update on international terrorism, implications in Pakistan, loose federation of interests, etc. Book it with my PA, will you?'

Harry agreed and left the Deputy's office, only pausing to speak to the PA to confirm the meeting for the 11th.

Over the next few days he studied a considerable number of Intel reports from many of the overseas posts, in particular those countries clearly identified on the international list as containing elements of, or receiving assistance from, Al-Qaeda. Additionally there are many militant Islamist terrorist groups working in a loose federation, or under an unproven, but perceived, Al-Qaeda umbrella. Countries, including both scenarios, in addition to Pakistan, are Turkey, Lebanon, India, Malaysia, Indonesia, Somalia, Sudan, Yemen, Iraq, and, of course, Afghanistan.

By the end of the week Harry felt that he had an initial, but reasonable, grasp of the increasing complexity of the international terrorist cells operating in various parts of the world.

The main problem was identifying the linkage between the various groups and whether there was any clear strategy, whether for operations, or forward planning in their individual jihads.

Whilst reading a significant number of reports from the High Commission in Islamabad it became clear that a problem of internal security existed within the Commission. A number of local Pakistanis were employed in various administrative positions, and although checks had been carried out before employment it was obvious that a considerable amount of 'porosity' existed. Certainly judging by the way Islamabad newspapers seemed to second guess Her Majesty's Government position on a number of issues!

Harry thought that there would be increasing complexity, within any given situation, in this sort of environment where truth and loyalty would be at a premium, but ambiguity and lies would be the staple diet.

The situation with the First Secretary would be difficult.

Would he 'assist' Harry when he could, or leave him to make mistakes which would not enhance SIS in any way? Would he play the game of double bluff, assisting Harry but leading him into conflict, real or imagined, with himself or others in the High Commission hierarchy? Or, more dangerously, on the ground in ops, involving conflicting elements within Pakistan's fragmented government or terrorist groups?

The Deputy's words 'watch your back' would be good guidance!

--

Following his meeting with the Deputy, Harry decided, as it was a lovely May day, to walk over Vauxhall Bridge and along the Embankment towards Chelsea.

As he passed Dolphin Square, engrossed in his own thoughts, he heard his name called out with an American accent.

'Harry, over here,' a man called from the other side of the road.

Harry located the caller, and his eyes widened as he recognised Jack DeCosta, in jogging gear, now crossing the road.
'Jack, what the hell are you doing here?'
'Well that's a nice welcome I must say', said Jack with a smile. 'It's about three years isn't it? Hamburg. Trying to get a proper handle on those arrested bomb makers and placers.'
'Yes, you're right,' said Harry smiling in return. 'Operating as part of the CIA team based in the US Embassy in Germany. What are you doing here?'
'CIA Head of Station, US Embassy, London. Promotion and responsibility, liaison with some of your opposite numbers this side of the river. Trying to see how much of the rubbish we can stop crossing the pond to cause unnecessary havoc to Homeland Security.'
'Congratulations,' replied Harry, 'Where are you living?'
'Sharing an apartment in Dolphin Square, presently,' said Jack, indicating the building behind him, 'until I can get a place of my own.'
Harry thought quickly,
'I'm off to my overseas posting in a few days, what about dinner tonight or tomorrow?'
'Tomorrow would work, yes.'
'OK', said Harry giving him a time and place, 'let's have a real catch up then.'
Jack threw up a mock salute and a 'See Ya', as he turned and jogged off in the direction of Dolphin Square.
Harry, as he continued his walk, reflected on his previous contact with Jack and their co-operative efforts in Germany three years previously.
The CIA had stumbled on some Intel in Germany which, linked with some shared activity with SIS

(MI6) had prevented a Jihadist bombers attack on a German express train. Subsequent investigation indicated this type of covert attack was to be 'exported' to the United States.

'Tomorrow evening should be interesting', Harry thought.

--

Harry and Jack met in the small Italian restaurant, Rocco's, in Earls Court at 7.30pm, and were shown to a discrete table at the rear.

Jack was one of those Southern European looking men; could be Italian, Spanish, maybe Greek, who knows, with skin than tans very easily, 5feet 10inches tall, a friendly face and disposition.

A good international cover.

Brought up in New York in an Anglo-Italian family they later moved to California, when, in his late teens, he joined the Marines. Noted for his application he was sent to university where he gained a degree in International Relations, which then led to him applying to join the CIA. The rest, as they say, is history (covert).

After they had chosen food and wine the conversation turned to current events.

'Well Jack, what's your focus now you're based in London?'

'OK Harry. Remember, some of this stuff is classified so I can't go there, but I will give you what I can, alright?'

Harry nodded.

'Without being too critical, the US of A is pretty hacked off at the UK with what, we consider, a far too liberal and lax view of some of your immigrants and asylum seekers.'

At this point Harry opened his mouth to speak at which Jack raised his hand and said, with a half-smile,

'Let me finish, then we can debate.

We are concerned that the UK could be a stepping stone for some of these jihadists only to eager to export some of their ideas and terrorism to the US.

You and I know a lot of them are going back for weapon training/brainwashing, and bomb making. That involves Pakistan, Iraq, East Africa, etc.

We know that Pakistan and Iran are hooked up on a deal for specialist rockets for Hezbollah in Lebanon. We are also concerned that some of these might find their way to Europe.'

Harry indicated nothing in his body language, just intently listening.

Jack continued, 'With what's happening in the Middle East and Gulf region at the moment the outcome is anybody's guess.

We are, mostly, reacting after the event, which often means it's too late. Somebody has already lit the fire. Then we're trying to find the source and put it out! Not easy!

I know you are operating in the same way. Unfortunately in our democracies we cannot be pro-active in dealing with some of these situations, themselves hugely undemocratic, but the World's press often doesn't quite see it as that, and we get targeted in the cojones!'

At this point Jack paused, aiming a questioning look at Harry.

'Jack, I hear what you say, and as I said to somebody else, not long ago, 'We are on the same side'. Thank God.

My present posting is Islamabad, chasing much the same agenda as yourself. In fact I fly out shortly.

As we say, we are on the same page as to Focus, therefore could I ask a favour?'
'You can ask, but I may not deliver', said Jack smiling. 'No, hit me!'
Harry continued,
'Either you make the contact direct to our Deputy, or get your diplomatic channels to ask officially, but let's, if sanctioned, share the Intel that covers Pakistan, at least. In that way we might make some short cuts, plus my feedback will help your overall assessment when looking at stuff trying, or succeeding, in crossing the pond.'
Jack reflected for a few seconds,
'Seems useful to me. Let me run it past my boss in Washington. Let us do our job. Let the diplomats do theirs!'
They continued their meal covering some old situations, and expanding a little further on their current responsibilities.
When they left at about 10.00pm, and started to walk eastwards along Cromwell Road, they did not notice the motorcyclist parked about 50 yards behind them, who watched them briefly, checked his watch, and left in the opposite direction.
The watchers were being watched.

--

The following morning, at 0800hrs, the motorcyclist logged his report electronically to his immediate superior at the Security Service (MI5) HQ.
[Dinner meeting: London Head CIA with SIS operative, duration: under 3hours.]

IV

Wednesday 3rd May – Thursday 4th May 2006

Islamabad

On Wednesday morning, the 3rd May, the British High Commissioner, Sir James Bollington, sat in his office reading a report, received that morning, from his First Secretary.

In bare detail it advised him of the appointment of Harry Baxter as Defence Advisor, who would be arriving on Monday the 15th May. A short summary followed of Harry's previous roles, both in the UK and overseas, sufficiently expansive in scope, but vague in specific detail.

'Civil Service Speak' was brilliant in this area, saying sufficient, but giving nothing.

It was accepted that the most senior ranking, namely the High Commissioner, would not be party to, or have detailed knowledge of 'security' operations or covert appointments, in order that ignorance could be professed, when publicly challenged, at any time in the future.

Responsibility for supervision, detailed knowledge of operations, whether covert or otherwise, Intel gathering, initial interpretation and distribution would rest, theoretically, with the First Secretary.

In practice, First Secretaries tried to keep their hands clean as far as possible, bearing in mind the possibility of appointment as Ambassador or High Commissioner at some future date, linked with a highly desirable K.

Why dirty the hands at all, if it could be avoided?

This meant that Defence Advisors were generally left to their own devices, running covert operations under their direct control, collecting Intel, establishing 'working relationships' with interested parties and 'assets', additionally trying to stay one step ahead of the almost incomprehensible game of terrorism and Pakistan politics.

He closed the file and picked up the next. He now knew the man's name; not much else. He telephoned the First Secretary to come and see him. Fifteen minutes later the First Secretary, Charles Urwin, walked into the High Commissioner's office.

'Good morning Charles, sit down. Coffee?'

'No thank you, I'm almost caffeined out this morning,' he responded.

'Charles, give me some background, or what you know, of this new Defence Advisor who's arriving later this month. Questions I have are; Why? Something specific we should know about? The urgency that has been applied to his appointment? Probably covert, but I don't need to know that.'

Charles coughed gently before proceeding to reply. He was nothing if not the consummate professional.

'I am aware that his appointment was carried out with almost indecent haste, and under a non-attributable basis, would confirm that there is a covert element within his brief.

As far as I can determine, with respect to both internal and external sources, there is nothing specific, of which we should be aware, that has influenced this decision.

Naturally under our operating and reporting rules, all activities, whether overt or covert, will be known to me, as will copies of all reports and transmissions between here and London.

I will, of course, keep you informed, on a need to know basis, of any event, action, report, etc., that, I believe, should be brought to your notice.
As is understood, such notice will be kept to an absolute minimum, in order that your public integrity is secure, whatever the eventuality.
I would hope, that beyond a brief meeting on his arrival, your contact with him would be almost non-existent, except, perhaps, at a High Commission reception.
His reporting line is to me. Any efforts to avoid my line control and constraint will be flagged to his London department for disciplinary action and withdrawal.'
'Thank you for that Charles. I was confident you would have a firm grasp and appreciation of the appointment.'
Charles nodded in agreement before asking, 'Is there anything further at this time? I have a small group of important businessmen arriving for discussions with our Commercial Advisor in about ten minutes. I would like to be there to kick off the meeting, and press the flesh.'
'Of course. Must keep the wheels of commerce oiled Charles, see you later.'
Charles Urwin left the High Commissioner and returned to his office, quite pleased with his handling of the situation.
The High Commissioner (HC) would stay in the background on this one. He, the First Secretary, would dictate what information went up to the HC. Additionally he had established reporting lines and disciplinary recourse.
First signs of this planted Attaché not playing ball and he would come down like a ton of bricks, early. If the Attaché's boss was the man that had rejected

his transfer to SIS some years ago it would be a double pleasure.

To some, in the High Commission, Charles Urwin had gone native. He had served two separate periods in Islamabad, split by service in the EU and Moscow. He had married a Pakistani he had met whilst in Islamabad, who was now with him on his present tour.

His wife came from an important Pakistani family, related, ultimately, through to the ruling elite which was of enormous value to him. Both in background gossip, Pakistan government position and intentions, plus some discrete lines of contact to certain organisations, some that were government supporters, and others that were not. It was a fine line he trod, but one, that due his obvious excellent local knowledge and intelligence, would do nothing, he thought, but assist in his career path.

Tel Aviv

At about the same time in Tel Aviv Anna was working at her desk on Intel analysis, but she was bored.

Trawling myriads of documents, transcripts of telephone, mobile, or satellite conversations was not her idea of satisfying employment. However, as she admitted to herself, ruefully, under the circumstances she was fortunate not to find herself on the streets of Tel Aviv looking for employment.

Her thoughts were interrupted by her phone ringing. It was her immediate senior asking her to come to his office.

Entering, she saw him poring over a report, with a small map which, from an upside down viewpoint, looked like Lebanon.

'Sit down.'

She complied, waiting for him to say something.
'Anna, you have been working on Intel Analysis since the 16th April and probably expected to be doing this for a couple of months.' At this point he smiled grimly.
'However, as you know, in our world things seldom remain static for long. A situation has arisen in Lebanon. Quite simply one of our embedded assets has been killed. We believe by Hezbollah. Our people on the ground are few in number, and in this particular scenario we are going to need someone who is totally unknown to any of the international agencies operating in Lebanon.'
Anna made no comment so he continued.
'You will recall the terrorist attack the killed 11 and injured 70 on the 17th April?'
'Yes, that was the day I started here.'
'The Islamic Jihad claimed responsibility. Their HQ is in Damascus but they have offices in Beirut. As you are aware they are funded from Syria and Iran. They are not large in numbers, but obviously effective. Additionally we need to get closer to Hezbollah who are planning a new initiative, judging by 'chatter' we have picked up recently.
Our embedded asset was uncovered, and we now know he was murdered three days ago.
We need someone on the ground with a good cover story to get reasonably close to them. We need to be able to gather very fresh Intel as to planned operations. How that is to be done has yet to be decided. What I need to know is whether you would be prepared to take on this mission. If you say No it will not be held against you, as the operation is considered high risk, and is on a voluntary basis.

Do you fully understand what I am saying?'
'Yes', Anna replied quietly.
'I do not require an immediate answer, but certainly by 0900hrs tomorrow.'
'Understood.'
'Because you are unknown in Lebanon we will be able to construct a failsafe background which will give you the flexibility on the ground. If the situation deteriorates we can pull you out in hours.'
Anna nodded her head, clearly understanding what he was saying.
'I'll get back to you by 0900hrs tomorrow.'
She got up from the chair, returned to her desk, and gazed blankly at the screen whilst jumbled thoughts filled her head.
Shaking her head to clear her thoughts she applied herself to the Intel reports on her screen, vowing to think the request through in the peace and quiet of her apartment that evening.
Not an easy choice to make, but I will have to make it, she thought. The memory of her father came flooding back, and the sacrifice he had made in the Six Day War.
The day passed quickly enough, and Anna then hurried home to eat, reflect, and make a decision.

Islamabad
That evening Charles Urwin was sitting with his wife drinking tea on the terrace of their villa in the guarded, security conscious, diplomatic compound. It was the quiet of the evening, the peace only broken by the distant hum of traffic, now evening prayers were over, on 4th Avenue and Isfahani Road.
Each was content with their own thoughts. His wife, Zahira, broke the silence first.

'Charles, can I ask you something?'
'Of course.'
'I know you are a typical Englishman. It was one of the things that attracted me to you in the first place.'
Charles turned and smiled, 'And?'
'When we have children,' she noticed his face darken a little at this comment, 'we have agreed that they would be brought up as Muslims.'
'Yes', he replied somewhat curtly.
'Would you ever consider converting to Islam?
His face turned quickly towards her.
'Where has that come from, might I ask?'
'It was raised to me by my family.'
Charles did not answer immediately, his face expressionless. When he did, his diction was slow, deliberate, and with a hint of controlled anger.
'When I asked you to marry me I made it abundantly clear that my professional career in the Foreign Office is what comes first, second, and third in my life. I also said that any children could be brought up as Muslims, as long as no attempt was made to challenge or change my own British habits and customs.
I thought that was clearly understood?'
'Yes, I remember all you have said on the subject, but my parents were concerned that I was becoming too Western in outlook and custom, and that it might work against their grandchildren being good Muslims.'
Charles, still looking straight ahead, replied,' I respect your parents, but frankly having agreed to our marriage they should be content that I will keep my side of the bargain with respect to their future grandchildren. Is that clear, and can we now finish discussing this matter?'

‘Yes’, she said quietly, holding back the tears that were forming in the corner of her eyes. She rose from the chair and disappeared inside, leaving Charles to his thoughts. Her identity as a Muslim was very strong, linked with her love and obedience to Islam, the two being just the obverse faces of the same coin.

Tel Aviv

Thursday 4th May 2006 dawned clear although Anna certainly did not feel much sympathy with the day. She had slept badly after turning things over in her mind the evening before, whether she should agree to the assignment proposed by her line officer, or whether she should reject it.

She was at her desk by 0830hrs, and knocked on her officer’s door promptly at 0900hrs.

He indicated a chair as she entered. Having sat down Anna opened the discussion.

‘I’m prepared to be considered for the operation you outlined yesterday. However you are aware of my limitations in operations. Quiet covert intelligence gathering, seeking out political and actual intentions as opposed to public declarations, gaining confidence of targets to achieve access to confidential and classified documents, etc. No training or experience in ‘wet ops’ whatsoever, and no wish to. If I can be used in the manner of my training, fine. If not, then I must refuse.’

Her officer sat back and replied, ‘OK, restrictions noted. You have responded as I thought you would. You will be working in Beirut, in contact with others, but your assignment will be a solo operation, to do exactly what you are trained for, and what you have just described. Full briefing and any other specialist advice/training will take place over the next week. You will be arriving in Beirut around the 25th May. Understood?'

'Yes.'

'Well finish today. Complete your Intel analysis reports, file any hard copies, complete sign off on the IT system with the engineer including security issues, passwords etc., shred any loose notes, general deep clean, OK?'

Anna nodded.

'Report here 0900hrs 7th May for training as I indicated. Have a good weekend.'

Anna left and returned to her station to close down one chapter of her life, and then start another, on this occasion largely unknown.

V

Monday 8th May – Friday 12th May 2006

SIS (MI6) London

The Deputy's PA called Harry at 0915hrs and asked him to come and see the Deputy at 1100hrs.

Harry was expecting some further briefing concerning Pakistan when he entered the Deputy's office at 1100hrs, but was surprised by the subject matter when the Deputy started speak.

'Harry, breaking news, and this conversation never happened. Alright?

There are changes taking place, as we speak, at the very top of SIS. A new Director General, James Readman, is being appointed, and without appearing too cynical, it appears to be more of a political payback appointment, than either operational or strategic necessity.

As an added ingredient in the mix is the fact that this individual and I have crossed swords on many occasions. He comes originally from across the river but latterly chaired the JIC. Mutual respect is not a phrase that springs readily to mind. Plus, he is close to another individual that could affect particularly you, and perhaps me, namely Charles Urwin!

Two of a kind, who run with the same pack. Politically professional and professionally political. Experts in climbing the greasy pole and gaining and influencing the ear of those who can say Yes, or No!'

Harry was somewhat nonplussed by the degree in which the Deputy had opened up concerning changes at the top, but recognised that such competitive enmity can last for decades.

'I appreciate your briefing me on this and, of course, recognise the complete confidentiality. Obviously at my level there is not a lot I can say or do, but I shall keep my scanner going, and my wits about me,' he said, half smiling, in an attempt to reduce the Deputy's tension.

'You're right. We will just have to see how the changes work out, what new brooms will be employed in the Aegean stables, then allow the dust and sh*t to settle, and crack on as best we can, providing our political masters with the sort of service they expect, but rarely listen to, as their strategic view, timescale, and attention span is somewhat less than a gnat's!'

Harry, realising the Deputy was quietly steaming, said, in a semi-joking way, 'I've often thought about applying for promotion, but really think I couldn't handle the extra pressures that you seem to take in your stride.'

The Deputy, slightly red faced, glared at him, before laughing out loud.

'God, you're right Harry. I just dust myself down and start all over again! Go on; get back to your appreciation of Pakistan and all that it will entail in fairly short order. I'll keep you up to speed on developments here. Just make sure you remember the relationships that exist, and which might impact on your activities. If they don't I will be very surprised!'

Harry smiled and returned to his office where he saw Tom Denman who had just returned from some leave, and was now involved mostly on administration following the recent operation.

'Morning Harry, any gossip?'

'Not that I'm aware of. Anything going the rounds?'
'Some whispering over coffee this morning. Seems there are some possible admin changes afoot. Have you heard?'
'Nothing yet', Harry lied. ''Anyway I'm off at the weekend, new posting, so it won't bother me.' Like hell it won't, he thought.
'Where?' asked Tom.
'Pakistan.'
'Why?'
'Change of scenery, plus the old man has seen and heard too much of me over the last six months!' he joked.
They parted, Tom to Admin Control, Harry more background briefing and local Intel.
Tom wondered why Pakistan, but then reminded himself that 2 + 2 in their game seldom made 4!

Tel Aviv
Anna had just started her second day of briefing/ further training and was surprised to be told that she would be placed in Beirut at one of the international aid agencies, in this instance Agence Francaise de Developpment (AFD).
It was explained to her that Mossad had strong connections with the French security service, DGSE, and it was common practice for national security organisations to use aid agencies as cover for operatives from time to time. Her role would be identifying potential social and welfare projects for AFD.
Her French was good and the scope of operations of the agency, AFD, meant that there would be no

problems entering the various regions in Lebanon, and any militia controlled districts of Beirut.
The relationship with DGSE meant that any useful Intel would be shared, and operatives were aware that there would always be additional resource and backup if required.
Anna took some comfort from the detailed explanation, realising that she would not be completely ‘flying solo’.
Her training officer took some time to explain how DGSE operatives were either embedded in the aid agency, or that certain aid agency employees were ‘sleepers’ or assets, working under direct or indirect supervision of DGSE.
It was normal, for agency employees employed in this manner by DGSE, not to be aware of other DGSE operatives embedded in the agency. This form of ‘Chinese walls’ prevented ‘leakage’, and also kept all operatives or employees within ‘a need to know’ discipline.
Anna realized she had a lot to learn, and applied herself diligently to all areas of the training, spy craft, communication systems, critical situation analysis, survival techniques in hostile environments, elementary interrogation techniques and response to them, red alert and exit, message handling, local control and reporting. Last and by no means least, an understanding of the risk levels involved, and that a situation could occur over which she had no control, resolution, or timely exit. She must be aware that this could happen at any time.
It could well be the case that Mossad could provide no assistance at that time. Was she fully aware of the consequences? Yes, she was.

Paris DGSE

That morning, in the DGSE HQ, 141 Boulevard Mortier, Paris, a briefing meeting was taking place involving a number of interested parties.

One was Alain Dubois. Alain had been involved in providing 'discrete' assistance to Harry Baxter in London in a delicate counter-terrorist operation which had culminated in a less than discrete explosion 'engineered', by Alain.

His 'Chef' had dealt with the aftermath of this operation, who, when questioned by SIS, with a typical Gallic shrug and wry smile, suggested, that as the operation had been successful, it seemed a pity to waste time trawling over one big bang, and what caused it! He suggested that the operation had shown how well certain agencies could work together, and that was what should be applauded! He could never really understand the Anglo-Saxon obsession of trawling over past events that had obviously been successful, but which then produced a high level of civil service paranoia in terms of trying to apportion responsibility (or blame!).

Every month such meetings were held giving regional senior officers the chance to update their peers verbally, above and beyond the normal lines of electronic comms or databases.

It would have been interesting to compare respective appreciation by both senior SIS and DGSE officers of global terrorism threats, and see that the nature of fragmentation in various regions raised the same levels of frustration in both agencies. In essence, globally, there was no common thread. Just haphazard operations carried out under the guise of Al-Qaeda, Hezbollah, Shia v.

Sunni, or vice versa, or the constant jockeying by world powers, creating localised resistance or revolution.
Concern was raised over heightened tensions in Lebanon. Sabre rattling continued from Hezbollah, aided and supported by Syria and Iran, indicating, perhaps, yet another armed intervention, either internal or external.
One observation that came from the Asian region concerned technical co-operation between the Indian and Russian governments in the aeronautical field where a Russian designed fighter (Sukhoi Su-30MK1) was being built in India. Over 120 aircraft have been ordered. It is understood a further order of 40 aircraft is to be placed. The aircraft incorporates Indian systems and avionics which, in turn, incorporate French and Israeli sub-systems.
At one level, such incorporation of avionic sub-systems by France and Israel gives cause for concern. However, this is more than counterbalanced by the embedded technology being able to transmit performance data back to the two countries, so that the aircraft's performance and capabilities, under normal operational conditions, are well known.
Concern was also expressed concerning the balance of power in the region, and continuing posturing and aggression between India and Pakistan, focussed on Kashmir.
After about 75 minutes the meeting broke up and Alain started to return to his office. On the corridor he fell into step with his Department Head who called him into his office. Alain, who had been posted back to Paris after the London operation, was now awaiting his next posting, and wondered

whether this conversation might provide some background.

Gilles Deniaud poured two strong black coffees before speaking.

'Bien Alain, so, where do we, and you, go from here?'

Alain shrugged and pulled a questioning expression.

'No idea. I was hoping you might be able to assist me with that!' he joked.

'There are several options Alain. Let's review them.

I could, of course, just assign you to a particular station or operation, but think it would be more productive to agree something which you would find interesting, stimulating, and where your profile indicated an appropriate match,' he said with a half-smile on his face.

'Also, perhaps a theatre which could give freer rein to your enthusiasm for pyro techniques, and which, perhaps, would be less obvious than your recent exercise in London.'

Alain smiled in response, not, at this stage, contributing comment. Not, at least, until he could see where this discussion was going!

'Firstly, do you want to remain in Europe, or are you interested in an overseas posting?'

'Definitely overseas.'

'Why?'

'I have spent the last two and a half years in Europe and need to broaden my scope and experience. Although interesting, Europe can a little bureaucratic, whereas I think overseas requires you to be more creative, and it can, without doubt, be more stimulating!'

'Fine. How about the Middle East? Lebanon? That you would find stimulating because nobody really knows from one week to the next what is going on! Perhaps your presence there will provide me with some solid intelligence that will assist our Ministère des Affaires Etrangères et Européennes in his macro-stratégique analysis and deliberations within a global framework.'

On this occasion Alain really smiled. He appreciated his boss's light hearted cynicism which he could relate to.

'Why not?' he replied, 'Would I be based in the embassy or elsewhere?'

'I think elsewhere. The reason for that is that I think the embassy is extremely 'leaky,' and everybody knows everybody's business. It would soon be common knowledge in the embassy and the streets of Beirut who, and what you are. We'll get you some interesting secondment. Let's discuss this next week when I've given it some further thought. D'accord?'

'Bien sûr!'

Alain was quite satisfied with the way the meeting had gone. Clearly the London operation had not gone against him. His career, for the present, was progressing.

London

Later that week Harry was starting his packing for his time in Pakistan. Always difficult. Not sure as to how long he would be there. Hot summers, cold winters.

Perhaps the basics, and a change or two. He could always pick up more in Islamabad.

He sat down at about nine, after pouring a beer, and let his head lie back on the couch, his eyes open, staring unfocussed at the ceiling.
His mind wandered disjointedly over a number of issues; career, imminent posting, Anna. Yes, that thought kept reoccurring. What was she doing? Would they meet up again? Had they just been passing ships? He pictured her face, her smile, the soft touch of her hand on his arm, their intimate and happy snatched times together, when they were able to shut out their respective professional worlds for a few hours.
He wondered what her career move would be. The one thing he did know was that he had no idea if, and when, they might see each other again.
He shook his head to clear his thoughts and focus on his career.
He would have a final discussion and briefing with the Deputy tomorrow, Friday, and then fly to Islamabad via Lahore, with PIA, leaving London Heathrow on Sunday the 14th May at 2000hrs, arriving Monday the 15th at 0740hrs.
A small step in the scheme of things; a larger step for Harry Baxter.

Islamabad
Charles Urwin couldn't sleep. He lay on his back staring at the dark ceiling.
The recent conversation he had had with his wife had upset and rankled him. How many times would he have to repeat himself? There was no way he would convert to Islam. If anything he was a devout atheist!
His sole driver was getting to the top of the greasy pole in his chosen career. He had little or no respect for his contemporaries, believing they lacked the

intellectual rigour to win, relying on the 'club', the sycophancy, or kissing appropriate posteriors to achieve personal advancement.

He believed in his own appreciation of the 'big picture'; the labyrinth of understanding and finding a way through, round, under/over, geo-political scenarios being a personal and particular skill, enabling him to have, in his own hands, what he perceived as the levers of power. In fact, just what he was doing currently with the High Commissioner.

Distractions, such as the one raised by his wife, contributed nothing to his personal plans or advancement.

Through her family he had established a number of contacts and lines of communication that any security service would give their eye teeth for. Over a period of time he hoped to develop this network and the relationships within it, so that one major diplomatic coup would secure his professional standing at the highest level.

His wife lay quietly beside him, her eyes closed, facing away, aware that he was restless and awake, wondering to herself if, and when, she should raise the question again that had clearly angered her husband. If he did not convert then unforeseen problems could well arise from some of her family connections.

He could see the sky lightening at the edge of the window curtains, so got up slowly and carefully from the bed, as not to disturb his wife, and moved noiselessly into his dressing room, where he slipped on his trainers and jogging gear.

Exiting from the back of his villa Charles jogged slowly down the lane to the road where he turned right and picked up his pace a little. He could feel his heart rate increasing slightly, enjoying the sense of wellbeing that comes from regular exercise.

He had taken to the habit of listening to light classical music on his iPlayer as he ran, at times his running matching the sequence of the piece.

His mind was running around a number of complex issues relating to some Pakistan Government opposition connections and the obvious sensitivities that he must not allow to impact on the High Commission in any way.

The next second his heart was pounding as he was hit from behind and fell heavily to the dusty ground, disorientated with the breath knocked from his body, losing partial consciousness as an evil smelling bag was slipped over his head and tightened around his throat. He felt himself being picked up, his wrists and ankles tied together, then thrown into a vehicle which started its engine and moved off. His heart was racing as he slowly regained his breath and composure.

Thoughts filled his mind; hostage taking by major and minor crime syndicates was common in Pakistan for ransom monies. Was this what had happened? Or was it by a terrorist group for interrogation as to HM Government intentions?

Whatever the reasons he must emphasise one thing; he was worth more money to the kidnappers if he was returned alive.

The vehicle bounced along unmade roads, he thought for about half an hour, before coming to a halt. He could hear a muffled conversation taking place with, from time to time, one voice raised above the others.

Then he was lifted from the vehicle and bundled, his feet dragging and stumbling, until he was thrown to the floor in a room where his hood was ripped from his head. He squinted in the dark to try and see his captors but the two men were wearing headscarves that covered their faces.

The door banged shut and was locked. There were no windows. There was no light.

London

Harry had seen the Deputy on Friday for a last briefing and best wishes for success in his new role. The Deputy had cautioned him more than once to 'watch his back', and to send any reports or observations, that he did not wish to go through the normal channels, by secure satellite link laptop that he would carry in his briefcase. Secure encryption was necessary and essential, bearing in mind the sensitivity of the role, the region, friends and enemies.

Tel Aviv

Anna had completed most of her training by that weekend, and was resting in her apartment going over some of her briefing notes on the current political situation in Lebanon. The influence of terrorist groups within that sector was high, with external funding and control adding a further confusing dimension to an already highly fractious and divided country.

Islamabad

Charles Urwin was left for 24 hours without food, water or contact by his captors. His mind tried to cover all the possible permutations that could arise when they did make contact. Parched, hungry and worried he found the exercise useless except for preparing himself for the worst if it should arise.

In the dark room, he lay on the hard floor trying to conserve his energy, his throat bone dry, his thoughts confused.

Suddenly the door opened, and two masked men entered, one carrying a bottle.

They pulled him roughly into a sitting position against a wall before speaking in Urdu.

Urwin, who was fluent in the language, asked for water, which was given to him. He was only able to take a couple of swallows from the bottle before it was ripped from his hand.

He was weak and he knew it. Questions were thrown at him. If he did not respond quickly one of them would slap him hard around the head.

They knew he was from the High Commission. Who was he? What job did he do? Who was his boss?

Slowly, and painfully, he gave them the information they wanted.

They left, leaving the bottle.

VI

Sunday 14th May – Tuesday 16th May 2006

London Heathrow

Harry sat in the departure lounge at Heathrow waiting to board his PIA flight to Islamabad. His mobile pinged.

He saw it was a text from Vauxhall Cross advising that the First Secretary in Islamabad had been kidnapped, by persons unknown, and that his first task on arriving there would be to manage the internal Incident Team, including liaison with the local Pakistan Police.

'Bloody marvellous', he thought, 'Land, and get chucked in the deep end! Some acclimatisation I don't think!

Well, at least it puts a different complexion on the future relationship with the First Secretary!'

He deleted the text and shortly afterwards his flight was called and after an uneventful and boring 7¾ hours landed in Islamabad, Monday morning, just past 7.45am.

Harry was met by one of the High Commission staff and with diplomatic status passed quickly through Immigration and Customs.

The car journey to the High Commission was slow and erratic due to rush hour, but Harry found himself sitting in front of the High Commissioner by 9.35am.

The High Commissioner looked tired, drawn and worried.

'Welcome Mr Baxter. You will excuse me, I am sure, for keeping my welcome brief, but you are aware, I believe, of the possible kidnapping of the

First Secretary, Charles Urwin, that took place on Friday morning?'
'Yes, I was advised by text at Heathrow before departure, but no details were given.'
'The incident took place, we understand, early on Friday morning as Charles went for a morning run. His wife raised the alarm when he did not return and also contacted the local police. She is Pakistani, and comes from a well-known and influential family with contacts at the highest levels in the Pakistan Government. We understand the local Police Commissioner is demanding direct line reporting to him concerning this diplomatic incident.'
Harry interjected at this point, 'Has any contact been made, either to the Police or the High Commission, by the captors or any group claiming responsibility?
Additionally what is the makeup of the Incident team, and has anybody carried out a thorough questioning of the First Secretary's wife?'
There was slight pause before The High Commissioner replied. When he did Harry recognised the tone as formal with a cool undertone.
'When we finish this meeting you will go the Incident Room, meet the team, and assume overall responsibility.
You will determine what needs to be done in all areas, including a review of overall High Commission security. However the safe recovery of the First Secretary is your prime responsibility, and I expect updates on your progress at least twice a day, or more, if you consider any particular event or occurrence should be brought to my attention.'
Harry recognised the instruction.

The usual initial briefing to make sure the boss man's backside was flame and bullet proof, and responsibility was clearly defined in the event of failure. If successful, however, take one step back as the 'Sun King' takes one step forward to garner the glory! It never changes, Harry thought.

'Of course Sir,' Harry replied, establishing a tone of formality for the current discussions, and for any subsequent actions that may require a similar response.

The meeting finished the High Commissioner rose from his desk, gesturing Harry to follow him to the Incident Room, where he introduced Harry to two people who had stood up hurriedly as the High Commissioner had entered.

'Rabbits caught in the headlights', Harry thought to himself as he looked at them.

One was a young woman, obviously records and secretariat, the other, a rather supercilious looking individual of about 28, probably 3rd Secretary grade, no doubt from a 'good' university and with previous family connections with the Civil Service, Harry thought cynically.

The young woman smiled nervously when introduced to Harry as Marion Simpson, the other, retaining his disdainful expression as he proffered his hand, a trifle limp, as Jeremy Hollingworth.

Harry turned to the High Commissioner, thanking him for the introductions, and saying he would report back to him later that day with an update.

Turning to Marion and Jeremy he said, 'Can you please give me, on an accurate time line as possible, events as they have happened, including interventions by us, local police, etcetera.'

Jeremy responded immediately.

'We,' nodding at Marion, 'were advised of the suspected kidnap on Sunday, and asked to maintain liaison with the local police and to provide any assistance or counselling, if required, to the First Secretary's wife. Also deflect any conjecture by the Press if that should arise.'

His response was couched in a manner and tone that Harry instantly disliked, but did not immediately react to.

'Right, not a lot to go on then,' Harry responded pleasantly, 'Let me give you some views and guidance on how this *might* unfurl in the next 48 hours.'

For the next half an hour Harry explained the likely scenarios that could follow from such a kidnapping. There had been complete blackout of any news or comment by the Police and High Commission, as the respective parties waited for any announcement from possible kidnappers or particular terrorist groups.

Harry was keeping an open mind as to whether this was a straight ransom kidnapping or perhaps terrorist backed, in which case demands could be very different to ensure safe release. Release of political prisoners was often the request; non agreement would result in murder, or euphemistically, political assassination.

He sensed that Marion Simpson was worried that she was contributing little to the current situation but encouraged her to keep a timeline report from now covering all events, meetings, comms, phone, email whatever, which would keep her busy.

Jeremy Hollingsworth was a different mix. He gave the distinct impression that this was something that he should not be involved with. An effete, semi-languid air surrounded him, linked with a faint condescending manner in speech and approach that clearly indicated a level of intellectual, or, perhaps, plain arrogance. He obviously regarded Harry as of a 'lower rank'; people of his station should concentrate on policy and strategy, leaving 'doing' and implementation to the likes of Harry.

Behind his veneer Jeremy could not give a damn for the First Secretary, Charles Urwin. Frankly, if Charles did not return this could perhaps provide some local promotion for him.

Bluntly, Jeremy and Charles were very similar. Focussed, totally selfish in pursuit of their career advancement, such incidents should be regarded as opportunities. If played correctly, indicating concern and co-operating with all the appropriate agencies, then good annual reviews would follow. If success was not achieved by others then equal concern at outcome linked to capacity to handle additional tasks would ensure beneficial reviews and enhanced promotion prospects. Anything remotely considered a problem or a challenge should then be converted into an opportunity.

Harry drew the meeting to a close by asking Jeremy if he had interviewed the First Secretary's wife.

'Not as yet, although I thought of seeing her this afternoon. Perhaps we could go together?' he artfully suggested.

'Good idea. Will you telephone and organise that for this afternoon?' Harry responded putting some indication of seniority in his request.

Jeremy nodded his agreement impassively.

Just as they rose from their chairs the H.C's PA entered carrying an envelope.

'This letter, addressed to the High Commissioner was handed in about 30 minutes ago at reception.

He has read it and told me to bring it straight to you Mr Baxter.'
'Thank you', said Harry, gesturing to the others to sit down.
He took out the letter and read it aloud. The English was not good, almost comic in parts, despite the seriousness of the situation and the threats contained in it.
The message was simple and straightforward.

A ransom was to be paid, or the First Secretary would be killed. If the ransom was agreed to the Union Flag was to be lowered to half-mast the following day, Tuesday 16th May, at 2pm.
The amount demanded was 14,000,000 Pakistan Rupees, roughly £100,000.
No other demands were made, no political prisoners to be released, no political statements to be made. A straightforward ransom demand.
The letter finished by saying that if the Union Flag was seen at half-mast further instructions would be received at the High Commission within 24hours.
Harry turned to the Jeremy and Marion.
'Any comments?' Before they had a chance to reply he put up his hand and continued, 'Jeremy get that meeting set up with his wife, would you? Marion, start logging from Day One up to present. OK? Give me half an hour. I need to do some thinking.'
The others nodded and left him to think how the operation should be handled.
Firstly, how to get confirmation that Charles Urwin was still alive, and, more importantly keep him alive up to and through handover of the ransom.
Harry went straight to the HC's office and asked what current policy in terms of ransoms was.

'Officially H.M. Government does not pay ransoms. However in order to achieve safe retrieval of persons it is unofficial policy to pay, subject to a suitable operational plan being in place to ensure return of such monies. Subsequent trial of the criminals, particularly in regions such as this, is frankly secondary, bearing in mind fatalities often occur to the criminals during the rescue operation. Do you get my drift?'

'Yes.'

'Therefore as the 'expert', compared to the rest of us, I would be obliged if you would proceed as quickly as is prudent to recover our First Secretary. You will be seeing his wife Zahira this afternoon? Good, although I doubt she will be able to add much to the mix. However it will give her some comfort that we appear to be doing the best we can.'

At this point Harry interjected.

'Do I now have your authority to fly the Union Flag at half-mast tomorrow? I don't want to be chasing around tomorrow morning asking you for it. In situations like this things can change quickly with unforeseen consequences so I like to clear all approvals as they arise.'

The H.C's response was slightly testy.

'Mr Baxter, you have my authority to proceed as you see fit. The planning and execution of this recovery operation is in your hands. Good luck!'

'One other thing Sir. I intend to speak to the Police later this afternoon. Do we have any particular operational contacts with them? Somebody who would have good knowledge of local Intel? Local mafias, Mr Bigs?'

'Our contact is Inspector Irfan Chaudhry, Federal Investigation Agency. I suggest you start there.'

With that their discussion finished, and Harry hurried back to the meeting room where he met Jeremy in the corridor.
‘The meeting with Zahira Urwin is scheduled for 3pm at her villa.’
‘Good. Jeremy, we need to organise a meeting with the Police, following that, say at 4.30pm. Can you do that? At as senior a level we can get. Ask if we can see Inspector Chaudhry.’
He turned and entered the room, leaving Jeremy quietly fuming in the corridor.

Harry smiled to himself as he sat down and collected his thoughts which he quickly noted down in staccato form in his notebook.
Start as you mean to continue, he thought, knowing that he was irritating Jeremy, and starting to get under his skin.
However there were more important issues to resolve than concerning oneself with a junior diplomat’s sense of injured self-importance.
At 2 pm he collected Jeremy and they walked over to meet Zahira Urwin in her villa.
Although an attractive woman, she looked pale and drawn, which, bearing in mind the current stress she was under was perfectly understandable.
Introductions were quickly made and Harry started his questioning of Zahira in a low key way, giving her plenty of time to think before responding.
The usual conventional lines of enquiry were followed, yielding nothing. Exceptional or different activities leading up to Charles Urwin’s disappearance produced nothing. Had anything in their conversations indicated any sort of concern by her husband? None.

Harry then asked Zahira directly what her own thoughts were as to why her husband had disappeared.

With her head bowed and with a voice just above a whisper she said that it was either a kidnapping for a ransom, or by a terrorist organisation wanting to make a statement.

At this point she broke off, covering her face while she silently cried.

Harry apologised for his line of enquiry, but she shook her head, saying she realised that such investigations are necessary, and have to include awkward questions.

At this point Harry excused himself, and he and Jeremy left to go to the FIA and meet Inspector Irfan Chaudhry.

During the short drive to the FIA Harry expressed sympathy for Charles Urwin's wife Zahira and the feeling of helplessness that normally overtakes someone in this predicament. Jeremy murmured his agreement, somewhat lacking in conviction, but which did not surprise Harry.

At the FIA they were quickly taken to the Inspector's office where introductions were made.

Harry decided to take the initiative in starting the discussion.

'Inspector Chaudhry, may I thank you for agreeing to this meeting at such short notice, and which I greatly appreciate'.

The Inspector nodded.

'One of my difficulties is that I only arrived in Islamabad this morning to take up my appointment as Defence Advisor, so my background knowledge is sketchy to say the least', he said smiling wryly.

‘I will need to rely on your support and your local intelligence if we are to find and recover our First Secretary.’

The Inspector nodded again before he spoke with a half-smile.

‘I think it would be best, Mr Baxter, if we could be completely open with each other, otherwise in situations such as this, if facts are not shared, then the law of unintended consequences could kick in, often with unfortunate end results.’

Harry, somewhat surprised at the command of English, commented on this, to be told that the Inspector had spent a year in London with the Metropolitan Police on immigrant terrorist group recruitment, corresponding surveillance, mosque and madrassah propaganda, and community relations.

Inspector Chaudhry also advised that some of his briefings had been carried out by a section within the Security Service (MI5).

‘You will probably have had dealings with them?’ he suggested.

‘Not really,’ Harry lied, ‘Somewhat out of my league as most of my service has been overseas.’

Quickly changing the subject he said,

‘To deal with our present situation we received this letter today, demanding a ransom, which, if we agree to, should be indicated by our Union Flag being flown at half-mast tomorrow.

We are not aware of any specific political group being associated with this kidnapping, but this is where your guidance would be invaluable.’

Harry handed over the letter which the Inspector read.

He looked up.

'It's a straightforward kidnapping for ransom, and by the way we don't pay ransoms here in Pakistan.'
'What do you do then?'
'We make them believe they will get the ransom, arrange a handover of hostage for money, and then arrest them.'
'It's that simple, is it?'
'No, sometimes the hostage or the kidnappers get killed. The luck of the draw, I believe you say?'
Harry for a second or two was speechless. When he responded he spoke slowly.
''This man, the First Secretary, is important to HM Government, and is married to a Pakistani whose connections go to the very top. I don't think she, or her family, would be very pleased to hear what you have just said.'
Inspector Chaudhry replied in measured tones.
'You must understand that Islamabad is not London, nor is Pakistan like the UK.
Five Police Cadets were killed and a dozen injured by terrorist bombs in Quetta recently on the 11th May. A complete waste of life and we do not even know why. Nobody has claimed responsibility.'
He paused, reflecting before continuing,
'We do not have trained negotiators who can psychologically influence the hostage takers. They are invariably poorly educated, low grade, criminals. Money is their driver. They are not sophisticated and invariably are fatalistic in outlook. Their religion guides and helps them in that area. Their life is in God's hands.'
He fell silent, then,
'My comments are realistic knowing what has happened on many occasions before.'

Harry looked at Jeremy who said nothing, but gave a small shrug of his shoulders, which indicated nothing.

Harry spoke.

'I am recommending to the High Commissioner that we fly the Union flag as instructed tomorrow. We have been told in the letter that further contact will be made as to time and place for payment of the ransom, within 24hours of the flag flying at half-mast.

At this time, therefore, I am asking that you and I agree a plan to recover, alive, our First Secretary, in which I will participate.'

At this point the Inspector opened his mouth to say something, but was forestalled by Harry who raised his hand.

'In the absence of such an agreement then I, with others, will mount our own rescue attempt and no information contained in the subsequent ransom letter will be passed to you. Also you will have no idea as to where or when the rescue and ransom exchange will be taking place.'

Inspector Chaudhry looked at him with exasperation.

'Do you realise how many protocols, international agreements, local laws, etc., you will be breaking here in Pakistan if you proceed in this way?'

'Probably about the same number of protocols, international agreements, local laws, etc., that significant numbers of your fellow countrymen break on a daily basis in the UK, I would think!'

A short period of silence followed as both men mentally measured up their options.

Inspector Chaudhry broke the silence.

'If I allow you to participate you will not be carrying any weapon, and you must remain at the rear of the recovery team at all times. I do not want to have to report the death of the UK Defence Advisor as well as the First Secretary', he smiled grimly.

'Agreed', was Harry's response. 'I will brief the High Commissioner, on my return, of our agreed understanding.

Now can we discuss and agree what will be the preferred ops for recovering the First Secretary?'

The discussions took about an hour, each outlining their op of choice, raising counter proposals until a firm and final outline was agreed.

Harry knew that when a recovery squad went in, invariably the best laid plans went out of the window in the seconds that followed. However he was happy with the final agreed tactic.

He agreed to contact the Inspector as soon as contact had been made following the half-mast drill and shook hands firmly before they left.

Harry and Jeremy walked to their car without speaking. Once seated Harry said, 'I will brief the High Commissioner on what has been agreed and confirm with a report. You will *not* prepare a report or brief him. There will be no confusion or different interpretations on what has been decided. Do I make myself clear?'

Jeremy nodded, 'Yes, but it is normal for all parties to submit a report following such a meeting and is considered the correct protocol in case any matters, of whatever nature, are raised following that or related events.'

'I obviously haven't got it across yet, have I Jeremy?

I don't give a sh*t what is the accepted protocol, and that is the last time you start quoting Civil Service guidance notes at me.

Get this in your head. I'm running this op from the UK side, working with the FIA, and keeping my fingers crossed that their trigger happy hit squads don't kill our First Secretary and anybody else, including me. To minimise confusion there will no written or verbal brief to the HC other than from me. For the second, and last time, do you bloody well understand me?'

Jeremy nodded sullenly.

'Good, now let's get back to base.'

The short car journey was completed in silence and Harry went straight to Sir James to bring him up to date, whilst keeping detail to a minimum about the recovery operation. Sir James seemed content to leave things in his hands and wished him luck, whilst offering any assistance whatsoever, which, by the nature of a High Commission, is frankly very limited.

Harry thanked him for his offer, but replied that he had every confidence in the FIA and their experience of similar kidnappings in the past.

He also thought it was fortunate that Sir James could not see his crossed fingers behind his back!

Back at the FIA HQ Inspector Chaudhry was in discussion with the leader of the Recovery Team, and also detailing significant numbers of men to be put on the ground, on immediate and nearby roads to the High Commission.

These plain clothed observers were checking on their local Intel as to currently active ransom, or politically motivated, kidnapping gangs.

Judging by the wording in the ransom letter they were probably dealing with a ransom kidnapping, and focussed their attention on a number of low grade criminals.

Whoever, or whatever, they would be prepared, and as the Inspector thought to himself, the UK Defence Advisor would be pleasantly and professionally surprised at the outcome.

VII

Wednesday 17th May – 18th May 2006

Paris

In the DGSE HQ in Paris on that Wednesday morning, the 17th May, Alain Dubois had received a call from his chief confirming a meeting for 11am.

He thought this would probably be a further discussion on his posting, so was looking forward to it with some interest, and admittedly some trepidation.

Alain presented himself at Gilles Deniaud's office at 10.55am and was called in immediately.

'Bonjour Alain, ça va?

'Pas mal, merci.'

'Well, we have come to a decision on your posting, which I hope you will appreciate, and which we think will provide a suitable challenge to your skills. All we ask is that your actions do not precipitate a further civil war!'

Alain smiled, a shade weakly. 'Where?' he wondered?

Gilles Deniaud continued. 'Beirut is where you will be stationed. Not at the embassy but in the AFD (Agence Francaise de Developpment) as a logistics expert. Sufficiently vague, but detailed enough to enable you to travel anywhere in Lebanon and with sufficient justification to neighbouring Syria, bearing in mind the number of 'asylum seekers/immigrants' crossing its porous borders.' The last few words were accompanied with a lifting of his right eyebrow, and a cynical half smile playing on his lips.

'You and I are aware of the funding and support of terrorist/political groups in Lebanon from both Syria and Iran. Until the supply line of funds and weapons is cut we will experience, from time to time, the eruption of civil war, which is hugely destabilising for the region.'

Alain agreed, and started to respond.

'What exactly do you..........?' he started to say, before his 'Chef' interrupted him.

'Exactly. I shall expand. As you are aware we have a working relationship with Mossad who have a number of embedded assets in various Government Agencies around the world, incidentally not only in French agencies.

It works on a collaborative basis where Intel of every sort, political, financial, personal, military, including terrorist groups, is pooled, then analysed from a number of different perspectives, and is then acted on, in the best interests of La Belle France, we hope and trust, by our political masters.'

The eyebrow was lifted once again.

'You will remember the case of a few years ago where a foreign government official, sitting in Washington, a position of discretion, in charge of major funds, was able to influence an award to a French company of an international contract in Africa in exchange for 'un petit cadeau', a commission.

When tne abuse was discovered we had two options. Firstly, pressure on the official to ensure further contracts for French companies. NO, I joke!

Or more likely, pressure on the individual with the threat of personal exposure to his government, or pressure on his government to co-operate more closely with France, against the threat of international exposure of corruption by one of their placemen.

With every government trying to influence others, and increase their standing on the world stage, there is little room for niceties, where we have to play! We must use any weapon/device/threat to improve our spheres of influence.

Never ever forget, others will have no compunction in doing the same, or even worse, given the chance.'

Gilles fell silent whilst Alain absorbed what he had said.

Alain had heard similar things before, but Gilles felt a reminder was in order, bearing in mind where he was being posted.

'There are a number of scenarios in Lebanon and elsewhere, where we need to have better Intel and analysis. That is your brief. You will be advised of the names of embedded Mossad operatives. However they will not know yours.

I anticipate you will be going to Beirut in about two weeks. I suggest you bring yourself up to date with all available Intel and also with current AFD activities.

I will provide your background cover for ADF tomorrow. Learn thoroughly. We will talk again next week, same day and time.'

The meeting over, Alain returned to his office thinking that there was a different angle to this posting that he had not experienced before, namely, being embedded in a government agency. A first for him. This would also dictate a different method of Intel 'harvesting' coupled with a 'cover' that would have to be carefully maintained. New skills to be learned quickly.

He started to compile a list of Intel sub headings covering Lebanon, Syria and Iran, plus Israel for good measure, bearing in mind the embedded Mossad agents.

AFD was included, but he thought he would wait for his detailed 'cover' from Gilles before compiling that list. Current Intel updates started scrolling onto his screen after he had punched in the necessary passwords, and country demand codes.

'Volumes', he thought, 'Focus and apply yourself. If you don't Gilles will no doubt trip you up next week!'

He made himself a large mug of black coffee.

Islamabad

That morning, Harry had advised Sir James, the High Commissioner, of the broad contents of the meeting with Inspector Chaudhry, including their agreement as to the type and scale of their recovery plan for the First Secretary.

Sir James insisted, briskly, he did not wish to know specific details; just that maximum effort was being made to recover Charles Urwin safely.

Harry, maintaining his apolitical facial expression, was quietly thinking to himself that, on the one hand, ersatz concern was being publically expressed by Sir James, whilst prime focus was exercised in ensuring cast iron protection against any possible subsequent criticism in the event of failure.

Pushing those thoughts aside, he reminded the High Commissioner that the Union flag would be flown at half-mast that afternoon, which was acknowledged.

At the due time the Union flag was lowered, and the waiting began for the next contact from the captors.

Tel Aviv
Anna was being briefed in detail on her role in ADF and the particular training she would receive in Paris in about a week's time.
This would be necessary for two reasons. One, specific training to act as a convincing cover for her operational role, and two, that her journey to Lebanon was on an Air France flight, which no doubt, could, and would, be checked by interested parties.
Before she left, additional small arms refresher training would be included, a purely defensive measure, but necessary under the given set of circumstances.
Over the next few days Anna must familiarise herself as to ADF operations and structure, whilst at the same time bringing herself up to date on current political activities within Lebanon, and the tangled web of connections across borders influencing events.

Damascus, Syria. 1900hrs
The Committee for World Jihad was meeting in a private room in a hotel, not far from the International Airport.
Debate and argument had waxed to and fro between groups either intent on establishing their position, or those wanting to retain the status quo.
Elements of Hezbollah and Al Qaeda had delayed many issues by their petty bickering, but there appeared to be some sort of consensus emerging.

The basic strategy was to focus on Lebanon, with Israel on its southern border.
With Hezbollah firmly established and controlling many areas in Lebanon it would be comparatively simple to inflame the situation by a pre-emptive strike against Israel, which would bring an automatic response by both army and air units.
As The Jihadists would possibly be able to acquire at some time in the near future Spent Uranium 238 tipped rockets, their attacking power against Israeli Land Forces would now be significantly increased.
A sub group would now plan the overall strategy, following which various area commanders on the ground in Lebanon would be briefed in order to plan their particular operations.

Islamabad

Inspector Chaudhry had flooded the streets around the embassy district with plainclothes officers who had been briefed about the kidnapped senior British official. Their task was to infiltrate all known suspect cells, gather any relevant intelligence, and also observe any actions on the streets, however tenuous, that might lead the authorities to the kidnappers.
During this 36 hour period Harry had sent, to the Deputy, by encrypted satellite comms laptop, a truncated report of what had happened since his arrival. This would be read against the usual High Commission reports sent to London. Harry wanted to fill in a few of the gaps, which would get lost in the official version, with a number of personal observations, which could expand some of the background for the Deputy.

Since the Union flag had been placed at half-mast, there had been no contact from the FIA, or more importantly, from the kidnappers.
The lull before the storm, thought Harry. Whatever sort of storm that would turn out to be!
On the streets the plainclothes team was digging for information, some leading to dead ends, others merely a distraction.
Purely by chance, one of them then had a piece of luck. Nothing to do with intelligence gathering, just observation.
As the agent crossed a street near the embassy district he noticed a truck stopping, and the driver gesturing to one the old men standing in a group on the side of the road. He saw them talking, the old man shaking his head from time to time, but changing to nodding agreement when some money changed hands. The driver handed him an envelope and pointed in the general direction of the High Commission. The old man set off at a slow pace in that direction.
The truck turned round and moved away slowly, the driver looking back at the old man's slow progress.
The officer, following his hunch, mounted his Ravi motorbike, and gently followed the truck down the road, keeping it in sight about 50 yards ahead. Traffic controlled the speed of the truck making it easy for the officer to maintain station.
After about half an hour travelling in a NE direction the truck pulled of the main road, then making several left and right hand turns before pulling up in front of a dilapidated industrial one storey building.

Watching, from a comfortable distance, the officer saw the truck driver look around before entering the building through a side door.

Maintaining a safe distance, but keeping the building under surveillance, he reported his suspicion and position to HQ FIA, who ordered him to maintain observation and report any entries or departures.

Additional specialist officers would be sent to assist, and determine whether there was any basis to his suspicion.

Inspector Chaudhry called the High Commission to enquire if a package had been delivered, and spoke to Harry following his brief conversation with the High Commissioner.

'My officer followed his hunch, and perhaps we might be lucky, bearing in mind we think the kidnappers are fairly low grade, and are probably not fully aware who they have.

However, we must assume they're serious and respond accordingly.

You requested your own participation in the rescue attempt. I will make it clear again. You will stay at the back, in reserve. Is that clearly understood?'

'Completely.'

'Good. I will revert once I have more information and corroboration, or otherwise. Goodbye.'

Inspector Chaudhry assigned a surveillance team to be on standby to investigate the factory if, and when, confirmation was received from the High Commission that a communication had been received detailing demands.

Harry, meanwhile, at about 2pm, was keen to find out if a package had been delivered, and went to Sir James's office to see if anything had arrived.

With the number of letters and packages arriving daily it took some time to filter out the one, crudely addressed to the High Commissioner.
Its content was stark.
The captors were now aware that they had the First Secretary and the ransom demand was the equivalent of about £150,000.
The instruction was to bring a case containing the money to a particular point on a road leading SE from Islamabad, at a particular time, the following night. The First Secretary would be handed over at that time. No police, no army. Any sign of either would result in the death of the First Secretary.
Harry was straight on the phone to Inspector Chaudhry.
After giving him the details of the letter he continued,
'We've probably got less than 24 hours max to deal with this, subject to your views on the local villains.'
'Mr Baxter, exactly my thoughts. Now will you give me a little time to confirm our intelligence, speak to the officers on the ground, evaluate the strength of the report, confirm by my surveillance teams that this is indeed correct, review the locale and prepare an outline plan for action? Having done that I will contact you soonest. Do you agree?'
Harry recognised the irritation under the line of questioning, and readily agreed. In Pakistan there was not much else he could do, other than agree!

--

In the totally dark room, where he was chained to a wall, Charles Urwin had now been fed and watered. That meant the door had been opened briefly to allow a bottle of water and a sandwich to be thrown in, generally in his direction.

His thoughts to then were totally confused due to significant dehydration and no food; at times a dreamlike state overtook him, challenging the barrier between sleep and reality.

He heard murmurings from the adjoining room, a distant sound of traffic from time to time, nothing that helped him identify where he was, and what was going to happen.

In his villa his distraught wife Zahira had contacted her family, who in turn were now using their connections at the highest and, in some cases, the lowest levels, to try and determine who were responsible for his kidnap.

Inspector Chaudhry had sent in his surveillance team following the initial sighting, and was waiting impatiently for their radio report as to whether positive ID had been established.

Harry, meanwhile, had briefed Sir James as to his conversation with Chaudhry, and promised to provide updates as they occurred.

The waiting was always the killer in situations like this, Harry thought.

In his own mind he was worried as to the professionalism and experience of the 'rescue' squad, but there was absolutely nothing he could do about that. He was dependent on Inspector Chaudhry and his team. Whatever the Deputy's opinion of the First Secretary, Charles Urwin, Harry didn't need some fatality in his first week in Pakistan, plus the ensuing international headlines and recriminations that would follow.

Later that day, at about 8pm, the telephone rang in Harry's office whilst he was updating a far from interested Jeremy Hollingworth.

It was Inspector Chaudhry.

'In brief. We have identified and confirmed the location of your First Secretary.

It is planned that the rescue operation will commence between 2 and 3am. Be here by midnight for briefing. Also, remember my words concerning your position in this operation. No participation, merely observation. Understood?'

'Yes, I will see you later as arranged. Goodbye.'

'Some movement?' queried Jeremy.

'Some. I'll catch up with you tomorrow, OK?'

Jeremy nodded and left, wondering what had been said during the telephone conversation. He shrugged mentally, and thought no doubt he would be briefed tomorrow.

Time passed slowly for Harry after he had briefed the High Commissioner that some progress had been made, and that he would be able to provide further detail the following day, after he had seen Inspector Chaudhry.

He had been somewhat economical with the truth, but felt that with such porosity in the High Commission it was probably more secure not to explain that a rescue operation was planned for that night.

At 11.45pm he arrived at the FIA HQ and was taken to Chaudhry's office.

After formal greetings Harry asked,

'How are you going to handle this operation? How many men on the ground? What numbers are we dealing with?'

The Inspector responded, 'Briefing will commence shortly. Listen to what I and my officers have to say, and if you feel that your observations are relevant then you will have an opportunity to contribute. OK?'

Harry took the point, 'Yes, excuse my concern, but I'm sure you can appreciate my reaction in such a situation.'
'Of course. Please follow me to the Ops briefing.'

In her villa, Zahira Urwin was sitting discussing her husband's capture with three members of her family.
She was tearful but composed as she listened to her father, Nadeem Kirmani, give words of encouragement, and details of his efforts to try and track her husband's capturers down.
Her grandfather had established a trading company, which had grown exponentially since partition, and which had served as a springboard for her father to enter the murky, but money influenced, arena of Pakistan politics.
The trading company was a figurehead in the Pakistan business world with its reach extending into every area of commerce, and, as a consequence, general and political society.
Her father had served two terms as a senior Minister in the Government, his influence extending much further than his ministerial brief. He took pride in this, claiming that his 'king making' ensured compliant policies from the very top.
'I have spoken to the Chief of Police and he has assured me that everything that can be done is being done. He did say however, that the Federal Investigation Agency (FIA) is the lead agency on this matter, as it involves a foreign diplomat. I have asked him to speak to his equivalent in the FIA, and put as much pressure on that force to secure your husband's early release.

I shall also raise the matter with all relevant ministries.'

He paused at this point, looking to his two sons, from his second marriage, to provide some additional moral support.

The elder brother, Kamran, thirty two, reiterated in the main what his father had expressed, adding his own words of commiseration, and invoking the blessing of Allah on any rescue attempt.

His younger brother, Azmat, aged twenty seven, mumbled a few words of sympathy, but thinking very different thoughts.

Although only twenty seven he had been radicalised from an early age, school/madrassah having played an important part in his life.

His conversion to the cause had been gradual; the drip feed of propaganda over the years, laced with an iron connection to Islam and the apparent world persecution of his 'brothers', coupled with the pervasive mentoring by one of his 'teachers' had ensured that his real thoughts remained hidden, a solid link to his faith, and a fostered hatred of most things Western.

He was now a committed jihadist, in a prime position in Pakistan society, protected by his family name and social standing with easy access to Government information, whether confidential or otherwise. Nowhere did he appear, currently, on any presumed list of agitators, or government opponents. On the contrary, with his father's reach and influence and his own quiet nature, the complete reverse.

He worked in his father's international operation, new business market development, an ideal cover for connections across the jihadist spectrum, his travels encompassing Afghanistan, Iraq, Iran and

various other Middle East, Gulf and East African countries.
As to his thoughts concerning the British First Secretary, he could not be bothered whether he lived or died. He was an irritant who had married his half-sister, and only hindered the ultimate success of the Caliphate.

Harry climbed into the blacked out Nissan van, indistinguishable from the hundreds that fill the street of Islamabad.
The seven men of 'A' team sat silently as the van drove through a succession of back streets for about twenty minutes before it stopped and switched off its engine and lights.
The team leader consulted his watch. It was 1.30am.
'B' team should now be in position not far from the rear of the building where the First Secretary was kept.
It had been agreed to assault the building at 1.45am from the rear, effectively driving the captors to the front, where, hopefully, they would be arrested by the 'A' team.
Harry had smiled to himself, thinking that this 'A' team was some way from the American TV series, but keeping his fingers crossed that they would be just as successful.
The team leader indicated that they should take up positions, so, leaving the van quietly they moved into their allotted positions.
Harry had been given strict instructions to stay with the team leader at the rear which he complied with.
They settled into their agreed positions, and as their watches showed 2am a loud blast, probably a stun

grenade, heralded the start of the rescue operation at the rear of the building. The first was quickly followed by a second, as 'B' team broke into the rear of the building.
Shouting could be heard, and smoke drifted across a partial moon, as suddenly the door at the front of the building opened and a small van, without lights, accelerated out, scattering members of the team in its way.
Harry, unarmed, who was standing about 50 yards back from the building, reacting purely instinctively, looked around and spotting a half-brick on the dusty ground picked it up, as the van, engine howling under acceleration, came towards him.
The driver could not see Harry as he took aim and threw the brick as hard as he could into the windscreen from a range of about 15-20 yards. The force of his throw and the speed of the vehicle shattered the windscreen into the driver's face, the van then swerving left, hitting the edge of a building opposite, and causing it to tip over onto its side.
Harry ran over and yanked open the door to look at a bloodied and unconscious driver.
He turned to the back of the van, opening the door to see a tied and gagged body; eyes wide open with fear over the gag, staring at him.
He guessed it was the First Secretary as he gently peeled back the gag.
'Charles Urwin, I presume?' he said trying to introduce some levity into the situation.
The First Secretary's voice was croaky as he replied.
'Who the hell are you?'

‘Harry Baxter, Military Advisor, arrived this week.’

‘Help me out of these ropes.’

Harry pulled him to his feet and quickly untied him.

As he finished untying the First Secretary, the Team Leader came over, advising that most of the captors had been arrested, one had disappeared, and the driver of the van was still unconscious.

In the next ten minutes two ambulances appeared, one to take the van driver to a prison hospital, the other to take Charles Urwin to a private hospital for a full examination following his ordeal.

Harry had commiserated with him about his capture and wished him a speedy recovery from any after effects, this gesture being met with a curt nod.

The team leader tried to indicate to Harry that what he had done had not followed the Inspector’s instructions of observation only, no involvement.

Harry pointed out that what he had done was an instinctive reaction, in fact just a close fielder’s throw to wicket, this making the team leader smile and shrug his shoulders.

Radio communications ensured that Inspector Chaudhry, The High Commissioner, and the First Secretary’s wife were advised immediately of the First Secretary’s release, and location of the private hospital.

Harry returned with the teams to FIA HQ to debrief Inspector Chaudhry. He was able to clarify his own role, being both fortunate and due to position, inevitable. The half-brick was merely opportune.

This raised a quizzical eyebrow from the Inspector but no comment. After the debriefing, and after ensuring that details would be given to him concerning the captors' background, he returned to the High Commission at about 5.00am to grab a couple of hours sleep before personally briefing the High Commissioner at 8.30am that Thursday morning the 18th May.

Tel Aviv

Anna was advised to prepare and pack ready to depart to Paris on Sunday the 21st May. This would enable her to settle in, prior to training and briefing with the Agence Francaise de Developpment (AFD), which would commence on Tuesday, the 23rd.

Monday would be spent with Mossad Bureau, Paris, providing her with her new identity, background details and necessary documents, Carte D'Identité, Carte Grise, etc.

She would fly in to Charles de Gaulle as Anna Harrison on El Al, but fly to Beirut on Air France as whom?

*

Islamabad

The High Commissioner looked considerably relieved after Harry's briefing and said he would be visiting Charles Urwin in hospital, as soon as the doctors advised that he had recovered sufficiently from his kidnapping.

'Well Harry' he said, in an unusually friendly tone, 'A satisfactory outcome to something that otherwise doesn't even bear thinking about.

You now see, I am sure, why our security strategy needs a complete review and the establishment of a series of protocols to ensure that such a similar incident does not occur again.'

Harry nodded as Sir James continued, 'Assume that task is your first priority to the exclusion of anything else, until completed. Is that clear?'
Harry nodded again.
'Good. I shall telephone his wife now.'
He paused.
'Of course she is probably at the hospital presently. I will call later.
Thank you. I am sure you will have plenty to occupy you now on your Review.'
With that Harry was dismissed.
Returning to his office he called up Jeremy Hollingworth and Marion Simpson for an update.
Marion seemed genuinely pleased at the news; Jeremy's look of indifference spoke a thousand words.
'Right, where are the written orders for Security issues covering the High Commission?'
'Somewhere in the Registry, I think,' Jeremy replied languidly.
'Well I think you had better go and bloody well find them in the Registry,' Harry snapped, very tired after the night's activities.
'We have to do a complete strategic review of all security issues in the High Commission, soonest. So chuck along and don't come back until you have them. That is not an excuse for several cups of coffee and a gentle look through Records.
After what happened to the First Secretary we don't want a repeat in the next few weeks. Might be a Third Secretary next time, and we might not be so lucky in finding him, or, as keen to rescue him as we were on this occasion.'
The last comment was accompanied by a glare at Jeremy, who got up from his chair and hurried away.

VIII

Monday 22nd May – Sunday 28th May 2006

Paris France

Anna was being briefed that morning in the Mossad Paris office, situated in an innocuous looking building not far from the Israeli Embassy at No 3, Rue Rabelais, Paris.

Her detailed cover and background would be fairly easy to provide; English mother. French father, both deceased.

Long periods in the UK in her formative years accounted for her, not quite, bi-lingual French.

However, her French Passport, Carte D'Identité, and Carte Grise, all added authenticity to her cover.

Her new name was Anne Hardy, both forename and surname being French, with obvious English connection.

Her roving brief, when operating with the AFD (Agence Francaise de Developpment) in Lebanon, was to cover as many bases as possible in areas where contacts were most likely with units or representatives of Hezbollah.

One particular region included the southern suburbs of Beirut.

Hezbollah completely dominated this particular area. The terrorist organisation's military infrastructure was embedded in the civilian population, and their word was the law.

In Lebanon, Hezbollah controlled, in addition to the Beirut suburbs, the south and North East of Lebanon. Their sources of funds and political support were Iran and Syria.

A dangerous area in which to try and recruit an informer, or to gather reliable Intel without suspicion. A very slow and delicate grooming operation would need to be mounted. Time was critical, both in establishing a source, and also in obtaining relevant and timely notice of any likely operations by Hezbollah, whether within Lebanon's boundaries or external attacks against Israel.

Hezbollah had infiltrated into the social and military fabric of the Gaza, supplying rocketry and training personnel to aid Hamas, whilst also arming Fatah and Islamic Jihad.

Paradoxically Hezbollah is Shia Muslim, whilst Hamas and Fatah are Sunni.

Her Controller was talking her through part of her assignment remit,

'Rapelle Anne, we are not expecting miracles from Day one. We have always played the long game and in that region it is the only game.

To get the sort of Intel we are looking for will require a dedicated approach to pull together a credible cell of perhaps two, or maximum three people. They will have to be kept in isolation from each other; overspill could be fatal. Understood?'

Anne nodded.

'There is another Mossad agent working in Beirut but with a totally different agenda. You will not be told his name.

'You also understand that there is another agency operating within AFD, namely the DGSE?'

Anne nodded again.

'You should be aware that whilst your level of operation is Intel gathering, the role of the DGSE officer is somewhat higher, and in many ways more hazardous. He will be operating on a close surveillance and counter terrorism basis and all that entails.

He will know your identity, but you will not know his for the obvious reasons I have just stated. Clear?'

'Perfectly.'

'Good. Then let us carry on with the regional background briefing and the specific operations of AFD.'

The detailed briefing continued, Anne aware that tomorrow she would be starting her induction with AFD at their offices near to the Gare de Lyon.

Islamabad

In Islamabad Harry had received an encrypted message from the Deputy via his satellite laptop.

Briefly he had commented on the rescue operation gleaned from official High Commission reports back to the Foreign Office in London.

However, the main thrust was that the new DG of SIS was carrying out a complete review of strategy and operations, and that it may be necessary for Harry to return to London for a few days to assist in preparing answers to detailed questions that may arise.

He smiled to himself as he read the 'official speak' of the Deputy's message. He could imagine the unprintable verbal comments that were much more likely!

At this point Jeremy entered his office, wearing his usual semi-truculent, diffident expression.

Harry looked up.

'Shut the door Jeremy.'

Jeremy complied and sat down.

Harry looked at him for several seconds, just long enough for the subject to start to feel uncomfortable and wonder what is going to be said.

In a quietly firm voice Harry then explained in concise terms what his Military Advisor role in the High Commission meant, and in addition the review on overall security that needed to completed soonest.

'Just be quite clear Jeremy, that if you co-operate with me in completing this exercise in short order, then we will have no problems in term of communication and relationship.

However, if you intend to operate at half-cock, and with little or no enthusiasm and commitment, then I need to know now, and I will go straight to the High Commissioner to get your replacement. I will also give him a report of your current attitude and ineffectiveness.

So it's quite easy, work with me, and let's get the job done, or continue as you were, and you can bugger off now!

Understood?'

Jeremy, looking somewhat startled started to speak.

'I don't think I've been spoken to like that before,' he said in a somewhat surprised voice.

'Well if you're working with me, get used to it,' replied Harry,

'We haven't got the time to sod about. The job needs to be done, now, and well. Are you up for it, or do I go and see your boss now?'

A short pause followed.

For the first time the expression changed on Jeremy's face as he spoke.

'Yes, you're right. I have been unprofessional. I apologise. I am happy to work with you and get this project done. Plus, I do know some of the

physical and electronic gaps in the High Commission.'
He stood up and extended his right hand to Harry, who also stood and shook it firmly.
'Good,' Harry smiled, 'let's get Marion in and start drawing up a plan and to-do list.
And, if you haven't got all that bumf from the Registry within the next two hours I'm definitely going to see your boss!'
Jeremy smiled, turning away pretending to run out of the office door.
Who knows, Harry thought, perhaps I've got at least one on side now!
Marion arrived, carrying a large number of files, which did not fill Harry with keen anticipation.
'They are?'
'All the files in General Admin that contained some element of Security. These are the hard files before we became IT smart.
I've brought them along because I'm not sure all were then put on our database.'
'Great,' said Harry, somewhat despondently, thinking of the cross referencing that would have to done.
'Actually I've done some of the cross referencing already,' said Marion, as though she'd guessed what he was thinking.
'Great,' said Harry in a more positive note.
Marion opened up the PC on his desk and pulled up the current Security files.
The next few hours were taken up with determining current security protocols against the most recent audits, and determining their effectiveness against the classified Security Strategy documents that Jeremy had brought from the Registry.

These were now some years old, and clearly in need of revision and transfer to a secure electronic platform.

It was clear considerable work needed to be done, top to bottom, left to right.

Tedious, boring, but very necessary, and when all that had been done translating such protocols into physical operating systems that could be clearly understood by all within the High Commission.

SIS (MI6) London

The Deputy had been asked to attend a meeting with the DG, James Readman, that afternoon at 1400hrs.

When asking his PA what the subject matter was, she replied that her opposite number in the DG's office had said' just bring an open mind!'

Metaphorically, the Deputy's stomach sank as he realised that a number of his concerns were about to be realised.

When the appointment had been announced internally, and knowing the particular individual's background, the Deputy was convinced that this was payback time and most definitely further evidence of the politicisation of Civil Service establishments.

There had been some well-founded gossip, about 18 months previously, concerning the ready co-operation of the now DG with the government of the day, corroborating certain Number 10 and Foreign Office statements, which had been shown to somewhat economic with the truth.

Rumours indicated that his appointment as DG was appreciation of his co-operation.

The Deputy checked through his current Ops list to highlight, or otherwise, those that might be raised in discussion, and asked his PA to produce a bullet point Sitrep for him to take to the meeting.

At the due time he entered the DG's office to be greeted, somewhat effusively, by James Readman.

They shook hands, the Deputy instinctively putting together in his head a short description of what he was experiencing.

The DG was a sleek, well dressed, in a restrained style, somewhat oleaginous individual, a little too warm or familiar in approach at first meeting.

An intense focus on the recipient, a style to include and make the 'us' at that moment, be both important, and feel important.

'Norman, let's take these more comfortable chairs by the window, I get fed up sitting at conference tables in the inevitable formal structured meetings.'

His hand rested lightly on Norman's shoulder as he propelled him gently towards the windows.

'Not a bad view, eh?' he said as they took their seats.

The Thames was spread in front of them, disappearing under Vauxhall Bridge immediately to the West, whilst the river view to the East extended to Lambeth Bridge.

'Norman, let me say initially that although I have been made DG, and you were probably hoping for that appointment yourself, your position as Deputy is absolutely fundamental for me, and for what we are going to have to carry out over the next two years.'

The Deputy immediately noticed the 'we', thinking collective responsibility for any future cock ups was being established on Day One.

The DG continued, 'I have had long and detailed discussions with the PM and certain members of the Cabinet concerning our role moving forward, the size and shape of the Service, both for now and the future, say the next 10 years, and the profile of its structure, both technical and human resource elements.'

The Deputy said nothing, maintaining his professional demeanour.

The DG, expecting some comment at this stage, paused briefly before continuing,

'It is very obvious and has been for some time that the game is changing. The threat is equally placed both here at home and overseas, and the link is clear to see with Islamic fundamentalism and Jihads. The increasing numbers of UK born Muslims going overseas for Jihad training; Pakistan, Africa etc.; whether to bring it back to the UK, or to be used in some insurrection in the Middle East or Africa.

It is going to be necessary for us to recruit a totally different agent and officer mix, than what was the recognised profile less than 10 years ago.

We are going to have to change our recruitment agenda to attract a more diverse, ethnic cadre. One that be easily located in local UK ethnic communities both here, and through family relatives, in overseas territories.

Inclusivity is something the Government is stressing across the board, and it is absolutely necessary for us to adopt its best practice here.'

The Deputy had been listening carefully, and had been wondering, during the latter comments, how their current security and background checks would have to be modified, and improved, in order to weed out the rogue elements.

'In brief, Norman, we have a major challenge. We need to make the service completely 'Fit for Purpose', for a time timescale extending up to 10

years, plus ensuring that we adopt those social policies being promoted and encouraged by the Government. Inclusive, multi-ethnic, reaching across social boundaries, the promotion of equal opportunity from both private and public sector.
Will you help me map out the strategy and implement what is required in our service for the 21st century?'
The Deputy paused, collecting his thoughts.
'As you are aware I have been here now for over twenty years, and yes, there have been some basic changes along the way. Pre and post-Cold War tactics and antics, industrial espionage on an industrial scale, etc., before 9/11 changed everything.
I operate by our charter. 'Defence of the Realm' sums it up.
Yes you have my support, although I can see some real problems along the way.'
'Norman, that's what I need. Identify the problems so we can fix them.'
The Deputy saw the 'we' again.
'Can you put together some outline proposals and an organogram that we can then start to flesh out?'
'In amongst the Ops I can hack something out.'
'Good, let you and me kick it around in about 10/12 days' time before we pull in others. OK?'
The DG rose from his seat, indicating the meeting was over.
The Deputy returned to his office wondering where exactly he would start and what sort of hybrid animal the DG wanted to construct.
The DG had returned to his seat by the window and was reflecting on the meeting with the Deputy.
He would never have got my DG role, he thought, a typical career officer, born to serve, not savvy

enough for the political infighting, which is always present, and always a significant component, in the path on the way to the top slot.

Regretfully he will have to go. What's needed is somebody with the drive and political antenna that can carry out the changes required. Tough enough to take the tough decisions, ruffle a number of unnecessary feathers, but a man who can navigate well through choppy waters. A man who will carry out what I want him to do. Misplaced loyalty, and an old fashioned view at a time like this, I do not need.

How to gently ease him out is the question. No rush at present. May make a fatal mistake. Early retirement perhaps? Who knows what will happen in the next few months?

He returned to his desk making a few personal notes in a file which he locked securely in his safe, before telling his PA he was off to the Foreign Office for a lengthy meeting. Do not wait for him.

The Deputy had returned to his office and was sitting staring into middle distance when the telephone rang.

It was an old colleague, Frank Stansfield, a senior field agent, who, some three years previously, had taken early retirement, to take up a position in an international security firm, providing close protection and support in a number of countries, particularly the Middle East and Africa.

They kept in touch, for old time's sake, a coffee, or sometimes something stronger.

This time, after the usual exchanges, Frank asked the Deputy to come to dinner one evening; he wanted to ask a favour of him. The least he could do was offer dinner!

‘Frank, I’m happy to come to dinner and have a friendly chat, but you know I cannot discuss anything concerning ops, or the Service. Is that clearly understood? Incidentally, you do realise that although you are now in the private sector you are still covered and responsible under the Official Secrets Act? But why am I telling you that?’

Pause.

‘Fine.’

They agreed to meet for dinner on Thursday the 25th May. Frank would contact the Deputy’s PA with time and place.

Replacing the phone the Deputy wondered what Frank wanted to discuss, but dismissed it quickly as he focussed his thoughts on the recent discussion with the DG.

It was a scenario he had expected. Leopards don’t change their spots, and the new DG was no exception.

His reputation, both public and private, had preceded him.

A man, whose mastery of ‘flexibility’ in the pursuit of advancement in the political arena matched that of the very best of Indian contortionists, was unlikely to remain satisfied with the old guard for very long.

It was a certainty that younger, more malleable and modern followers, unelected but committed placemen, convinced of the rightness of their broad social message, would gladly fill any of those positions.

Norman thought that in all probability his days as Deputy would probably be numbered, but he, sure as hell, would not make it easy for anybody to politicise the Service for political expediency, or favour.

His personal mantra was clear. Defence of the Realm.
Take each step as it comes; play the long game if he can. Bureaucracy can be a great leveller and time consumer when played as such, and he would certainly play that hand if required.
However he had been asked to prepare an outline paper and organisation for discussion. That would take a little time bearing in mind the confidential nature of such a document.
He smiled to himself. This could be quite stimulating in its own way!

Paris
Wednesday, the 24th May, was a glorious, warm, classic Parisian day, which Alain Dubois fully appreciated as he walked to the DGSE HQ that morning.
Plus différent que Liban, he thought as he entered and made his way to his office.
He re-read a number of his documents and briefings before presenting himself outside his Section Head's office at 11.00am.
He knocked and was called in by Gilles Deniaud who rose to shake his hand before indicating a chair and then coffee.
'D'accord Alain, let's get your briefing started.
Your responsibility, avec souplesse, will be to two Mossad agents embedded in the AFD. The first, a man named X, should not concern you at all. He is well trained and can really take care of himself, and I mean really!
The second is a different proposition. A woman called Anne Hardy. French father, English mother. Both deceased.

Her role is Intel gathering, on the broadest front. Hezbollah activities, current or planned. Funding and weapons supply and distribution; Syria and Iran in particular. Routes of both into Liban, middlemen, types and quantities, all the usual suspects.

Additionally, and this is the most difficult and dangerous part of her mission, is to establish a reliable informer in the South who can indicate if any specific operations against Israel are planned, and even more importantly if Hezbollah is likely to gain access to any spent uranium tipped missiles.'

At this point Alain looked somewhat perplexed.

'Spent uranium tipped missiles?'

'Yes. We are not talking ICBMs, but short range tactical weapons, ground to air, and specifically ground to ground.

This has arisen because a rogue Pakistani nuclear physicist in 2004 passed details of the Pakistan nuclear programme and critical scientific information to Iran, Libya, and North Korea.

He gave, as his excuse, the idealistic statement that all should benefit, but it was a clear breach of the International Non-proliferation Treaty.

We believe a lot of the information had also been passed from Pakistan to certain Al Qaeda elements in Afghanistan who have strong links through to Hezbollah, so we have a pincer effect including Iran who actively support, fund, and arm them as well.'

'This is a real hornet's nest then?'

'Yes it is. Hence the sensitive and dangerous nature of what Anne Hardy will be trying to establish as an Intel source, plus adding to that with her regional brief, which includes Syria.

Fortunately your respective operations are complementary, which will mean fairly regular contact in order to carry out your designated functions.
Your role will be to shadow her at all times; keeping your AFD cover intact as you monitor her activities within the organisation, whilst having a full perspective of her real operational assignment.'
'One question.'
'Yes.'
'In an emergency I need to know the identity of the Mossad agent who really knows how to take good care of himself. It's only backup if things turn really nasty.'
'Very well. His name, his operational name, is Georges Gagnier.'
Gilles then took Alain through a number of communication protocols, passwords, encryption systems, all contained in the highly confidential satellite laptop, which would serve as his prime communication tool for contact to both Mossad station chief in Beirut and Gilles in Paris.
It was decided that he would fly Air France to Beirut the following Saturday, the 27th May 2006.

Islamabad
Harry had gone to the hospital to see how Charles Urwin was recovering from his ordeal, and was surprised to find him dressed and in the process of discharging himself despite concern from the doctors.
Having introduced himself, Harry offered to drive him home, but Charles insisted on being taken directly to the High Commission.
Conversation was brief during the journey, and Harry noted a certain coolness in Charles' manner.

Perhaps some delayed reaction to his experience, perhaps his usual demeanour, or perhaps because of what the Deputy had suggested initially.

The First Secretary thanked Harry, albeit somewhat curtly, for driving him to the HC, where he disappeared in the general direction of the High Commissioner's office.

Harry returned to his office to see that Jeremy and Marion were heavily engrossed in the manual transfer of security issues and protocols to the IT platform, using Foreign Office and GCHQ encryption and password protected software to provide level six security.

Progress at this technical level was being made, but it was clear that elements of security involving the physical perimeter of the High Commission were still unresolved.

Harry's telephone rang.

It was the High Commissioner calling him to his office.

Entering the office he saw that Charles was sitting across from the Sir James, looking none too happy.

Sir James greeted Harry pleasantly, and told him to sit in the vacant chair.

'I have just been saying to Charles that he has been extraordinarily lucky, and, judging by what Inspector Chaudhry had to say, owes you a significant debt of gratitude.

In addition I have been explaining to him your immediate role in reviewing and updating all our security protocols whether internal, external, IT, telecoms, etc. It is also to include the security issues covering all staff, whether Foreign Office or locally recruited.

Morning jogs, unless properly organised, are now off the agenda.'

This last remark was made with a half-smile in Charles' direction, but the point was clear.

'I have suggested, no, instructed that Charles spends the next few days with his family, to recover properly from his most unfortunate experience before returning to work.

I would hope Harry, that you will be some way down the track towards completion by then.'

This last comment being made with a quizzical look in Harry's direction.

'Some way is correct,' Harry replied, 'the amount of physical transfer to an IT platform is significant before we start looking at High Commission security.'

'If you require additional support I will allocate it.'

'I would prefer to complete it with a small, tight, secure team even if it takes a little longer. Frankly, I don't want the world and his wife to be chattering about what we are doing.'

'It is your decision Harry, but keep the timescale as short as you can.'

Charles had said nothing during this exchange, until now.

'I would remind you, Sir James, that, as was agreed before his posting to Islamabad, Harry's direct reporting line would be through me to ensure operational issues would not interfere with your High Commissioner's duties.

This will therefore commence on my return next week, when I will review what has been achieved to date, and whether or not additional resource should be allocated to ensure speedy resolution.

I do not think we need waste your time on speculative issues.'

There then followed a short silence whilst Sir James and Harry took in what had just been said.

The High Commissioner spoke first.
'Charles, one of the problems of bureaucracy is its rigidity, and inability to appreciate flexibility. This is such an occasion.
The set of circumstances that were discussed before Harry's arrival were rendered obsolete, and produced a totally different agenda, once you had been kidnapped.
I, for one, am completely relieved that you have been recovered, uninjured, from a frightening situation that could have turned into something with a fatal ending.
For that I thank Inspector Chaudhry and Harry for their best efforts culminating in your release.
One thing I have learnt over the years, to paraphrase Winston Churchill, is that one must never be surprised at the intervention of the unexpected.
Or, to sum up what I have been thinking, is this.
The distinct advantage of the obverse of bureaucracy is its capability of infinite amendment.
That is what I am now doing.
I will be taking a keen and direct interest in security and related issues until further notice. Is that understood?'
The HC continued without waiting for an answer,
'Charles, take your rest and re-join us next week, invigorated and ready for work.
Harry, you will report to me on a regular basis, critical issues as they arise. Is that clear?'
Harry nodded.
'Right, I think that covers today. I look forward to your return next week Charles.'
Charles and Harry, having been politely dismissed, walked down the hallway, Charles toward his office, Harry towards his.

Without looking at him, Charles addressed Harry in a low menacing tone.
'When I return next week, you and I will have a meeting, at which you will understand that your reporting line is through me.
Sir James will lose interest in your regular reports, and whatever consequences you raise, because they will interfere with his normal diplomatic duties. Do I make myself clear?'
He turned to look at Harry.
Harry stared straight back, his set face betraying no emotion.
'Absolutely clear Charles. I look forward to the meeting when you return at which I will be able to update you on progress so far. The initial Status Report will have already been submitted to Sir James. Enjoy your few days leave.'
Harry turned and walked off down the corridor to his office.

Thursday 25th May

London
Frank Stansfield was waiting in the restaurant when the Deputy, Norman Spencer arrived.
It was about 7.30pm, the restaurant not yet having filled, and the table picked was in a quiet corner giving them some privacy.
After the usual exchange of pleasantries and ordering a couple of gin and tonics, Frank suggested they order their meal before he mentioned various press reports covering a number and variety of terrorist activities around the globe.
Norman immediately cautioned him.

'Frank, I'm happy to see you, but if you're digging for any Intel, I told you on the phone, forget it!'

'Don't worry Norman; I'm not tapping you for anything, just drawing your attention to all that's happening in the big wide world, not that you need briefing I'm sure!'

'I'm glad about that,' he replied, smiling.

Over their meal they discussed some old reminiscences and colleagues since retired.

When they had been served coffee Frank spoke.

'You recall our telephone discussion the other day?'

'Yes,' Norman replied guardedly.

'You can forget the Intel worry. What I want to do is offer you the chance of a career change.'

'What!'

'Don't be so surprised. Let me explain. I am now a director of an international security firm, the Tutis Group. Tutis? It's Latin for Safe, Secure, Protected,' noticing Norman's somewhat questioning look.

'It was formed after a merger of three separate companies, one UK, one French, and one small US. (Here Frank described the three companies, their history, expertise, and regional activity).

'Each had a particular niche with respect to skill and region, which therefore made the grouping logical.

I'm 2i/c UK based operations, and I was asked by my boss to look out for a heavy hitter to take over from him when he retires in twelve months.

The group's aim is to build on what we've got, bolt on a number of specialist companies in the IT, comms fields, and attract some of the disaffected service personnel aware of the likely reductions in all theatres.

Obviously the group is going to increase dramatically in size over the next 2-3 years hence they need somebody to head up the UK, and be on the main Group board assisting in the international development.
There would obviously be a significant improvement in earnings, plus profit share, so that's why we are meeting tonight!'
Norman was silent for a few seconds before replying.
'Obviously I'm flattered to be asked but you know the rules as well as I do. Permissions, authorities, Official Secrets Act constraints, and, speaking personally, transfer of pension rights!
No, being serious, it's tempting and the way things are being organised at present leaves a lot to be desired. However I've been in this game a long time and do I want such an upheaval? I'm not sure I do.'
'Norman, I realise that this has come out of the blue but promise me you will, at least, give it some thought? You owe it to yourself.'
'Fine. I know you won't want to take no for an answer, so I will promise to think about it. OK?'
'OK. Now how do you think England will do in the Tests this summer?'
They both laughed, then ordered more coffee, this time with a brandy.

Islamabad
Friday the 26th May was not a good day for Charles Urwin. He was not sleeping well, with recurring bad dreams and nightmares, the black circles under his eyes being proof of that.

His wife Zahira had made a fuss on his return, but had gone today with her family to the mosque.
This had irritated him. One Friday missed would not bring down the wrath of the Iman on the family.
He sat, holding the newspaper, not reading, thinking about the High Commission, Sir James, Harry Baxter and what his plans may be for the following week.
He was a control freak, that he knew, confirmed to him on many an occasion by his peers in his early years at the Foreign Office, when all were struggling to gain a foothold at the bottom of the greasy pole.
He had made a commitment to himself that nothing, repeat nothing, would be allowed to stand in the way of his professional career and his pursuit of the perceived Holy Grail of Ambassador, and the K that normally accompanies it.
His respect for the current High Commissioner was minimal, linked with his somewhat warped perception that the appointment was certainly a rung down from Ambassador.
He felt that some of the appointments to Ambassador or High Commissioner were only rewards for diligent time servers. It also included those that had mastered the ability to nuance and finesse their views with delicate adjustment, so that their socio-political views were always apparently aligned to, or were fellow travellers with, their political masters, whatever their hue or persuasion.
Their grasp of the geo-political issues were, he thought, at best elementary.
Under no circumstance would he allow this SIS operative Baxter, to sidestep his control, and he

was not in his debt either. The Pakistan FIA had saved him.

He must ensure his wife's family were aware of this, and that appropriate thanks were passed to the relevant authorities. This would further strengthen his contacts within a number of Government Departments, and also some significant private sector organisations. Politically this would assist with his own career, indicating his numerous and successful relationships across the Pakistan spectrum.

His mental exercise was then disturbed by the return of his wife who enquired as to how he was feeling.

His response was curt and impersonal.

Zahira turned away without continuing the conversation, biting her lip as tears formed in her eyes.

Meanwhile Harry had received a further encrypted communication from the Deputy advising him that he would probably need to be back in London the second half of June for a few days, maybe a week, to assist in putting together the short to medium term strategy document. This would then get discussed, torn apart, rebuilt, before being broken down into chunks, which would be further dissected and argued over, by the various vested interest groups in SIS (MI6).

Not something that filled him with keen anticipation, but he realised that the Deputy needed support from people he could trust. Also it would be good to catch up with Tom Denman and others, and compare some regional Intel.

Paris

Anna was completing her briefing at AFD and had been advised she was flying to Beirut on Sunday the 28th May by Air France arriving in the evening. She would be met by AFD representatives.

At this point, after a few days of familiarity, Anne Hardy was used to her new identity, and had no real problems when being addressed in this way.

As she packed on the Saturday she wondered what her new assignment would bring, and momentarily her thoughts focussed on Harry, wondering what he was doing, and when they might meet again.

She mentally questioned herself on what she would have to do in Beirut, and the delicacy of establishing such an Intel cell. Be very sure; in this game one mistake is all it takes to be fatal.

IX

June 2006

London

As Harry was spending a few days at Vauxhall Cross he had contacted Jack DeCosta at the number he had been given.

A message was taken with a promise that contact would be made within 24hrs.

Jack called him, within an hour, and they met briefly for a drink one evening.

'I've just been back for a few days. Restructuring discussions,' Harry explained, 'what's happening with you?' he enquired.

'Middle East is the preoccupation at present. I bet I'll find myself out there soon.'

'Well if you do, don't forget to call!' Harry joked.

'Oh I will, have no fear!' Jack replied.

SIS (MI6) London

The strategy meeting in London that Harry had to attend was almost a complete disaster.

At times he could only just control his impatience at the stupid intransigence of certain parties.

Fortunately for him he was only required to attend for four days. On his last day, late morning, he saw the Deputy for about an hour, giving him a verbal update on the situation in Islamabad, plus snapshots of the main personalities involved.

'OK, Harry. I appreciate your filling in some of the blanks in your official reports. I realise it's early days, but I think you are going to have to start digging sooner than we thought.

We've got a lot of confusing Intel concerning Pakistan involvement in Afghanistan, arming of militant groups, turning a blind eye to the drug trade feeding down a conduit into Europe. All that whilst trying to get a firm handle on the factional fighting for the top dog positions in the Pakistan Government.

In the Middle East there are some signs that the fragile peace in Lebanon may not last much longer. Both sides, and particularly Hezbollah, are upping the rhetoric. Only words so far, but that's always the overture.

The other part of the muddied mix is the co-operation being extended by Syria and Iran, in turn receiving help in various forms from Russia, armaments, funding, training, whatever.'

Harry responded, 'I appreciate the confusion concerning Pakistan, but to be honest it's even worse on the ground, feet in treacle, plus, with a general hearty dislike of the truth, why ruin a good story with the facts! You know what I mean?

I'm trying to get close to certain sources to differentiate truth from fiction, but it's taking time.'

'Of course. Do the best you can Harry. There are clearly changes coming here. Keep in close communication. A week in politics is a long time!'

Russian Embassy Islamabad

In a small office, at the Embassy of the Russian Federation situated in the Diplomatic Enclave, Stepan Volkov was reading a report.

His position, as a designated Commercial Attaché, was the usual cover for intelligence gathering, and he reported directly to Moscow, two levels down from the Head of the FSB, Nikolai Patrushev.

His contact, inside the British High Commission, kept him up to date with all the general gossip, plus staffing appointments, both from the UK and locally. More importantly, any specific matters covering intelligence gathering, investigations or operations, the subjects of prioritised internal reports, became high priority in terms of analysis and transmission to Moscow.

What was interesting him now was the review of all security within the High Commission, electronic and written records, the physical perimeter of the Commission, personnel security, all telephone or electronic communications, encrypted or otherwise, both nationally, between Islamabad and Karachi, and internationally between Pakistan, the UK or other countries.

Responsibility for this rested with Harry Baxter, Defence Attaché, a new arrival from the UK.

He decided to run checks on Baxter, both with Moscow and the Russian Embassy in London.

What concerned him was the possible exposure of his tame internal mole in the High Commission.

Not the public reaction that might follow, but the grooming and training of a replacement. That was the negative, and it takes considerable time, bearing in mind the usual paranoid security measures that are then introduced as a result of the first failure.

He smiled to himself.

His mole, he considered, was secure for some little time yet.

With all that activity in the High Commission his mole's reports would make interesting reading, and also give an indication what was happening under the heading of 'Security' at UK Embassies and High Commissions.

Moscow would like that.

X

July 2006

Islamabad

Harry flew back to Islamabad at the end of June wondering how he could break the apparent impasse and start to get some meaningful information and intelligence that was at least credible.

Further conversations with Inspector Irfan Chaudhry might produce some possible co-operation, or at least determine whether he was linked to any active group, political or otherwise.

He wondered whether there was any mileage in pursuing any connections that Charles Urwin's father-in-law, Nadeem Kirmani, might throw up. Well connected, a Minister in two administrations, owner and chairman of a well-known Pakistan conglomerate.

If that connection could be made, and assuming willingness to contribute, then useful indicators in both political and commercial fields, could help build a part of the matrix.

An early discussion with Chaudhry could include reference to Kirmani. It would be interesting to gauge the reaction.

Following his return to Islamabad Harry called the Inspector to make a convenient appointment.

'Anything specific you want to discuss?' queried Chaudhry.

'I thought an update would be sensible, plus a general discussion, now I am getting my feet under the table.'

'Getting your feet under the table?'

'Sorry. British saying, meaning getting more comfortable in a new assignment.'
'Understood.'
The meeting was made for 10.00am, Monday the 3rd July 2006, at the Federal Investigation Agency (FIA).

Beirut, Lebanon
During June Anne Hardy had been diligent in her AFD activities, establishing a conscientious profile amongst all the local groups that she had contact with.
Building trust is vital to gain confidence before the slow and delicate game of entrapment.
No moves had yet been made, that was the game plan. Nothing for at least two or three months. A number of different eyes would be focussed on her. AFD, her unknown Mossad colleague, local intelligence gatherers for the Lebanese Government, Hezbollah, PLO, Syria, and probably DGSE of France.
Her own particular group included a number of specialists, feasibility, financial, operational, logistics, staffing, training etc.
There was an easy rapport and team spirit within the group, and due to their respective responsibilities Anne had worked on several occasions with Alain Dubois, a logistics expert.
He had, she thought, an easy Gallic charm, linked with an ironic sense of humour that helped soften and overcome some of the apparently insurmountable bureaucratic obstacles that the country presented.
On one occasion, when driving in a 4x4 to a village east of Beirut, the conversation turned to her family.

'Your family are not concerned with you working in Lebanon?'
'Both my parents are dead. I was their only child. So I can go and do what I want,' she said lightly.
'Well, you certainly picked something and somewhere interesting.'
'And you?' she replied.
'A little of the gypsy in me, I think. A grandfather on my mother's side that nobody wanted to talk about!' he joked.
The conversation carried on for about an hour, each giving away very little, with one having no real idea of the other. The other, however, watching for any cracks in the adopted identity.

Islamabad
Meanwhile Harry was trying to determine the links between the FIA and the Inter-Services Intelligence (ISI) and the extent to which Intel was shared, or kept within each department.
He assumed that little was shared, bearing in mind the number of departments within ISI, and the cultural paranoia that normally inhabits such organisations. Information is power, so why share it?
Prior to his departure to Islamabad he had researched a number of relevant Pakistan Government Departments, including the ISI.
The current Director General was Lieutenant General Ashfaq Parvez Kayani, appointed in 2004.
The overall reputation of the Directorate was suspect, at best.
National politics manipulation, malfeasance, Taliban support from 1994 to 2001, bribery of political figures to influence policy, active support of Indian insurrection groups, and clear counter-

intelligence operations against the CIA operations, in both the lawless regions of the country, and Afghanistan.
In addition, the release by the Pakistani nuclear physicist of sensitive information to a number of unstable regimes, including Iran, a close friend and ally of Pakistan, had significantly raised the status to high alert of certain countries in the Middle East, including Lebanon, exacerbating its tensions with Iranian supported groups, particularly Hezbollah.
The ISI Directorates had always followed an aggressive intelligence model, including espionage, psychological warfare, subversion and sabotage. Its agents were often embedded in Non-Governmental Organisations (NGOs) and international cultural or aid programmes. It also maintained connections and professed collaboration with a number of Security Services, including Saudi Arabia, paradoxically the CIA, Chinese Intelligence, and MI6.
A classic case of running with the hare and the hounds!
As SIS (MI6) had determined a long time ago, view any actions with ISI involvement with considerable care and caution.
Despite significant reservations, it will be necessary to get much closer to the centre, in order to ensure that a considered judgement prevails, rather than an ill-informed guestimate.
Harry wondered who would help him with his attempt to contact ISI, and thought a general conversation with the High Commissioner would be a starting point, although he guessed that he would soon be pushed down to Charles Urwin.
'Co-operation or hindrance? I'll soon find out', he thought, as he reached for the phone.

Twenty minutes later he was sitting in the HC's office where, after explanation of his request, found the meeting terminated.
'Harry, such matters are always in the remit of the First Secretary, and I would ask you to discuss this matter with him.
Do not put him under undue pressure at this time as I want him fully recovered and back in post, firing on all cylinders, without any relapse. Understood?'
'Completely.'
'Good. Is there any other area I can assist you with at the present time?'
Harry shook his head.
'Well, good luck.'
Harry returned to his office thinking that he would see Inspector Chaudhry again before requesting any assistance from Charles Urwin.

Bint Jbeil, Southern Lebanon
A meeting was in progress involving senior Hezbollah military and the political section of the organisation which included two members of the Shura council.
A military commander was speaking, 'My brothers, in our continued fight and struggle against the Zionists I am proposing that we take the first step again. Why should we wait when they are living on our land taken from us? Why should we tolerate them a moment longer than we need to?
I have a diversionary attack that I believe will work well.
I do not want to waste the valuable time of the Shura, but ask for their approval, so that I might discuss and agree the attack with my fellow commanders.'

It was a formality. Permission was granted.
The commander withdrew, taking with him two other senior Hezbollah military personnel, with whom he would discuss the details of the attack, timing, logistics, etc.
The three men sat down at a table in an adjoining room on which the commander unrolled a map.
He outlined a number of alternative scenarios that he knew would interest his colleagues.
What was being planned was a pre-emptive strike. Initially another thorn in the Zionist side. A rallying call to all Muslims to try and regain their Holy Land. To focus world opinion on the fragile state of the region, perhaps then forcing a compromise by the major powers involved, who in turn could bring pressure to bear on Israel, and her supporters.
Hezbollah exercised control of three areas in South Lebanon through its operational commands, North, Central and Western units; the last being adjacent to the Israeli border giving frequent opportunities for infiltration, hit and run, mine laying and hostage taking.
With the agreement of his unit commanders the senior Hezbollah Commander decided that the action would take place in the next few days. A date was fixed.
Wednesday the 12th July 2006.

--

In a Beirut suburb Anne was sitting with a young family discussing the education and medical needs of a young daughter, eight years of age.

The wife was Lebanese, a Muslim, but had been born in Greece, prior to her family and a cousin's family in Beirut bringing her and her second cousin together in an arranged marriage.

Having spent her formative years in Athens the stricture of an arranged marriage was wearing her down, whilst at the same time her husband had become increasingly radicalised and involved in the strident politics that pervaded the Muslim suburb where they lived.

This was another area controlled by Hezbollah, with those, not involved with the military or political hierarchy, being careful to keep their opinions to themselves. Intimidation and fear ruled.

Gulshan, the child's mother, was sitting talking quietly to Anne, obviously unhappy as tears started to form in her eyes.

'My daughter needs special medical treatment for her legs and I want her to have a proper education. It is unlikely that she will receive either here, or if she does the treatment will not be long term and the education will be very limited and restrictive. You know what I mean?'

Anne, nodded her head, all too aware of the societal pressures on Muslim women and children, particularly girls.

'Yes, I understand, but there are only certain areas in which I can help. You do realise that, don't you?'

'May I be frank with you Anne? I grew up in Europe with all the normal freedoms of thought and society. Here it is claustrophobic and only a man's world. You have seen it, and the control over everything. The arguments I had to be able to see you. It took over two weeks, and my husband was still very suspicious.

I want to leave Lebanon with my daughter and return to Europe, probably Greece.'

She fell silent, realising the enormity of her statement and the possible repercussions that could arise.

Anne did not reply immediately, keeping her head lowered as if in thought, and probably embarrassed. She was thinking that perhaps this might be an opportunity for information if the situation could be played for a period.

Sympathy, followed by gentle questioning leading to possible Intel (wrapped up in concern for the child and the possibility that mother and daughter could be evacuated at some future date. Information needed about developing situations that could impact on their current safety and eventual flight from Beirut).

'Gulshan, you have taken me completely by surprise with what you have said. I realise that you are under enormous emotional stress and I would ask you to consider the short and long term effects that your wishes may bring. I don't know how I can help at this stage, but will investigate what can be done with, or through ADF.

Maybe nothing, but I promise I will see if we have any similar previous experience of this sort of situation.'

Gulshan nodded meekly.

'I appreciate your help, whatever it is. I don't know what is going to happen to us as a family, or what the men are planning. Frankly I don't want to know. All that happens is usually death and destruction for someone.'

She sounded bitter, but Anne was starting to think that maybe Gulshan was more aware of events than she had first thought.

'Let us meet again in a few days. If you wish to telephone me, this is my mobile number.'
She scribbled it on a piece of paper and gave it to Gulshan.
They said their farewells and Anne made her way back to the AFD HQ where she sought out Alain to run the Gulshan situation past him.
After Anne had explained the situation where an unhappy wife and child wanted to get out of the country, leaving her husband as well, Alain responded that extreme care should be taken.
Major points to bear in mind included the volatility of the present political climate, plus the reaction of the husband, once Gulshan's wishes became known. A toxic mix without doubt.
Anne kept her thoughts to herself concerning any Intel harvesting.
By raising the issue with Alain, Anne had ensured that no accusation could be made that the matter had been kept confidential between her and Gulshan.
Now, perhaps, would start the nurturing stage, drawing Gulshan closer, rather like the spider and the fly.
Purely pawns in the larger game, Mossad officers, or any other intelligence officer for that matter, could not allow sentiment to cloud their operational judgement.
A few hours later Mossad Control Lebanon was reading Anne's encrypted report, and the suggestion that this could be used as a possibility of establishing the first link in an intelligence cell.
Having considered the potential, Mossad Control ruled it out. Not sufficient, and early enough payback, driven essentially by personal wishes for lifestyle changes, fraught with risk. Denied.

In this game sentiment had no place. Raw intelligence was what was needed. They needed all the material they could get, bearing in mind the confused indicators coming from a number of disparate sources.

Certainly a number of locations, including sources external to Lebanon, were showing increased traffic between Syria, Iran and Hezbollah.

However, the game plan was confused.

Islamabad

At 1600hrs Sunday the 9th July Harry received a coded and encrypted report from the Deputy.

He read it once, and then again, not quite believing what he was reading, but the source and quality of the evidence was undeniable.

The Deputy concluded the report by saying that Harry would have sole discretion as to appropriate action to be taken on the ground, and that he would receive full backing and support from him.

In essence the report was based on GCHQ intercepts of mobile phone conversations of certain individuals in Pakistan.

GCHQ is located in the UK, but there are a number of listening posts around the world, one on Ascension Island, another being based in Cyprus, this giving coverage, by satellite, over the Middle East, Gulf and Indian sub-continent, including Pakistan.

This is a vital source for intercepts in that region including Iraq and Afghanistan, particularly focussed on Al Qaeda traffic, and related terrorist groups.

GCHQ had, over a few weeks, picked up traffic from the mobile of Azmat, son of Nadeem Kirmani, father of Zahira, wife of Charles Urwin.

This, in itself was not surprising. Surveillance of parties, both direct and indirect, is common place when diplomatic and political sensitivities are involved.

What was surprising and shocking was the content.

Azmat was a committed jihadist deeply involved in a number of areas. He was able, due to his position as International Sales Development Director in his father's group, to include many of his activities under the cover of his frequent and necessary travelling to most Middle East countries. One was the support and supply of arms and munitions to Al Qaeda backed insurgents in Afghanistan and Iraq, others included Iran backed Hezbollah in Lebanon and anti-government elements in Pakistan, whose ultimate aim was the overthrow of the elected Government and the establishment of a Muslim state based on strict Sharia law.

Passionately anti-Western, Azmat was highly critical of his father and sister. More worrying was his hatred of Charles Urwin, and what he stood for.

The Deputy had spelt out the seriousness of the situation and the risks attached.

There was also the risk that some intercepted conversations had been a deliberate smoke screen. Because of his marriage to Zahira, and the connections through his father-in-law, a certain amount of suspicion would naturally fall on Charles Urwin. What did he know? And if not, why not? Some mud may stick. More confusion.

Harry needed to think long and hard about this one and how it should be handled.

'Bloody nigh impossible,' he thought. 'The High Commissioner is going to love this one!

Let's see what the conversation brings with Inspector Chaudhry tomorrow. A few flies placed

delicately on the water may produce something or nothing.
After that, HC? We'll see. Tomorrow is another day!'

--

Inspector Chaudhry rose from his desk, his hand outstretched and a slight smile on his lips.
'Good morning Mr Baxter, we meet under quieter circumstances this time.'
'Indeed we do, and incidentally Harry is my name,' Harry replied, smiling, whilst shaking the Inspector's hand and sitting down in the chair indicated.
He remained silent whilst coffee was brought in and poured.
Chaudhry broke the silence.
'Well, you asked for this meeting, would you like to start the event?'
'Yes, but I must emphasise that I hope our discussion can be regarded as completely confidential, and not taken any further up our respective chains of command. Can we agree on that?'
'Yes, so far as it does not affect Pakistan's security and political integrity.'
'I understand your concern, and hope that my comments and questions are taken in the spirit they are intended, namely that they are being asked in order to further enhance our respective countries security and, hopefully, co-operation.'
Chaudhry nodded. 'Let us proceed on that basis and understanding.'
Harry spoke hesitantly, 'As you are aware the High Commission's First Secretary, Charles Urwin, is married to a Pakistani, the daughter of Nadeem Kirmani, an ex-government minister and a very

influential businessman with significant commercial interests in Pakistan and overseas.

He has two sons, one of whom is of particular interest to us. We were wondering if we shared a common interest.

Additionally we have been looking at a number of other areas, which impact on our concerns of global terrorism, and therefore, ultimately, UK security.

We need to have a more detailed grasp of the relationships between the main groups, such as Al Qaeda and Hezbollah, particularly funding, and the covert support being provided by Syria and Iran.

Instability in Afghanistan is a major concern, exacerbated by the opium crop production, now showing an overall increase compared to a few years ago.

My question is therefore a comparatively simple one. However I am sure it's response may cause significant difficulties!

Question. Are these areas in which we could assist each other, or at least recognise the extent that such areas of concern impact on both our respective countries, in a number of different ways?'

Chaudhry had been listening carefully to what Harry had to say, and after a slight pause responded, choosing his words carefully.

'May I call you Harry? Fine. Please call me Irfan.

What you have just raised is something that is covered by both the FIA and the ISI. You are aware of their spheres of operation?

We have a joint operational board that ensures, we hope, cross dissemination of relevant security matters.'

At this point he smiled.

'We hope, because the impression received is that ISI is very keen to keep matters confidential to itself, and at times is very slow in releasing information or intelligence that could be of assistance to the FIA.'

He paused.

'We are now getting into areas of discussion that probably require authorisation from a higher level than myself, but I feel at this stage, that as it is only exploratory, we can continue a little further.

You are aware, I know, through the media, of the political situation here in Pakistan, which is very fragile and sensitive, with many voices of different political views as to the direction the country should take.

Some have strong elements of democracy, others the opposite. A difficult balancing act for all concerned, particularly when it is evident that radical elements are in place in most government institutions. Not easily identified, but still able to influence direction and policy.

Yes, it is a difficult question to answer, but I will ask for authority for us to continue our discussions on those areas you mentioned. I will explain that our discussions are in the best interest of co-operation. Subject matter I will leave blank. Let us hope some good will come to us as a result.'

'I appreciate your response Irfan. Let's leave it at that today. Could I ask you to contact me at the High Commission when you have the necessary clearance?

I look forward to hearing from you.'

The meeting ended, Harry made his way back to the HC, and asked to see the High Commissioner on an urgent matter.

He was shown in immediately, and Sir James asked him to explain what was so urgent.

'You will be aware Sir, that I receive regular reports from London on matters relating to my current posting, and the most recent raises a number of questions concerning internal security here at the High Commission.'
'Explain.'
At this point Harry handed over a transcript of the encrypted report and sat back whilst the High Commissioner read it with an increasing frown. He obviously read it again before lifting his head, and continued with a tired voice,
'Where, exactly, will you be taking this now?'
'That's what I wanted to discuss with you. I fully realise your position with respect to security matters, but obviously you would need to know, in advance, if an internal investigation is to take place. My own view is that Charles is in no way connected with the subject matter. It is purely an accident of marriage that has resulted in this unfortunate connection.
I am sure, once the security review has been completed, he will be totally exonerated, and no impact will felt on his career. However, the review has be carried out and your instruction to that effect must be issued.'
The High Commissioner, after a short pause, then said, 'You will ensure that the review is carried out with suitable and appropriate sensitivity, bearing in mind Charles is not yet fully recovered, and his wife will be distraught at the revelations concerning her brother. Is that clear?'
'Yes, but I will be requesting that Charles does not discuss with his wife, either the review, or her brother.
Additionally you must recognise that whilst questioning will be conducted in a fair manner,

there has to be a considerable amount of searching and digging along the way. You are aware that review protocols demand a robust search for the truth?'
'Of course,' he replied testily. 'Just make sure you don't overstep your remit by one inch, or I will demand your recall immediately.'
'If I may say so, High Commissioner, that would not be a good policy decision, particularly if I had not completed the investigation.
All that would happen then is a new team would arrive, ignoring all requests for sensitivity, and be tramping around rather like a bull in a china shop. Not to be recommended.'
'Understood Baxter,' he replied sarcastically, 'Assume my official instruction is given. When do you intend to start, and with whom?'
'I had planned to handle this in a very quiet low key way, with discussions with Charles first. Take him through the report. I want him on side, not fighting it.'
'Well you'd better get started then. Keep me informed of all interviews.'
'I will. I plan to see Charles tomorrow morning.'

XI

Two months earlier. May 2006

Tehran, Iran
The car stopped in front of the hotel and the young man alighted, making his way quickly into the foyer where he was met by two men.
After cursory greetings they made their way to the lifts and a second floor room.
There they sat down and talked softly between themselves, until the coffee had been brought and the door locked.
One man then circled the room checking pictures, lights, telephone, TV, cupboards, bed and bed head for any listening devices.
Initially satisfied, he then turned on the sound of the TV to a level sufficient to drown out their conversation.
The discussion covered the supply of spent uranium from Pakistan and its conversion and incorporation into rocket heads currently planned for manufacture in Iran.
Concern was being expressed that insufficient material was being received from Pakistan, this in turn holding up production, and therefore final numbers of tipped rockets.
Azmat Kirmani listened patiently whilst the concern was stated.
'Could I remind you of a number of things that impact on the production you are talking about?
The base material is not something that is produced in large quantities. In order for amounts to be diverted for our cause a number of people have to be organised who sympathise with us.

Documentation has to be adjusted, and then reconciled. Finally, there is a considerable logistical exercise that has to be carried out, covering export documentation, avoidance of sample testing, and security of transportation to Iran.

Do you understand it is not quite the same as sending a few Iranian carpets to Dubai?' he said sarcastically.

The two other men looked at each other and changed tack.

'We realise, my brother, that it is not simple or easy, but, Insha'Allah, we shall prevail.

There are certain plans in preparation where will need large numbers of these rockets. For that we need the material to make them in good time.

Can we ask that you try and improve on the quantity and frequency of the deliveries?'

'I will try my brothers. I promise I will do the best I can. My wish is your wish to see our land under our control again, and the thieves driven into the sea.'

The discussion then went into some detail concerning recent shipments, delivery times and cost before Asmat said, 'Now I must go to another meeting. Trading business, but it does contribute to our more important plans.'

The meeting broke up, Azmat driving to an adjacent office, the two other men leaving by a side door of the hotel, hopeful that deliveries of the raw material could improve. This could then significantly affect the success of the planned assaults in the future.

Damascus Syria

The Committee met again. This time one of their members requested permission and funding to revenge the deaths of their two brothers in London. It was a simple plan, but if successful, very effective. The world would take notice.

XII

Wednesday 12th July 2006

Lebanon

The diversion started at 0900hrs.

Hezbollah fired rockets onto several Israeli towns.

Whilst this was happening Hezbollah militants crossed from Lebanon into Israel and ambushed two Israeli Army vehicles, killing five soldiers and abducting two of the soldiers. Another four soldiers were killed in a failed rescue attempt.

Following this action, Hezbollah demanded the release of Lebanese prisoners held by Israel, in exchange for the release of the abducted soldiers.

Israel refused, and launched a large-scale military campaign across Lebanon, in response to the Hezbollah incursion.

This marked the start of the *2006 Lebanon War*.

Within 24 hours in Beirut, news and TV bulletins announced the start of hostilities, some cautionary, some exultant. The man in the street was polarised, dependent on where, and how he lived.

The first 24 hours saw small localised military activity, but everybody knew the Israelis would counter attack.

What they did not appreciate was the extent to which Lebanon would be affected by Israeli air strikes, artillery fire, port blockades and significant damage to Lebanon's infrastructure, including Beirut's Rafic Hariri International Airport.

Traumatic times indeed. A literal baptism of fire for Anne, being on the receiving end of Israeli Army actions, not necessarily the preferred location for an undercover Mossad officer!

Difficult times, difficult decisions.
AFD operations management decided on a current suspension of operations, and possible exit routes for staff during hostilities.
All activities were halted, and AFD teams in isolated regions of Lebanon were advised by radio of the start of hostilities and to take appropriate action. In some cases, where they were near the Syrian border, they were given the option to cross.
In such a febrile atmosphere the true situation on the ground was difficult to determine, changing by the hour, with no advance warning of what may occur.

Islamabad
At 10 o'clock Harry contacted Charles Urwin and asked if he could see him to discuss a confidential matter.
The response was curt, but suggested that straight away would be most convenient, the latter part of the remark carrying a hint of sarcasm.
Harry entered the First Secretary's office and closed the door behind him.
'Well, what is it you wish to discuss.'
'Firstly, this discussion is to be kept completely confidential, the subject of which is already known to Sir James. Secondly, it is to be covered under the Security Check Level, LOCSEN (Local Sensitivity), and in documents, written or printed, UK Eyes Only.
Is that clear?'
'Sounds rather melodramatic, but I suppose somebody considers it necessary.'
'Sir James certainly does, and suggested that I have an initial discussion with you to outline what has

arisen, and decide how the investigation and subsequent actions are to be progressed.'

Charles raised an eyebrow and said, with a slight smile on his lips,

'Before we begin I feel I must say, officially, that I appreciated your assistance in obtaining my release when I was kidnapped. I'm sure Inspector Chaudhry appreciated your participation as well.'

Harry ignored the comment, looking impassively at Charles, before handing over a document.

'I suggest you read this before we start our discussion. I'm sure its contents will present a few challenges. The questions it raises will be what we need to answer, and how we will deal with them.'

He then passed to Charles a truncated version of what Sir James had read.

Harry watched Charles's face as he read the document, it gradually changing from mild incredulity, to one where reddening of the neck preceded a look as black as thunder.

Finally, with a sound of exasperation, he threw the document back to Harry,

'Pack of lies, distortions, absolute rubbish. How do we know this is genuine? It could be completely false. People posing as others, phone tapping and hacking, network intervention, any one of a dozen reasons. Designed to create inward looking suspicion. Breakdown of trust, classic ploy. You and I are supposed to discuss this rationally? What a bloody stupid, pathetic joke!'

He paused, whereupon Harry spoke quietly.

'I'm not surprised you have reacted as you have. In your position I would do the same.

However I am assured that GCHQ carried out all the usual checks and investigation, including voice profiles and identity over a period of time, with

cross checking against networks, both terrestrial and satellite.
As far as one can determine it is genuine.'
Charles suddenly got up and left his office, leaving Harry sitting there.
Off to Sir James, I'll guess, thought Harry.
He remained there, until about 20 minutes later Charles reappeared, and sat down behind his desk.
Charles spoke first. With an edge to his voice that Harry had not heard before.
'Sir James has said I must fully co-operate in this investigation.
Let me make my position quite clear. My career is my number one priority, and no investigation, such as this, is going to detract from my single minded effort to perform my duties in the most professional manner possible.
I would state, at this juncture, that I have had no previous knowledge, or contact with my brother-in –law with reference to the matters raised by this investigation.
Lastly, once this has been completed, I will make every effort to ensure that you are recalled to the UK as quickly as possible.'
The tenor of his voice hinted at an increasing level of stress which caused him to pause.
Harry interjected, 'I get your drift, and frankly with your attitude and complete lack of co-operation, so far, I will be delighted to get back to the UK.
However, there is a job to be done and I will bloody well do it, despite your imagined intellectual superiority and position in life.
I have already said to Sir James that I believe you are completely innocent of any possible connection with the activities of your brother in law, but we have to go through the process in a professional

way. That I am going to do, and if it takes a long time, then tough.
Get used to the idea. That's my position. Understood?'
Charles stared at Harry without replying. His face said it all. Harry, expressionless, stared back.
Almost a minute had passed when Charles spoke.
'Right, get on with it,' he said quietly.
Harry then started a timeline investigation going back over two years, logging the times Charles and Azmat had met, singly or in groups(other persons present), any discussions and content, any telephone calls, whether landline or mobile, observations of the rest of the family including his father-in-law, Nadeem Kirmani, and his other brother-in-law, Kamran.
After about three hours Charles was visibly irritated and increasingly petulant, so Harry suggested they meet again the next morning, this giving Charles some time to catch up on his normal activities.
He agreed with bad grace, and they went their separate ways.
When Harry returned to his office the latest Intel reports were waiting for him on his satellite laptop.
One caught his eye immediately. Lebanon.
Hezbollah and Israeli army units were engaged in a cross border action which appeared to be intensifying.
On the ground feedback was sparse. Most information was being gathered by satellite observation and military bandwidth radio intercepts.
Initial reaction was that this was a typical Hezbollah incursion which, normally, would be quickly repulsed and equilibrium restored.

However on this occasion it appeared that Israeli artillery and other units were being mobilised and moved towards the Lebanese southern border.
Israeli F-15s and F-16s had also apparently been scrambled, and were keeping mid to high station over the border area.
On this evidence it would seem that significant escalation was taking place.
Open hostility at this level would cause huge instability within Lebanon, with a profound knock-on effect for the region.
He wondered to himself if Anna was involved, as Mossad could be monitoring events in the border area, little knowing she was sitting in the middle of Beirut, wondering what the next stage of the conflict would bring.

Islamabad Diplomatic Compound
The front door of Charles Urwin's villa slammed shut, with a force and sound that was heard throughout the building, as he entered and made his way to his study.
His wife, recognising the sign, this not being the first occasion, remained in her dressing room on the first floor.
The study door slammed shut, as he slumped into his desk chair.
He was having difficulty in controlling his anger and frustration, compounded by the after effects of his kidnapping.
His career could be severely damaged by the security review, if only by implication a question mark would arise.
Her blasted brother was the problem, start to finish.
GCHQ would have checked, and double checked, before raising a review.

Thinking back he kicked himself for not initiating some security checks on *all* the family. He'd accommodated them all due to the father's position and previous Pakistan Government Ministerial roles.
Perhaps it was time for him to call in a few favours within one or two Pakistan Government departments in order to provide himself with some intelligence as to what was going on in the life of Azmat Kirmani, his brother-in-law.

SIS (MI6) Vauxhall Cross London
The Deputy, Norman Spencer, was working on a future organisation document when his telephone rang.
It was the UK Ambassador, Lebanon, Jonathan Peters, calling from Beirut by satellite link.
They had met on a couple of occasions at the Foreign Office, when the Gulf and the Middle East had been the focus of a Strategic Review, exploring passive and active relationships in the continuing challenge of organised terrorism.
'Jonathan, good day. But I would suspect it is not a particularly good day for you at present. I have just been reading the latest Intel reports. Things seem to be developing quite quickly and with some significant escalation.'
The ambassador then updated the Deputy as to his reading of events on the ground, after which he asked for some specific assistance.
'As you are aware we try to maintain a neutral position within Lebanese politics and with the various combatant groups.
This is difficult to achieve, but, as a consequence of our strategy, this means that we are light on the

ground with certain specialist skills, when such current events occur.
We need to have a well experienced operative here that can assist in the repatriation of British nationals, plus good negotiating skills in order to maintain our perceived neutrality. Hence my phone call. Additionally, and off the record, that person could greatly assist us, and therefore London, in terms of intelligence interpretation, and a better understanding of what is actually happening. Can you assist?'
'I think I can, but it will obviously depend on availability, and how we can get this person into Lebanon.
I would guess he would have to enter from Syria. Currently no flights into Beirut. No passage from Israel, and by sea would take too long.
Leave it with me. I will revert within 24hours by satcom. Alright?'
'Norman, many thanks. I await your call.'
The Deputy had already thought of the 'operative'.
Harry Baxter was made for this assignment. Well experienced in the region, and comparatively close at hand.
He would be able to fly to the UAE from Islamabad, and then take Syrian Air to Damascus. From there it would be comparatively simple to cross into Lebanon and make his way to Beirut, a distance of no more than 100kms.
First he would need to contact Harry and see if he would be prepared to leave Islamabad for about a month. If so, then a discussion, through the Foreign Office, with the High Commissioner, would hopefully result in agreement.
He reached for his telephone and arranged for a satcom connection to Harry later in the day, whilst

asking his PA to call his contact at the Foreign Office.

He jotted down some salient points whilst waiting for his FO contact.

His telephone rang.

Islamabad

It was about 8pm when Harry's satcom beeped.

It was the Deputy.

Harry listened with a wry smile on his face as the Deputy explained the details of the Lebanon Ambassador's request.

When he had finished, Harry countered with the present state of the investigation involving the First Secretary and his wife's family, and what the interruption might mean to those enquiries.

The Deputy responded by suggesting Tom Denman could replace him in the meantime, continuing with slow and methodical questioning of all parties, plus a holding action mode until Harry's return.

Harry was happy with Tom's participation, they had worked well together in the past, and he knew he could rely on him.

Agreement was a formality, as the Deputy had insisted that he make himself available soonest, once agreement had been reached by the FO with the High Commissioner.

Harry thought wryly that they would probably be happy to see the back of him for a month, that feeling only being tempered by the fact that they did not know Tom's persistence in the face of bureaucratic obstruction!

He was fully aware of his likely route into Lebanon bearing in mind the current military activity so started checking airline schedules for suitable connecting flights via Abu Dhabi/Dubai through to Damascus.

--

18 hours later he was called into Sir James' office.
'Well Harry, I'm not completely in the picture and I can't say I'm best pleased, but I understand you are leaving us to go to Beirut. Time there, as yet, not specified.
I have read our FO intelligence reports so am aware of the very difficult situation that prevails, and the request that has been made for your services.
I further understand that a colleague of yours, Tom Denman, will be here within a few days to carry on the investigation you had just started.
I trust you will brief him before your departure, and also reconfirm my request for a kid glove approach. We do not need explosions here, mirroring Lebanon,' he observed dryly.
'Fully understood, Sir James. Tom will be well briefed, and advised as to the style of the investigation.
He's a good man, and thorough.
I anticipate that I will leave sometime in the next 24hrs so would thank you for your assistance whilst I have been here, and look forward to my return in about a month.'
At this point they shook hands, Sir James wishing Harry good luck, and advising him to keep his head down.
Harry walked back to his office thinking of the encrypted briefing notes he would send Tom, complete with observations on the various players, characteristics, style, pressure points, rough psychological profiles, etc.
Not an easy holding operation in his absence, but probably quieter than where he was going!

He briefed Jeremy and Marion on his departure and the imminent arrival of Tom Denman.
He made it quite clear that he expected the same degree of co-operation with Tom that was now extended to him, and if not, they would hear about it when he got back in a month's time!
They both wished him luck and assured him of their support for Tom in his absence.
Later that evening Harry received another detailed encrypted report from The Deputy concerning the Kirmani family, Azmat in particular.
Further electronic surveillance and analysis had thrown up further corroboration of his activities, also confirmation of a Pakistan – Iran link which, in turn, extended into the Hezbollah operations in Lebanon.
Initial illegal sharing of nuclear processes two years earlier with Iran had ensured that such information had been passed to the terrorist organisation, who wished to inflict, with such technology, major destructive attacks against Israel.
In its simplest form 'dirty' devices could be manufactured, however, on a more sophisticated level, spent uranium tipped rockets could be used to devastating effect.
Uranium 238 tipped rockets do not rely on the radio activity of the material, but its density, which is two and a half times that of steel. The rockets can therefore blast through the very best tank armour. Once through, the uranium splinters and ignites, with obvious consequences.
Its effect on structures, high rise buildings and non-armoured facilities is terminal, on humans catastrophic.
It was understood that the trail from Pakistan, with active Iranian support, led to Hezbollah, with

supplies of such rockets planned to be supplied in the near future.

The transfer of manufacturing technology, implemented by Azmat, linked to Iranian production, ensured that such a capability would be part of the Hezbollah arsenal in the near future.

'Dirty' devices could also be deployed, inserted during cross border incursions, and then activated by either delayed timers or mobile radio devices.

Essentially the report and suggested action was instructing Harry, once he was in Lebanon, to investigate, if possible, routes and timings for the deployment of the rockets from Iran into Lebanon.

Air, sea, land? How, where, when?

Because of shared Intel with 'friendly' nations it was essential to try and understand the modus operandi and, most importantly, timing.

It was possible that Israel already had Special Forces on the ground who, linking up with Mossad operatives, already had some indication of possible routings.

The next few days would be demanding as he travelled to Beirut, but certainly not as demanding as the operation facing him, whilst maintaining an embassy cover.

As Harry was organising his flights, Sir James was briefing Charles Urwin of his imminent departure and the continuation of the investigation by Tom Denman, who would be arriving within 48 hours.

'I think Charles, that with the arrival of Tom Denman, the level of the investigation will have been reduced by at least one, in terms of priority.

I instructed Harry Baxter to brief his man that the investigation will be continued with sensitivity, and certainly no browbeating.'

'I appreciate your intervention Sir James, but frankly there is nothing that can adversely affect me, save for the unfortunate family relationship that includes my brother-in-law, who is the prime suspect of the investigation.
Additionally, I cannot believe that my father-in-law would be involved in any way, bearing in mind his Ministerial, Government, and international commercial group activities. He abhors terrorism.'
Charles tried to maintain an air of calm confidence, despite feeling that his options were severely limited. Perhaps his contacts in a couple of Government departments might bear fruit, if pushed hard.

XIII

Sunday 16th July 2006

Damascus International Airport Syria
Harry came down the steps of the Syrian Air Airbus and stepped into the bus taking the passengers to the terminal.
He had taken an Etihad flight from Islamabad to Abu Dhabi, then joining the Syrian Air flight from Abu Dhabi to Damascus.
He was met by one of the UK diplomatic staff and taken to the Embassy where he met the current Defence Attaché, Major Mike Thompson, Royal Artillery.
'I believe you have received an outline of my assignment, so any help and advice in getting me across the border into Lebanon would be of great assistance.'
'Not too difficult at present if you're carrying a Diplomatic Passport,' he replied.
'I can get you there, but at the border you may get some slight hassle. They're all a bit jumpy now things have kicked off in the South. As you know the Hezbollah Shia strongholds are in the South and North East of Lebanon, so hopefully you should get to Beirut without too much grief.
You can pick up a car and driver on the Lebanese side who can take you straight to Beirut. Should take between two and three hours.'
'Thanks for the advice. Can we leave very early tomorrow morning?'
'Certainly.'

At 0400hrs the following morning the two men left the embassy, and made their way by car to the border, an uneventful journey of about 90 minutes.
Disinterested border guards waved Harry through after a cursory examination of his Diplomatic Passport.
Picking up a car and driver on the Lebanon side of the border was no problem, and the journey to Beirut started shortly after 0730hrs.
Harry sat in the back, thinking through what the likely scenarios could be, idly taking in the scenery as it changed from craggy mountains to cultivated fields and then back again to hills and mountains.
He noticed the driver looking at him frequently in his rear-view mirror, quickly returning his eyes to the road when he realised the look was noticed.
As they climbed one particular hilly section, turning to the right around a bluff, the driver braked hard to avoid hitting the rough barrier set across the road between two Toyota Land Cruisers.
Bearded men in camouflage uniforms, carrying AK-47 weapons, moved from behind the barrier, shouting in Arabic for the driver and passengers to get out of the car.
The driver emerged quickly, Harry more slowly.
He spoke the usual greeting in Arabic, 'Salaam Alaikum'.
The obvious leader of the group demanded identity documents of the driver, and the passport of Harry.
After much studying of his passport the leader asked, in stumbling English, where Harry was going and why.
Harry slowly explained that he had come from the British Embassy in Damascus and was travelling to the UK Embassy in Beirut. Reason? A liaison visit

because of concern of what was happening in the south of Lebanon.

Shouting and waving his AK-47 the leader pushed Harry towards one of the Toyotas and pushed him into the rear seat.

At this point the car driver was told to sit on the ground by his vehicle, an armed guard standing close by.

The group leader by now was on his radio checking, with some argument, Harry's credentials, travelling under a diplomatic passport.

Finally the discussion finished and he turned towards Harry, indicating sullenly that he could leave.

The driver scrambled quickly into his car whilst Harry took up his seat in the rear, but not before extending his hand to the leader, who shook it reluctantly.

The rest of the trip was uninterrupted and uneventful.

Arriving at the British Embassy Harry met initially with the First Secretary, a man with a totally different profile to Charles Urwin, who explained, as far as he could, the status of the fighting in Southern Lebanon.

The next meeting was with the Ambassador, Jonathan Peters, to whom Harry explained frankly what his main task entailed, as directed by the Deputy, notwithstanding the Ambassador's concern for Embassy staff if the fighting escalated. It was made clear the priority was to determine routing of the tipped rockets.

However it seemed a connection had already been made.

Local radio news had said that on the 13th July, at approximately 6:00 a.m. local time, all three runways of Beirut International airport sustained significant damage from missile strikes directed at it by the Israeli Air Force. The Israeli Air Force claimed at the time that Hezbollah had received a weapons shipment there. The runways were rendered inoperative and the Lebanese Government declared that the airport was closed until further notice.

Information and intelligence coming from Lebanon's southern border was confused, with no clear picture as to what was actually happening.

Harry asked if he could drive to various quarters of Beirut to try and determine which groups were evidently in control, and the extent that movements were restricted or monitored.

It was agreed that an Embassy driver, in a civilian car, would take Harry on a limited tour of certain areas of the city to determine the current position. This would take place early the following week.

Monday 17th July 2006.

SIS (MI6) HQ London

The Deputy had received an internal call to attend a meeting with the DG scheduled for 11am.

No content had been discussed, just the irritating phrase, 'bring an open mind', delivered in a half-joking manner.

The Deputy pulled his file together on initial reorganisation thoughts and added a few bullet points for consideration.

He arrived a few minutes late, deliberately, apologising as he entered the DG's office.

'Apologies, got caught just as I was coming to see you.'

‘No problem Norman. Sit over here with the view. Coffee?’

The first couple of minutes were taken up with inconsequential chat, before the DG then explained the reason for the meeting

‘I wanted to expand further on our recent discussions concerning the future shape, structure and focus of SIS.

I have been giving it some additional thought following discussions with both the PM’s Office and the Treasury.

As you can imagine there are a number of constraints arising within Budgets, plus a very different Focus, moving forward, as to our specific areas of operation, staffing levels and mix, and therefore, structure and organisation.

Within budgetary constraints we cannot cover the world. Therefore our future relations and Intel sharing with ‘friendly’ countries, and to some extent with ‘not so friendly’ countries will increase in importance, and will form an important part of future strategy.

In essence the Service will be embarking on a paradigm shift, which will probably take a minimum of three years to implement.

‘You understand what I am saying?’ he queried.

‘Yes, so far.’

‘To continue then.

As I indicated to you we must start this process with no preconceptions as to where it should finish. We must start with a clean canvas and be prepared to think the unthinkable. ‘Undiscussables’ must be brought onto the table and discussed.’

The Deputy, by now, was thinking that if he heard any more management or jargon speak the embryonic headache would turn into a real humdinger.

'I hear what you are saying, but if we are going to start somewhere on this canvas we are going to have to agree some basic elements as a starting point.

Countries in which agents will be placed, countries we consider 1st Division for Intel sharing, a basic idea of what Treasury thinking is, and/or what they think will be our budget, what are the priorities for intelligence gathering, any linkages to home grown terrorism, relationships with GCHQ, our 'friends' across the river. That sort of thing.'

At this point the DG looked a little disappointed as he replied,

'Norman, what you have just said is perfectly true, but is only appropriate at the tactical level.

What I am talking about is the strategic level.

That's where I want you to concentrate. Bring forward a number of scenarios that we can then flesh out. Once we have got some idea of shape and form we can then start to create the sort of structure that we will need.

Do you recall that in the '60s when the Army was being reduced in numbers, and before they knew what were the challenges of the '70s, the MOD took out a considerable number of Majors under the 'Golden Bowler' scheme in order to free up promotion to younger officers? That was the sort of bold stroke that was implemented then and which transformed the Army structure.

Norman, bring your experience to bear on what might be, the options that could be considered. You understand?'

'Absolutely.

Let me go away, put my thinking cap on and come back to you with some ideas in about 2-3 weeks. Current ops are still pressing!'

'Of course Norman. When you have some thoughts in outline let's meet and discuss.'

The Deputy went back to his office having a very clear idea of what the DG wanted.

The last comment concerning 'Golden Bowlers' summed up his thinking.

If you took out a layer of senior officers there could be a significant saving in budgetary terms.

At the same time younger, more 'flexible' officers could be promoted, or given additional responsibility in the same rank, which would suit their political masters looking for a more malleable cohort.

The downside was the loss of experience contained in the cadre of dismissed officers.

How to write my own retirement ticket, the Deputy thought grimly.

Beirut Lebanon

Harry and the civilian driver left the British Embassy at about 8.30am, and drove cautiously in an easterly direction towards the centre of the city.

The traffic was sparse as many Lebanese were fleeing the city as indiscrimate shelling took place.

They could hear the crump of artillery and rocket shells landing nearby, and suddenly a particular salvo peppered the road about 50 yards ahead, the last, of a group of four or five, landing directly in front of a six storey office building.

At the same time a Toyota 4x4 drove round the corner of the building, and took the secondary force of the explosion, lifting the front end of the vehicle

5 feet off the ground, before tipping the vehicle violently onto its side.

Harry's driver had skidded to a halt whereupon Harry leapt out and ran to the 4x4.

He clambered up onto the right side of the vehicle and pulled open the passenger door to see the driver, obviously unconscious, slumped over the wheel, on the left hand side.

Broken glass from the side window and windscreen covered the driver and passenger.

The passenger, also unconscious, had, by the force of the explosion, been turned and pushed partially over the front seat into the rear of the vehicle.

Harry called to his driver to come and assist, and two Lebanese, who had appeared from a side street, also came over.

He started to gently lift the passenger, who softly groaned, and realised he was lifting a woman as he saw the long dark hair as her head came from behind the front seat. A thin line of blood stretched from her mouth to under her chin.

His stomach lurched as he realised it was Anna.

Having got her out and laid on the ground a short distance away, he returned to the vehicle to try and extricate the driver.

His head was racing with confused thoughts as he clambered into the Toyota to try and extricate the driver who had a severe cut on his forehead, currently seeping blood across his face.

With help from his driver and others he was able to pull the unconscious form from the vehicle and carry him to the same sheltered spot as Anna.

As the driver was laid on the ground Harry realised, with another shock to his system, that he was looking at Alain Dubois, his old friend from the DGSE in Paris.

He quickly felt their respective pulses whilst at the same time asking a local to call for an ambulance, which he found out had already been done.

With siren wailing the ambulance arrived after about twenty minutes, and took both Anna and Alain to the nearest hospital. Both, by then, were starting to show signs of consciousness, and Harry followed with his driver.

In the short ride Harry was trying to make sense of the pairing, not having paid particular attention to the damaged signs on the rear windows of the Toyota, denoting an AFD vehicle and activity.

Once in the hospital Harry lied that he was a colleague of the two casualties, and had been following in his car when the accident happened.

The doctor responsible for the examinations queried as to what had exactly happened in order to consider the appropriate treatment.

Harry was able to give an honest account of what had happened, and asked when it would be possible to see them.

He was advised no earlier than 5pm that afternoon.

He decided to wait at the hospital in case that time changed and sent his driver back to the embassy.

Sitting in the reception his mind was racing through any number of permutations covering Anna and Alain.

Some were completely off the wall, but others made some sense.

Mossad was keeping a very focussed eye on Lebanon, and in particular Hezbollah control and direction. Therefore he could understand, in one way, why Anna was there.

Alain was different. French DGSE in Lebanon. Doing what? That was a strange one. Perhaps some angle, he, Harry, wasn't aware of?

Yes, DGSE and Mossad shared Intel from time to time, but operating together, not a usual scenario.

Time will tell all, he thought grimly.

The situation in the hospital was fairly chaotic as an increasing number of casualties were arriving on a fairly regular basis.

Demand, on the doctors and support staff, was intense, and normal administrative conventions were being put on one side.

Harry knew the general area where Anna and Alain had been taken, so at about 2pm he went looking for their ward or room.

Walking down a long corridor, with rooms off each side, he eventually saw, through one of the open doors, the form of Anna on a bed connected to a drip with some bandaging on her head and arm. She appeared to be asleep, so he entered quietly and closed the door gently behind him.

At this slight noise her eyes partially opened and then widened as she recognised him.

'Harry', she said in a strained voice reaching out her hand to him.

He took her hand in his, squeezing it gently and at the same time smiling down at her.

'We really must stop meeting like this. If we don't people will be starting to talk!'

Anna smiled weakly at him, 'Don't try and make me laugh Harry, everything hurts too much. What are you doing here? Don't answer that, just please listen to what I have to tell you.'

At this point Anna then explained her cover in AFD, her identity, and what her tasks were, as directed by Mossad.

Harry listened carefully until she had finished, and then innocently asked who the driver of the Toyota was.

‘That is Alain Dubois, an AFD logistics man from Paris. Why?’
‘Nothing really. Just joining up the dots,’ he said, smiling.
She smiled back, ‘Just a colleague in AFD. We work together. That’s all. Nothing more.’
Harry started to gently protest in a humorous way, whereupon she squeezed his hand and said seriously, ‘I’d never have guessed you were a jealous man Harry Baxter, but you have to promise me if you speak to Alain that you respect and maintain my cover. Agreed?’
‘Yes’, he said, smiling.
‘And don’t forget my name is Anne, not Anna!’
Harry smiled, ‘Absolutely, but in Alain’s case I can still keep an eye on possible competition!’
They sat quietly, each with their own thoughts, until Harry said he would go and see if he get any news on Alain.
Harry bent down and kissed her briefly on the cheek.
‘Back soon.’
A couple of rooms further up the corridor Harry found where Alain was situated, apparently asleep, or perhaps sedated.
His head was bandaged and his pallor was grey. A nasty knock and probable concussion at least, Harry thought.
A nurse appeared and shooed Harry away, telling him to come back at 6pm.
Returning to Anna’s room he told her of Alain’s condition, and then asked her what plans AFD had made about their staff in Lebanon. Were they going to stay, or try to get out as quickly as possible?

'We were returning to AFD HQ when we were hit. We had received instructions to leave as soon as possible, probably by road into Syria.
It was necessary to get those who were leaving together, and put together a mini convoy. We hope safety in numbers, particularly when crossing the border.'
'I know similar plans are being considered at the UK Embassy leaving only a skeleton staff behind.
How long this will go on for nobody knows, but it's building up by the hour.'
Anna nodded.
'How long do they think you will be here in hospital?'
'I don't know, but not a minute longer than necessary.
I need to get information on Alain, as soon as he regains consciousness.'
'Look', said Harry, 'I'm going back to the embassy now, but will come back here at six o'clock as told by that nurse.
I want to find out if I've received any further instructions from London, and secondly what plans are being made about embassy staff. Also give me the name and contact number of your boss at AFD.'
Harry wrote down the details Anne gave him, then said, 'Look after yourself, rest up. I'll be back later.'
'Fine Harry, I shall still be here', Anne said smiling weakly.
Harry kissed her on her forehead whilst squeezing her hand and left.
Picking up his driver they made their way back to the embassy where Harry checked his recent encrypted messages received via satellite link.

The only one of real importance was from the Deputy.
In summary it instructed Harry to assist in the evacuation of British nationals from the embassy via Syria, the only feasible route at present.
Forget possible routing and delivery into Lebanon of uranium tipped missiles. They were already being used.
Lastly, return to Islamabad as soon as possible to continue investigation into the Kirmani family, Azmat in particular, and connections with Charles Urwin, which may have compromised his position as First Secretary.
Tom Denman was carrying out a holding brief in this connection, but was running up against a significant lack of cooperation from Charles Urwin.
Harry then met with the Ambassador to discuss evacuation plans. A late night departure was discussed, arriving at the border at dawn.
Harry briefed him on the parallel evacuation of French nationals in AFD, and suggested that a joint convoy would perhaps be best, safety in numbers, etc.
The Ambassador, worried by reports of significant escalation in the Southern border region of Lebanon concurred, and instructed Harry to organise it as soon as practical.
At 6 pm Harry returned to the hospital.
He stopped off briefly at Anne's room before going to see Alain.
He had regained consciousness, but was clearly weak with a broken arm and two cracked ribs.
Harry explained what had happened in the accident, the escalation of the fighting, rocket attacks, indiscrimate shelling of residential areas, and the

outline plans for evacuation, and that Anne was recovering in another room.

Harry explained, in very general terms, what he was doing in Lebanon, and also asked Alain if Anne knew that he was DGSE.

Alain then asked that Harry keep that strictly confidential, Harry smiling inwardly to himself, thinking of the double games that are played at all levels. Alain expanded the reasoning behind such confidentiality, to which Harry concurred.

Harry then explained the idea of a joint convoy, once all individual vehicles had left Beirut and made a rendezvous on the main road to the Lebanon/Syria frontier. Marshalling a number of vehicles in Beirut could be fatal.

Speed would now be of the essence. Would Alain be strong enough to travel?

Alain had initially expressed surprise at seeing Harry and had tried a Gallic shrug, which brought an expression of pain to his face, when he said,

'Mon vieux ami, why should I be surprised to find you here? In the games we play there are no real rules as to where we go, or what we do.

I am very happy to see you. What next?

Am I OK to travel? D'accord! I certainly do not want to remain here with increased bombing. Je suis prêt à partir!'

As he was speaking Alain was trying to lift himself but was restrained by Harry who said,

'Alain, hang on. We are not leaving in the next few minutes! It will probably be tomorrow sometime at the earliest. Rest up for God's sake. You have been injured. Get your strength back. OK?'

Alain nodded and leant back against his pillows.

'Bien sûr! À demain! Do not forget me!' he said, smiling, and wagging his finger at Harry.

Returning to Anne's room Harry explained Alain's condition, and his insistence on travelling when it had been organised.
Anne asked if Harry had kept her cover intact which he confirmed.

Islamabad 19th July 2006
Tom's first meeting with Charles Urwin was not going well.
There is always a problem with the law.
The assumption of innocence must be maintained until proven guilty.
However, in an investigation such as this, where evidence appears to implicate the subject under investigation, it is hard, if not impossible, to assume innocence, and there is a tendency to believe that there had to be some connection, however tenuous.
The connection could have been allowed to develop in a passive way, by not taking a strict enough line covering security issues. Perhaps by indiscrete remarks made at a social level.
Charles Urwin was taking the offensive.
'Mr Denman, I am surprised, bearing in mind the seriousness of this investigation, and the subject matter, that is was felt that somebody of your grade was sufficiently experienced to handle it with appropriate sensitivity.
Additionally, bearing in mind that the intelligence gathered so far is focussed on my brother-in-law, I would have thought that your efforts might be directed at that part of my family, through marriage.
What you have asked me so far could have been handled by a simple question and answer document

which could have saved considerable time, and been considerably less tedious.'

Tom, who had been taking notes, paused, put down his pen and looked hard at the subject of his questioning.

After allowing several uncomfortable seconds to pass Tom spoke.

'Mr Urwin, let me acquaint you with a few facts concerning yourself.

Someone in your position is so keen on 'position' that you can often be blind as to what is actually happening. From your lofty 'position' you tend to adopt a helicopter view. The problem with that is you actually have no eye for detail. Broad brush strokes carry you along.

I have the stamina and persistence of a dripping tap, and if I find one gap in your evidence, yes evidence, I'll chase your tail until you beg for some relief.

Let me jog your memory of your time in Moscow.

A satisfactory tour I believe?'

Charles gently nodded his head.

'No. During your watch, and at your grade at the time, you allowed certain information to leave H.M. Embassy which was quite useful to the FSB.

Not critical but sensitive. Could have been used against the UK at some point.

The Ambassador glossed over it, gave you a good end of term report, and off you went.

Why? Because he was fed up with your style, manner, arrogance, and career focus, to the exclusion of anything, and everybody else.

He was delighted to see the back of you, so let me tell you this.

This investigation will drag on as long as it needs to, and if you don't cooperate then, I personally, will raise the Moscow issue, and ensure it enters your file for all to see.

Do you understand?'

Charles Urwin stared at Tom Denman, his mind racing, a mix of hatred and fear at what he had just heard. Something, he thought, lost in the mists of time and unlikely to ever surface. Until now.

His defence mode kicked in with appropriate verbal and physical reactions.

'Tom, may I call you Tom?' He spoke cautiously.

Tom ignored the question.

'What you have just described was in my early days in the Foreign Service, and I fully admit to the error on my part. I thought one was allowed one non-critical mistake as a young man', he said smiling weakly.

'I realise from what you have just said that all misdemeanours are noted and recorded, to be produced on occasions such as this, in order that enquiries can be pursued relentlessly.'

He added hastily, 'A process I fully understand and support, and which is only right and proper under the circumstances surrounding my related family.

From this point on you can depend on my full cooperation in this investigation so that it can brought to a satisfactory conclusion.'

Tom did not answer. His look more than adequately conveyed his thoughts.

Russian Embassy Islamabad

Stepan Volkov was reviewing the latest updates from his mole in the British High Commission.

He smiled at the description of internal investigations taking place concerning the First Secretary's in-laws family.

His brow furrowed when he read that Harry Baxter was currently in Lebanon, having travelled via Syria, following up on specialist munitions. Starting to get a little closer to Russian/Syrian/Hezbollah relations.

Advise Moscow, maintain watching brief, ensure updates are obtained on a more frequent basis. Every two days up from weekly.

XIV

Friday 21st July 2006

SIS (MI6) HQ Vauxhall Cross London

The liaison meeting with the CIA Head of Station London had started well.

The Deputy had been briefed on the previous working relationship of Harry Baxter and Jack DeCosta, established on a joint-op in Germany.

Whilst recognising that the CIA's global reach far exceeded that of MI6, there was a professional respect as to the quantity and quality of Intel that was mined by MI6.

'Well Jack, as you know Harry is based in Islamabad, currently about to go back there after a short stay in Beirut, which, as a current theatre, is not looking at all good.

What Intel we are getting is very confused, and there is a lot of tit-for-tat flying around the ether between Hezbollah and Israel.

Israel are saying HB started it, but bearing in mind they want to wind back or significantly reduce its capability, they would say that wouldn't they?'

Jack immediately countered by saying, 'Our Intel so far indicates that a cross border incursion by Hezbollah was the trigger. The Israelis are quick to respond, and I for one don't blame them one little bit.

When you are surrounded as they are, I'm sure you would be jumpy too.'

'Agreed, but what is likely to be the escalation, and will other adjacent countries get pulled in? Plus indiscriminate shelling by both sides is going to rack up a significant number of fatalities. Plus the usual blame game.'

Jack DeCosta then observed, 'Could I change the location back to Pakistan?'

The Deputy nodded.

'Fine.

As you said, Harry was trying to get a handle on the source and set up of some of the Pakistan based groups, whether involved in internal destabilisation, funding and training of jihadist groups, exporting of terrorism, cross border excursions into Iraq or Afghanistan. Correct?'

The Deputy nodded in agreement.

'OK. When Harry and I last spoke he was suggesting some sort of Intel sharing which I ran past my boss for approval. That was given, so here we are today. The question now is analysis and distribution. We need to ensure it gets to the right agents, in time, so that it can be properly acted upon.'

'Not one single argument there Jack. Suggestions?'

The discussions then covered a number of scenarios and the involvement of parts of the Service in order to maximise results.

If Harry had been listening, he would not have been unhappy.

UK Embassy Beirut Lebanon

On Saturday, the 22nd, the Ambassador had pulled the embassy staff together and decided who, as UK nationals, would be leaving Beirut.

The locally employed Lebanese had also been given the opportunity to travel to Syria if they wished, some to join families who had already left, others to stay in Beirut.

Arrangements were made concerning vehicles required, particularly bearing in mind two people, Anna and Alain, who were not yet fully recovered from their injuries.
It had been decided that vehicles would make their way, singly, to a rendezvous point on the Beirut to Damascus road, leaving at approximately 5 minute intervals from the embassy.
Departures would start on Monday the 24th July, at about 0500hrs, aiming to RV at approximately 0630hrs. Eight vehicles were assigned to the trip.
Assuming sensible progress then they would expect to cross the border into Syria between 1030 and 1130hrs. From the border to Damascus about 1-1½hrs max.
Diplomatic passports, vehicle documents, food, water, some basic vehicle spares, shovels, etc., were organised, together with full tanks of fuel and a number of full jerry cans.
After receiving agreement from the French Embassy and the AFD, it was decided that Alain and Anne would be brought to the UK Embassy on the Sunday afternoon using the vehicle they would be transported in to Damascus. Any 'comfort' problems could be sorted out at that time.
Harry went back to the hospital to advise them of the plan and timing.
Anne was happy to see him, and held his hand tightly as he outlined what would be happening over the next two days.
Visiting Alain, who shook him by the hand and appeared to be in good spirits and recovering well, Harry gave him the basic timings for the planned departure.

‘Alain, we will collect you about 1600hrs on Sunday, take you to the UK Embassy, from where we leave about 0500hrs Monday morning.

It won’t be the most comfortable journey you will have had, but we’ll do the best we can. OK?’

Replying with a straight face, Alain said,

‘Perhaps I can take my turn at driving. My last experience has taught me to be a little more cautious when turning corners!

Incidentally, have you got some coffee for the journey? I don’t think I could stand tea all day!’

‘You’ll be lucky if you have water to drink, my friend’, laughed Harry, gently slapping Alain on the shoulder, which made him wince slightly.

‘I’m sorry’, said Harry, concerned, noticing the reaction.

‘Pas problème, mon vieux, I’m making good progress.’

Returning to Anne, Harry mentioned, with a mock solemn face, the fact that he would probably take a few days leave in Damascus, just make sure she was being properly looked after!

Anne laughed and said, ‘I think that is an excellent idea. Do you have anywhere in mind, and preferably not a hospital?’

‘Well, I have it on good authority that there are a couple of great hotels, the Beit Al Wali and the Beit Zafran. Not the usual international monster concrete boxes, but medium size, with loads of character and great service. Why don’t we try one of them?’

‘Sounds ideal, but you realise I’m not going to be very mobile?’

‘Of course. We, and particularly you, can relax, have some good food, and then go back to your French op in Paris!’

‘Well Mr Baxter, you’ve convinced me. Just make sure we get to Damascus in one piece. Obviously Alain will be travelling with us to Damascus. What will happen when we get there?’

‘He will probably go straight into the St Louis, the French hospital for a thorough check up, and any remedial treatment that needs to be done on account of his injuries.’

Anne nodded.

‘I’d like to make sure he’s OK and fit to fly back to Paris, as we would probably travel back together.

At least we need to make sure our reports match before we put them in to the Big Boss!’

‘Don’t worry about that,’ said Harry in a jocular mood, ‘let’s get to Damascus first, *then* we can worry about the reports!’

Anne laughed and took his hand in hers, looking at him intently.

‘You’re a good man, Harry Baxter. I’m glad I know you, and I’m *very* glad you’re here. Now go and do what you have to do, and I will be ready Sunday afternoon.’

Harry bent down and kissed her on each cheek and her forehead before saying,

‘Behave yourself, see you Sunday.’

Sunday 23rd July 2006

1600hrs UK Embassy Beirut

There were no problems in collecting Anne and Alain from the hospital. In fact, doctors and staff were grateful for their removal as increasing numbers of injured were arriving for treatment.

Anne seemed to be recovering well, some colour had returned to her cheeks, but Alain was still in some pain; concussion, a broken arm, at least two cracked ribs, and severe leg bruising were making movement difficult and painful.

Sleep was grabbed early as a first light departure was planned.

Monday 24th July 2006

0430hrs UK Embassy Beirut

The eight vehicles had been loaded and fuelled (with some difficulty), but dollars still spoke loudly enough in the region.

Drivers and passengers started to climb on board at the scheduled departure time.

Leaving at 5 minute intervals the 4x4s set off for the RV point on the main Beirut to Damascus road.

At this hour the city was comparatively quiet and the vehicles made good progress towards the RV, at Louaize, roughly 6 kilometres outside Beirut.

The first 4x4 waited there for the others to join up, keeping a good 50metres between each vehicle as they arrived.

Harry was driving the fifth vehicle, with Alain and Anne, able to keep in contact with the other drivers by radio. Silence was to be maintained unless absolutely necessary.

Having accounted for all vehicles the convoy set off, maintaining 100metres between vehicles.

With luck and steady driving they could be crossing into Syria in about two hours.

The convoy was making reasonable time, only delayed from time to time by slow moving refugee traffic, and had already passed Sawfar.

After about another 9 kms they were passing Dahr Al Baidar, which is the exact point of the junction between the regions of Mount Lebanon and the BeKaa valley.

Due to a few vehicles ahead of them which were stationary at what appeared to be some sort of check point, they too slowed down, and stopped.

Harry got out and moved up their convoy to see what the reason was. From about 50metres he could see bearded, camouflage dressed members of Hezbollah shouting and waving their AK-47s around, whilst obviously haranguing some poor unfortunate.

Eventually it was clear money had passed hands and the queue moved forward.

Harry, retracing his steps, advised each vehicle to rightfully claim diplomatic immunity before any negotiations as to money arose.

Getting back into his 4x4, he told Alain and Anne to look as ill as possible. Anything to get through the roadblock.

However, his 9mm was wedged under his seat, if things took a turn for the worse.

The convoy edged forward, each vehicle being quizzed, and documents being carefully examined.

Arriving at the check point documents and passports were demanded and examined.

Harry was explaining that eight vehicles were in their convoy, and that the two persons in his 4x4 were seriously ill and being taken to a hospital in Damascus.

He was ordered out of his vehicle whilst one of Hezbollah stuck his head in to check on the two occupants.

Harry looked left and right at his fellow travellers and shrugged.

At that point he saw, standing about 25metres away, the leader of the group of Hezbollah controlling the checkpoint. It was the same man who had stopped and quizzed him when travelling from Damascus to Beirut.

He indicated to the paramilitary inspecting his papers that he wanted to speak to the leader, and was led over with his papers.

Harry reminded him of his previous trip, his checking of his diplomatic passport, and the fact he was now taking embassy staff and injured persons to Damascus.

The leader of the Hezbollah group recognised him, and with a surly nod of the head instructed his men to let the vehicles through.

Breathing a sigh of relief Harry waved to his convoy drivers and they moved slowly through the checkpoint.

The convoy passed through the Lebanese border post at Masnaa with no problems and drove on a further 10kms, before passing through the Syrian border post, Jdaidit Yabws.

From there it was a comparatively easy run to Damascus taking about 1¼hrs.

Seven vehicles headed for the British Embassy, Harry meanwhile, driving Alain directly to the St Louis French Hospital.

Alain was quickly admitted and taken to a room for a full examination.

Harry promised to return the following day.

'Get some rest my friend, and don't keep trying to talk to the pretty nurses!'

'Harry, mon vieux, don't forget I am French! Anyway all these tests are boring. I just want some painkillers, some sleep; 24hrs and I will be fine! After that the thought of a glass of a good Bordeaux will keep me going!

Va bien! À Demain!'

You can't keep a good man down, Harry thought, as he drove with Anne to the Beit Zafran Hotel.

Harry said he would telephone the hospital and give a hotel number once they were checked in.

They found the hotel, situated in Old Damascus, a short drive south from the hospital.

Having checked in, Harry went into the bathroom and sent an encrypted satcom report to the Deputy advising of safe passage of embassy staff, current position Beirut and Damascus, condition of Alain, etc., and that he expected to return to Islamabad within three days, logistics permitting.

He suggested that some of the data sent should be shared, or discussed with Jack DeCosta, CIA London Head. Bearing in mind the difficulty for every agency on the ground to be up to date, sensible sharing was to be encouraged.

He and Anne/Anna ate early that evening, being fairly tired from the journey, and with her not fully recovered from her accident.

On retiring to their room, no words were exchanged whilst she showered and changed.

As she came out from the bathroom Harry stood up and opened his arms.

She stood against him with their arms around each other.

They stood like that for a few minutes, she feeling his hard body against hers.

She looked up at him. He kissed her gently before turning her around and pushing her gently towards the bed.

'I think Anne/Anna, you had better get some well-earned rest, otherwise, I might forget that I'm a gentleman, and be tempted to take advantage of a beautiful young lady!'

She laughed softly.

'Mr Baxter, if I were slightly fitter than I am now, I could well forget that I'm supposed to be a lady!'
They both laughed gently, comfortable in the unspoken knowledge that they were both back on track.

Tuesday 25 July 2006

Damascus
They both slept well and in the morning Harry went down early to the hotel reception to see if he could organise his flight back to Islamabad.
Walking towards the lobby, which was quiet at that time, he saw a man enter from the street, cross the lobby and start to climb the stairs.
Harry thought he recognised him but could not recall a name.
Whilst discussing flights with the concierge he suddenly remembered who it was.
Harry had seen some old CCTV footage and photos from France, provided by DGSE about 18 months ago.
DGSE had been monitoring a number of Syrian 'persons of interest', all using a particular hotel in Paris, just off the Etoile, in Avenue Hoche, which had been acquired by Arab interests some 25 years previously.
His name was Omar Najjar. He was, or still is, an important member of the Committee, committed to the continuing Jihad against perceived Western attacks against the Muslim world.
Harry wondered what the reason was for the visit to the hotel, co-incidence perhaps, or was the Committee meeting?

He decided he would raise it with Alain when he saw him later in the day. Decisions would have to be taken as to Alain's fitness to travel, and how soon. Obviously Anne would travel at the same time.

As dawn had broken over Damascus they had discussed their relationship, and had caught up on a lot of things that had remained unsaid, over the previous months. Lying comfortably in each other's arms they knew they had reached that point in the relationship where it either moves forward strongly, or, with huge regret, they go their separate ways.

They had agreed that that no mention would be made to Alain, unnecessary complications at the present time are best avoided!

Having determined flight options Harry told Anne to rest whilst he went the French Hospital to find out how Alain was recovering.

Arriving at the hospital Harry was shown to Alain's room.

'I understand there are already complaints of pestering some attractive nurses by some French chap, or so the Head Nurse told me', Harry said with a smile as he walked in.

'Oui, mon ami, but there is always temptation when one is unable, or incapable, of doing anything about it!' he replied stretching out his hand, his face wincing slightly with the effort.

Harry shook his hand carefully.

'Well, how soon do you think you could travel?'

'Tomorrow, I'm sure, but carefully and properly looked after by some Air France hostesses!'

Harry shook his head.

'Unbelievable. He thinks he's God's gift to women, and he's not even handsome.'

‘What do you mean?’
‘Well, I bet the day you were born your mother looked at you and thought what an ugly little brute, BUT I love him! And nothing’s really changed over the years has it? Except you don’t dribble quite as much!’
They both laughed, happy in that adolescent way that men can bond, and become friends.
‘OK,’ Harry said, ‘there is an Air France flight tomorrow, leaving at about 1600hrs, my Etihad flight leaves at about 1730hrs.
I can get you both on it, so Anne can give you some assistance, plus telling you to behave when you start pestering the hostesses!’
‘I will at least get their sympathy when I tell them of my accident, and I shall blame my *older* sister for spoiling my fun!’
Harry smiled, ‘Just be careful you don’t find out you have more injuries by the time you reach Paris!’
‘Touché, my friend! That is something I must consider. My personal safety!’
‘Putting your personal safety to one side, there is one item I’d like to raise.’
Alain nodded. ‘Bien.’
‘This morning whilst I was talking to the concierge a man came into the hotel and went upstairs. I thought I recognised him and I did. It was Omar Najjar, a member of the Committee. It was your CCTV and some photos that you had sent to us in London that triggered it. It was definitely him. Have you got any recent activity for him?’
‘I don’t think so, but will certainly do some checking when I get back to Paris. Thank you for your good memory. I will contact you through our usual channels when I have some information.’

Having agreed that, Harry told him to be ready to leave the hospital about midday on Wednesday, and looked forward to seeing him at that time.
'In the meantime just make sure you get as much rest as you can. And I'm not joking, alright?'

--

In the Beit Zafran Hotel Omar Najjar knocked on the door of room 105.
After a short pause it opened and he was invited in.
He saw that there were three other men, seated and talking quietly between themselves.
Seeing him, they rose as one and greeted him in the familiar Arab embrace, mouthing their greeting.
After an initial exchange of pleasantries they moved on to the main item for discussion.
The broad outline of the plan was to try and organise a simultaneous attack in two world capitals, to draw attention to their cause, and highlight their ability to strike at will.
Various suggestions were put forward as to which cities should be targeted, and after some debate it was decided that London and Paris would garner the most world-wide publicity.
How this would be carried out and the level of funding required were dealt with in broad terms, Omar requesting overall approval, after which he would then investigate method, and cost to be sanctioned later.
It was agreed by the Operations unit that there would be a further meeting in Paris in two weeks' time to consider final plans and funding.
Other matters were discussed, particularly the ongoing situation between Israel and Lebanon, casualty numbers mounting and the increased

support levels required by Hezbollah to maintain the initiative and advantage.
At this time there was no clear idea how long the war would continue, but the Committee was very clear that maximum propaganda must be achieved for their cause, and to gain worldwide Muslim support in their actions.
Omar left the meeting and made his way to his hotel, he too, catching a flight to Paris the following day.

Wednesday 26th July 2006

Damascus
Harry and Anne dressed quietly that morning, each in their own thoughts, wondering, without questioning out loud, where events would take and shape them over the next few weeks and months.
Before dawn they had lain quietly in bed, each sure the other was awake, but neither breaking the silence.
Later that morning, as they were packing, Harry started to speak,
'Look, I'm sure you know how I feel about you, but the one thing we don't know, is, what the hell is going to be happening over the next few weeks or months, before we can meet again.'
Anna turned and placed her hand on his mouth.
'Don't say anything more Harry.
You also know how I feel about you. I'm already looking forward to when we can meet again.
In our line of work this is an occupational hazard, but if it is going to last, it will. Believe me.'
Harry nodded. 'Yep, you're right, but it doesn't make it very easy, does it?

Anyway, we'll both crack on, and think of the next time we are going to meet, wherever and whenever that may be!'

They held each other for a short while, Harry finally kissing her on her forehead.

'Let's go and pick up 'appy Alain, and no doubt submit our apologies to the hospital for his conduct whilst he's been there!'

Anna laughed, 'He's a good man and definitely a friend of yours. However I'm glad, or hope, you are not as flirty as he is!'

Arriving at the hospital they saw Alain was ready, looking a little pale, but with a smile.

'Bonjour mes enfants, let us go before I get into more trouble!'

'More trouble?'

'Oui Harry! I asked the lovely, but older, Matron if she would come to Paris with me to assist in my recuperation!

I'm not sure if she wanted to laugh or slap me! Fortunately she laughed!'

The taxi ride to the airport was uneventful, and Harry wished them a good trip, and a professional goodbye to Anna at the Air France Check In, before making his way to the Etihad desk for his flight to Islamabad via Abu Dhabi.

The flight was on time, and after take-off Harry drifted into that half sleep state, his thoughts mixed up with recurring images of Anna, and jumbled dream scenarios including Charles Urwin, the Deputy in London, and Beirut rocket attacks.

Changing flights in Abu Dhabi he wondered if Anne and Alain's flight had arrived in Paris yet, little realising that she and Alain were sitting two rows behind Omar Najjar as Air France started its descent into Paris Charles De Gaulle Aeroport.

XV

Thursday 27th July 2006

SIS (MI6) HQ, Vauxhall Cross London

The Director General had called the Deputy for a meeting that morning on an urgent basis.

What was so specifically urgent, wondered the Deputy, as he made his way to the DG's office.

Once greetings were dispensed with the DG opened up.

'Norman, I have been having a series of meetings at number 10, and it is fairly clear, and it has been made very clear to me, that we need to accelerate the process that I outlined to you recently.

What is self-evident, is that there is an increasing public focus on our activities, linked with, and one may think, an unhealthy pre-occupation, with any perceived, or mistaken political bias, or influence being brought to bear on our activities.

Our independence of political influence or bias is paramount to our credibility in the eye of the public, and one that I will strenuously defend.

Therefore I believe, that in terms of thinking what our structure and shape may be in the future, and which you have started to consider, under a medium term strategic review, is a requirement to break this down into bite-sized action plans.

By this, I mean that we can drip feed to the JIC, MP groups, Press, etc., that we have taken on board some of the public concerns, and are expediting a number of pro-active programmes that will address the particular concerns in a very transparent and sustainable manner.

Can you see where I am coming from Norman?'
'I think so,' Norman acknowledged.
His mind had already absorbed the general points made by the DG, and only by substantial muscular control had he avoided either smiling or laughing out loud at the 'strenuous defence' of political influence.
The man, sat before him, trotting out the usual politically inspired mantra, was himself a political appointment, having served his masters well in a previous intelligence role.
'Do you have any short term specifics in mind?' the Deputy enquired.
'Not sufficiently precise at present, but I thought that if you had kick-started an outline, following our recent discussions, then we might use some embryos from that. What do you think?'
'To be honest, current ops have taken up the majority of my time, so progress in that direction has been minimal. Additionally the activity in Lebanon has demanded our current focus, so I was hoping to spend more time on it once the readiness state there had been downgraded.'
Two can play this sort of game if required, he thought.
The DG's face darkened.
'I'm disappointed Norman, that you didn't give a higher priority to what I requested previously. As the emphasis has changed I am prepared to ignore your oversight on this occasion. However, may I be sure that you understand the level of urgency that should be applied to the new task in hand?'
'I am assuming the 'political influence' response to take priority over Lebanon?' replied Norman, keeping his face as expressionless as he could.

'Yes Norman. Delegate. You've got some good men. Let us meet a week today for an update and discussion.'

This signalled the end of the meeting, and the Deputy returned to his office where his PA advised that Frank Stansfield, his old colleague, had telephoned.

The Deputy returned his call, if only to hold a semi-lucid conversation compared to his recent experience.

Frank suggested meeting for a drink that evening to which the Deputy agreed; the rendezvous being a pub they both knew well, just off Victoria Street.

Later that day

As the Deputy entered the pub at 6.45pm he saw Frank sitting in a small alcove towards the back. Frank waved to attract his attention, and stood up to shake him warmly by the hand.

'And your poison tonight is?' Frank enquired.

'A large gin and tonic, and very easy on the tonic,' was the reply.

They both sat down and exchanged the usual pieces of conversation that occur in situations like this, before Frank said,

'Well, have you had any further thoughts on what we were discussing previously?'

'Yes I have,' the Deputy said, pausing before continuing.

'Firstly, let me say that I was flattered that your organisation thought that an old hand, such as myself, would be an appropriate choice for the position they had in mind.'

Frank opened his mouth to interrupt, the Deputy's raised hand indicating that he wished to continue without comment.

‘Additionally, I am sure you are aware of a number of different scenarios playing out at present, some in the Middle East, and some in the Indian sub-continent. You know them as well as me.

Mix those various ingredients with an increasing level of public scrutiny, plus interference from the political establishment, whether good intentions, influence or control, then the challenges facing our Service are increasing on an exponential basis.’

He paused again, collecting his further thoughts.

Frank said nothing.

‘Tasks facing me at present are obviously operational with limited resources, and how best these are prioritised.

Increasingly difficult with more overseas, and home grown, potential martyrs on the loose.

To say that your offer is not tempting would be the big lie! However tempting that is, I am going to say No!

Reason? Simple. You know my credo. Defence of the Realm. Somewhat undervalued at present within our current crop of masters.

I intend to stay, and do my level best to defend and maintain the standards, for which our Service has been known since its establishment.

I do not intend to allow it to become, either a political stepping stone for some short term unworthy, or for its values to be diluted and made less effective under the guise of so-called ‘transparency. My dander, as they say, is well up!

When I came into the Service I did so with a mixture, obviously, of career interest, enjoyment and advancement, but that was also tempered with a dose of idealism. ‘Service’ in the broadest sense, with responsibility and loyalty to country. Some

might say idealism. I frankly don't give a damn how they describe it! I know what it means to me!'
He put his hands behind his head and smiled.
'Go on, tell me I'm a complete idiot!'
Frank spoke slowly.
'When I was discussing you with the Group Chairman, I said that you would be the best man for the position. However what I didn't tell you when we met last, was that I also said it was very unlikely that you would move, for exactly the reasons that you have just given me.'
The Deputy smiled.
'Delighted I have confirmed what you thought and said!
My shout this time, same again?'
They spent another hour together, the Deputy enjoying his time with 'well-informed opinion' or at least somebody on a similar wavelength!
As he sat on the Tube, rattling its way to the suburbs, he reflected on what he had said to Frank.
He had chosen his words carefully, diplo-speak perhaps, but in essence true.
Yes, he was going to stay and fight for the Service, and to hell with the politics! Defence of the Realm. Don't see why I should be the one to help to change that!
He reflected on his own career, now standing on the tee of the 18th hole, a bumpy road from time to time, a *very* bumpy road on some occasions.
He turned his thoughts to operations, and wondered how Harry was getting on, safely out of Lebanon, on his way back to Islamabad.
Frying pan and fire spring readily to mind, he thought wryly. The train slowed and stopped at his home station where he alighted, walking the 330 steps that he had walked, most nights, for 15 years.

Islamabad

Harry's flights had been uneventful and he arrived back at the High Commission at about 2.00pm.

There he met Tom for a progress report of the investigation so far. Tom brought him up to date including the specific issues whilst interviewing Charles Urwin, and the exchange of words.

Whilst discussing various lines of questioning Harry received a call from the High Commissioner requesting an early meeting, including Tom, at 4.00pm.

Entering the HC's office Harry saw that Charles Urwin was already there, seated to the right of the HC.

The HC formally welcomed Harry back from Beirut before quickly moving on to what was, obviously, the main reason for the meeting.

'Harry, this meeting is to be considered confidential for all parties. There will only be a written note by myself to record subject matter and agreed solution. Do you understand and agree?'

'On the basis of the decision you have already made, I assume that my agreement is a given.'

The HC looked hard at him for several seconds before continuing.

'There are two items I wish to discuss with you.

Firstly, the ongoing investigation into Charles' brother-in-law.

Secondly, a matter of internal security and clear leakage of such information from this High Commission.

Mr Denman, in your absence, has been continuing the investigation into the first item, with all necessary due diligence.'

With this comment the HC permitted himself a wry smile, which was, in no way, reciprocated by Charles Urwin.

'I hope that this will be brought to a speedy conclusion, so that Charles can devote 100% of his time to his wide ranging duties and responsibilities, which by the current intervention have been somewhat, if not severely, curtailed.

Now, secondly. Internal Security. It has been breached.

In your absence Harry, I received a number of advices from our colleagues in London and Cheltenham concerning clear breaches of our security.

There were a number of intercepts of traffic from one of our non-friendly embassies here in Islamabad, back to their intelligence HQ.

Information concerning internal activity, planning and personnel movement here at the HC, known only to myself, Charles, you Harry, and perhaps two others, was known in detail by the country embassy concerned.

I recognise that the opinion in Whitehall of our general security is low, but the detail contained in the captured transmissions is at a significantly higher level, and would indicate a high level of professionalism.'

He paused to allow the information to sink in.

'I was wondering if, and I say if strongly, the current investigation is completed shortly, whether the same resource could then be focussed onto the matter I have just raised?'

Harry and Tom looked at each other, Tom giving an almost imperceptible shrug of his shoulders.

Harry spoke slowly, considering his words carefully.

'I am not up to speed on the current investigation, so the security issue could only be started when that is completed.

Now I am back the timescale can obviously be shortened, but I need some time with Tom to update and review, etc.

Once that is done I could obviously put Tom on the security issue, subject to approval from London. An official request from you would help in that direction,' he said, looking directly at the HC.

'Of course,' the HC replied.

'Can I revert after my review with Tom as to status and timing?'

'When would that be?'

'Max three day should cover it.'

'Good. Charles do you have any comments at this time?'

Charles had been sitting quietly and expressionless whilst the discussions had taken place. Inside he was fuming.

He felt side-lined, without any sense of contribution or, more importantly, a feeling or sense of control.

He looked across the room at these two mavericks, in his eyes free agents, seemingly, in this scenario, only answerable to themselves.

'I have answered, I believe, to the best of my ability, all the questions put to me by Mr Denman, plus providing a detailed timeline over the last two years of meetings, discussions, telephone conversations, etc., that took place with my brother-in-law, whether private, family or public.

I shall be delighted to return to my official duties as soon as I am able.

Beyond that I have no further comment.'

Harry ignored the look thrown in his direction by Charles, instead suggesting that the sooner he could be updated, the sooner the initial task would be completed, and the second- started.
The HC agreed, adding that he would see Harry on Tuesday the 1st August, at 1000hrs.

Sunday 30th July 2006

Islamabad
Harry and Tom met at 9.00am to start the update on the current investigation into Azmat Kirmani, Charles Urwin's brother-in-law.
'Well Tom, how have you got on Charles Urwin?'
'To begin with I think I was given the Urwin professional 'look down the nose, who do you think you people are?' treatment, until I reminded him of one of the less than professional faux-pas he had committed in his early days.
After a very frank and fair exchange of views the communication channels then appeared to clear somewhat, and since then we have proceeded with appropriate speed.
My report is in the file and also filed on the database, and I will say, here and now that I do not think he is connected in this matter with his brother-in-law.'
'Why', said Harry.
'Well, he may be a self-opinionated smug b****d, career driven, but on following through in all areas of his life, the only connection that I can find he has with Azmat, is through his wife.
He is desperate to get to Ambassador or High Commissioner level and that is his obsessive focus.

Nothing else matters, and certainly not a family based and terrorist linked supply chain!'

'OK Tom. Let me read up and we can meet again tomorrow morning, same time. Alright?

Now what about the HC's request to start digging in to Internal Security?'

'I'm happy with that if you and the Boss agree.

It shouldn't be too difficult to trace, once we have sight of the specific GCHQ and London Intercepts. Plus we can narrow it down a lot when we know the specific embassy involved.'

'Agreed. Leave that with me. I'll contact London to get clearance after the HC has sent in his request.

Let's assume that clearance is forthcoming, so you can start putting on your thinking cap. Probably a bit rusty after a few days of not doing very much here in Islamabad!'

Tom feigned injured innocence, before smiling and asking about Lebanon.

Harry gave Tom a very brief staccato version, omitting any reference to Anna and Alain, finishing by saying that that it really had been a bit of a waste of time, but exciting at times, none the less!

Harry then called in Jeremy and Marion to ensure that they in turn were up to speed within their respective areas, plus aware of the likelihood of an investigation into High Commission security.

Both queried what form this would take, Harry responding that form, depth, and parameters would be advised, once clearances had been received.

He then sent a brief Satcom request and recommendation to the Deputy concerning Tom's involvement in the proposed Security trawl, adding that the HC would also be making a similar request.

Russian Embassy

Later that day Stepan Volkov received a short coded message by mobile advising that a specific Security investigation was likely to start soon at the High Commission. Reason and scope; not known. Would advise when further information available.

He wondered what had triggered this. Something specific or a routine investigation?

Care must be taken to protect his mole. Too valuable to jeopardise.

Charles De Gaulle Airport Paris

Alain and Anne had landed and were proceeding slowly towards Passport Control when they saw a disturbance slightly ahead of them.

Two uniformed police had detained one of their flight's passengers, and were on the receiving end of some less than perfect French mixed with Arabic.

The individual was trying to resist arrest and was being very loud about it, which was, apparently, having no discernable effect whatsoever on the arresting officers.

Alain and Anne were now level with the group and Alain suddenly realised that the man was Omar Najjar, the subject of the brief discussion between himself and Harry the day before.

Because of his injuries and incapacitation he would not intervene but would certainly raise the matter at the earliest opportunity with his Director, Gilles Deniaud.

After passing through Passport Control and Customs Alain and Anne went their separate ways, Alain to hospital, Anne to a hotel.

--

Monday 31st July 2006

HIA Val-de-Grâce Paris

Val-de-Grace is a military hospital sitting in the 5th arrondissement in Paris; not far from the A1 and the Péripherique, no more than 35-45 minutes from CDG airport on a clear day.

Alain had been taken there by ambulance taxi on the Sunday, examined, treated fed, administered medication, and slept soundly for perhaps the first time in many days.

He awoke on the Monday morning feeling refreshed, however, still aware of some very tender parts of his body, indicating he would not be jogging in the Bois de Boulogne any time soon!

His Director arrived at about 10.00am, enquiring as to his health, his self-discipline, with respect to the nursing staff, and for a verbal update on recent events and likely direction.

Alain avoided dwelling on the first two, skipping quickly over events that had brought about his early return to Paris.

Instead he concentrated on his conversation with Harry, concerning the sighting of Omar Najjar in Damascus, and the subsequent arrest at CDG the previous day.

Gilles Deniaud was not aware of the full background of Najjar, but immediately put through a telephone call to DGSE HQ and the French Border Directorate, to ensure that Najjar was not released until further questioning was carried out by DGSE, in addition to the matter of his apprehension.

Alain requested to be released from the Hospital as soon as possible, in order to attend any questioning sessions with Najjar, but was instructed by his Director to do what he was told. Get well first. He would be able to catch up quickly following his treatment.

He was also advised that the Director would keep him up to date so no time would be lost.

He was thinking of liaison with Harry depending on what was uncovered, particularly if the tentacles stretched across the Channel. International jihadists were no respecters of borders.

After the Director had left Alain felt drowsy and fell asleep, contradictory images filling his head, so when he awoke he rang for a nurse and blamed the medication.

He tried his charm approach in trying to find out when he would be released, and despite enjoying his efforts, his nurse indicated that only the doctor had access to that information, and No, she would not be free for dinner on the evening of his departure!

Anna, meanwhile, had checked into a hotel close by the AFD HQ. Then she had contacted the Israeli Embassy.

A meeting was arranged for the following day so that secure contact could be made with Mossad HQ in Tel Aviv, whilst updating Paris Head of Station on recent events.

She wondered what would happen now. Continuation with AFD? Reassignment to another country? Recall to Israel? Many options.

Meanwhile retain cover within AFD, maintain contact with Alain, wonder when she would see Harry again. Put that last thought out of her mind, for now, anyway.

--

In a Paris Holding Centre not far from CDG Airport, Omar Najjar was still berating officialdom for his arrest on entering France.

The reason given so far was that he was 'an undesirable alien', not permitted into France, and should be put back on the next plane to Damascus.

His lawyer, contacted by phone, arrived at the Centre and proceeded to 'prove' that it was a case of mistaken identity with a similar sounding name contained on the Undesirable list.

The lawyer insisted that his client be released immediately, passport returned, in exchange for providing a cash bond, and the address of the hotel in Paris where he would be staying.

After further investigation the officials agreed, reluctantly, to his release, after which his lawyer drove him into Paris and deposited him at the hotel in the Avenue Hoche.

His lawyer suggested that he enjoyed himself for a few days as a tourist because, no doubt, he would be under surveillance initially. Business should be put on ice for a few days.

The mass exodus for 'le mois d'août' was starting, Paris would be deserted.

'À la rentrée' was the cry, as Paris and other major cities disgorged to the beach, mountain and country.

--

Tuesday 1st August 2006

Islamabad

Harry met the HC, at 1000hrs as arranged, to discuss the current status of the investigation concerning the relationship between Charles Urwin and his brother-in-law, Azmat Kirmani.

London had indicated concern, based on intercepts by GCHQ, of any possible breaches of security which would have, or could have, damaged the UK position in the country or region.
'Well Harry, where are we currently?'
'As you are aware I started the enquiry before going to Lebanon, handing over to Tom to continue the investigation.'
The HC replied, somewhat testily,
'Of that I am fully aware, as I have been here during your absence, whilst Mr Denman continued his research and questioning.'
'My reason for raising this, is that in both instances, namely myself and Tom, without collusion, both arrived at the same conclusion.
By checking mobile phone records here in Pakistan, diary notes both private and official, source and respondent on GCHQ intercepts, individual interviews and responses, we are both confident that Charles Urwin is in no way connected to any activity involving Azmat Kirmani. This is despite a significant reluctance, initially, for Charles Urwin to cooperate in the investigation. Thankfully, common sense prevailed, and we were able to conclude the investigation in good order.'
The HC, after a short pause, commented,
'Harry I am delighted that this matter appears to have been resolved. I am aware that Charles can be somewhat prickly when his integrity is questioned, but this is only because an aspersion is being cast on that, and his undoubted professionalism. I hope you can accommodate his shortcoming in this area.'
Harry nodded, not wishing to get into the minefield of personal observations.

'Sir, may I ask if you have sent a request to London for Tom to remain here and proceed with the internal security question?

I have sent mine, and said that I understood you were also sending such a request.'

'Yes, I expect a response today.'

'If that is all I would like to check with Tom on the form and depth of the security review. Perhaps you would brief Charles Urwin on our discussion and findings?'

'Indeed I will Harry. I am sure that will be a matter of some relief to him.'

Harry left, returning to his office to discuss the security issue with Tom, whilst the HC mused on what he had heard, and what would be Charles' likely reaction.

Paris DGSE HQ

Gilles Deniaud was reading the file online of Omar Najjar, which was light on detail, heavy on conjecture.

Over a number of years the department had received a number of leads from Middle East and Gulf stations as to his activities, but little in the way of corroboration of involvement in a number of attacks, some political, some designated as terrorist, others merely power plays between competing groups.

DGSE had initially collaborated with DCPAF (Direction Centrale de la Police aux Frontieres), itself a Directorate of Police Nationale, at CDG Airport.

Database entries had thrown up a detention instruction, which had then been circumvented by Najjar's lawyer using name similarity, but different

spelling, and a close, but different passport number to obtain release.
The subject was being tailed and kept under 24hour surveillance, but, as Gilles knew from previous experience, it is impossible to maintain 100% cover.
Alain Dubois had more background knowledge on Najjar, so Gilles was hoping he would soon be released from hospital and resume duties which would greatly assist in their current operation.

HIA Val-de-Grâce Paris
Alain was getting restless. Despite some residual mild pain he was frustrated, lying on his bed, unable to get any information from his nurse, who continued to refuse his invitation to dinner, thus becoming more impatient by the hour.
F0rtunately, at about 11.00am, the doctor arrived, whereupon Alain cajoled him into letting him leave the next day at midday, subject to a final examination at 10.00a.m.
He contacted his Director to advise him, that with luck, he should be in his office by 2.00pm the following day.

--

That morning in Paris Anna made her way, by a slightly circuitous route, from the hotel, close to the Gare Saint-Lazare, to the Israeli Embassy in Rue Rabelais, where she was met by the Mossad Head of Station.
A thorough debrief followed with considerable questioning as to observed infrastructure damage in Beirut, public attitude to the attacks, fear/defiance, level of refugees on the road to Syria, cooperation or otherwise of Lebanese and Syrian Border Posts.

Following this Anna then enquired as to what her likely role and location would be, bearing in mind she would have to report to AFD within the next few days.

The response was uncharacteristically vague, indicating no decision had yet been made, no doubt final determination resting in Tel Aviv.

She was advised to maintain her existing cover until ordered otherwise; contact would be made fairly quickly as to whether she would continue as at present, or a different role was decided.

Returning to her hotel, she reflected on the meeting.

If she remained with AFD her only use would be another posting to the Middle East/Gulf region. No real benefit being stuck in Paris. Unless there was, what? Wait and see, she told herself.

Mossad Head of Station Paris was wondering where Anna could be placed to be of some benefit to their overall Intel gathering when a thought struck him.

Would Tel Aviv support it? Could it, in fact, happen?

'If you don't ask, you don't know', he thought.

He decided to put a brief proposal together and submit it to Mossad HQ Tel Aviv. If they don't like they'll say No. If they like it, things could be very interesting!

The basis of his thinking was the close relationship and cooperation between Mossad and DGSE that had existed for many years.

Why not propose Anna to be Mossad Liaison Officer with DGSE in Paris?

Her position would therefore be transparent, and she had already worked with AFD in Beirut, where he knew DGSE operatives were already embedded.

Additionally, bearing in mind the increased focus on Pakistan and Iraq in particular, plus the Middle East and Gulf as a whole, she would be in prime position as a valuable add-on to any team activity in that region.

Mossad HQ in Tel Aviv may not like the disclosure of her background, but bearing in mind the long term shared interest in that region's diverse and complicated terrorist groupings and activities, such Intel could be vital and priceless.

HQ could only say No!

He put forward a short but cogent proposal, a robust justification, a bit outside the box, but there again, they often said that one should think creatively!

Coded, it was sent that day, asking for an initial agreement in principle. Detail could be filled in following that confirmation.

Why not, he thought, at least it would give us an even better inside track!

Islamabad

Harry and Tom sat down in Harry's office with the door locked.

Harry outlined the Security breaches that had occurred, not hyper-critical, but certainly important, and if embarrassing major policy had been leaked publically, then heads would have certainly rolled.

It was very clear that a person or persons working together, had access to, or were gaining access to, strictly confidential information, and were bypassing security level protocols already in place.

Harry had already said to Tom that he was sure permission would be granted for Tom to stay and proceed with the Security investigation, and was sure both he and the HC would receive confirmation that day.

Such investigations can be extremely boring in operation.

Who has access to such information, and who, in turn, are colleagues or friends of those who have access?

The pyramid is starting to build.

Why is the leak happening? Political point scoring? For money? An undercover agent? What is the driver? How is the information taken and delivered externally? Mobile, download to memory stick, memory?

Appropriate Personnel files to be reviewed, background checks, political affiliations, potential sleepers.

Often slow, at times boring, work. But it has to be done; checked, reviewed, discarded, and started again.

Whilst Tom and Harry were setting up their starting sheet, the HC had called Charles Urwin to his office.

The HC was on the phone as Charles entered his office, waving him to a seat as he finished his conversation.

'Well Charles, we make good progress.'

He looked enquiringly at the HC.

'I have had a very reasonable discussion with Harry Baxter concerning the investigation into your brother-in-law, his alleged illegal activities, and his personal relationship with you.

Mr Baxter assures me that with respect you own position with Azmat Kirmani your security clearance level is in no way affected, and that you been given a clean bill of health in that regard.'

The HC then added hastily, 'Both he and I, from the onset of this investigation, had both held the view that you were in no way implicated with Kirmani's activities, which is now proven.'
Charles in a well-modulated manner then spoke.
'This is the first and last time that I intend to be an unwilling party to a farcical sideshow, where despite our fundamental legal premise of presumption of innocence, a process of investigation is instigated, not on the basis of proof, but requires a demonstration, beyond doubt, of such innocence.'
He paused, turning his head to the window whilst he collected his thoughts.
'Frankly, Harry Baxter had to do what he did.
He and I inhabit, I suppose what could be described as parallel universes. Seldom meeting in an operational sense, but occasionally, the gate is left, or forced open, between our two worlds.
I am, as you and I would say, 'considering or reserving my position' at present.
I have been acutely embarrassed by the investigation. Bad news travels fast in the Foreign Office, and naturally all my actions, past and present, have thus fallen under the microscope of suspicion.
I am therefore asking for a period of leave to consider what I should do. At present I have no firm ideas whatsoever, so please do not ask what I am considering, as I am considering everything, and nothing.'
He stopped at this point, looking sadly out of the window.
The HC recognised that further discussion was pointless. It could be the man was close to a nervous breakdown.

'Of course Charles. Take at least three or four weeks, initially. Perhaps we could meet at that point for lunch or dinner and have an informal discussion?'

Charles nodded his agreement, turning to the HC, bidding him good day, and leaving his office with no further word.

Harry, in his office, was reading an Intel report of the terrorist bombing that had been foiled in Germany. Undetonated suitcase bombs had been discovered on a train from Cologne between Dortmund and Koblenz. The reason for non-detonation was assembly error.

Intensive investigation by the Bundeskriminalamt (German Federal Police) was already in place; CCTV footage at Cologne was providing some early leads as to how the suitcases were placed on board.

Indiscriminate slaughter avoided, Thank God, he thought. What possible justification can there be?

He pulled his thoughts back to the Security leak op that Tom would be pushing forward. Come on, focus.

XVI

Wednesday 2nd August 2006

London Grosvenor Square CIA offices US Embassy
Jack DeCosta was on the Satcom network talking, on a secure line, to his Director in Washington.
'We have established a good, I think, working relationship with our friends at Vauxhall Cross.
Certainly the Intel sharing has gotten off to a good start, with plenty of feedback and cross-fertilisation in specific areas in the Gulf and Indian sub-continent, particularly Pakistan.
Problems occur when we are trying to pin down special relationships between certain terrorist, insurgent, and militant described groups.
To me they're all the same. The Opposition.
It may well be necessary for me to pitch up somewhere in the region to assist our local guys, and for me to get a better feel being on the ground.
I assume your agreement on that, without further referral? OK?
The real pain in the a**e is the loose, apparently, leadership of these groups. They seem like spectres at time. Trying to pin these goddam S.O.Bs down is damn near impossible.
I also made contact with an old Limey working buddy at SIS of a few years back, Harry Baxter, who's sitting in Islamabad presently. If I go there I will certainly have some solid support, background and corroboration from him.'
The conversation finished shortly after this point, and Jack sat back, thinking through possible actions and planning of a potential visit to the region. There were too many blank spaces in the overall

picture. They had got to be filled in and at reasonable speed.
The problem with most security agencies was that they were, on most occasions, working off their back foot.
Electronic, satellite, conventional intercepts and surveillance were starting to speed up the process, but as in most things, timing is of the essence.

Paris Hotel Avenue Hoche
He had made two telephone calls, using a remote Syrian village dialect that was almost impenetrable.
Omar Najjar had spoken to two contacts, one in France, the other in the UK.
The essence was that an unforeseen delay had occurred. Therefore planned meetings would be pushed back at least a week.
New dates and locations would be advised.
Omar was frustrated and angry by the delay caused by those immigration pigs at CDG Airport.
Paris was quiet, except for the gawping groups of foreign tourists that filled all the usual places. Waiters in restaurants provided a less than average, if not poor service, disappointed and bored that they had to remain in Paris in August, and fed up with explaining bills and service charges to large Chinese groups who spoke no French.
Omar had no intention of playing the tourist. All he would do is pick up a tail from either DCPAF or DST (Direction de la Surveillance du Territoire), which would result in absolutely nothing for both parties, plus being particularly unpleasant in the hot, humid conditions.
Instead he read, slept, and ate, and occasionally, after dinner would walk up Avenue Hoche to the Etoile, and then down the Champs Elysees to

Fouquets' for a coffee, sitting outside watching segments of the world walk by. At least slightly less boring than the hotel.
Little did Paris know what would be happening in the autumn.
DST surveillance teams were also bored. Nothing was happening. M.Najjar was completely predictable. His routine was unchanging, including most evenings for coffee at Fouquets.
Najjar was aware of this, and after a week, he thought, they might get sloppy. He would see.

Paris DGSE HQ 141 Boulevard Mortier XX
At 1400hrs Alain was sitting in the outer office of his Director, Gilles Deniaud.
On time Gilles entered, smiling and extending his hand to Alain.
'Bonjour Alain, tu va bien?' he enquired.
'Pas mal, presque d'accord!'
'Viens, what was the doctor's prognosis?' Gilles asked, waving Alain to a chair.
'Some rest, keep taking the painkillers, and adjust my driving style to Paris!'
Gilles smiled, before picking up the file in front of him.
'What to do now bearing in mind the sort of reports and Intel we are getting back from the region?' He paused, the question being rhetorical.
'We have to decide where to deploy our resources, bearing in mind the threat from terrorism is not confined to one, two, or three countries. It has been internationalised. Regional activities in the Middle East is one thing, but now home grown support in Europe and other Western countries is making this a global struggle, when viewed from either side.

Ethnic and immigrant communities are being targeted to support varied forms of global Jihad. Sharia law now rules in some communities in our major cities. Our politicians are reluctant, under EU rules, to pursue strong policies whether on immigration, deportation, or the lawyers dream, Human Rights. This in itself compounds the problem, as offenders and their lawyers use every clause to evade justice.'

He was silent for a few seconds.

'However, we have a job to do so we had better get on with it.

For your information we are reviewing current strategy, and how we intend to respond both now, and in the future.

We are going to have to think somewhat differently, if we are going to keep La Belle France safe and secure.

Come and see me next Monday, same time. Meanwhile get some rest. I need you fit and able. Comprends?'

'OK, je comprends. One thing though. What about Omar Najjar? What are going to do with him? Also will you clear my 'resignation' with AFD before they come calling?'

'Yes indeed. AFD have already been advised. With Najjar we have him under 24hr surveillance, plus phone and mobile intercepts. Very quiet so far. If it picks up speed before next Monday I'll contact you.'

They shook hands and Alain left, trying not to limp too much, Gilles smiling gently at his attempts.

--

Thursday 3rd August 2006

London SIS (MI6) HQ Vauxhall Cross

The meeting with the DG was not something that the Deputy was looking forward to.

However, they met at 11.00am for the Deputy to sketch out a rough outline of the future structure of the Directorate. Merely a skeleton on which flesh could be added to the bones over the ensuing weeks.

'Norman, good morning, I trust you are well?'

The greeting was given in the style and manner that required only the briefest of responses, if one at all.

That done they sat down, coffees were poured, whereupon the Deputy opened his file, and handed several documents to the DG.

'I would like you to look at Organograms one and two, with the accompanying Strategy Notes, on sheets three and four.

These are, of course, very preliminary ideas without any real idea of budget, or accompanying analysis.'

The DG looked at him quizzically.

'I was hoping Norman that you might have some ball park figures that I could digest, particularly in relation to the overall current budget, the proposed Treasury constraints, all linked to some sort of strategic and manpower model.'

The Deputy looked at him, before saying very slowly, 'I hope you will take this in the way it is intended, but bearing in mind we only met a week ago, impossibilities I can deal with straight away, miracles will take a little longer.'

The DG's face darkened.

‘In these critical times Norman, flippancy is something I can live without.
There is significant pressure from our various masters to achieve a higher success rate than hitherto, whilst at the same time recognising comparable pressures on our budget.
I will go through these first ideas with you, but I will certainly require something significantly more robust and detailed in the fairly near future.’
A short silence followed, whilst each man reflected on how, and what, had just been said.
The Deputy then spoke in a fairly flat and measured tone,
‘If you look at Organogram One, you will see that I have merged certain departments that contain complementary skills. Some silo thinking and activity, perhaps, will be removed, or at least reduced.
Decisions will have to be made both at a strategic and operational level as to those elements which will have our focus. In turn these will impact on budgets.
You will also see that, on page Four, I have listed a number of questions that require answers, or at least some parameters, in order that there is a partial, if not definitive baseline to work from.
For example, plans on ethnic mix, under the heading of your inclusive structure? Plus, and obviously, security clearance measures and depth?
To what extent officers can be embedded in government departments, Aid agencies etc., both in UK, mainland Europe, and overseas?
With the continuing extension of electronic surveillance, linking with GCHQ, does the skill set require review in light of this? And, will this

therefore have an impact on overall staffing levels in the field?

To sum up, therefore.

Either you will need to give guidance in a number of these areas, or whatever I prepare will be a hotchpotch of possible scenarios, all incapable of proper budgeting until clearly defined.'

The Deputy sat back and looked squarely at the DG.

The DG continued to read for several minutes the pages handed to him.

Slowly putting them down on the desk he then looked up at the Deputy.

'Norman,' he said, the tone now more mellow, 'I appreciate what you have prepared and, in addition, recognise the significant gaps that need to be filled before we can properly construct the new model for the 21st Century.

Perhaps I was expecting too much, too soon. I recognise that this has to be fitted in to your already crowded schedule, so please go away and complete, in essence, the questionnaire that I need to consider in some detail before you are able to build the operational matrix.

Let me have that within the next few days.

These documents you have given me will assist me in those deliberations.

I suggest we meet sometime in the next four weeks for an update, and a review of my thoughts, in answer to those questions.

Do we understand each other now?'

The Deputy nodded.

'Indeed. I will prepare the questionnaire and get it to you by Tuesday next week.'

The meeting finished, the Deputy returned to his office.

The DG sat reflecting on their meeting, thinking that he had the outline of where he wanted this to go.
As he had originally thought, the Deputy was past his sell-by-date.
Timing will be critical but if, and it is a substantial if, a paradigm shift were to take place in the Directorate then significant decisions and changes would have to occur.
During a confidential discussion with one of the Defence/Intelligence MPs, currently sitting in Cabinet, it had been suggested to him that if the final structure and operations were to be operationally and financially in line with both Foreign Office and Exchequer expectations, then he could be assured of their joint appreciation, at an appropriate time.
He was well versed in such coded indicators, so the success of such reorganisation, and no doubt recognition, was clearly within his remit and responsibility.
Do not be impatient, he warned himself. Allow events, under his control, to dictate the timing.
As a previous PM had been asked, what did he most fear, responded, 'Events dear boy, Events!'
The present strategic and financial review could easily serve as an indication of non-commitment by the author (Deputy), lack of understanding of current political strategy, old-fashioned structures and recruitment, insufficiently lean and pro-active in the present ever-changing environment, etc, etc.
It would be interesting to see what was presented to him next Tuesday. Play the medium length game for this one.
Meanwhile the Deputy in his office was carrying out his own review and likely outcomes.

It was clear the DG wanted him out. Transparently so.

The political animal had made it to the top of the greasy pole, and wanted a more pliant Deputy.

However, the Deputy thought, why should I make life easy for him? Two can play that game, and I've been around the Government circus a lot longer than he has.

He may have his political supporters, but they can be fair-weather friends, ready to dump him in a nanosecond, if their position is threatened.

No, he had built up some strong allies over the years, and he was sure they could be more than a match for the DG and his gang!

Let battle commence, however remember we're still at the skirmishing stage!

Telling his PA to take his calls, advise them he would only be available the next day, and please get him a sandwich, the Deputy shut his door to do a little planning.

Wondering if the DG had any skeletons in his cupboard, he started to work on a list of possibles/ probables, his own past and current friends and colleagues, who could, perhaps, add something to his research. First, however, was the list of questions requiring answers, in order to establish the basic footprint of the Directorate for the foreseeable future.

That would certainly take him all afternoon as the list and the accompanying options would be extremely detailed, requiring considerable thought by the DG in formulating his responses.

The Deputy was sure that this would, perhaps, create in itself, another set of questions for the DG, when proposing such fundamental changes to his political masters. This, in turn, would contrast with their own, somewhat amateur views, of how both MI5 and MI6 could best serve their political ends, whilst maintaining Defence of the Realm.

Monday 7th August 2006

Paris Israeli Embassy Rue Rabelais

Mossad Head of Station, Eran Lang, had received a response concerning his proposal for 'Anne Hardy'.

It was positive, and suggested that he approach DGSE, in an unofficial capacity, to determine their likely reaction.

From a Mossad perspective, an embedded asset such as 'Anne', within a friendly agency could provide unparalleled amounts of useful data and Intel, plus similar levels of co-operation in the field, wherever that is required or requested.

He called his contact at DGSE, one Gilles Deniaud. They had worked together in previous years, once in Eastern Europe, the other in South East Asia, establishing a good working relationship, and importantly, a high level of trust.

Gilles had moved up to Director level, he to Head of Station.

'Gilles, Bonjour. Comment va-tu?

Can we meet to discuss a particular opportunity that I think could benefit us both?'

'Both?'

'Yes. Both our organisations, and both in the short and medium term horizons.'

'OK. Demain à midi.'

'À Demain.'

He sat, wondering how surprised Gilles would be at the suggestion. Who knows? À Demain.

Islamabad

Tom had started the security investigation.

Who had access to the information leaked? The substance of the intercepts gave a clear message as to subject matter and dateline.

Transmissions occurred, on average between 24 and 48 hours after information had been dealt with and securely filed on the IT database in the High Commission.

Password protocols controlling access were robust, and held only by a small number of security screened personnel.

Had any of these people been compromised? Personal relationship, blackmail, ideological or political beliefs could all feature in such a scenario, plus a few more besides, he thought grimly.

Such investigations often leave a nasty taste in the mouth, for all concerned.

The taint of suspicion has its own particular odour, and always hangs around longer than one anticipates, even for the innocent.

He called in Marion Simpson to collate all files of security vetted personnel, currently holding approved access to the main database.

In addition to that, he asked for all related files, husbands, wives, family, annual reviews and any examples of similar lapses that may have occurred at other postings, Embassies, or High Commissions.

Fairly tedious trawling work that has to be done; if only to try and eliminate the vast majority of potential suspects.

He suggested that Marion set up a desk in his office with secure filing, PC/laptop, etc, so that by working together some time could be saved.

Marion set about this whilst Tom started his initial fishing through the old personnel files. Were there items in them that had not been transferred onto the IT database?
He looked at the pile of files on his desk, about a foot tall.
He sighed, stretched for the top one, and started to read.

--

Tuesday 8th August 2006

12 noon Paris DGSE HQ
Gilles shook Eran Lang by the hand, at the same time offering coffee, which was politely refused.
Initial pleasantries were exchanged, before Gilles asked, with a slight smile, what Eran's proposal was.
'Well Eran, you indicated that your, as yet, undefined proposal would be advantageous to both of us in the short to medium term. I'm intrigued.'
Eran then described, in measured tones, the background, experience, and recent activity of a particular Mossad agent.
Bringing it up to date, he said,
'I believe one of your officers kept a watching brief on our agent during her time with AFD in Beirut, and who was also injured in a rocket attack that hit their 4x4. We believe her successful exit from Lebanon with your officer was organised by a UK Intelligence officer, via Syria.
Let me now outline my proposition.
Bearing in mind her considerable experience including the UK and Middle East I am proposing that she is appointed Mossad Liaison Officer, here in DGSE Paris.'

Gilles opened his mouth to speak, but Eran's raised hand stopped him interrupting.

'Please, let me finish.

With the sort of joint assaults that are being made against our democratic governments and institutions, deliberate terrorist attacks against innocent civilians, and a comparative inability of our respective services to be pro-active, I believe that a major re-think of our method of operation is required.

Intel needs to be pooled, inter-service silo thinking is to be rejected, and we need to consider our response to this world-wide attack from a team perspective.

That is why I am proposing the appointment of Liaison Officer.

Through this we can share, discuss, prepare and respond in a much more effective manner, and let's be honest, you and I have talked along very similar lines before, a few years ago.'

'Eran, in principle I agree with you. Whether 'Mon Chef' will agree is another matter.

Obviously I can submit it with my recommendation, but before that we need to cover a few details of security levels, operational parameters, etc.'

'Naturally Gilles. But I cannot stress too strongly what I consider the benefits in the short to medium term.'

At this point they then started putting together the sort of framework which would cover such a Liaison Officer, including reporting lines, clearances, legal obligations, and operational restrictions. The minutiae that dictates 'the devil is in the detail!'

At about 2.30pm the meeting broke up, Gilles having enough detail to prepare a strong proposal for his Division Director.

They shook hands firmly, Gilles clapping Eran on his back, as he promised to get back to him as quickly as possible after submitting the proposal to his chief.

Eran crossed Paris back to his Embassy, hoping that his proposal would be recognised as something where most would gain, with the downside minimal.

--

At 4.00pm Alain made his way to his Director's office where, as he entered, Gilles smiled at him, a little knowingly, he thought.

'Take a chair Alain.

I am going to discuss something with you now, which is purely embryonic, not hypothetical.

Our conversation stays in this room, is that understood? Bien.

You will recall, I am sure, your recent activities in Beirut, in the company of Anne Hardy? Of course you do!

You will also recall that she is a Mossad agent who had been placed in AFD; your task to observe, monitor, and lend a helping hand in an emergency.

However, your status as an officer of DGSE was not known to her.'

Alain nodded, not knowing where this was going.

'Subsequently, following your unfortunate accident in Beirut, she, and you, spent time with a British agent, known to you, who assisted in your exit to Syria.'

Alain nodded again, still somewhat bemused.

'You are now back here in Paris, she is currently located in the Israeli Embassy, Mossad section, and I have just had a very interesting meeting with Mossad Head of Station, Paris, Eran Lang, who, incidentally I have worked with over the years, in a number of different scenarios.'

By now Alain was wondering where this was leading, as Gilles had been looking somewhat serious whilst updating him.

At this point however, Gilles smiled, and said,

'Ne panique pas! Écoute! En bref!

The Mossad Head of Station, who I trust, is proposing that a Mossad Liaison Officer, Anne Hardy, is placed in DGSE, here in Paris. The role would be to assist in joint activities, shared Intel, a shared perspective and response in various regions; all, as Mossad, Head of Station said, for the common good.

Now what do you think?'

If Alain had been standing this would have certainly rocked him on his heels; however seated, and still in some pain in his legs, his facial expression was one of amazement.

'Incroyable. Are they serious?'

'Yes, and I think we will push it to a higher level with my recommendation for implementation soonest.

I will prepare a brief summary proposal. You, meanwhile, overnight, will give it some operational thought, which we will discuss tomorrow morning prior to my submission to the Division Director.

Remember, this is completely confidential.

I like it because it's creative, but it also gives us an entrée into Mossad workings. That's worth something.

See me at 9.00am tomorrow morning.

By the way, are you keeping in touch with your UK colleague? What's his name?'
'Harry Baxter. No I haven't been in contact with him since Damascus.'
'Keep that warm, Alain. You worked together before. You may work with him again, bearing in mind where he is based. À Demain.'
'À Demain.'

London CIA Office US Embassy Grosvenor Square
Engrossed in what he was planning, Jack was startled when his secure line to the Pentagon rang.
It was his Director.
'Jack, the Intel from the field, intercepts, satellite surveillance, you name it, are giving us a very cloudy picture.
We are going to need some sensible, on the ground, analysis.
Based on our previous discussion I suggest you plan to get out there soonest, and hook up with any friendly agencies and individuals with whom we can share our perspective, and see if their view is as opaque as ours, or if they have shone some light into the dark areas!'
'Understood. Co-incidentally I was roughing out some ideas in that area. I'll copy you in this evening, and plan to get moving within the next few days.'
'Fine. Keep me in the loop and updated. Good luck.'

Wednesday 9th August 2007

Paris Hotel Avenue Hoche
The DST teams monitoring Omar Najjar at the hotel were bored stiff.

Absolutely nothing was happening.
The previous evening, the 8th, he had followed his usual pattern of a walk to Fouquets, a coffee and brandy for an hour, and a gentle walk back to the hotel.
However, when they made their morning check at 8.00am at the hotel, consternation followed.
It was the practice to enquire if M.Najjar was available. The response normally, was that he was still sleeping, and would they like to leave a message? No they would return later.
On this occasion they were advised that M. Najjar had left hurriedly, just after midnight, destination unknown.
Leaving by a rear exit, Najjar had taken a taxi to the Gare de Lyons, briefly resting in a seedy hotel nearby, before taking the TGV to Marseille at 6.30am in the morning, arriving there about 9.35am.
There he quickly made his way to an area adjacent to Le Vieux Port, populated by a significant number of North African Arabs. Arriving at a nondescript apartment block he made his way to the third floor, where he knocked at number 32.
The door was opened partially, by Nabil Selmi, Algerian, but on a specific exchange in Arabic was fully opened, and Najjar invited in.
Omar Najjar discussed, in some detail, the basis of a plan he had scheduled for the autumn in Paris. It was bold, and would draw attention to the fight of Islam against the Kuffars, the unbelievers.
He knew Nabil to be a true believer and a warrior for Islam, and that he could count on his bravery in this war.

He spent some time with Nabil, repeating the plan and the glory that would go with it, lifting the spirits of Muslims everywhere.

He left at about 2.00pm, returning to Marseille railway station.

This time he took a TGV, leaving at 2.45pm for Lille, changing there to another TGV to London, arriving at about 6.00pm local time.

The journey was uneventful, his only cause for concern was the passport check on the TGV, when travelling from Lille to London.

The checks were cursory, another of his forged documents easily passing scrutiny.

London later that day

Having arrived in London Najjar stayed in a modest hotel not far from Waterloo Station, eating at a local Italian restaurant, before retiring at about 10.00pm.

The following morning, the 10th of August, he made his way to an address in South London, an area well known for its ethnic mix, with a few Arab families.

In a street which led down to Brixton Hill, he rang the bell of number 16, to be greeted cautiously by Amri Behar.

They exchanged certain words in Arabic, followed by the usual greetings.

Amri had prepared coffee, so whilst drinking it Najjar outlined his similar plan for London, which would mirror Paris, same day, same time.

He spoke also of the sustained attack by western powers on Muslims as a whole, and their responsibility to fight back to protect their faith, and advance the position of Islam to the ultimate world Caliphate.

Amri, whilst acknowledging some of Najjar's entreaties, was also keen to measure his faith by the amount of money that he and his family would receive.

Potential martyrdom is one thing, but it comes at a price.

However, much emphasis was laid on the plan for autumn, synchronisation with Paris as to date, time and method.

A simultaneous strike against two major western governments. The publicity for their cause would be registered world-wide.

Time now was critical in planning and sourcing of materiel.

Timing and location for the attack must be decided, investigated, and planned to ensure success. That must be Amri's first task.

After about three hours of discussion Najjar took his leave, returning to his hotel near Waterloo Station.

He would have a couple of days 'relaxation' before returning to Syria; not via Paris, but by an Etihad flight from London to Abu Dhabi, and then Syrian Air from Abu Dhabi to Damascus.

Never retrace the same steps if that can be avoided.

As he travelled back to his hotel, thinking of alternative 'relaxation', Najjar was also thinking about the materiel required, and how it could be shipped to both Paris and London.

The easiest route would be for two relatively small boxes to be shipped from Damascus to Algeria or Morocco, then into France, one by road transport to Paris, the other by similar transport into the UK through, for example, Portsmouth.

Dover was too obvious, and was invariably congested, due to attempts by illegal immigrants to gain entry into the UK.
Though Portsmouth had similar concerns to Dover, the volumes were lighter; one relatively small package at the back of a 45tonne container lorry would attract little attention, travelling under a manifest labelled, 'Replacement Agricultural Machine Parts'.
He would need to expedite those two separate shipments from Damascus immediately on his return.
He spent a heady night somewhere off the main streets near St Pancras Station and Kings Cross. In the badly illuminated bars and clubs he toured that evening he spent money unwisely, but convinced himself it was for a good cause, him!

Thursday 10th August 2006

London
***New York Times**. LONDON, Aug. 10 — British authorities said today that they had thwarted a terrorist plot to launch a wave of attacks on airplanes between the UK and the United States that would have caused, what one senior police officer called, "mass murder on an unimaginable scale."*
The plotters had planned to use liquids in drink bottles, smuggled in hand baggage, to combine into explosive cocktails aboard flights high over the Atlantic, British and American officials said. British authorities raised its terror threat assessment by one notch to its highest level — "critical" — meaning that an attack was imminent.

The British announcement, reinforced by warnings in the United States, set off a huge alert security alert that grounded hundreds of flights and turned Heathrow airport outside London into a maelstrom of stranded, complaining, but often resigned passengers. Flight schedules were left in turmoil.

Najjar woke on the morning of Thursday the 10th August, and took his breakfast with an aching head, and much black coffee, before seeing the headlines in the morning papers. What he read made him extremely nervous.

A significant number of arrests had been made overnight, by the Metropolitan Police and other Police Forces, of both British born Pakistanis and others born in Pakistan, allegedly involved in a mass bomb plot to bring down a number of different airlines aircraft flying from London to New York.

He decided to extend his stay by 48hours. London Heathrow airport would be very jumpy. He could not run that risk with his forged documents, despite them passing all checks so far.

Perhaps take a train from London to Harwich, a boat to Hook of Holland, then a train to Paris? No, why not Schiphol? Worldwide connections from there. Wait a couple of days. Let the initial reaction die down.

Time to recover, and get rid of the blinding headache.

--

Friday 11th August 2006

SIS (MI6) HQ Vauxhall Cross London

The Director General was very angry. Somewhat red faced, and decidedly grumpy.

The Deputy was sitting in front of him in his office, listening to an ever increasing tirade about the competition across the river, and how they would be lauding their expertise in nipping this, potentially, very large terrorist attack, in the bud.

Bearing in mind, the Deputy thought, the silo thinking and turf war attitudes that still existed between MI5 and MI6, it was a minor miracle, that at times, attacks were thwarted.

The DG threw the Guardian newspaper across the desk to him.

'Read that.'

The Deputy slowly picked up the paper. He'd already seen the papers that morning, plus some police reports available to the agency.

He knew the details, but quickly scanned the paper.

The Guardian*. LONDON, 11 Aug. - British suicide bombers were within days of blowing up 12 passenger jets above five US cities in an unprecedented terrorist attack designed to commit "mass murder on an unimaginable scale", counterterrorism sources claimed last night.*

Anti-terrorist agents said they had uncovered the plot from surveillance of a group of young British Muslims, which began nearly a year ago and was on a scale never before undertaken.

United States and British counterterrorism officials claimed the men, the majority British Muslims of Pakistani descent, were going to disguise liquid

explosive as bottles of soft drink and carry them in their hand luggage on to US-bound planes leaving British airports.
When the jets were in midair over American cities, they planned to combine the explosives and detonate them using an electric charge from an iPod, the security services believe. BA flights were among the targets. US officials said the bombers had been seeking to hit New York, Washington, San Francisco, Boston and Los Angeles. Other airlines targeted were thought to be United, American and Continental. Loss of life might have surpassed the 2,700 killed in the attack on the twin towers in New York five years ago. "This was our 9/11," a British security source said.

The Deputy slowly put down the paper.
'Frankly, a minor bloody miracle, if that is indeed the case. Unsubstantiated as yet, but there appears to be some very credible Intel backing it up.'
The DG interjected, 'Why did we not have any indication of this from any of our Joint Intelligence Committee meetings, the 'boy scouts' kept this one close to their chests?
With our current officers on the ground in Pakistan, then, at least, there could have been some joint co-operation and liaison with input from Islamabad.
As it is they are trumpeting success, and, as far as I can see we have had no involvement whatsoever.'
It was clear from his tone, the Deputy thought, that the DG was somewhat upset at missing out on some of the praise from the World press.
Tough! That's what can happen from time to time. Events, Dear Boy, Events!

‘Well, you know how sensitive they are when the action is home grown, and they hate to have us pushing in, even if there is an overseas connection.

Bearing in mind their Intel sources, here in the UK, they were no doubt keen to keep it on a ‘need to know basis’, so that there were no leaks.

I shall contact Islamabad to check on current status, also local Intel that may have some connection with the current arrests here in London.

With your agreement I will get onto that straight away, and come back to you when I have further information.’

The DG agreed, somewhat truculently, adding, ‘Put some pressure on. I want some indication, if any, by late afternoon. Both Whitehall, and across the river, will be asking for any corroboration from the region.’

Returning to his office the Deputy put through a satellite Sitrep request to Harry, and to contact him soonest.

He studied recent report summaries from Pakistan and the region, for any indications or links that may be connected to the recent developments.

About one hour later Harry came through on the secure line from Islamabad.

Saturday 12th August 2006

London

The newspapers were full of the recent arrests and conjecture, lockdown had occurred at most UK airports, as severe security measures kicked in.

Public suspicion was being aired as to possible connections with Pakistan, and whether assistance and training may have been provided in, or by, that country.

Omar Najjar decided he would travel on the Sunday and booked his train and boat tickets, leaving at 2.30pm from Liverpool Street station to Harwich, then boat to the Hook of Holland, arriving about 8.00pm local time.

He would stay overnight before catching a train the following morning, from the Hook of Holland to Schiphol airport via Rotterdam.

From there he would have many airline route choices back to Damascus, Syria.

--

In a London suburb the Deputy was mulling over what Harry had told him during their conversation on Friday.

Local intelligence was confused, but what was clear was the training of terrorists, taking place in the mountainous regions of Pakistan.

Many rumours were circulating about European and American Muslim recruits entering Pakistan to train, and take up their own personal jihad against their home countries, as a direct protest against foreign policy.

Al-Qaeda was known to be funding these groups, sources of such funds difficult to pin down, but solid evidence was mounting.

It appeared there may be an opportunity to deal directly with an informant, who was prepared to provide solid evidence, (in exchange for a substantial fee, a new passport and identity in a suitable country) of who, where, what, and why, were involved.

Firstly, however, credibility would have to be rigorously tested on the informant, and subsequently on any Intel arising. There had been too many instances of informers trying to sell fake intelligence in exchange for US dollars. Some had been very sophisticated, others laughable!

If any was confirmed as credible, then this in turn could then be used as leverage by HMG against the Pakistan Government, to try and ensure that the State returned to its 'neutral' position in dealings with such groups.

Harry was proposing that such a relationship be pursued, but as he advised the Deputy, it would not happen overnight. Slowly and softly; so as not to frighten the animals!

Yes, the Deputy thought, but I've got the 'reforming' DG on my back, and he'll be wanting something he can wave at the Foreign Secretary or PM! However, I can stretch something out of that to keep him vaguely happy in the meantime!

XVII

Week commencing Monday 14th August 2006

US Embassy Abu Dhabi UAE

Stopping over in Abu Dhabi, Jack DeCosta spent two days with CIA Head of Station getting up to speed with his overview of the region, before he travelled on to Karachi and Islamabad.

He accepted the analogy put to him that trying to follow all the obvious currents of Gulf politics, and then trying to determine the hidden ones, was rather like attempting to play three dimensional chess in a fog.

However impenetrable the view might be, they had to try and make sense of it, and, more particularly, weed out the bad bits that impacted, literally at times, on Homeland and European security.

He spent a day and a half in Karachi before flying on to Islamabad where he was met by Head of Station and taken to the US Embassy, where he would stay during his time in Pakistan.

After an Embassy briefing his first discussions would be with senior officers of Pakistan's Security Services to determine their take, approach, public stance, etc, on the varied and challenging security issues facing them.

Pakistan is racked internally, at a political level, with savage in-fighting between parties; this, in turn, is exacerbated by obvious or hidden alliances with groups linked to terrorist organisations, including Al-Qaeda.

One of his first contacts on Saturday was Harry, who sounded surprised, but pleased, to hear he was in Islamabad.

‘Don’t let anybody know you’re coming, will you?’ Harry said jokingly.
‘It was all slung together pretty quickly so no chance to advise you.
Anyway when can we get together for a fair, but frank, exchange of views?’
‘Why don’t you come to the High Commission and meet the HC as well. I’m sure he would welcome that, and be able to report back on our collaborative efforts.’
‘OK, Next week, say Tuesday the 22nd, if that’s convenient?’
‘Fine. I’ll check with the HC, and get back to you.’

Wednesday 16th August 2006

Mossad Station Israeli Embassy Paris
Anne Hardy was called to Eran Lang’s office. She wondered what was to be discussed.
In the previous days Eran had received confirmation from Mossad HQ Tel Aviv, and also from DGSE in principle.
He smiled at Anne as she entered his office.
‘Anne, good morning.
I think, or I hope, I have some good news for you.
It is something which will, I am sure, enhance your standing in our organisation. It will also be extremely interesting and challenging, plus, be of enormous value to Mossad in our continuing fight.’
Anne was certainly interested in seeing where this was going, so said nothing, whilst retaining a look of interest, she hoped, on her face.
‘What we have done is to see how we could gain from your recent experience with AFD in Lebanon,

and at the same time benefit from the fact you are currently located here in Paris.
As you are aware, we maintain very close working relationships with a number of friendly countries agencies.
This enables us, at times, to pool our respective resources when faced with a common challenge. As, I am sure you know, we have good working relations with DGSE; in fact at least two of their officers were embedded in AFD in Lebanon.
One was Alain Dubois, with whom you worked with fairly closely, I believe?'
Anne's surprised look confirmed to Eran that Alain's cover had been secure, as he continued,
'After discussions with DGSE, which followed agreement From Tel Aviv as to my proposal, it has been mutually agreed that you will take up the role of Mossad Liaison Officer with DGSE here in Paris.
Yours will be a roving brief, not solely confined to Paris or France, but active in whichever theatre of operation is agreed between us and DGSE.
Do you understand so far?'
'I think so.'
'Good.
Understand this. Within your role as Liaison Officer there are obviously going to be areas of extreme sensitivity, both from DGSE and ourselves.
Therefore you should understand, that if there is the slightest doubt in your mind as to whether a piece of intelligence is to be shared, then you must act with caution and seek approval from your senior officer.
Is that understood?'

‘Yes, but I have a number of questions at the appropriate time.’

‘I would be very surprised if you did *not* have a *large* number of questions,’ Eran said, smiling.

‘Perhaps now I should ask you an important question?

I am assuming that you are prepared to be appointed to this role? If not please indicate accordingly.’

‘I would be extremely pleased to be appointed to this role. No question.’

‘Good. I will continue, and you can ask questions when I have finished.’

There then followed a more detailed description of how the role was envisaged, method of operation, collection of intelligence, upper and lower security levels, reporting criteria and frequency, line officers and protocols, secure networks, codes, etc.

At the end Anne had a number of questions that Eran was able to answer with little problem, the last one being start date.

‘Apart from briefing and update here on joint operations, which can be completed in a day, I would think introductions could be arranged for next Monday, the 21st August, assuming DGSE agree.

I will advise you no later than Friday.’

Anne left the meeting with some excitement caused by adrenalin flow, mixed in with a soupçon of trepidation.

This was certainly pastures new, and completely unknown. However she felt that it would be more satisfying, and that she would be contributing more than her previous role as a Minister’s PA in London.

She would need to organise where she would live, but in this regard Mossad had several 'safe' houses and other properties around Paris.
Anne returned to her hotel and reflected on where her next steps would take her. DGSE, and all that entailed. Hand-in-hand with Mossad. The Intelligence world never ceased to amaze. It would be good meeting Alain again. They had got on well, on a professional level. That's all she wanted.

Islamabad UK High Commission

Tom was not having a good day.
Check, double check, cross reference, annual reviews, associates, friends, hobbies, relatives, possible political affiliations, any observed peccadillos, internal relationships; the matrix had grown exponentially.
However the analysis was ongoing, and although significant amounts of data were being run through a number of algorithms, there did not appear be a chink anywhere. No red flag was being waved.
It had to be somebody very close to the centre.
In the afternoon he called in Marion Simpson for an update.
'Marion I've been going through all available data, whether hard copy or electronic, on all persons involved in the High Commission.
I've also checked it all against the data we have in the UK, MI5 data, GCHQ, the works.
There has been no blip or mild hiccup against anybody whatsoever, one level down.
In my mind this means that the leak must have happened at a senior level.
If so, then life starts to get embarrassing. We will then have to consider other factors, such as

blackmail, honey traps, money worries, you know the sort of thing.'

Marion looked a little embarrassed at this, which caught Tom's eye.

'Any ideas or speculation in those areas?' he asked.

'Well, I suppose we can rule out the HC', she joked weakly.

'The First Secretary has gone through a couple of traumatic incidents, but he is such a loyalist I could not imagine him being responsible', she added hastily.

'Jeremy, the Third Secretary, might be bit strapped for cash at his level, but is quite lazy. Just don't see it happening with him.'

Tom interjected, 'What about the Charles Urwin's wife? Pillow talk and then onwards transmission, or communication to either of her two brothers?'

'Unlikely, as I believe the First Secretary, as a principle, never discusses anything concerning the High Commission with his wife.'

Tom fell silent, reflecting on the recent comments.

'Well Marion, thanks for your observations. I will continue to search and filter and see what, if anything, is thrown up.

Unfortunately we have now reached the stage where the investigation starts to dig really deep into those dark areas people never talk about, and hope never surface.

I've not been beaten before, and won't be this time.'

Islamabad Diplomatic Area. Charles Urwin Villa

The room was almost dark, the shutters closed, and one small light flickering in a corner.

Charles Urwin sat in his armchair, his face expressionless.

A jumble of thoughts were racing round in his head as he struggled to come to terms with his recent experience.

He raged at his family, in particular his brother-in-law who had precipitated the investigation into his conduct.

This rage was also directed against his wife. She must have had some idea of what her brother was doing, similarly her father, and older brother.

He was somewhat ambivalent towards Harry Baxter; means well, goes by the book, and yes, had been part of the operation that had saved his life.

The High Commissioner; was playing the game in the proper way, hands kept clean, studied consideration for his welfare, take some time off, as much as you want, let's meet for lunch in a month. Condescending bastard. Basically couldn't give a sh*t, as long as the problem is contained within a nice orderly file.

Now how am I going to react? What am I going to do? What do I want to do?

I want that bastard brother-in-law to suffer in the biggest possible way, and if that means elimination then so be it.

By the book, conventional means? Not at all. This is going to involve a number of my not so official contacts. Time to call in one or two favours. I need to think this through carefully. No rushing.

Remember, revenge is a dish best served cold.

Let's get some of my ideas in order.

He reached for a pad and pencil.

Writing some broad headings on the page, he stared at it for some time, before tearing it into small confetti sized pieces.

That done he rose, moving towards his desk and picking up his mobile.

Islamabad Russian Embassy

Another short message from his mole at the UK High Commission was occupying Volkov.

It indicated a root and branch investigation as to the recent security breach, and the sense that it might not be too long before suspicion fell on the mole.

He sat musing on possible outcomes.

If the identity of the mole was uncovered diplomatic immunity in Pakistan could take care of any redress.

It was unfortunate, but in the event of discovery the mole would just have to be another casualty in the continuing intelligence gathering war.

Coming in from the cold here in Pakistan would not be an option.

Perhaps he should look for potential recruits within the US or French embassies?

As one door closes, another opens.

Monday 21st August 2006

1030hrs DGSE HQ Paris

Eran Lang and Anne Hardy were shown to the office of Gilles Deniaud where, after being seated, Anne was suddenly confronted by a beaming Alain Dubois entering with a slight limp, with his hand outstretched.

'Bonjour Anne, comment va-tu?'

'Très bien, merci', she replied smiling in return, 'I see you are almost fully recovered.'

'Paris air, excellent nursing, and a glass of Burgundy all help.'

'D'accord, let us get on', said Gilles, waving Alain to a chair.

The discussion focussed on initial areas of co-operation, and where best for Anne to start as Liaison Officer.

Regions; operations, past, but still active; current activity etc; were all reviewed until Gilles threw one specific example on the table.

'Alain, this is not far from where you were operating before.

The recent foiled terrorist attack on several airlines operating out of London has a clear Pakistan profile, linked to Al-Qaeda funding and training.

Let us be quite clear, such an attempt will, I'm sure, encourage similar thinking among our own ethnic groups with Jihad in mind.

It may not follow the same pattern, idea, method, whatever, but it will certainly encourage them to try.'

Alain nodded in agreement, 'Certainly.'

Gilles continued.

'Anne, you carry both UK and Israeli passports? Good. This means you can enter the UK without problem, particularly bearing in mind your UK passport will be in the name of Anna Harrison.

Alain, why don't we send you both to London for a short period? You can both be based in the embassy, and perhaps you, Alain, will be able to pick up some ideas and information from your old friend, Harry Baxter. Eh?'

At this comment Anne looked sharply at Alain.

'Excuse me. How do you know Harry Baxter? I thought you had only met him in Lebanon?'

Alain, a little sheepishly, explained briefly and quickly, the circumstances of his operation in London with Harry, and how effective it had been.

Anne then commented, with a little edge to her voice, 'Well I do know he is not based in London at

present. He is operating out of the UK High Commission in Islamabad.'
Alain made no comment. He had said enough.
The discussion then covered some initial training of DGSE methods and systems to be undertaken by Anne in Paris, before they both transferred to London.
That would start on Wednesday the 23rd, with a planned transfer to London, week commencing Monday the 4th September.
Anne thought that Alain had been somewhat 'economic' with the truth concerning Harry, but there again, hardly surprising in their environment.

Inter-Services Intelligence (ISI) Islamabad
In Pakistan there are essentially two Security agencies.
One is ISI (Inter-Services Intelligence), headed by Lieutenant General Ashfaq Parvez Kayani, the other the FIA (Federal Investigation Agency), Director General Tariq Parvez.
In broad terms ISI is operationally similar to MI6, with FIA in the role of MI5.
Charles Urwin, both in his function as First Secretary, and also through the connections of his father-in-law, Nadeem Kirmani, was known to, and was on good diplomatic terms with, a number of the senior officers in both organisations.
Sitting in the offices of ISI he was holding a general discussion with one of the divisional heads, Deputy Director General Aatif Durrani, responsible for both internal and external operations.
Charles had used all his diplomatic skills to justify his request for a meeting. He had suggested, that bearing in mind that there were a number of

disparate interests involving both their countries at the present time, it would therefore be appropriate and sensible to share such thoughts and possible remedies.

He was adept at touching lightly on a number of current issues, such as the recent London arrests, as well as extending sympathy to the ISI in keeping track of individuals and groups, who by their actions were impacting on both homeland security, and also the negative perception of Pakistan that could arise in the wider world context.

'If I may, I would like to raise another matter that has crossed my desk recently, and which is highly sensitive, both in familial and security aspects.'

DDG Durrani nodded his head in agreement.

'I would like to ensure that at this stage our discussions remain completely confidential, and I am sure that would be your wish also.'

The DDG nodded again, whilst Charles was thinking to himself that he could guarantee the conversation was being recorded, and would be distributed to all interested departments within one hour of the meeting ending.

'We, that is the UK High Commission, are aware of certain trading activities being carried out by Azmat Kirmani, youngest son of Nadeem Kirmani. In the main the majority, apparently, give little or no cause for concern. However certain 'products', involving foreign powers, both for raw materials and manufacture, are causing considerable anxiety. The familial connection is, of course, extremely embarrassing to both myself and my family, particularly my father-in-law, Nadeem Kirmani, who, I am sure you are aware, has been a Government Minister in two previous administrations.

You can, therefore, recognise why I wish to keep this matter on a strictly confidential basis at this stage?'

The DDG opened his mouth to speak, but Charles ignored him and continued.

'Naturally I will provide as much detail and background information as possible to assist in your investigation, but Her Majesty's Government will want to ensure that this is viewed as a normal ISI investigation, once any information is released to the public and world press.

Naturally, before that point, HMG would like to work with you in agreeing the sort of presentation that would be to the mutual benefit of both our countries.

I do hope I am making myself clear at this stage, and that we could have the joint benefit of HMG working with a renowned international intelligence organisation.'

Finally the DDG spoke.

'It may not come as a surprise to you that many security agencies around the world share and exchange information on relevant security issues.

It is very sensible, bearing in mind the somewhat fragile foundation in certain countries on which their own form of government or democratic institution is based.

Therefore I would not be at all surprised if we did not have some intelligence on the person you have referred to.

What I would suggest is that you leave the matter with me whilst I run some checks through our database, and, with your permission, confer with a small number of my co-Directors who would be specific to what you have described.'

'Of course. I would be delighted if we could work together on this matter, and look forward to our further joint discussions and deliberations in the future.

If there is any further information that you may think I could provide, please do not hesitate to contact me through the High Commission, or on my mobile telephone. Being currently on leave for the next three weeks, I think the mobile would be best.'

At this point the meeting finished and Charles Urwin left, thinking quietly to himself that Stage One was now under way. With a slow burning fuse and the addition of some flammable liquid from time to time, he was sure he would achieve what he wanted.

He already knew from past experience that ISI had a somewhat chequered reputation.

External views ranged from, that it was a state within a state and too powerful, to having too close a relationship with certain political parties, and also various assorted militants and terrorist groups.

However the structure was very clear. Within the ISI there were about ten Bureau or Directorates.

Accepting the usual areas of intelligence and counter intelligence, both overt and covert, 'aggressive' intelligence gathering included espionage, sabotage, subversion and psychological warfare.

The fields of operation included diplomatic missions, multi-nationals and NGOs, international media centres, and collaboration with other agencies, in countries such as, Saudi Arabia, China, USA CIA, and the UK, MI6.

Third Country technique included Afghanistan, Nepal, Sri Lanka, Iran, Turkey, Bangladesh and

China, producing additional intelligence and operational data.
Charles was confident that what he wanted to achieve would come to pass in due time. No hurry. Patience will be a virtue.

Tuesday 22nd August 2006

High Commission Islamabad
The High Commissioner rose from his desk and strode forward to shake Jack DeCosta's hand.
'Welcome to a small part of the United Kingdom, Mr DeCosta. It is extremely pleasant to extend the hand of friendship to our closest ally.'
Shaking hands, DeCosta reciprocated with similar words, whilst Harry stood back, a small smile playing on his lips.
You had to hand it to him, Harry thought, he's always got the words and music, and keeps a straight face when saying them!
There must be a lexicon they insert at birth, or when they get to a certain level in the Civil Service. The ersatz sincerity comes pouring out, on cue, on demand, whenever needed. Brilliant!
Small talk was made covering a number of general areas of mutual interest which lasted about half an hour, at which point Harry glanced at his watch and said,
'I think Jack and I should get back to our desks now, High Commissioner, we've taken enough of your time.'
'Fair enough Harry, it's been a pleasure to meet Mr DeCosta. I wish you Mr DeCosta, and, including us, all success in our future joint endeavours.'
Walking back to Harry's office Jack commented,

‘Seems a pleasant guy. OK to work with?’

‘Fine, no problem. Let’s me get on with it and do it my way. Unless it impacts on his public position. Then he can get a bit arsey!’

Jack then raised an item that pricked Harry’s curiosity.

‘You said the First Secretary is on leave for the next few weeks?’

‘Yes. Why?’

‘I was hoping that I might meet him.’

‘Again. Why?’

‘Just some tenuous connection and ‘chatter’ we picked up on the airwaves that involves his family. We don’t think he’s involved, but one of his family could be.’

‘Can we sit down and discuss this in a bit more detail?’

‘Sure, but let’s do it at the embassy. I can pull off some details from our database. OK?’

‘Fine. When?’

‘Give me a couple of days. Let’s say Thursday. 1000hrs, OK?’

‘See you there, Thursday, 1000hrs.’

They entered Harry’s office to see Tom Denman sitting waiting for Harry.

Tom rose as soon as Harry and Jack entered, and was introduced to Jack.

‘Something specific?’ Harry queried.

‘Yes. That security issue we were talking about the other day.’

‘Fine, give me a few minutes, whilst I see Jack off the premises.’

Tom sat down again, whilst Harry escorted Jack to reception, saying,

'Let's follow through on what you've raised when we meet on Thursday, plus any other titbits that take our fancy!'

Returning to his office he sat down with Tom for an update on the Security issue.

'Where are we, Tom?'

'Thin ice, I think.'

'How so?'

'I've covered it all. Top to bottom, left to right. You name it, Check, double check. Vauxhall Cross, GCHQ, the boys across the river, here, files, telephone records, intercepts, any dead drops, whatever.'

'And?'

'I've got it down to no more than two people.'

'And?'

'Number one, local recruit, but I don't see it. Just sufficient access, but perhaps not enough overall understanding of how politics work. Could not really do the summary we picked up. I don't think.'

'The other?'

'Well if it is, it's odd as to motive. That's what's stopped me pushing on. I wanted to run it past you first.'

'OK. What do you want to do?'

Tom outlined his thoughts and how the approach might be made.

Harry gave it some thought, and then said,

'What you are saying in terms of suspicion, and how you arrive at that answer is highly sensitive, and could prove very embarrassing if proved wrong.

Only if you are confident that you have exhausted all other possibilities, and are prepared to carry that responsibility will I proceed in concert with you.

Just remember this, I don't want my head in the noose and neither do you, do you?
I'll back you, but if you're wrong there could be two careers down the tubes, comprendo?' he said, smiling at a very concerned Tom.
'OK, 1500hrs today. My office here, AND get your ducks in a row. Prepare for ugly, and anything better is a bonus.'
Tom went away to prepare, conscious that it really was thin ice!

1500hrs Harry's Office High Commission Islamabad
Tom came into Harry's office with Marion, who was carrying a number of files and a small recording machine.
Harry greeted them both, and joined them at the separate table where the files were stacked adjacent to the recorder.
'I see you've included Marion in the meeting.'
'Yes, it seemed sensible bearing in mind she's been helping with some of the spadework all through this investigation.'
'Good. Where do you want to start?'
'Probably where I left our conversation this morning.'
'Fine. You have the floor.'
'You will recall my comments concerning the two possibilities? One not sufficiently experienced enough in my mind, the other problematic when considering motive.'
'Yes, I recall. Have you made any progress?'
'I think so, but I would like Marion to chip in here, bearing in mind some of the researching she did for me.'
At this point Marion looked a little puzzled.

‘Such as?’
‘You will remember Marion, when we were going through all the background of possible sources of the leak, one area which was particularly important was motive.’
‘Yes I remember.’
‘We did some considerable probing in that connection.’
‘Yes, we did.’
‘What were the main areas for motive?’
‘The usual; money, blackmail, sex, politics.’
‘Yes, and we were not really able to tag anybody with any of those motives. Why do you think that was?’
‘Well, probably because we could not find any of the potential suspects fitting the criteria.’
‘Yes I agree, but had we really exhausted the full list of potential suspects?’
‘I think so. We went over all areas with a fine toothcomb.’
‘Yes we did, but there were two people we did not investigate, other than superficially.’
‘Who are they then?’
‘One is Harry,’ Tom said, at which point Marion burst out laughing,
‘The other one is you.’
The laughter ceased abruptly and the room fell silent.
Marion said, half smiling, ‘You don’t really think that I had anything to do with the leak?’
Tom spoke,
‘Let’s examine that scenario Marion, in a hypothetical way. If you were involved in such a breach of security, what would be your motive?
Money, relationship, political? Why not give us a hypothetical answer?’

Marion looked at him as the expression on her face changed to one of anger.
'Firstly it wasn't me, and secondly what do you mean hypothetical?
'I mean just that, or if you prefer, let's deal with it in a factual manner.'
'What was your motive, and what do you think you would gain from such actions?'
Harry had been silent so far. Now he spoke quietly.
'At this point Marion, you should consider yourself under caution. Tom, carry on.'
'Marion Simpson, we believe, with the evidence collected, that you are the source of the security leak from this High Commission, in passing classified information to the Russian Embassy.
This was carried out mostly by mobile telephone provided by the Russian Embassy, which had incorporated within its software, a voice distortion element to cover your own transmissions.
However GCHQ UK, and listening posts elsewhere, picked up those transmissions, and using specialist software, were able to reverse the voice distortion and identify your voice as a match.'
Marion's face at this point seemed to crumple and she partially slumped in her chair.
Tom continued,
'Why? Give me an answer.'
Marion slowly pulled herself up.
Speaking in a flat monotone she started her explanation.
'When I was at university in the Midlands I did politics and sociology.
I was extremely idealistic and believed that social policies could make a real difference. I joined certain political societies that had a great effect on

my own moral compass, plus, I felt, when I had gained entry into the Civil Service, that there had to be other ways of doing things.

Our own government's conduct in the Gulf and Middle East, over the last few years, makes me sick.

I decided, that in my own small way, I could assist other countries in acting as a brake on some of our activities and the excesses at present.'

She paused, and her voice became stronger.

'There, that's the reason. Idealism. And I don't regret my actions.

All you people chasing your tail, or some person or organisation that doesn't agree with you. For what? Some brief success before another problem rears its head. Didn't Winston Churchill say Jaw, Jaw, is better than War, War?'

Harry and Tom had listened without interruption, but Harry now spoke.

'Marion Simpson, you are now effectively under house arrest, and will be confined in your room under guard, until you are returned to the UK to face an appropriate court.

You will speak to no one other than Tom Denman or myself in the interim, unless specific permission is granted.

Once in the UK you will have access to a lawyer for your defence needs, your trial and any appropriate appeal.

Speaking personally, I am bitterly disappointed at your actions, and what has been revealed.

Tom, would you remain here with Marion whilst I inform the High Commissioner, and organise security details to cover her house arrest.'

Harry left Tom with Marion, who was now sitting with her head in her hands, quietly crying.

Whether with frustration, anger or self-pity, Tom was not sure.
Things like this were always messy. No winners, only losers.
Bad taste in the mouth for a little while. Friends like these, who needed enemies? Disruption, destruction, hand in hand.
One had to believe that what one did was right, in every sense of the word.
Harry saw the HC who was shocked, mortified, and disappointed, but ever the professional, complimented Harry and Tom in resolving the issue in a "timely fashion". His words.
He placed responsibility with Harry in returning Marion Simpson to the UK, organising escort and security, and all necessary waivers, visa, compliance with local and airport police, and official arrest in the UK.
Harry prepared, and sent an encrypted report to the Deputy providing the salient facts, resolution, and possible date for the return of Marion Simpson to the UK under escort.
He also recommended that Tom Denman act as Senior Escort, returning to the UK at the same time, his two assignments having been completed.
He also wrote a commendation for Tom to be logged in his career file.

XVIII

Thursday 24th August 2006

Russian Embassy Islamabad
Volkov was not happy. Messages had abruptly stopped from his mole. This was causing concern. He was not aware of the current status involving the security leak, the CIA visit, the First Secretary, in fact anything.
Trying a test connection achieved nothing. The equipment was totally off air.
That evening the Russian Embassy was hosting a reception for a number of other embassies situated in the Diplomatic area, including the UK, USA, Canada, France, Egypt, and India.
Perhaps information could be gleaned as alcohol loosened tongues? It's happened before, and will happen again!
Work the room well tonight, he thought.

United States Embassy Islamabad
At 10 o'clock Jack DeCosta welcomed Harry into his temporary office, and sat him down with a steaming cup of coffee.
'Well my friend, what gives in your world?'
'Judging by the mix in the region, an inverted game of 3D chess being played in dark glasses with one hand tied behind your back!
What's it like in the sunshine world of the CIA?'
They both gave a small ironic laugh. They had both been here many times before.
I don't know about the patience of Job, Harry thought, but I could do with a couple of bucketsful right now!

Harry opened with, 'You wanted to discuss some relation of the First Secretary, Charles Urwin? Anything specific?'

Harry wanted to see what Jack would tell him. No point in offering anything at this stage.

'Yes. We've collected a certain amount of traffic involving his brother-in-law, Azmat Kirmani, who is obviously involved in international trade.

However, some of the international trade is clearly not of a peace generating kind. Weapons, rocket launchers, uranium tipped rockets, all apparently linked through to Hezbollah in Lebanon.

You must have seen some of this when you were there recently?'

'Yes I did, but did not have any knowledge of the connection with Kirmani', he responded glibly, 'What are you gangbusters going to do about him?'

'Nothing at present. Keep up the overall surveillance, monitor, and see where this leads.

However I'd like to share whatever Intel we have with a cross check against yours. Can your guys agree to that?'

'I would think no problem. I'll double check, but within usual operational limits that would be signed off.'

'Great. Anything from your side.'

'One thing. We've just uncovered a small security leak in the High Commission. Apparently a lot of low to medium grade stuff was being passed to our friends at the Russian Embassy here in Islamabad.

The person concerned is being shipped back to the UK tonight/tomorrow.

Incidentally the Russians have a reception tonight. I'm going. Are you?

I want to drop a small brick into their pond when I see their FSB man, Stepan Volkov, who carries the title of Commercial Secretary.'

'Yes I'm going too. The Ambassador thought it would be a good idea to see at close hand what they were like, and try and get a feel from where they are coming!'

Harry and Jack covered a few other areas of mutual interest before Harry left, saying he looked forward to seeing Jack at the Ruskies reception.

Could be an interesting evening, was his parting comment!

Damascus Syria

The Committee had met to hear the report of Omar Najjar on his return from the UK and France.

Before his update Najjar suggested that the 'warriors' who had been caught in the UK in the attempted mass plane bomb plot should be blessed, and their place reserved in paradise.

Turning to his plan Najjar advised that two Jihadists, willing to give their lives for Islam, had been recruited, one in Paris, the other in London, to carry out the synchronised attack on the seats of Government.

He explained what weapons would be used and how the attacks would be carried out, however some local details were being left to the Jihadists.

Discussions followed with close questioning by some members of the Committee. Despite this, the general mood and reception was encouraging, with some restrained admiration for the plan, subject to success.

The meeting broke up with two sub-groups, one finance and one materiel, now involved in the detail.

A further meeting was arranged for the following Sunday, the 27th August with the weapons supplier, one Azmat Kirmani.

Najjar returned to his hotel, the Beit Zafran, one of his favourites, content that progress was being made, and that his own personal return would be wrapped up in the overall financing of the planned attacks.

Russian Embassy Reception Islamabad

Just after 6.30pm the first guests started drifting into the embassy.

Teetotal and alcohol drinkers mingled easily with each other, studiously ignoring what was contained in their respective glasses.

Conversation and chatter was inconsequential, and contention free. Some arm hugging and air kissing prevailed among a few nationalities, a firm handshake sufficed for the remainder.

Harry and Jack arrived a few minutes before their respective High Commissioner and Ambassador, protocol observed.

The evening was passing in a familiar pattern as the guests circulated.

At one point Harry found himself talking to Volkov, the Commercial Secretary.

Both men maintained the pretence that exists, whilst commenting on industrial development in Pakistan and the hoped-for contribution this would make to the economy.

Volkov, at one stage, was expressing the hope that there could be a move towards more of a technology base for the economy, away from the trading and agricultural dependency that seemed to exist.

Harry leant forward, and said,

‘I agree with you, but there would appear to be some pockets of technical progress already.’
‘What do you mean?’ queried Volkov.
‘Well’ said Harry, ‘In our High Commission we found we had some very high tech foreign pieces of communication kit, which really were ahead of the game. Unfortunately, we have had to stop that development, as I think in the short term it could have been damaging to us, if it was allowed to carry on unchecked, and without proper support or review.
The other problem was that as it contained one or more foreign manufactured parts, we obviously couldn’t accept non-British components.
An unfortunate find of course, but I’m sure you would agree with our decision, wouldn’t you?’
At this point he looked directly at Volkov, holding eye contact.
Volkov returned the look, whilst speaking in a very measured tone.
‘I agree. Such developments could be harmful to a number of people, and perhaps could give technology a bad name.
Very interesting talking to you Mr Baxter. You do understand, I must circulate.’
With a slight smile Volkov turned away, and walked over to the Indian Ambassador.
Harry turned and caught Jack’s eye, before walking over, and introducing himself to the US Ambassador. After introductions he turned to Jack,
‘Small brick delivered. Volkov received and understood message loud and clear. Job done, I’m away. See you very soon.’
Jack smiled, ‘See ya very soon.’
Volkov maintained an air of diplomatic neutrality as he chatted to the Indian Ambassador, whilst

reflecting on his brief conversation with Harry Baxter.

Obviously a clear indication that the mole had been discovered, plus the Russian manufactured mobile. Hence the sudden termination of any reports.

Unfortunate, but always a likelihood in the game they played.

As he had previously thought, perhaps a focus on the US, Canadian, or French embassies. There must be a few more 'idealists' wanting to share their country's intelligence knowledge with the wider world?

Time will tell.

--

Harry returned to the High Commission to organise the necessary documentation and escort for Marion Simpson back to the UK.

It had been decided that Tom Denman would act as escort as his role was now finished in Islamabad, with another female staff member from the HC handcuffed to Marion Simpson. All would travel Business Class on Emirates via Dubai to London. She would be taken to a local police station under caution, where she would be charged with aiding and abetting a foreign power.

She would be extensively de-briefed by MI6 between the time of her arrival and appearance in court.

Saturday 26th August 2006

Baluchistan SW Pakistan & Islamabad

Tribal leader Nawab Akbar Bugti was killed in a battle between tribal militants and Government Forces. 30 rebels were killed and five soldiers.

As a direct result of this, there followed five days of rioting in the vicinity of the Marriot Hotel Islamabad, which itself is very close to the Baluchistan Mosque. 6 people were killed, dozens injured, and over 700 arrests. Just another event in the Pakistan political arena.

This, in turn, created significant disruption in the vicinity of the Diplomatic area, causing some inconvenience, but no delay in the return of Marion Simpson to the UK, by Emirates via Dubai, which was scheduled for departure, Islamabad, Monday 28th, 9.00am local time; arrival London Heathrow, 8.00pm local time.

Damascus Syria

The two small groups responsible for finance and materiel met that Sunday afternoon the 27th August with Omar Najjar.

The extra man was Azmat Kirmani.

Discussions and wrangling followed covering weapons, value, price, shipping, bribes, timing, etc.

Finally agreement was reached. Part payment now, balance on safe delivery, fees, commissions, etc. All the tawdry issues that go to make up terrorist activity in the West.

Azmat left satisfied. His 'products' had generated a handsome return, and the circuitous delivery routes would leave no connection traceable to him.

At the hotel reception a well-trained agent from DGSE recognised him from a previous Observation report. Later that evening he posted his report by satcom to Paris.

It being a Sunday, and with no Priority indication on the message, it would wait for action until Monday the 28th August.

Week commencing Monday 28th August 2006

SIS (MI6) Vauxhall Cross London

The Deputy had read Harry's report and had detailed a team to handle the arrival at London Heathrow Airport that evening.

He had advised the DG by sending on a copy of Harry's report which later in the day resulted in a telephone call.

'Norman, Good Day.

I've read Baxter's report, and although recognising it is very early days with respect to any legal case, do you think that some judicious comment may help us in the public domain?

I was thinking along the lines of a successful surveillance and apprehension of a UK mole in one of our overseas embassies.

Rigorous analysis and interrogation produced a confession. Defence of the Realm in far flung territories, etc.

Do you think that is possible, or too early at this stage?'

The Deputy responded in a controlled fashion, thinking that this suggestion was probably caused by the publicity achieved by the boys across the river, and the DG wanting to get something positive out there as soon as possible.

'I think it's a bit early, bearing in mind the accused is not yet back in the country.

I suggest delaying anything for at least a week, or at least until we have some sort of signed confession or a clear suggestion from the prosecution.

Clearly it would be appropriate in the current climate to get some positive publicity, and I will

ensure that I revert to you soonest, once I have a clearer idea and timescale.'
'Very good Norman,' the DG replied, a note of disappointment in his voice, 'I look forward to hearing from you in the next few days.'
The Deputy put down the internal phone and wondered how this current situation would proceed, or unravel.
He knew, only too well, the tactics employed by defence lawyers in similar cases.
All the usual excuses.
Undue pressure being brought to bear on the accused.
No legal representation when first detained.
Appeals, in public, for all related security files to be made available, under the guise of openness and transparency.
Clemency to be extended to the accused due to idealism and naivety.
Human Rights.
Yes, he could well see what would happen once trial was under way.
He sent an encrypted commentary to Harry, confirming that it would be necessary for him to return to the UK at some point, as he was present when the confession was obtained, and was the senior officer attending with Tom Denman.

First Secretary Charles Urwin Islamabad
Over a week had passed since Charles had met with ISI, so he decided he would visit Inspector Irfan Chaudhry at the FIA, who had organised his rescue when he had been kidnapped.
It would give him an opportunity of registering his thanks for the rescue, and also appreciation for allowing Harry Baxter to be in attendance.

His thinking was, that although ISI were briefed as to his brother-in-law, their operations were essentially external to Pakistan. FIA on the other hand were solely Pakistan.

It would seem appropriate for the left hand to know what the right hand was doing.

The meeting had been arranged for 2.00pm the 29th August.

After the usual pleasantries Charles took a similar tack to that he had adopted with ISI, only on this occasion focussing on Azmat Kirmani's frequent business trips to Iraq, Syria, Afghanistan, and most interestingly, Tajikistan, whose increasing and main commodity exports are, cotton, aluminium and uranium.

He led up to these matters via his rescue, (a huge debt he therefore owed to FIA), enormous sympathy with the efforts being made to deal with militant and terrorist groups both internal and externally (despite the international criticism of insufficient effort), and the continuing pressure from political masters wanting results yesterday from decisions taken today, (his sympathy for both countries, UK and Pakistan, that invariably suffered in similar ways).

He floated a few flies on the water when he raised certain issues concerning the other countries, including Tajikistan, and dwelt on his concerns on the increasing sophistication of terrorist attacks and bomb making, including 'dirty' devices.

He then outlined the general intelligence he had shared with ISI, concerning materiel, foreign governments, funding, manufacture and distribution.

He baited his comments concerning Azmat Kirmani with references to the enormous concern within the family, and the hugely embarrassing impact this could have on the family name, and on his father's reputation as an ex Minister.

Knowing the levels of competition, if not distrust, between ISI and the FSA, he did refer to a 'brief' discussion he had held with one of the Deputy Director Generals, merely as a matter of course, and to ensure that the most important Pakistan Government Departments were fully aware of the current 'embarrassment'.

Inspector Chaudhry listened intently to what was said, making brief notes from time to time.

When Charles had finished he thanked him for bringing the situation to him, but wondered, in terms of specifics, what he could do.

Charles, not wishing to be seen to be taking a vendetta approach, suggested that all the usual surveillance methods could be adopted in Pakistan, together with a careful analysis of foreign trips and perhaps meetings in those countries.

Perhaps Pakistan embassies could possibly be alerted to listen for any local news or gossip?

Chaudhry thanked Charles for bringing this to him.

FIA was, of course, limited geographically, but liaison with embassies was a definite possibility.

He would like to review his options, and then revert to Charles, perhaps in a week to ten days?

The meeting ended, Charles repeating his thanks and looking forward to a further discussion.

He smiled to himself as he made his way back to his villa.

He would make Azmat's life Hell, and additionally he would do anything to hasten his departure to that place!

Thursday 31st August 2006

DGSE Paris

The report covering Azmat Kirmani had been reviewed but no action taken. Purpose of visit? Unknown. No further details. Filed in database.

It was late afternoon and the briefing session was drawing to a close. It was still warm outside, and the A/C was humming in the background.

The original plans for Alain Dubois and Anne Hardy to go to London on the 4th September had been cancelled, as it was clear no real benefit could be made for either of them with the absence of Harry Baxter.

Alain suggested to Anne that she might like to join him for an early dinner, raising his hands as he said it, to emphasise that it was just two colleagues having a meal!

Anne smiled at his actions, accepted in good grace, and said she fully understood that that was what was intended!

Alain recognised his and her position, and her relationship with Harry, a little jealously, if truth be told. But there was no way he would ruin either friendship.

Sitting in a little restaurant, Le Bistroquet, later that evening, they relaxed over their coffees, and quietly discussed their respective positions and thoughts.

Alain, the perennial charmer, admitted that some years previously he had met someone, with whom he thought he could spend the rest of his life.

'Charmante, sophistiquée, pleine d'humeur, I thought this was the one.

We spent many happy days together. She knew I worked for the government. That was all. There were no problems as far as I could see.

After about six months I was preparing myself to propose.

You know, a romantic gesture on the Tour Eiffel, or a bon weekend in the country.

Well, two days before le bon weekend, she told me that she was going to marry somebody else!

In fact she went off and married Monsieur Le Comte de whatever, I forget his name, who was a Fund Manager, or something like that, here in Paris!

You see, an old title, *AND* new money!'

He laughed, cynically.

'Since then I decided I would be the charmeur, no risk, no problem, no disappointment, but a little lonely from time to time, *BUT,* not very often!'

He laughed, this time relaxed.

Anne smiled at him.

'Yes, I remember your charmant actions in the hospital in Damascus! The French Embassy is still fielding complaints!'

This time they both laughed, confident in their unambiguous relationship.

Anne then said,

'I wish in some ways my relationship with Harry could be so straightforward, but I suspect it never will be,' before adding hastily, 'we know what we mean to each other, but, my god, our profession makes it difficult.'

'When do you hope to see him again?' asked Alain.

'I've no idea. We have not been able to talk since Damascus. But I hope soon', she said, smiling.

SIS (MI6) Vauxhall Cross London

The flights had been uneventful from Islamabad via Dubai to London Heathrow, landing a few minutes early.

Little or no conversation had passed between Tom Denman and Marion Simpson. She had been handcuffed to a female officer from the High Commission during the flight, and she had mostly read or slept during the trip, the only communication being whether she wanted any of the meals served.

Special Branch officers were on hand to take them to Vauxhall Cross, where Marion Simpson was formally charged and arrested.

She was then given access to a lawyer for an initial briefing, after which she was taken into custody, prior to an appearance in front of a local magistrate the next day.

Tom Denman then spent some time with the Deputy, verbally briefing him on the investigation, the planned discussions with Marion Simpson in front of Harry, the accusation of collaboration, and the subsequent admission.

Admission was achieved without any undue pressure or coercion, merely a short sequence of questions.

On wrapping up the Deputy commented,

'Tom, good piece of work. You will, of course, no doubt have to give evidence at the trial from behind a screen, and will also no doubt be vigorously questioned.

See our own lawyers soonest, and go through everything with a laser. I don't want some smart arse lawyer tripping us up. Alright?'

Tom agreed to follow through quickly, but pointed out recordings and transcripts had been made of the investigation and questioning, and also the distortion software evidence.

However, he recognised that the prosecution needed to have a tight, well substantiated case to succeed against the defence.

The Deputy enquired as to Harry's situation, particularly the recent imbroglio with the First Secretary, and members of his wife's family.

Tom, who had carried out the latter part of the review confined his comments to Charles Urwin; Harry had, and was, following through with the Kirmani family.

The Deputy also confirmed that Harry would need to be back in London for the main trial of Marion Simpson.

Israeli Embassy Mossad desk Paris

On Friday the 1st September, Anne met with her Mossad chief to review her role and induction into DGSE, plus an update on current thinking of areas of particular interest.

After the review her Director sat back and said nothing for about two minutes, which seemed like an eternity to Anne.

He then raised the matter of her role as Mossad Liaison Officer within DGSE, the understanding within DGSE of her scope of operation, and the difference between that, and what Mossad expected from such a placement.

'Anne,' he said quietly, 'I am sure that with your knowledge of our country's history, and your own father's sacrifice during the Six Days War, I do not need to stress the necessity for ensuring that we know as much about our friends intentions as our enemies.'

He paused.

'Your placement as a Liaison Officer within DGSE requires you to, in effect, compartmentalise your mind.

There will be those occasions when you will be working very closely with your DGSE colleagues on some important joint operation.

There will be other occasions when it may be possible for you to understand, that although you are working with a close ally, that ally will be working to establish, perhaps, a type of rapprochement with one of our enemies, which will be of no assistance to us in the defence of our country.

That is when you have to adopt a different mind-set and understanding of your role, and where your first priorities must lie.

Do I make myself clear?'

Anne nodded.

He continued.

'We do know from a historical perspective that there is a keen interest by the French Government to maintain a position of equilibrium for France within the region. That, at times, pushes them into a position of public Government rhetoric, which is neither helpful, nor encouraging to us.

On occasion they will give advance notice to us of such statements and actions, at other times, none.

You must understand that *any* advance notice of any action is of benefit to us, strategically.

Therefore I wish you to understand the delicate position you will find yourself in from time to time. It is not only the French and France that are looking for equilibrium!

The last point I wish to make at this time can only be described as very sensitive.
There may well be many occasions when you are not included in discussions or reviews of either 'wet or dry' ops.
These are areas of particular interest as they may cover incursions, either by DGSE operatives across borders, or by terrorists into Israel, or other countries, in the Middle East or Europe.
This is information we wish to know at the earliest opportunity.
The gathering and reporting back of such activity I will leave to your choice of method, and discretion. Is that last point completely understood?'
'Yes', Anne replied. 'One point?'
The Director nodded.
'What is Mossad's position if my particular 'research' is uncovered, and DGSE take exception to my methods?'
'You will be pulled immediately. Profuse apologies will be extended to DGSE at the highest level, and your enthusiasm will be blamed for overreaching yourself, or words to that effect! Clear?'
'Completely.'
'Good luck. Yishar koach!'
Anne reflected on what was expected of her over the coming months. Some good, some bad, some not so bad, and some not so good! Running with the hare, and looking over the hounds shoulder. A delicate mix, that at least was correct!

--

Week commencing Monday 4th September 2006

ISI HQ Islamabad Pakistan
Deputy Director Aatif Durrani, was discussing with his opposite number at the FIA, Director Tariq Kassar, his recent meeting with Charles Urwin.
Durrani was outlining the salient points, when Kassar interrupted him,
'Co-incidentally, Inspector Irfan Chaudhry, also had a meeting with First Secretary Urwin on the 28th August concerning the same individual and similar concerns. Inspector Chaudhry had briefed me following his meeting,'
There has always been a certain, if not considerable, sensitivity between the ISI and FIA, not least the apparent huge difference in the budgets allocated to them by the Pakistan Government.
Whilst accepting the increased geographical reach of ISI, there has always been an apparent difficulty in reconciling and justifying the difference.
'Perhaps we should consider how this matter is to be resolved?' suggested Durrani, 'particularly if we want resolution to be external of Pakistan.'
'What is your thinking?' enquired Kassar.
'First, if this to be resolved externally are you in agreement? Secondly, in order for us to be absolutely clear as to current activities, we will have to rely on your department for internal Pakistan surveillance and monitoring.'
'Full agreement on both points. What have you determined from your own intelligence so far?'
'We have been monitoring the individual probably for about eighteen months to two years.

In that time we have accumulated a considerable amount of detail on his activities throughout the region.'

Kassar interrupted,

'Why has no action been taken before and what detail do you have on his 'business, activities?'

'I'll deal with the second first.

His activities involve a number of countries, a number of disparate groups and individuals including politicians and militant groups with a number of products and services including weapons, training, bombs, financial services, including brokerage with the opium drug trade in order to pay for weapons, etc.

Why no action? You are as aware as I am of the conflicting interests and influences within our own political environment.

We apply pressure, instructed to back off, leave alone, bigger fish to follow, limited resources prevent us, of no real consequence, you know the words that are thrown at us.

How to prioritise in this situation is almost impossible.

However, with this one we now have very good reason.'

'Why? In what way?'

'We have now a much clearer picture of where and with whom he is operating.

Countries; Iran, Iraq, Afghanistan, and Syria to name the most important ones.

Weapons, bombs, drugs, money; Militant groups such as Al-Qaeda, Haqqani Network Iraq, Taliban, Harkat-ul-Mujahideen, Palestinian Islamic Jihad, the usual suspects, with strong or loose relationships.

The individual, well trained and indoctrinated as a boy and young man, is a committed to his cause. That is to the Caliphate, and making himself rich.'

'And to resolve this problem, you propose what?'

'If you are prepared, as you previously agreed, to leave the detail to me, but with current intelligence provided by you, then I can promise a satisfactory outcome to this problem.

I shall probably brief a unit of our Special Forces, well trained for such an eventuality.

The operation to be carried out externally and, in one of the countries I am thinking of, it would not raise an eyebrow. Merely another casualty of terrorist action taking place on almost a daily basis.'

Kassar indicated his acceptance, and was more than happy to be only involved to the extent indicated.

The FIA had a more than difficult job, navigating through the inky, but turbulent waters of Pakistan politics.

The plus, of course, was the clear agreement and co-operation between the two departments. Not an everyday occurrence!

Kassar promised some swift action in updated current intelligence and monitoring, both for telephone and data, bank records where available, and surveillance of meetings in Pakistan. Airport checks and flight details would be logged and passed to ISI on a daily basis as occurring.

Following Kassar's departure Durrani organised a meeting with a senior officer of Special Forces to discuss a future operation, date to be determined.

The Deputy Director sat thinking of what was likely to happen. Despite the dirty political dealings that ISI was often party to, he detested people like Kirmani; religious hypocrites, tainted money merchants, bringing nothing but death to so many innocents.

British High Commission Islamabad
With Tom returned to the UK, Harry was reviewing what he had been originally sent out to do.
Intel gathering on militant and terrorist groups in the region, relationships, funding, interdependency, hierarchy, positioning, political relationships.
Enough to keep one man occupied for years.
One of the main areas of militant activity, terrorist and suicide attacks, was Afghanistan.
A number of different groups were operating almost with impunity, as the ISAF (International Security Assistance Force), a multi-national NATO led group, had expanded into the North, South, East and West of Afghanistan.
With an unidentified enemy, containment was almost impossible, ISAF had been invariably reacting to circumstances; thinking now was for a more pro-active approach. In known militant controlled areas take the fight to the militants.
This was why Jack DeCosta was going there.
US interests, assets, support of the present regime, and political justification for US involvement were critical, and solid Intel in support of all those factors was vital.
He touched on these aspects in his report to the Deputy. After his recent 'activities' in the High Commission he had also decided to ask for some leave back in the UK, incorporating that as a last item.
He also inferred in the report, that during his leave, he would like to discuss an operational plan going forward. His thinking was that current Intel

gathering, whilst having some benefit, was not getting close enough to the militants on the ground. Therefore a new tactic should be adopted. That required discussion, design, and method of implementation.

He was sure the Deputy would see the logic behind his suggestion.

Sitting in his room that night Harry sent a text to Anna asking if she could call or text him.

He was just dropping off the sleep at about 11.30pm when his mobile beeped. It was a text from Anna, saying that she was in Paris, her mobile was on, and if he was awake he could call her!

Needing no encouragement he dialled her number. She answered immediately.

'Hullo Harry, how are you?'

'A whole lot better hearing you on the end of a phone.'

The conversation was slightly stilted due to the slight time delay over satellite, but nothing could disguise the warmth between the two of them.

'How's everything in sunny Paris?'

'Certainly interesting, if somewhat challenging,'

'I won't ask what you're up to, as long as you're keeping that French lothario Alain at arm's length.'

Anne warmed to his obvious concern.

'Well, we had dinner the other night. He told me about his charmed existence with the women of the world, and I told him about you and me, so he's very happy for us. You have a real friend there, who likes and respects you.'

'OK, but I'm here and he's there' he joked.

'I'm probably going to take some leave shortly. Can we get together, if only for a weekend?'

'I'd love that, but dependent on timing and planning I may be going abroad within the next three weeks.'
'Damn, but I'll try and bring mine forward.
Look, if I can, I will come via Paris, and we can grab a long weekend or just an ordinary weekend. How does that sound?'
'Fantastic. Just make it happen. Please?'
'I will try. Trust me. I will text you within 3 days.'
They finished their call reluctantly, and with expressions of their feelings. Both were aware of the strain surrounding their relationship, but determined to try and make it work.

DGSE HQ Paris
Discussions were going on between Alain and his Director, Gilles Deniaud, as where it would be appropriate for himself and Anne Hardy to be posted, now that the London proposal had been cancelled.
Alain was pushing for something under the AFD (Agence Francaise de Developpement) banner under which he and Anne had previously operated, albeit then, without Anne knowing of his DGSE credentials.
AFD operates in over 70 countries, including Afghanistan, Syria, Yemen, and Pakistan.
Why not Afghanistan?
Tough, challenging, difficult for AFD, and everybody else for that matter!
His Director was not convinced initially, until Alain reminded him of her capabilities in Lebanon and Syria. Plus, her professionalism whilst there, having no knowledge of his pedigree.

At this point Syria was considered as an alternative bearing in mind knowledge of the Committee, international funding of terrorism, recent experience of Omar Najjar, and other intelligence reports indicating significant activity by terrorist groups, including Hezbollah, financially and weapons supported by the Syrian Government.

A discussion ensued on the relative merits of an AFD cover in the two countries.

AFD, as an organisation, would be able to accept the Syrian option, bearing in mind the exit plan from Lebanon was executed through Syria.

Therefore, on balance, and bearing in mind major security issues in Afghanistan, it was decided by Director Gilles Deniaud that they would both go for a four or six week assignment, on the pretext of an operating audit of that country. Budget, value for money. Was Aid getting to right areas; Checks and balances, corruption index review? That type of thing.

An outline review thought that something could be set up in about two/three weeks. Take some leave before departure. Get a good update on AFD Syrian operations, visas, flights, all the usual preparations.

Anne, when she heard of country choice, was hopeful that something could be organised with Harry prior to her departure.

First Secretary Charles Urwin BHC Islamabad

Charles was seated opposite the High Commissioner explaining that he was rested, relaxed, with batteries recharged, ready to resume his role and responsibilities.

'Charles, I am absolutely delighted that you have fully recovered from such an unfortunate situation.

I, for one, felt for you throughout such a distressing experience, and would reassure you that in no way has your current role, or career been affected or jeopardised by it.
May I suggest you ease yourself in gradually? Do not try and 'catch up', it is not necessary and could be a retrograde step in your progress after such a stressful time.
Do I make myself clear?'
'Absolutely, and I appreciate your kind thoughts and consideration at this time.
As I am sure you understand, there are still a number of residual factors that affect my family, and its internal relationships.
Specifically, my wife has, in many ways, been traumatised by the recent events, plus worrying about her father's health, which has been adversely affected by his son's actions, and which, of course, also impacts on his reputation.'
The HC looked appropriately concerned, whilst slowly nodding his head in agreement.
Charles continued, 'Therefore I would ask for your understanding in the next few weeks if my attendance here is spasmodic, whilst I assist in my wife's recovery, and lend some moral support to my father-in-law and his reputation.'
'Of course Charles, fully understood.
Be as flexible as you like. Just ensure that your staff are fully up to speed with any outstanding matters, and in your absence and an emergency, they should bring any relevant matters to my immediate attention as a matter of urgency.'
Charles felt at this stage that he had laboured the point adequately, and that he would have sufficient 'flexibility' to pursue and harass his brother-in-law over the next few weeks.

Having thanked the High Commissioner he excused himself, and went into Islamabad to see his father-in-law, Nadeem Kirmani, at his office.
Sitting opposite him, Charles saw a deflated man, a face now heavily creased, with a sickly pallor in place of what had been a picture of confident rude health.
His voice, which previously had had a strong timbre, was now lower in tone, and with little inflection, almost a monotone.
A man showing, at present, every sign of defeat.
Charles decided, that trying to shake him out of his emotional lethargy would not be productive, so took a gentle commentary line, dwelling on family bonds, the need to stick and pull together.
'Please call on me for any help that you think I could provide', he suggested.
'Surely that would be limited bearing in mind your position here in Islamabad? You must, due to your diplomatic status, remain ambivalent if not neutral?'
'Yes, you're right, but I was thinking along family, commercial, and perhaps your political connection lines.'
'What are you thinking?'
'Well, your son has brought disgrace on the family name. We need a convincing story to reduce or remove that stigma from your name. We need your friends and political allies to rally round and put out some positive commentary to support you.
If that means we have to blacken Azmat's name any more than he has done already, then so be it.
We need to discover his connections, good or bad, and focus on the bad. Get the good to step ten paces forward and express huge disappointment.

You know, the sort of thing that Government Press Departments are very good at!'

At this remark he smiled, wolfishly. Just enough to conceal his burning hatred of Azmat.

Nadeem stirred in his chair.

'You could be right.' His voice for the first time sounded a little stronger.

'Let me think on this. I have a number of friends in high places, and a few other friends that owe me certain favours.

If we could put together some sort of PR that would achieve what you have just said, then that could perhaps mitigate against any long term adverse effects.'

Charles having planted the seed, then said,

'Do you have any connections in your business empire who would know with whom Azmat has been dealing with in these various countries?

I realise, of course that the majority of his time was spent on your group's behalf, but he certainly found enough time for his own activities!'

'That is what is making me ill. The duplicity of a son with his father. I can never forgive him.'

Good, thought Charles, we are making some progress.

'Whilst we are discussing this have you had much, if any, contact with ISI and FIA?'

'Our intelligence agencies?'

'Yes.'

'Not really. The group's focus was commercial. I think I met one of their officers on one occasion, which agency I can't remember, but we didn't discuss it.'

Excellent, thought Charles, that will ensure no complications with either agency, if anything arises in the future.

'Do you think you could start to do some digging in your organisation, particularly in Afghanistan, Iran, and Syria, to see if anybody has any idea as to Azmat's contacts there, and perhaps what were his side lines?

It will probably take some form of financial inducement for them to co-operate, but I think it will be worthwhile in the long term', he said, smiling wolfishly again.

'But I don't have to explain that sort of thing to you, do I?'

This time Nadeem smiled wolfishly in return.

'Leave this to me now Charles, I did not get where I am today by following every straight line.

What is it you English say? Many roads lead to Rome? Well I have travelled many!'

They shook hands and Charles went back to his villa and his wife.

There still existed long periods of strained silence between them, not least because of her brother, but also her wish to raise their future children as Muslim.

In one outburst Charles had linked the two, pointing out the example of her brother where things can go catastrophically wrong.

When they are of age, he said, then their children can decide for themselves, until then the basics of right and wrong, good and evil, will suffice.

On his return his wife asked quietly if everything was alright, which he answered positively, but brusquely.

His wife, clearly upset and fragile, left the room with eyes glistening that turned rapidly to tears in the privacy of her bedroom.

Charles sat in his study reflecting on his conversation with his father-in-law, hoping that information could be added to the mix concerning his son Azmat, and his connections and contacts in some of the group's trading countries, particularly Iran and Afghanistan.

Any of this he could pass on to FIA or ISI which could help and assist in the resolution of the problem.

What he was not aware of was the operation being formulated by ISI.

--

The High Commissioner, meanwhile, had been updating Harry Baxter on the present circumstances of Charles Urwin.

As he opened the discussion the High Commissioner looked keenly at Harry.

'This conversation Harry is strictly confidential, and I mean confidential. Do you understand?'

'Absolutely.'

'Right, I will continue. It concerns our First Secretary, Charles Urwin.'

Harry registered no emotion or reaction as the HC continued.

'He and I have had a general conversation as to his wellbeing. He assures me as to his health, and willingness to return to his duties, whilst at the same time indicating he will need some latitude as to his daily commitment.

The reason for this is, as he described, concern for certain members of his family, particularly his wife and father, Nadeem Kirmani, previously a Pakistan Government Minister. The time required is to provide some form of comfort and empathy as they recover from their recent traumatic experience, involving brother and son, Azmat Kirmani.'

The HC paused at this point, clearly assembling his following words.

'Harry, I believe that reason is only half the story. Let me elaborate.
Charles is an extremely competent member of the Foreign Service, clearly destined, up to now, for a very senior position in the last third of his career.
He is incredibly focussed, one could say passionate in his dedication to the exclusion of external factors, including his family.
Psychologically, one could possibly describe him as a paranoid obsessive, with no lack of self-worth, which is of the highest order.'
He smiled gently at this point.
'On occasions I have often envied his self-confidence which borders on the narcissistic; he allows no room for doubt.
However he lacks charm in execution; perhaps megalomania is a better description.'
Harry sat there thinking he had never heard the HC talk in this way, or go down such a sensitive path before.
The HC continued, now holding Harry in eye contact, 'the reason for my comment is that I believe Charles is heading for, or is already experiencing, a severe nervous breakdown.
Link that with certain factors of his personality I have described, and I believe you have a potent mix.
Sequence and outcome I have no idea, but I would imagine that an element of revenge will be there.
In what form this will manifest itself I have no real idea, but would guarantee that Azmat Kirmani would be in his sights.
My question to you is this.
Is there anything that you know, or discovered, during the investigation that could throw light on my comments, plus is there any resource you could

bring to bear on maintaining some sort of surveillance over the next few months?
A, to ensure he does nothing stupid, and B, that anything he does do, does not heap embarrassment on HM Government?'
Harry was speechless for a few seconds, never guessing that the HC would open up in this way, but recognising now that there were clear grounds for concern.
'I cannot give you an off-the-cuff answer immediately.
Can I go away, consider what you have said, and come back with some suggestions?
I know, bearing in mind your concerns that sounds a little feeble, but there are a number of factors I must consider before proposing something.'
'Of course Harry. We must recognise the sensitivity of what we have discussed, and I would remind you again of the strict confidentiality surrounding it.'
'Noted.
Give me a couple of days, and incidentally, I will probably have to go back to London for about a week, sometime in the next three weeks.'
'Also noted Harry. See me on Thursday, the 7th September, about 10.00am?'

Azmat Kirmani Tehran Iran
Since some friends in high (government) places had gently warned him, Azmat had been keeping a low profile.
His current stay in Tehran was necessary as he was acting as broker for a significant arms transfer deal from one of the Iranian armament factories through to Hezbollah in the Lebanon and Hamas in the Gaza Strip.

At the same time, he was also trying to position himself as the preferred arms supplier between a Pakistan terrorist training group and an Al-Qaeda affiliate, Jaish-e-Mohammed, an active insurgent group in Afghanistan.

He was also aware that Pakistan Military and ISI were involved in 'support' roles with J-e-M, scope and definition unknown.

Most meetings were held in his hotel room, and short telephone calls conducted through a number of mobiles, never the same one twice.

XIX

Week Commencing 11th September 2006

Tuesday 12th September 2006

Harry Baxter High Commission Islamabad

Several decisions had been taken.

Following a meeting with the HC on the Thursday before, Harry was to organise some additional assistance under the heading of 'High Commission Security Evaluation'.

Selection would be left to Harry and probably confirmed during his meeting his London, linked with a few days leave.

Harry already knew who he would pull in, if available.

He had worked with this individual, Dai Evans, some years before; ex SAS, Welsh born, very competent indeed on those operations that are not strictly 'standard'.

A tough Welshman from Tiger Bay, Cardiff, fiercely proud of the Regiment, who had served in many capacities and operational theatres over the years.

Yes, absolutely ideal for what was wanted, namely keeping a weather eye on Charles Urwin, and 'interrupting', if things got bloody stupid.

He had submitted an encrypted report to the Deputy outlining his requirement, but leaving out the commentary from the HC, merely covering the matter under the heading of 'Internal Security'. This was to be expanded on during their face to face.

Lastly, he requested 4 days leave on his return to the UK, to be taken immediately prior to his meeting in London with the Deputy.
Permissions had been given.
Contacting Anna by telephone, he suggested that he travel to the UK via Paris, enabling them to spend their long weekend together, which he hoped would be the weekend starting Friday 22nd September 2006.
In his own mind he was thinking he could then confirm his meeting with the Deputy for Tuesday 26th September.
She hoped that it could be arranged, and promised to get back to him by the end of the week.

Wednesday 13th September 2006

Azmat Kirmani Tehran Iran to Kabul Afghanistan via Dubai
Azmat Kirmani knew in his heart that he was supping with the Devil, but the lure of money linked with influence and his concealed reputation, was too heady a mixture.
He had always dealt carefully, in his own particular sphere, aware that sensitivities injured in any particular group, can bring speedy retribution.
With his contacts at senior government level advising or warning of potential threats or investigations, he had acquired three different passport nationalities and names, this facilitating travel and removing the possibility of frontier apprehension or arrest.
The latest opportunity involving armaments supply from Pakistan to the Al-Qaeda affiliate, Jaish-e-Mohammed, in Afghanistan, would be a major step

in his commercial progress, and considerably enhance his various bank balances.
However there was a significant downside risk with his activities on both sides of the Muslim divide, namely Shia with the consignments to Hezbollah, and Sunni funding to the Salafi Jihadist groups in Afghanistan.
Under one of his assumed identities he travelled from Tehran to Dubai in the Emirates, spending a day there, before flying to Kabul in Afghanistan, on another of his three passports.
He stayed at the Heetal Airport Hotel in Kabul, adjacent to the International airport, conducting his business by meetings in the hotel, and alternate mobile telephone discussions.
On one occasion he went out for a meeting to the south side of Kabul, whilst the embedded ISI operative, within the hotel reception staff, noted his time of departure and return, along with other details of his visitors.
This information was in turn transmitted on a secure network back to Islamabad every 24 hours.
He flew from Kabul to Dubai on the afternoon of Monday 18th September.
In Dubai he had rented an apartment, under an assumed name, now no longer in communication or contact with his father or family.
Dubai, over a number of years, had become a centre for Russian oligarchs and criminals, East European organised crime gangs, major financial deposits of South American drug cartels, and a number of African despots.
The Asian subcontinent had also contributed a number of dubious commercial characters and organisations, and whilst hotly denying any culpability or encouragement, the authorities were

now recognising that the reputation of Dubai was sinking, not rising.

In the face of this mini-invasion of undesirables, the order had now come from the very top in Dubai.

Clean the Augean stables, and do it now!

The Administration was thin on the ground in terms of intelligence gathering, so free reign was the order of the day for most Western powers through their respective embassies.

Clutter, and tripping over each other, was often the recipe mix, however some sharing did occasionally produce some good results.

Everybody was looking at everybody else, so embedded observers and agents were the order of the day at most hotels.

Arrivals and departures were scrutinised for ‘regulars’, persons of interest on whatever list, Interpol wish lists, European Government ‘wanted’ lists. The lists were endless!

With such confusion certain agencies were prioritising. It was the only way.

Azmat’s profile was gathering interest. It was clear from his activity over a number of months that different passport identities pointed to the same individual.

He was now, to a number of organisations, ‘a person of interest’.

Thursday 21st September

Islamabad/Paris

Harry had agreed his schedule both with the HC in Islamabad and the Deputy in London.

He was planning to fly from Islamabad to Paris on Thursday the 21st September, either with Emirates, or Etihad, via Dubai, or Abu Dhabi.
He would arrive in Paris around lunchtime, and hopefully catch up with Alain Dubois in the afternoon.
He plumped for the Emirate flight and had about an hour's wait in Dubai before catching the Paris connection.
He was taking his seat when he thought he recognised a man across the aisle; 'Yes', he said to himself, definitely, 'a person of interest'.
It was Azmat Kirmani.
Why was he going to Paris? Harry thought. Give Alain a nudge when I see him. Almost certainly up to no good.
The flight passed uneventfully, and Harry saw Kirmani just ahead of him in the taxi queue.
Their respective cabs held station down the motorway A1 into Paris, Harry's taking the route to his hotel in the centre of Paris, on the Rue de Rivoli.
First he called Anna to say he was now in Paris, and hoping to see he that evening, about 7.00pm?
She sounded delighted to hear him, and readily agreed to the time suggested.
Then he mentioned he needed to see Alain to give him some specific current information. She laughed and he enquired why so funny?
She replied that Alain would probably explain, and if he didn't she would when they met!
He called Alain and they agreed to meet at 5.00pm at Harry's hotel, Harry commenting he had just seen an old 'friend' on the flight who could be of interest to Alain.

'Sounds interesting, mon vieux. I look forward to seeing you again.'

'Me too.

By the way I just spoke to Anne, and told her I wanted to see you to pass on some information, at which point, she then laughed.

Any idea what the joke is I'm missing?'

'Hasn't she told you what her role is now?'

'No.'

'Well I'll let her tell you later. It is quite amusing and I'm sure you will see why!

See you at 5.'

--

On the Avenue Hoche, just off the Etoile, Azmat Kirmani had checked into his hotel and was resting on his bed when the telephone rang.

The caller was confirming the meeting for Friday at 7.00pm.

That done, Kirmani thought of how he would approach the second part of his negotiations with Omar Najjar when they met tomorrow.

Part payment had been made, but he thought a premium might be required in order to complete the delivery.

If delivery was not made, then Najjar could lose face with the Committee. It all depended how far he could push in the negotiation. That could also be very satisfying.

--

Harry was resting in his room at the Saint James and Albany Hotel when his telephone rang just before 5.00pm to tell him his guest Alain Dubois had arrived.

They met in the lobby shaking hands vigorously, and a slap on the back from each of them.

Once seated in the lounge area Harry said,

'Let me fill you in on the co-incidence.'
'Bon, allez.'
'On my flight from Dubai to Paris I thought I recognised a fellow passenger. In fact I'm convinced.'
'Who?'
'Azmat Kirmani.'
At this Alain sat up.
'Are you sure?'
'Yes, I've seen the mug shots. No mistake.'
'Very interesting. I wonder what he is doing here. One thing is sure is that he will probably stay in that hotel, on the Avenue Hoche, that I have mentioned to you before.
Anything else you can add?'
'Not really.'
'Let me go and make a telephone call. I need to set something up quickly. Give me 20 minutes and then we can have that drink! D'accord?'
'D'accord', Harry replied, smiling.
On his return Alain quickly outlined what he had set up by way of confirmation of hotel, if so, then surveillance, engineer some phone taps, interception of mobile phone traffic, etc.
They caught up on their present operations and considered any overlaps or common ground, whilst enjoying their drinks.
Harry asked on one occasion whether Alain could explain Anna's role or function, but he refused, light heartedly saying it would be best coming from her.
At about 6.40pm Alain left, saying he had things to follow up on, determined not to be there when Anna arrived.
Shaking Harry's hand he said,

'If things start to happen with our mutual friend can I contact you?'

Seeing the slightly pained look that crossed Harry's face, he added hastily,

'Of course, it would have to be very important, or very serious for me to contact you. That I understand.'

'As long as that is clearly understood, then fine.'

Harry sat reflecting on a few permutations, his reverie then interrupted as Anna strode into the lounge, walking briskly towards him, arms outstretched.

She kissed him on both cheeks, whilst holding him tightly, which he reciprocated.

Reluctantly they released each other, but still held hands as they moved over to a settee by the window.

'Christ, it's good to see you again' Harry said softly.

'Yes Mr Baxter, I agree with you,' Anna replied squeezing his hand at the same time.

'First things first' Harry said, 'what time can you get away tomorrow?'

'Probably around lunchtime.'

'OK, that gives me the morning to plan where we could go for Le Weekend!'

'Second item. Monsieur!' he said catching the waiter's eye.

'Deux coupes de champagne, s'il vous plait.'

He smiled at Anna.

'I've been thinking about ordering that for a few weeks now!'

She squeezed his hand again.

'And all I've been *thinking* about is you.'

They smiled affectionately at each other, slowly sipping their champagne.

'Do you want to go up to my room?'
'That's a little early, even for you Harry' she teased.
'No, just in case you wanted to freshen up before we went out to dinner', Harry replied, reddening slightly.
She squeezed his hand again.
'I would love to go up to your room now Harry, but I want to enjoy you over dinner as well.'
They looked at each other, many things being left unsaid.
'I saw a nice looking bistro just around the corner from the hotel when I arrived. Shall we try that?'
'I'm happy with what and where you decide.'
'OK, one question.'
'Fine.'
'What is your present role that obviously some people find amusing?'
Anna paused before replying.
'Don't laugh, because my bosses have decided that there are a number of advantages in me agreeing to the suggestion.'
'Alright, tell me.'
'I have been appointed as Mossad Liaison Officer with DGSE. I will continue with the name I was given in AFD, namely Anne Hardy.'
There then followed a short period of silence.
'I suppose it is somewhat amusing. But are you aware of where this could take you?'
'Yes Harry I do. You know what happened to my father in the Six Day War. And, I also remember something you said to me in London.'
'What was that?'
'We're all on the same side.'
Another short period of silence followed before Harry said,

'Let me let those thoughts sink in. I think dinner calls, don't you?'

Anna agreed, never having let go of Harry's hand during the exchange.

Although there was still some warmth in the air, the odd breeze indicated that autumn was following, and not too far behind.

They were one of the first in the small bistro, only a few minutes' walk from the hotel, and as they were early, had a wide choice of tables.

Taking one that gave them a view onto the Rue de Rivoli, they chose carefully from the carte, both food and wine, relishing both, and their own company, after their recent enforced separation.

By about 10.00pm they had eaten, drunk, and taken coffee, before they took the short walk back to the hotel.

On this occasion they walked straight to the lift that took them to the second floor and Harry's room.

In the lift they had kissed only once, but it had carried a hint of eagerness.

Entering his room Harry turned and said,

I'm not happy with the role you have taken with DGSE.'

Anna was immediately deflated.

'How can you say that at a time like this?'

'Because I think I love you. That's why, and now I've said it' he said defiantly.

'Oh Harry', that was all she said, as she sat down on the edge of the bed.

'Don't you realise Anna, that in effect, both DGSE and Mossad will be using you?

They will both be very interested in what you know, or what you can find out.

I don't know what your operational brief is from your Director, but I can bet he will want anything and everything you can find out on current ops, strategic thinking, and where DGSE is trying to forge alliances, both overt and covert.

It's because of the way I feel about you that makes me worry about your new role.'

He paused,

'*And* by God, I'm sorry to have raised it and put a bloody great dampener on our day.'

Anna said nothing, just looking at the floor with a very sad expression on her face.

After about a minute she spoke.

'Harry, you know my family history and the sacrifice my father made. That is why I do what I do.

My country and its people are very important to me, therefore I will do what I can to defend them.

Yes, you and I feel the same way about each other, but if we are to continue, we are going to have to live with our respective loyalties.'

Harry was looking at her intently.

'Anna, I have not felt for any person like I feel for you. I may not have the words and music that some men may have, so my statements may appear somewhat naïve and simplistic.

When I got you out of the 4x4 in Beirut I thought initially you were dead.

At that instant I could have killed somebody, the feeling was terrible, something I had not experienced before.

Can I just apologise for being so brusque, not thinking, and allowing my love for you to bluntly put my opinion, without any thought for your feelings?'

At this point he put out his hands and took Anna's in his own, pulling her gently up from the bed, then wrapping his arms around her.

She laid her head on his shoulder as she gently shook with crying, and tears ran from her eyes.
'Yes Harry, you can', she said quietly.
Little conversation followed, but they lay in bed, bodies together and slept fitfully, each at times reflecting on what had been said, and wondering where their relationship would go.
In the morning Harry tried to lighten the mood with discussing where they might go for the weekend, both agreeing that they did not need to go far from Paris, as long as there was some countryside for walks, and some good dining in the evening.
Harry spent the morning organising 'Le Weekend', with Anna scheduled to be back at his hotel by 2.00pm latest.
When Anna arrived just before 2.00pm, her mood was lighter, she was smiling, and she clasped his hand in both of hers, as she said,
'I've been thinking about this all morning. Let's go and have a lovely time.
We know how we feel about each other. Put the other stuff away for at least 48 hours. It's us and our weekend that are important now. Agreed?'
'Damn right. Agreed!'
'So where are we going?' she enquired.
A surprise, wait and see, and your car awaits!'
Harry ushered her downstairs to the cab that was waiting for them, driven by a jolly character it seemed, who winked at Harry in a conspiratorial way, before driving away down the Rue de Rivoli, across the Place de la Concorde, and up the Champs Élysées.
Their driver had fun in the usual joust crossing the Étoile, before heading in a NE direction leaving Paris by the Porte Maillot.

After crossing the Pont Neuilly over the Seine, they then took the D913/991 through Le Vésinet and Le Peq, before crossing the Seine again, as the road climbed up towards St Germain-en-Laye.

Entering the town they turned right into Rue Thiers, shortly before the chateau, and at the end of the road entered the grounds of the Pavillon Henri IV, a hotel which had once been the residence of Louis XIV, the Sun King, now a superb hotel, situated high on the hill, overlooking the Seine, and Paris in the distance, surrounded by 500 acres of parkland.

Harry had done his homework well, and Anna gasped and exclaimed at the location and views, as she got out of the car.

Depositing their bags at the entrance, the driver gave Harry a departing wink and a deep chuckle, before leaving.

They were shown to their room on the first floor with windows on two sides, one giving a view of the adjacent chateau, the other the Seine, at the bottom of the steep hill.

It was about 3.45pm, so they went for a short walk in the grounds, marvelling at the Terrasse extending for 2 kilometres, used as a horse exercising run in Napoleon times.

Returning to their room they showered and changed leisurely, before descending to the Gallery Bar for an aperitif.

They sat, talking quietly, taking in the panoramic view of Paris in the distance.

The previous tension that had existed between them had slowly seeped away, leaving two people able to leave their professional world behind, albeit for the very short term, but, which would hopefully serve as some sort of balance against the chaotic environment they inhabited.

The meal and wines helped to reinforce the mood of the moment, coupled with their relaxation in pleasant surroundings, no time constraints, phone calls, or interruptions.

Back in the Gallery they sat drinking their coffee and brandy, looking at the lights of Paris and barges on the Seine, as night had now fallen.

Harry spoke,

'Well, if we are going to do those 500 acres justice tomorrow, I suppose we had better get some sleep.'

Anna looked at him with one eyebrow raised.

'Harry Baxter, Action Man, you made an excellent choice for our weekend. But, I am disappointed.'

'Why?'

'Here was I thinking, not only a weekend together, but with my rugged, romantic man in the City of Love, Paris, and all he can suggest is an early night, so we can get some sleep, in order to go for a long walk tomorrow!

Harry Baxter, you disappoint me!'

Harry smiled, somewhat ruefully.

'I did warn you that I don't have all the right words and music that some men have, so I have to approach certain things obliquely!

However, in the face of that accusation, can we please now go to bed so that I can make love to you?

Is that clear enough?'

'Certainly Mr Baxter, take me to bed!'

They both laughed gently, Harry taking her hand and pretending to drag her away.

As they walked along the corridor to their room he put his arm around her shoulder whilst her head inclined to his, with her arm around his waist.

At their room he exaggerated the finding of the key in his pocket that made Anna laugh, which turned into a small squeal, as, after closing the door, he picked her up in his arms and carried her to the bed. She lay looking up at him.

'Me Jane, you Tarzan?'

'No, Harry Baxter ma'am. At your service.'

As he was saying this, he was turning off the main and the bedside lights, so that there was only a soft diffused light coming through the curtains from a distant Paris.

'Mr Baxter, what are you doing?'

'Something, I hope, that meets with both our approval.'

She giggled, 'Well I approve so far!'

He swiftly undressed her, and they kissed several times with an urgency that was apparent to both of them, and which progressed and culminated quite quickly.

'Well, Mr Baxter, for the innocent abroad you seem quite well informed,' Anne said, with a catch in her voice.

'Thank God for some of the Self-Help books you can buy these days', Harry replied, causing another giggle from Anna.

Harry stopped the giggle with a firm kiss, which led to a gentler refrain, which echoed more than once, during that Friday night and Saturday morning.

Hotel Avenue Hoche Paris

Omar Najjar strode into the hotel on the Avenue Hoche at about 7.00pm.

Azmat Kirmani had told him which room, 412, so he took the lift to the fourth floor.

Knocking, he entered to the usual greetings, was offered coffee which he declined, and then sat down facing Kirmani for the discussion which he knew, by experience would not be easy.

Always there were 'extras'. Persons to pay off, customs problems, the usual mix.

Kirmani advised that both weapon systems were now in Paris. However there were complications in shipping one to London.

It could not be done direct, from Paris to London, either via Dover or Portsmouth.

Contacts had indicated increased security measures in those ports, suggested routing was now via another small port on the South Coast, and a lorry trip to London.

People had to be dealt with, seen to, brought on side, etc. Whatever the description it cost money. The amount? That is dependent on the negotiation. That is what was starting now.

Stamina was what is needed, thought Kirmani, plus a hint of advising the Committee on a lack of co-operation on a very important project.

Do not get heavy in approach, keep it light, but with sufficient emphasis so that the veiled threat is clearly understood.

The discussion was laborious, but agreement reached about 10.00pm.

They shook hands and Najjar left, grateful that the amount was within his budget sanctioned by the Committee.

Kirmani was grateful for the extra added onto a project, into which he had already added the contingency.

Smiling to himself, he called a telephone number to arrange a little 'light relief' after such a stressful evening.

Saturday 23rd September 2006

Islamabad

The meeting had been arranged by a circuitous route.

Nadeem Kirmani had served twice as a Minister in the Pakistan Government.

Whilst not a man to make headlines it was recognised that, among a highly dubious collection of fellow ministers, he was a comparative safe pair of hands.

Not exciting in headline grabbing policy, but steady and thorough.

Now no longer a Minister, but a very successful business man, he had, through a Ministry colleague, been able to arrange a meeting with a senior responsible figure in ISI.

He had outlined, in some detail, his concerns with his son, Azmat Kirmani, and his son's involvement with highly suspect militant groups with terrorist connections.

It was increasingly damaging to the family as a whole, and he was aware that both ISI and FIA had him on their radar.

He asked, in a roundabout way whether ISI had any plans to curtail his son's activities by arrest.

The senior figure in ISI had listened sympathetically to the father's concerns, and allowed him to finish before responding.

'Mr Kirmani, you should be aware that your son Azmat has been a 'person of interest' to us for some considerable time.

His activities, carried out under the aegis of your group, involve a number of countries that feature very high on a list of considerable concern to us.
Bearing in mind that fact, and I am sure you understand our confidentiality, we have number of operations currently running in various countries that could include, or not include, your son's activities and contacts.
I would assure that our actions will be taken in the best interest of Pakistan, and to neutralise any impact your son's activities may have on this country.
I hope that provides you with some assurance at this time?'
Nadeem Kirmani thanked him for his comments, and said he felt reassured that ISI were clearly on top of the situation.
The senior figure then reported verbally on the meeting to one of the Deputy Director Generals who nodded on completion, and said,
'This is to make no difference whatsoever to the assignment planned, of which I believe you have full knowledge?'
The man nodded.
'The operation and timing will proceed as planned. From our Government perspective Azmat Kirmani has become a significant nuisance, and is interfering with our own strategic and tactical plans for a number of our relationships with different political and militant groups. Therefore the man and his operations must be neutralised.
If Kirmani wants to hear soft words, be prepared to give them to him. Understood?'
The man nodded again. The meeting was over.
He returned to his office, and made a couple of data entries on the IT system. As simple as that.

Pavillon Henri IV St Germain-en-Laye

The September sun was forcing itself through the curtains in the early morning, as Harry stirred and rolled over to look at Anna.

She was lying on her side, a soft expression on her face, one that gave him a hint of what she had looked like as a young girl.

He lay quietly, watching her gentle breathing, considering himself a lucky man.

Suddenly her eyes opened, and she smiled at him.

'Good morning Ms Harrison, I trust you slept well?'

Anna did not reply, but raised one arm to encircle his neck as she pulled him towards her.

'Far too much talking Mr Baxter' she said, as her lips met his.

He felt her length against him, as they both responded to their mounting feelings.

At about 8.15am Harry called down to reception for breakfast, which they took leisurely sitting on their balcony with the Seine below.

Time, for a change, was on their side.

They decided to go for a long walk along the Terrasse, stopping from time to time to admire the views of the Seine from the top of the steep hill running down from St Germain-en-Laye.

The whole park and chateau was steeped in history, with the town's narrow streets and market place hardly changed for over a hundred years.

They took coffee sitting at an outside table of Le Soubise, a café directly opposite the chateau.

'You know, I could get very used to this,' Harry commented, 'It has a style I like, modern, but in many ways unchanging. The French tradition.'

Taking a light lunch at about 2.00pm they then walked slowly round the town, looking at some of the antique and art shops, and Anna, surreptitiously on occasion, studying some of the current women's fashions!
Returning to Le Pavillon Henri IV they spent a lazy late afternoon in their room, happy and content in each other's company, retracing and rebuilding their relationship.
Harry had made a reservation for dinner at the Brasserie du Theatre, situated directly facing the chateau, this being a about a 7 minute walk from their hotel.
The evening was still warm as they walked up Rue Thiers to the restaurant.
As they crossed the road from the chateau towards the restaurant, a man, sitting outside Le Soubise, was ostensibly taking a photograph of the chateau.
It was an excellent evening photo of the chateau, but also included was the image of Harry and Anna crossing the road hand in hand.
As they entered the Brasserie, the photographer, having transferred the shot from his camera to his mobile by Bluetooth, sent the image by email to an address in Paris.
All agencies like to keep up to date with any relationships, but are even more interested in those across agencies.
The evening passed slowly with both enjoying the classical restaurant with good food and service. Perhaps an occasion to recollect at some time in the future, Harry joked.
In Paris the photo attachment had been received and attached to the file electronically. Something to be raised at an appropriate time. No urgency at present. Both parties identified and known.

Harry and Anna walked back slowly to the Pavillon savouring the evening air, only too aware that time was moving on, and that they would be back in the real world in 24 hours.

Sunday 24th September 2006

Islamabad

Nadeem Kirmani called Charles Urwin and arranged that they would meet at 10.30am.

Kirmani was guarded on the telephone but, said he had some news concerning their joint problem.

They met at Kirmani's villa.

'Charles, good to see you again,' he said over heartily.

'Come through.'

They sat down in his study.

'I decided to use one of my contacts from my Minister days, and was put in touch with one of our agencies.'

'Which one?'

'That is Confidential.'

'And?'

'Having explained the situation from my own position and the family, I was told that our particular concern had been under observation for some time.

This had covered his activities, the countries involved, and the commercial relationships established, which are described as undesirable and certainly not in the best interests of Pakistan.'

'What are they doing, or are proposing to do, about it?'

‘They assure me that any effect or impact on Pakistan’s best interests will be neutralised, and that I need have no concern.’
‘And how are they going to achieve that?’
‘They did not go into any detail, but said I was not to concern myself in any way, and that I should reassure all my family that the resolution of the problem was in good hands.’
‘Hmm. Well, I suppose we will have to wait and see what eventuates. No doubt you will inform me if you have any further news?’
‘Of course. At least the matter is now in hand.’
Charles left, wondering which specific agency had been involved, whether the explanation was just a typical Pakistan Civil Service brush off, or whether something really was being done. Time will tell. All will be revealed in due course, he thought cynically.

Pavillon Henri IV St Germain-en-Laye
They had passed the day in isolated splendour.
At times completely oblivious to the rest of the world. Like a sponge they were as desperate as each other in soaking up all they could understand of the other.
At one point, mid-afternoon, Harry said,
Look, I don’t know how the hell we are going to do it, or, for that matter, whether you want to, but I want to spend the rest of my life with you.’
Anna looked surprised, but pleased, as she answered,
‘I haven’t a clue how the hell we can do it, as you put it, but it’s something I want too.’
They both started to speak, and Harry stopped first.
‘Harry, in the job we’re in, it’s going to be very difficult to do that, but let me tell you, I will really

work to achieve that, as I know you will. There has to be a way, somehow.'

Harry agreed, and they both fell silent as they realised a commitment had been made.

At 5.30pm their car appeared to take them back to Paris, the same driver winking irritably at Harry, when putting their cases in the boot, and enquiring if they had had a Bon Weekend!

Arriving back at Harry's hotel on the Rue de Rivoli brought about one of those moments that everyone has experienced at some time, when the bubble bursts, and reality kicks in.

However, as Anna started to say goodbye, she fixed Harry with a defiant stare,

'Harry Baxter, let me say two things, and then let me go.

One, I love you.

Two, we are both going to fight to achieve what we both said earlier today.

Now, give me a hug and kiss, and let me go before I bawl my eyes out.'

Harry kissed her gently, hugged her very hard, in a bear like grip, before releasing her with the words,

'I am in complete agreement with everything you have just said, so now let's come out fighting,' he said, with a big smile on his face.

She stroked his face once, before turning away, and getting in the first cab sitting in the hotel rank.

She turned and waved as it pulled out into the evening Paris traffic, before disappearing into the middle distance.

Harry, now feeling somewhat flat, turned and went into his hotel to prepare for his trip to London the next day Monday, for his meeting with the Deputy on Tuesday, the 26th September.

That was going to throw up a number of issues, including where the Service was going under the new Director General, resolution of the Marion Simpson case, current status and outcomes within Charles Urwin's family, and general intelligence on arms trade involving Russia, Iran, Pakistan and Afghanistan.

Week commencing Monday 25th September 2006

US Embassy Islamabad

The meeting was analysing recent intelligence and surveillance data, some satellite collected, the other by a UAV (Unmanned Aerial Vehicle), a drone.

Jack DeCosta was comparing results obtained by both, which clearly indicated an increase in terrorist group activities in the SE near the Afghan border, the other up near the disputed territory of Kashmir in the NE.

Langley, CIA HQ, was calling for more detail and some further interpretation.

Jack, working with limited resources in Islamabad, was heavily reliant on electronic surveillance. However, he had enlisted the help of a an ex-ISI officer, retired early on health grounds, but who was happy to receive dollar assistance for providing local knowledge and 'chatter' from his home region in the NE of Pakistan.

There were a number of village and town elders in the NE region highly suspicious of some of the moves and decisions made by the Government in Islamabad. The concern was, that as a region, they were being ignored, and of more concern, the

degree of hostility being shown in negotiations for regional development.
One elder in particular had consistently provided a good general overview of the situation within the region, and recently had hinted that further information may be forthcoming concerning weapons trading and distribution.
This is a major area that must be developed, Jack thought.
With Harry in London there would be no opportunity for cross checking until he returned, which would probably be at least 3-4 days.

Russian Embassy Islamabad
The military attaché in the embassy had just returned from a clandestine trip to the NE of the country where they were supplying arms and ammunition from the Indian side of Kashmir.
This duplicity fitted in well with their involvement in the region.
Russia was also heavily involved in supplying the Indian military with equipment, in particular completing the 140, locally assembled, Sukhoi Su-30MK1 all-weather, long range fighter.
Volkov was receiving an update on the sensitivities in Kashmir, and the likelihood of any confrontation between India and Pakistan over the disputed region.
Such local 'activity' can, of course be an ideal proving and testing ground for weapons operating in difficult terrain and climate. Reports would be sent to Moscow in due course.

Tuesday 26th September 2006

SIS (MI6) HQ Vauxhall Cross London
The flight on the Monday from Paris had been uneventful, except for the usual ATC delays, meaning the BA flight was 25 minutes late on its Stand at London Heathrow.
On the Tuesday Harry was at Vauxhall Cross by 9.00am, catching up on any communications and regional Intel, before meeting the Deputy at 10.00am.
'Welcome back Harry. Sit thee down. We live in interesting times, don't we?'
Harry agreed,
No doubt at all, but there again, that's what we're here for, isn't it?' he said smiling at the Deputy.
'Can I start with my report I sent you, and the first matter, Charles Urwin?'
The Deputy nodded.
Harry then took him through the meeting with the High Commissioner, and his concern as to the mental fragility of Charles Urwin.
As a subset of that, concern had been raised as to whether he might do something of a violent nature, as a direct result of a possible nervous breakdown.
The HC was of the opinion that a nervous breakdown had taken place.
Harry asked if an additional resource could be assigned to Islamabad, under the heading of Security Analysis, or Security Inspection.
He referred to his previous experiences with Dai Evans, ex SAS, and asked if he could be re-assigned.
The Deputy said he would investigate, and revert.

Harry explained that it was very obvious that the HC was extremely worried as to the mental state and stability of Charles Urwin, and he had been surprised at being brought into the HC's confidence on this matter. To him it indicated concern of a very high and serious level.

Discussions then covered operating relationships with the US in Islamabad, Harry confirming that Jack DeCosta and he shared, wherever possible, Intel covering Pakistan, Afghanistan, and other neighbouring countries.

Although significant drone activity continued against militant and terrorist groups, little knowledge or publicity of this was finding its way into the world press.

It would ultimately, but for now such remote actions were remaining classified.

Harry also covered the question of unfettered arms deals in the region, dealers, and recipients. It was like the head of Medusa. Cut one off, another sprang up in their place.

The Deputy interrupted Harry at this point,

'Before you continue, let me bring you up to date with activity here in the UK.

There is an ever increasing risk of home grown jihadists, courtesy of our Government's policy of unlimited immigration, and superficial checking of so-called mullahs.

However, as you and I both understand, we must carry out the wishes of our political masters to the best of our ability, despite the introduction of legislation, which is apparently at odds with our best endeavours, which is to safeguard our country from external attack.

Recently I have had two meetings with our new DG.

On both occasions he has stressed the need for a complete review, top to bottom, left to right, as to our modus operandi within this New Age scenario, of empathy, inclusivity, ethnic diversity, etc, etc.
What have I forgotten? Oh yes, creating an environment that is women friendly, and therefore attracting more of them to the Service.
To this end, he has asked me to draw up a skeletal strategic document that can then be discussed with all relevant sectors and disciplines.
Assuming that gets past the first post, then we will 'flesh out' the document in more detail, now applying numbers to respective resources, the 'mix' of those resources, and financial numbers that will be considered 'sensible and sustainable' by Treasury in both the short, medium and longer term.'
He paused for breath at this point, allowing a look of exasperation to cross his face.
'Make of that what you will, but you can see, I am sure, the 'challenge' ahead.'
'Yes. But I'm ops. But where do I come in.'
'It's because you're ops, so that when it happens, I want you on the team when we are considering strategy, structure, and systems. Sharp end stuff, that the numbers boys at Treasury have no idea about whatsoever.
Nothing significant will happen before year end, I'll make sure of that. But I will want you back here January '07. Right?'
'Fully understood.'
'Now then, what else do I need to know?'
Harry gathered his thoughts.
'You remember I started seeing Anna Harrison some little time ago?'

'Yes. And, if I remember, I also cautioned you on the risk of such a relationship.'

'Yes you did. But it has developed, and you are no doubt aware from reports of our experiences in Lebanon and exit through Syria.'

'Yes.'

'Well to put it simply, the relationship has developed, and we are intending to get together.'

'Excuse me, but how the hell are you going to do that?'

'We don't know at present, but we are going to work on that.'

'Jesus Christ Harry, you're not serious are you?'

'Yes we are, and we recognise the difficulties.'

Both men fell silent for a minute, then Harry spoke again.

'Let me bring you up to date as to her present assignment.

As you know she is Mossad, and I understand she did a good job in Lebanon working with my friend, Alain Dubois of DGSE.

Both of them were embedded in AFD, the French Aid Agency, typical cover for intelligence penetration on the ground in specific countries.

Now she is back in Paris, and I understand that Mossad and DGSE have been getting into closer co-operation together over the last few months.

Following discussions at the appropriate level between DGSE and Mossad a tactical decision was made.

Because of her specific experience she has been assigned as Mossad Liaison Officer within DGSE HQ in Paris. Her ops name will be the same as that which she had in AFD, namely Anne Hardy.'

The Deputy's eyes widened a little.

'*And* what do you think is the purpose behind that?'

'Well, bearing in mind we, that is most Western Agencies, are supposed to be on the some side, working together, and sharing Intel, it would seem to be quite sensible.'
'But Harry, you know that is not the case. They'd scratch each other's eyes out to get an edge, when it came to Intel.'
'I agree, but I haven't said that to Anna. My own personal view is that this is a fishing trip by both DGSE and Mossad. See what she can find out. Are there bits we will share that we wouldn't have shared before? Will we get a clearer idea of reach and size by this placement? Will Mossad get a clearer idea of some of the French Foreign Ministry machinations in Central Africa? Possibly. Will the French get a clearer idea of Mossad covert ops in the Middle East and Gulf? Maybe.
The permutations are endless from both sides.'
'I agree Harry, but if I may pose a personal question, how are you going to carry on a relationship within that perspective?'
Harry smiled, a little weakly,
'A very good question, to which I don't have an answer right now.
All I know is, we're both going to try and make it work, although we both know it's going to be a bit long distance to begin with.'
'Well Harry, I wish you well. You do realise this information will be on your file? Please ensure you don't put yourself in a position where Internal Investigation gets involved. Conflict of interest or whatever.
Lastly, any comment to make re the Marion Simpson case?'
'I have submitted my report, evidence, tapes, photos etc.

Tom handled the interrogation, I was only observer other than one comment. It's all on file.
Tom will be able to handle the case as he carried out the investigation start to finish. I don't think I will be needed back in the UK, but will come if ordered.
Lastly, could you call in a few favours, and try and get Dai Evans out to me as soon as possible?'
The Deputy nodded.
'When are you going back to Islamabad?'
'Thursday, then refreshed for a start on Saturday.'
'Fine. All the very best Harry. Keep me up to speed in *all* areas,' he said smiling.
'I will,' said Harry, also smiling, as they shook hands.
The Deputy sat reflecting on what DGSE and Mossad had agreed. A Mossad Liaison Officer in DGSE. Interesting. Who knows, maybe two can play that game?
Now where is Dai Evans, and what was he doing?
He reached for his phone.

Saturday 30th September 2006

UK High Commission Islamabad
Harry asked to see the High Commissioner as soon as was convenient and was told 11.00am.
At the meeting Harry confined his comments to the question of Charles Urwin, the concerns expressed by the HC, and the possible provision of a 'watching brief' he had requested in London.
The HC thanked him for his actions and asked to be informed immediately of any news as to possible assignment.

Harry did not expand on the person he had requested. He had additional plans or responsibilities for Dai Evans, above and beyond, the basic 'babysitting'.

Sunday 1st October 2006

Anna's Apartment Paris
After the high of the previous weekend with Harry, Anna was feeling down.
She could sense the hurdles that she and Harry would have to overcome, plus the disadvantage of distance, and snatched times together. The perfect recipe for a disaster!
She shook herself angrily. Pull yourself together. Think of your father. Think of the challenges he and your mother faced. In comparison you have a stroll in the park.
She felt better after giving herself that talking to.

Week commencing Monday 2nd October 2006

Somewhere in Germany
The close support team car spun in its own length before sliding sideways into the Minister's Mercedes.
The position of the support car prevented the Minister and his aide from exiting safely, compounding the problem.
At this point a man ran out from behind some scrub carrying an automatic pistol, which he stuck through the side window of the support team car.
'Where did you stupid bastards learn to drive? Toy Town?' he shouted.

'Get out the bloody car, and stand over there', he said pointing to a small hut.
He waved at the 'Minister' and his 'Aide' to get out the other side of the Mercedes and told them to join him and the others in the hut.
Dai Evans was completely pissed off with the collection of Close Security and Escort teams he was supposed to be training in Germany.
Basic skills were lacking; silk purse and sow's ear sprang too readily to mind.
He ranted at them in a very firm and quietly deadly way, indicating that if no real progress was made he would fail them all, following which he would suggest 'pram walking' as a starter.
His mobile rang.
It was London.
As an ex-SAS specialist he was on Reserve call. This was such a call.
Get his arse back to London PDQ. Overseas assignment. His replacement on the course would be there in two days. Tell the trainees to go and get some driving lessons in the meantime!
No encouragement was needed as he briefed the trainees on the revised programme, and then made his way to Dusseldorf to catch a flight to London.
He made his way to the M.O.D. on the Tuesday where he was briefed as to the request that had been made for him by Harry Baxter.
Dai remembered him well. They had got on well. No bullshit. Says it as it is. Competent shot, not as good as him, but who is?
Yes, he'd be happy to work with him again.
Where was he now? Pakistan? Oh well, could be worse. Where in Pakistan? Islamabad. Never been there before. Closest was Afghanistan. Probably the same mix of devious untrustworthy bastards.

Hey Ho, could be interesting. Anyway a bloody sight better than having to teach a bunch of incompetents how to avoid crashing cars!
Arrangements were made for him to fly out on Thursday 5th September, and then get a full briefing on the Saturday from Harry Baxter.

High Commissioner's Office Islamabad
The HC was wondering how he could raise and resolve the current matter with Charles Urwin.
He decided that there was no soft way of dealing with this. It would have to be done in a sympathetic, but firm way, not allowing any counter argument, for which Charles was renowned.
He arranged a meeting with him for 5.00pm, this would ensure that most High Commission staff would be leaving, hopefully keeping their discussion confidential.
On time, Charles entered his office and sat down with a slight querying look on his face.
'Charles' said the HC, 'I need to discuss with you a somewhat sensitive issue.
Please bear with me, as my comments and suggestions will be made to you, with your own best interests at heart.'
Charles looked at him with an expression combining faint irritation and mock surprise.
'And my best interests are?'
'Let me expand.
You have recently gone through an extremely traumatic experience that has affected you and your whole family.
Due to the illegal activities of your brother-in-law you found yourself under suspicion. Subsequently

you were thoroughly investigated, and completely exonerated.'
'Yes?'
'As I said at a recent meeting, I could understand your anger directed against your brother-in-law, and your wish for him to face justice for his actions.'
Charles opened his mouth to speak, but the HC raised his hand.
'I therefore find myself in somewhat of a cleft stick.
Firstly, there is your present state of mind caused by the trauma, and secondly the impact this is having on your current actions and performance, which in turn could impact on your career.'
The HC paused, to let his words sink in.
Charles, who been listening intently, was also silent, as he collected his thoughts from behind an increasing red mist of muted anger.
'May I now, in turn, make a comment or two on what you have just said?'
'Of course. I trust that we can be open and frank with each other in this exchange as the satisfactory outcome can only be for the common good.'
'You have no idea what I have gone through over these past weeks, and the conflicting emotions I have felt during my investigation, and realisation of the criminal activities within my close family.'
'I most certainly do Charles, which is why we are having this discussion today.'
'I don't think so, but there is no point in arguing about it.
What I am trying to do, within my High Commission role as First Secretary, is to support you and HM Government policy, and at the same time try to assist my father-in-law with the

embarrassment he is experiencing as a result of his son's actions.

Frankly damn difficult!'

'I admire your verbal self-control Charles', the HC said smiling, 'I doubt if I could have limited my words thus, in a similar situation.

Continuing, he said, 'Now let me now speak very frankly.

I am of the opinion, rightly or wrongly, that you have, and continue to have, a form of nervous breakdown.

I am therefore instructing you to return to the UK for a proper medical examination, and following that to take at least one month's leave before I will consider your return to Islamabad.'

Charles opened his mouth to speak again, but the HC continued,

'There will be no discussion about this. That is my decision, and I instruct you and your wife, to return to the UK soonest, in order for the necessary examination and tests to take place.

I have already sent my report to London containing my decision.

Charles, it is for your own good, both physically and mentally. See it in that light.'

Charles remained silent, uncharacteristically so, before replying,

'If, after tests and a medical, I am shown to be completely unaffected by my recent experience, and that this then, in any way, affects my career within the Foreign Office, then I shall personally hold you responsible.'

'Charles, I understand your frustration, but it is for your own good. All of us, and yourself, must be satisfied we have done the right thing.

Now please go and organise your travel arrangements for you and your wife.'

Charles left without saying anything further, quietly fuming at what had been forced on him.

A discussion with his father-in-law was first on his agenda.

Whether his wife would want to go to London was another matter, some way down the to-do list.

Charles Urwin met with his father-in-law and explained, in truncated form, that he would have to go to London for a series of meetings, for how long, he was not sure.

Unfortunately, due to the confidential nature of the meetings, he could not divulge the subject matter, but was sure his father-in-law understood from his own Government experience.

Could he please keep a close family eye on his wife during his absence? This would be much appreciated.

He was now comfortable with what he would tell his wife, now also being corroborated by his father-in-law.

He could also use his London visit to massage a few relationships within the Foreign Office. Career planning was essential, and fundamental.

Tuesday 4th October 2006

Islamabad

Confirmation had been received by Harry that Dai Evans was on his way, and would be arriving Thursday the 5th.

He saw the HC briefly to advise him of timing, but then found himself being briefed on a previous decision by the HC concerning Charles Urwin.

It appeared that the First Secretary would be returning to the UK shortly, so the 'overview', by Dai Evans could be quite short.
Harry countered that by suggesting he could fully occupy Dai Evan's time, bearing in mind some of the joint Intel and activities now occupying him and the US Embassy.
This was not something the HC wished to be briefed on, but took Harry's word for it, as long as he was happy to take responsibility.
Harry agreed, thinking that asbestos lined fireproof trousers are mandatory kit issue for most HCs or Ambassadors!!

Thursday 5th October 2006

Islamabad International Airport
Dai Evans arrived on the Emirates flight at about 7.30am, having left London Heathrow the day before at 1.30pm, arriving in Dubai just after midnight, and catching the connection to Islamabad.
Looking somewhat bleary eyed at Harry, he grasped his hand in a firm grip, and said in his strong Welsh accent,
'Well, what sort of a bloody mess have you got yourself into, that requires my professional assistance?
I thought, after our last little exercise, you were reasonably competent to be let out on your own, but current events seem to indicate otherwise!'
The last few words were accompanied by a broad smile, as he slapped Harry on the back, and said,
For God's sake, get me somewhere for a decent cup of coffee. My mouth feels a bit like the bottom of a

month old parrot cage, the occupant of which had continence issues!'

Harry smiled; Dai hadn't changed, still a social disaster in mixed company, but bloody good at his job and with a lively, if unpredictable, sense of humour!

If the proverbial was about to hit the fan, he was just the man to have around.

They got that cup of coffee, and Harry brought him up to official speed. No detail on the reason for the 'overview', but general security issues being the main reason.

Secondary issues could include what was likely to be learned on joint Intel working with the CIA, and any specific intelligence on arms trading and distribution, particularly near the disputed NE Kashmir region.

'OK', said Dai, 'Which, specifically, are the areas where my consummate skills can be put to the best use?'

'Let's discuss this when your brain has caught up with your body on Saturday morning. Don't forget tomorrow is Holy Day, so just take things easy, get some sleep, and we will go through everything then. Alright?

Nobody needs sorting out straight away!'

They both laughed, both knowing they could rely on each other, with their own very different skills.

XX

Week commencing 9th October 2006

DGSE HQ Paris

Intelligence had been coming in from various regions, Eastern Europe, Gulf, Middle East, and Africa, some with connections to major French cities, Marseille and Paris, in particular.

With immigrant population influx across the Mediterranean, Marseille had a significant North African Arab quotient, in the main trying to earn a living, others involved in any illegal trade, including drugs and armaments. A northern area of Paris showed a similar demographic mix and social order.

Surveillance of one individual in Paris had shown connection with a visitor, known to DGSE, as a person of particular interest.

Phone taps of landline and mobiles indicated transportation of weapons through France, one to Paris, the other to the UK.

Backtracking from Paris to Marseille brought another connection who was responsible for transhipping the packages to Paris and the UK.

Re-routing of the package from Paris to London was now in train, shipping data analysis was reducing the number of consignments down to almost manageable numbers.

Last minute changes in routing would identify possible target.

Alain Dubois was studying the timeline of a number of consignments, which led back from France to the Middle East. There were a number of ‘lost’ or ‘broken’ weapon systems in various countries that later appeared in full working order in militant or terrorist hands.

He collated as much data as he could before seeing his Section Head.

‘You will recall a conversation I had with my contact Harry Baxter who spotted Azmat Kirmani on a plane from Dubai to Paris?’

‘Oui, je me souviens.’

‘As far as I can see there is a clear connection between Kirmani and Najjar who met him at the hotel in the Avenue Hoche, and the two shipments of weapons, one to Paris, the other to London, we are fairly sure.’

‘And your conclusion or proposal is?’

‘We need to cut off the head of this supply chain, so I am suggesting that as the prime sourcing seems to be controlled from Pakistan, that I go to Islamabad, link up with Harry Baxter, share our intelligence and resources and cut that umbilical cord, as soon as is possible.’

‘I see your reasoning but if one of the weapon systems is destined for here, Paris, should you not liaise with DST (Direction de la Surveillance du Territoire) to bring this to their attention, and cover any eventuality?’

‘Yes, I agree; I’m actually thinking of the longer term, say in a few weeks’ time when we have a clearer picture of what is happening here in Paris. With your agreement I will contact DST and bring them up to date.’

‘Bon, allez!’

The discussions finished, Alain contacted DST for a meeting later that day.

--

In a Northern suburb of Paris Nabil Selmi had received his package. He had collected it from the depot and moved it by van to a lock up. But he was worried about a number of things.

Would he be able to carry out his Jihad? Would the arrangements involving his friend Salim Matoub be watertight? Would his previous training be sufficient to handle the weapon system?

His life is in Allah's hands. He must trust his faith.

--

The DST officer shook Alain Dubois by the hand and indicated a chair.

Three other DST colleagues were present as Alain covered old ground in his briefing.

With the division of responsibility between DGSE (External of France), and DST (Internal France), it was vital to have all the cards face up on the table, in a joint operation such as this.

Data from DGSE was fed into the DST computers, running highly sophisticated algorithms, giving the ability to pick up 'trace' connections, whether, verbal or message, and basic code. Date comparison and time lining of messages and meetings, coincidental or otherwise, would be thrown up, together with any surveillance reports carrying similar connections.

It became clear that DST had a significant number of suspects under observation, with several, perhaps, fitting the profile of committed jihadists, and in one or two cases, prepared for suicide missions.

Having narrowed down potential suspects, additional surveillance, electronic and physical, was initiated with an exchange of data and reports every 48 hours.

Alain returned to his office, completed a report for his Section Head, and briefed Anne Hardy on progress to date.

High Commission Islamabad

The HC called in Harry to his office on the Monday to tell him he was posting Charles Urwin back to the UK for a medical review and tests. It was anticipated that he would leave sometime this week.

He also said that it was not something that had been debated.

Therefore, the scope and role of Dai Evans was to be Harry's responsibility, something, incidentally, that Harry had already planned for.

On the previous Saturday Harry had given Dai Evans a full briefing of events that had led up to his arrival, whilst maintaining a certain level of confidentiality concerning Charles Urwin's return to the UK.

He dealt at some length with the activities of Azmat Kirmani, the illicit and extensive arms trade in Pakistan, the regional effects such as Kashmir in the NE, and the region in the SE close to the Afghanistan border.

In particular he described some of the approaches being made by certain village elders in the NE region to the authorities in Islamabad, who found themselves repeatedly caught between the militants and government Forces, often with severe loss of life.

One such village area was near Masjid.

In recent discussions Inspector Chaudhry of the FIA, had given his tacit approval for Harry to go to the area for a meeting with a village elder to hear of their concerns. The FIA must keep a neutral stance on this otherwise accusations at government level would be made.

To try and make sense of it all, is almost impossible to a Western mind. There appears to be the irreconcilable mix of tribe, region, and religion, which produces a sticky morass, totally devoid of logic and resolution.

Dai had some pungent observations.

'Well, my take on it is this.

If they are hurting us, anywhere, then in my book, I can hurt them anywhere.

I don't take too kindly to havin' the shit kicked out of me, when we are sending financial aid to these b*****s, for which we get no bloody Thank You!'

'OK, Dai, calm down.

We are having to play the Good Cop to their Bad Cop. AND we are not going to change how they carry on! That's genetic! Whatever we are doing it has to be low key.

Certainly no full frontal! Do I make myself clear?'

'Absolutely. But if push comes to shove, then I am not going to ask the bastards to sit down, and have a chat about it. OK?'

'Understood.

Now let me tell you what is happening in the disputed Kashmir region, and why you and I will be involved.'

Wednesday 11th October 2006

SIS (MI6) Vauxhall Cross London

MI5 had been in contact.

Their own electronic surveillance teams had been reviewing considerable amounts of 'chatter', some from the Midlands, some from SE London.

With initial information from MI6, who in turn, were sharing some data from DGSE in Paris, they had started to keep a closer eye on certain individuals in the Brixton area.
Indeterminate activity at present, but association with extremist groups and firebrand mullahs at certain mosques warranted the overview.
Preventative measures are very necessary.

Thursday 12th October 2006

DGSE HQ Paris
Tracking of the weapons packages was now very focussed.
The Paris one had been identified, and location confirmed.
DST were about to raid the delivery address.
The UK package routing had been changed, and was, as yet, not determined.
Several routes could be taken by lorry.
The usual short cross channel routes, Calais/ Boulogne to Dover/Folkestone, or maybe the Hook of Holland to Harwich.
Longer routes would be Dieppe/Le Havre to Newhaven, or Caen to Portsmouth, or Cherbourg to Poole/Portsmouth. An even longer routing would be Roscoff to Plymouth.
Would this be handled by a reputable logistic company, or would a small, no questions asked, operator be used?
Needles in haystacks spring to mind.
Local agents of DST were briefed, some embedded at ports, others within commercial organisations.

In a northern suburb of Paris, two unmarked black Citroen vans made their way down from opposite ends of a rundown street. It was 7.30pm.
They stopped about 50 metres apart, and both engines were switched off.
The rear doors opened, and a number of balaclava wearing DST officers, carrying small arms, moved quietly and quickly into position. Some of the detail moved down an alleyway to the rear of the building.
At a visual signal the front door of the building was smashed open, and the officers poured in shouting instructions to the residents, most of whom were staying behind locked doors.
Arriving on the second floor, the officers burst open the door into the one bedroom apartment, number 8.
No one was there.
They searched the room quickly. It was obvious that whoever had been there had left, with no intention of returning.
Interviews were then carried out with the remaining residents, who confirmed they had not seen the occupant of number 8 for several days.
Disappointed at no result the DST team withdrew, carefully placing the broken external door in an upright position adjacent to the opening.

In a lock up, about 400metres from his previous one bedroom flat, Nabil Selmi was now checking the weapon system in the back of his Renault van.
All would appear to be in good condition, and could be assembled, and disassembled easily.
He was now staying with a relative of Salim Matoub.

Therefore no trace of his present address.
This would be good for the period leading up to his Jihad. Allahu Akbar.

In the French Port of Cherbourg the lorry made its way slowly forward in the queue for the ferry to Poole.
It was fairly nondescript, not one of the big transport group trucks that routinely used this crossing.
The DST agent decided that it was probably worth noting this back to HQ, so telephoned the company name, registration number and manifest details immediately.
Checks were run. Shady company, several large question marks, no prosecutions or arrests, but due to lack of evidence still in operation. A strong possibility?
The Intel gathered was sent to the Security Service (MI5) London under their co-operation agreement.

Monday16th October 2006

SIS (MI6) Vauxhall Cross London
Intelligence received by MI5, cross checked and confirmed by GCHQ, indicated some possible attack on a government building.
It being mainland Britain, MI5 were taking priority, but in order to make sure the left hand knew what the right hand was doing on this occasion, ensured MI6 were kept in the loop.
Recent Intel from DST in France suggested initiating surveillance on a particular vehicle, passing through Poole.

However, electronic police checks on many thousands of vehicles produced nothing, suggesting perhaps, a change of the French number plate, details of which would not be thrown up on the UK system.

The trail had gone cold, and trying to find one French truck in the South of England would be a non-starter.

It was at about 11.00am that the Deputy received a request from the DG to see him at noon.

At the due time the Deputy entered the DG's office.

'Come in Norman, take a pew.

I was wondering how progress was being made on our embryonic restructuring, or making us 'fit for purpose', as some Ministers seem to want to describe us and others.'

'To be frank, not a lot.

If you recall, I submitted a list of criteria that would require some definition, before I would be able to, at least, get a feel for an outline structure.

You, very kindly, gave me some generalised responses that go some way in assisting me, but I was going to contact you, in any case, to discuss them further, and to get a sense of priority in a number of cases.

In changing from our present organisation to the sort of structure you indicated, it is not only the structural changes that are significant, and my, are they significant, but involve a paradigm cultural shift at one and the same time.

I'm sure you can see where I'm coming from?'

The DG had been listening carefully, and for once was lost for words.

He was not used to the Deputy using the sort of management HR speak that was second nature to him.

The content and flow would require a considered response.
'Norman, you're absolutely right. Let's make a date to meet, and discuss further some of those parameters and guidelines. Perhaps then, we might be able to get some more flesh on the bones of the body corporate!'
He chuckled as he said the last few words, putting a hand on the Deputy's shoulder, and guiding him out of his office.
'Let's say about 10 days' time, shall we?'
The Deputy went back to his office, thinking that a quick read of the 'HR Guide to Buzz Words' had certainly helped on this occasion!
Better box something together for 10 days' time. Another glance at the book might give him some more convincing phrases!

Wednesday 17th October 2006

FIA HQ Islamabad
A meeting had been arranged for Harry to introduce Dai Evans to Inspector Irfan Chaudhry.
Sitting in the Inspector's office Harry was giving him a précis of Dai Evan's experience both in the SAS and subsequently.
This was done to ease Chaudhry's concerns about the proposed trip into the NE region to hold discussions with a particular village elder.
Over a period of weeks, messages had been arriving at the High Commission, mostly guarded in content and tone, but still giving a clear message. In a village near Masjid, the villagers, in modern parlance, have found themselves to be between a rock and a hard place.

Not far away is the disputed territory of Kashmir, a running sore between Pakistan and India.

The region is home to independent militias, some being funded and supplied by each side.

Running concurrently is the thriving illegal arms trade, where for modest sums, sophisticated weaponry is bought and sold.

This particular village, had experienced tragedy in the deaths of a number of its young men, and the fact that its territory is frequently a battleground for factional interests.

One elder has had enough. Hence the guarded messages.

He had turned to the High Commission really as a last resort, perhaps hoping for some small breath of neutrality, in a hugely destructive issue.

Harry had explained the background in some detail to Inspector Chaudhry, which had also brought Dai up to the mark.

Harry had one last observation to make,

'I can understand, that after so many years the villagers are fed up to the back teeth with their country being used as a fighting zone, and so many families being severely hurt or destroyed.

From my own and the High Commission's point of view, we are looking at this as a situation that requires the intervention of say, an Aid Agency, not necessarily for funds, but a way in which focus can be brought to bear that will embarrass, perhaps, the Pakistan Government, to get involved and sort it out.

If, by our visit, we are able to get some lines of communication open, and people have a better understanding of what is happening, then we will have succeeded.'

Inspector Chaudhry then gave his own comments,

‘Harry, I understand completely the village contact that has produced your response.
However, there are certain things you should be additionally aware of before you go.
Whilst recognising the description of what the villagers have been suffering, be under no delusion of what is actually happening.
There are a number of very powerful men running these operations in that region, some with significant backing and support from friendly and unfriendly governments.
They will not take too kindly to interference from members of the British High Commission, whether well intentioned or otherwise.
Their reactions will not be at all diplomatic, and I am afraid to say, could be fatal, in an extreme case.
Therefore if you decide to go, you must realise that any support from my own Department would be limited in the extreme.
I am, therefore, very sorry I can’t be more helpful.’
‘Well’ said Harry smiling, ‘I am under no delusion that things may get a bit sticky, but my High Commissioner is happy for me to, at least, give it a go!’
‘I wish you the best of luck Harry. By the way, can I confirm your mobile number that you gave me previously?’
Harry provided his number, thanked him for his advice, and said he would give him a report after their visit to the NE region, which would probably take place in about a month’s time, due to other pressing matters at the High Commission.

Thursday 18th October 2006

Israeli Embassy Paris

Mossad Head of Station sat listening to Anne Hardy as she updated him on her current ops status in DGSE.

'One of the problems is the fact that I do not have, as yet, any real intelligence to give them from our side. What you have sent across is pretty low grade, and with not much detail.'

At this he smiled.

'Anne, I want to draw them out. See if they complain, suggesting it is unbalanced. We are getting more Intel from them than from us, you know the sort of thing.

If they raise it officially then our response will be something along the lines of; 'Tell us which regions are your focus, then we can focus on providing the right sort of Intel'.

It is very early in the relationship, so there are bound to be mini-problems like this.'

'OK, but I'm not exactly overstretched at the moment. In fact it is fairly boring. However there is one op that is occupying them at present, and that is a threatened attack on somewhere important.

It is clearly Arab/North African Arab in origin, but would appear to have a Pakistani and Hezbollah connection respectively for funding and weapon supply.'

Her Head of Station was interested in this, but said as it is a Metropolitan France op, then DGSE and DST would be involved. He did not think there could be any input from Mossad at this point.

Friday 19th October 2006

Foreign Office Whitehall London

They had lunched well at the Athenaeum Club on Pall Mall.

Now they were sitting quietly in a corner of the Morning Room, savouring a port and a brandy.

Charles Urwin was appreciating the gesture of the lunch invitation from a senior colleague, Quentin Horncastle, in the Foreign Office.

He respected the man, certainly someone of a similar intellectual capability.

Since his return to London, Charles had gone through the tiresome exercise of medical examinations and psychological tests, including the rather demeaning psychometric tests, which he found somewhat amusing, if not challenging, or even vaguely worthy of examination.

As far as he could gather from the medical staff, he had been suffering from acute stress, now receding, and which could be treated with a short term parcel of pills, and further rest.

The other tests had shown his normal mental state to be somewhat obsessive, but not overly so.

In terms of stress, the condition linked to recent experiences was to be expected. Some modest medication would certainly stabilise this in the short term.

Overall assessment concluded that full recovery would be achieved in the short term, with medication as prescribed, and further rest taken as leave.

The discussions over lunch had ranged far and wide, but now Quentin Horncastle brought some focus to them.

‘Charles, you have been in Islamabad now for over two years. What do you think you want to be doing next?’

Charles took his time before responding. No point in being hasty, gives the impression you have it all planned out. No, let the inquisitor think he’s guiding you, assuming that’s where you want to be led!

‘Well, I do have a considerable experience now in a number of regions, which must be of benefit down the line for the FCO.

I know what my own personal ambitions are,’ he said, trying to smile in a modest way, ‘but my career path is something that will be decided by others.

Naturally I wish to serve my country well, where my particular skills can be best employed.

As you know, I tend to thrive on challenges, albeit not every 24 hours, every day!

Perhaps in your position Quentin, you are able to advise, or guide me, in terms of my future appointments?’

Quentin smiled at this point, recognising that Charles was gently casting a fly on the water.

‘What I do know Charles, is that your name came up at a career review meeting last week, and I was asked to have a gentle conversation with you as to two alternative appointments.

Let me elaborate.’

Quentin outlined the two, one which caught Charles’ imagination, the other really more of the same that had gone before.

Charles, although sure in his own mind as to his choice, asked to be able to consider the alternatives and revert after the weekend. Measured consideration always looks better, he felt.

'Certainly Charles, let's talk next week. Make it Wednesday. Policy meetings Monday and Tuesday.'

Weekend 21st/22nd October 2006

Islamabad/Paris telephone link

Harry and Anne spoke at length on the Saturday.

The conversation started quickly, describing in a roundabout way, what they had been doing since their weekend in Paris.

After that exchange it softened, words coming more slowly, as the distance between them became more apparent.

'Missing you' was mentioned several times, carrying with the words the strong feelings each felt for the other.

Each was reluctant to end the call, but finally it was done, allowing reflection and comfort to take over, the strength of the spoken word being immeasurable.

Monday 23rd October 2006

UK High Commission Islamabad

Jack DeCosta was discussing the Kashmir region with Harry, and the possible meeting to be held with a specific village elder.

'Can you really see some major benefit from that?' Jack asked.

'Some. Let me expand.

The particular groups in that region rule by fear, coercion, and murder.

This is a man, we think, who is prepared to stand up and be counted. There are not many like him in that region.
The militant groups thrive on publicity.
We need to puncture that particular balloon with some publicity of our own. The meeting is the first step.
I'm sure it is going to be bloody difficult, but we need to make those steps.'
'Fine, but be very careful. You know they are capable of changing their minds in an instant, dependent on how many dollars, or whatever, are waved in their faces.'
Dai Evans entered at this point carrying a bulky MOD canvas bag.
'Latest welfare parcel from home, via the Diplomatic Bag,' he said smiling.
'And the goodies are?' enquired Harry.
Dai unzipped the bag and pulled out two SA80A2 assault rifles, 5.56mm calibre, plus several ammunition boxes.
'You requested these?'
'Well yes', Dai replied, 'you can't go up into that region carrying a pea shooter, can we now?'
Harry smiled.
'OK, but don't go waving them around. Keep them under lock and key until we go to the NE. Alright?'
'Will do.'
Jack suggested that he might come along as well, it being sensible to go in a two car convoy to the region, but Harry refused, saying this had to be a very discrete approach, and without drawing much attention to the visit.

Wednesday 25th October 2006

ISI HQ Islamabad

The officer had been fully briefed.

He would be driving from Islamabad to Kabul in Afghanistan, via Peshawar, crossing the border at Torkham, and then on to Kabul, via the Jalalabad/Kabul Highway.

A distance of 475 kms, taking about 6 hours by car.

The Dragunov SVD Sniper rifle, 7.62 mm calibre, in its special case, would be bolted underneath his vehicle.

Little or no checking takes place at the border, plus he would be carrying a legitimate Diplomatic Passport which would obviate any potential search.

Once in Kabul he would be accommodated in a safe house for the period of his mission, following which the car would be abandoned, and probably torched.

He would then take a flight from Kabul back to Islamabad the following day, (there are three flights a day), travelling on another Diplomatic Passport, this one showing an entry stamp into Kabul International Airport from the week before.

He would travel to Kabul on Friday, the 27th October 2006, roads would be less crowded, and border crossing guards less interested on the holy day.

Foreign Office Whitehall London

Quentin Horncastle had scheduled a meeting, starting at about 11.00am, for himself and Charles Urwin to discuss further the options he had outlined at their last meeting.

Quentin Horncastle was a classic Whitehall mandarin.
Educated at a 'good' school, he was destined for Oxbridge, reading PPE, and dutifully following in his father's footsteps, both at school and Oxbridge.
People like Quentin are mostly concerned with Policy or Strategy, hardly ever Implementation.
That can be fairly contentious, and a bit grubby, if major 'change' has to take place. It also, unfortunately, seems to gather the venal media reporters around like flies around the jam pot, asking either embarrassing or inconvenient questions, apparently only designed to hinder the change process.
No, people like Quentin Horncastle preferred to work quietly in the shadows of their political masters, creating a working policy or strategy, that is recognised for its worth in due course.
Publicity is not something they wish to garner. The reverse is indeed the case, as political masters may come and go; they, the permanent cadre must maintain stability at all times, whatever the political cost.
Quentin greeted Charles warmly.
'Sit down Charles. Trust you have had sufficient time to consider the content of our discussions last week?'
'Yes indeed.'
'Good. Would you like to expand?'
'Your first proposal certainly fired my enthusiasm, and I hope that I may be favourably be considered for that role.
May I say that the second option struck me as merely being a variation of what I have been doing currently. The challenge of the first is what attracts me.'

The discussion then pursued in more detail the scope of the preferred option, which in general terms covered the following.

Charles Urwin would now remain in the UK at the Foreign & Commonwealth Office in Whitehall.

His medical examination and other tests were considered satisfactory for his continuing career.

His appointment and grade would be as a Director, with specific responsibility for the Middle East and Gulf, plus Pakistan and India.

It had been indicated to him, by Quentin Horncastle, that there was a very strong possibility for advancement to the next grade, being Director General, within a comparatively short time scale, subject to his demonstration, which was not in doubt, of his professional competence, and the forecast retirement of an existing DG.

Naturally, his wife should return to the UK as soon as satisfactory arrangements could be made.

If he agreed then the High Commissioner in Islamabad would be informed immediately, so that a replacement could be considered as a matter of urgency.

Quentin wrapped up the meeting by saying, with a half-smile on his face,

'Well Charles, do I inform your High Commissioner that he needs a replacement First Secretary?'

'If, by that question, you are indicating that I could be fortunate enough to have secured the appointment we have discussed, then my answer is Yes!'

They shook hands, and then walked up Whitehall to Admiralty Arch, along the Mall and up the Duke of York Steps to the Athenaeum Club for a second lunch in under a week.

Charles now felt more content, thinking, that in his new position, this gave him a much closer view of the snowy heights, whilst providing him with enough power and influence to make certain individuals lives fairly unpleasant, if not miserable. Quentin Horncastle would signal Islamabad on Thursday the 26th, leaving Charles to contact his wife to advise her where his future now lay.

Sunday 29th October 2006

UK High Commission Islamabad

The High Commissioner called Harry to his office, where he was sitting at his desk, looking somewhat thoughtful.

'I received a missive from the FCO, sent Thursday, advising that Charles Urwin will be staying in London, having been re-assigned in a new role.

Therefore I should make representations to them for his replacement, and assist his wife in her return to the UK.

In veiled commentary it appears he passed muster in both medical and psychological examinations.'

Harry remained silent. There was not a lot he could say.

The HC observed, 'I must say, I find the workings in London, at times, extremely strange, and totally inconsistent.

I shall, of course, ask for a replacement. We will just have to see who that is.'

'If there is anything I can do to assist in the meantime, just tell me', said Harry.

'I appreciate your gesture Harry. I may well call on you in the following days. Thank you.'

Monday 30th October 2006

3.00pm Kabul Afghanistan

The man lay on the flat roof of the single storey house in the shadow created by the large A/C unit.

He was dressed in typical Afghan clothes and head gear.

Cradled in his arms was a Dragunov SVD Sniper rifle, 7.62 mm calibre, a weapon with an excellent effective range of 800 metres, and a maximum of 1300 metres.

He was looking thorough the telescopic sight at the entrance of the hotel, no more than 400 metres away.

The telescopic sight gave the effect that he was only about 75 metres away with superb clarity, as the hotel entrance was bathed in sunlight.

There was the usual traffic and city noise surrounding the area as two men exited from the hotel, walking quickly towards a private vehicle.

The man in front was looking left and right as he reached for the rear door to open it.

The second man, about 3 metres behind the first, wearing dark glasses, was looking straight ahead, as a single bullet caught him in his left chest.

As he was spun round the second bullet caught him in his back on the left side.

He was dead before his body hit the ground.

The first man turned in shock, as he heard the faint shots, and the sound of the body hitting the ground.

He looked around wildly, throwing himself to the ground, not knowing the source or direction of the shots.

No further shots were fired.

The sniper, by now, had quickly crawled round into the far lee of the AC unit, hidden from the hotel, and was disassembling his weapon back into a shabby workman's bag.

He waited for about 15 minutes, whilst initial help was provided by the hotel, an ambulance called, and two relatively ineffective policeman arrived on the scene.

Making his way downstairs he exited at the rear of the building, climbed into a shabby, nondescript small Toyota saloon and drove off, away from the direction of the hotel.

In Kabul the incident would probably receive no mention either on TV or in the press. At most a press reference to an unexplained assassination on a back page.

The sniper texted 'kar liyaa' (done) to a number, before stopping and destroying the phone.

In Islamabad, at ISI HQ, the message was received and noted.

The next day at a review meeting of current operations, one file was redlined through, and 'Completed' written across its front diagonally.

It was the file of Azmat Kirmani.

--

On the same day, 30th October 2006, in Pakistan, the Chenagai airstrike allegedly aimed at Ayman al-Zawahiri (the leader of Al Qaeda) destroys a madrassa in Bajaur area and kills 70–80 people. Pakistani military officials claim they were militants while provincial minister Siraj al-Haq and a local eyewitness said they were innocent pupils resuming studies after the Muslim Eid holidays.

Lies, counter lies, and somewhere, conveniently hidden, is the truth.

--

Thursday 2nd November 2006

DGSE HQ Paris

The team was facing a conundrum.

Electronic intercepts had picked up a considerable amount of traffic, but it was one conversation that was attracting considerable attention at this time.

The difficulty was the interpretation.

The language was mixture of North African French, mixed with the local patois or dialect.

The gist of the conversation, part humorous, part threatening, was saying, in effect that,

'The Hôtel will really top the Hôtel de Ville completely.'

Working on the assumption that there would be the possibility of a rocket attack against the Hôtel de Ville, then from where? There are no hotels in the immediate vicinity of the Hôtel de Ville, only the Ile de la Cité to the south, and clustered narrow streets to the north, with the exception of the Rue de Rivoli.

It would be impossible to launch an attack from the Rue de Rivoli, a one way street, with its very fast moving traffic.

It didn't make any sense, but at the same time they knew an attack was planned and probably imminent.

Alain discussed the latest situation with his Section Head,

'It doesn't add up. We know, or think we know, what they are planning, but as to target it is not at all clear.'

'Spread your view wider Alain. Look at other areas in Paris. Are there smaller municipal town halls that could be a target?

These jihadists don't give a damn as long as they get the publicity, and take out innocent people at the same time.'

[Translation: Hôtel de Ville = Town Hall]

MI6 HQ Vauxhall Cross London

The Deputy had been called by Tom Denman.

'Yes Tom. What is it?'

'I've been keeping a watching brief on a number of areas whilst Harry has been in Pakistan, as you instructed.

One in particular seems to have both a French and UK connection.'

'Specifics Tom.'

'Similar 'chatter' picked up would indicate some sort of action both in London and Paris. We have shared Intel with DGSE, etc, but unable to pin down specifics.

You said to keep you informed, hence my call.'

'Correct Tom.

As it's a home grown problem as well, keep the Security Service in the loop. If anything happens they will have to act.

Keep me informed if status moves up a notch or two.'

Tom was wondering what the likely targets would be, current chatter giving no clues, just the usual rants against the West, and the hope of a world Caliphate.

XXI

PARIS

Palais Bourbon; Assemblée Nationale Paris

Standing in front of the Hôtel de Crillon, looking across the Place de la Concorde and then the Pont de la Concorde, which crosses the Seine, one can see an imposing building, the Palais Bourbon. It is the home of the French Government, namely the Assemblée Nationale, in which 577 Deputies govern France.

From the roof of the Hôtel de Crillon there is a clear line of sight, of no more than 600 metres, to the Palais Bourbon.

2.30am Wednesday 8th November 2006

Hôtel de Crillon Paris France

Nabil Selmi drove the Renault delivery van into the reserved area at the rear of the hotel where he was met by Salim Matoub.

They conversed in low tones, the hotel being at its quietest at this time.

They quickly unloaded the box, roughly just over a metre long and 500mm square in cross section, from the rear of the van onto a small trolley and took it to an adjacent service lift.

Markings on the box indicated heating and ventilation equipment from a well-known French company.

Arriving at the top level, Salim looked out before waving to Nabil to carefully push the trolley along the narrow passage way between heating and air conditioning equipment. Further along they passed

a series of water tanks and pumps, plus a number of lift head mechanisms.
Steel steps at the end led to a door, which, in turn, led onto the roof of the hotel.
The box was manhandled up the steps and through the door, where, stepping out into the cool evening air Nabil could see, about 15 metres away, a small structure, which had been the top of one of the original lifts in the hotel, now empty except for storing some small items of maintenance equipment.
Salim helped him to move the box inside, and also assisted in ensuring that the top of the box was opening readily.
Nabil gave the Renault keys to Salim, who shook him by the hand and returned the way he came.
Nabil took care to lock himself in, and having rolled out a futon, which he had carried in the box, bedded down for the rest of the short night.
Salim, having retraced his steps, went back to the Renault, and drove it off in the direction of Paris Nord.
No notice had been taken of the small amount of activity in the delivery area, a common occurrence on any weekday night.
At 6.00am Nabil sponged himself and made his morning prayers, including some for blessings, support and courage for his jihad.
He ate the sparse rations he had brought with him, and tied around his head his old Hezbollah bandage.
At about 9.00am he started his preparations. Unpacking the crate, he laid out the components on the floor, carefully checking each one.
Then, very methodically, he assembled the unit.

It was an Iranian Saeghe, a reverse engineered copy of the American M47 Dragon Anti-tank missile system. A comparatively simple, but very effective shoulder fired weapon, designed initially as an anti-tank weapon carried by infantry. Comparatively low weight and simple in operation ensured its success.

With the ammunition he had, he could easily fire from this position over a distance of about 600 metres, maximum range of the weapon being 1000 metres.

He had three rockets. With careful sighting and execution they could cause enormous damage, death to a number of people, and public panic.

--

11.15am DGSE Team Hôtel de Ville Paris

Alain's team had prepared thoroughly for any eventuality at the Hôtel de Ville.

It is a huge building, so total lockdown is almost impossible.

Armed response teams were located at strategic points, with observers located on the roof with wide scan vision equipment.

All were linked by radio, silence being maintained at present.

Alain had located himself on one of the upper floor outer abutments which gave him at least a 270° view.

At about 12.20 his radio crackled into life.

It was one of his analysts back at HQ, asking if he could speak.

'Yes, but be quick,' he replied testily, knowing that the individual, although very bright, had no concept of the word 'brevity'!

‘I’ve been thinking a lot about the Hôtel de Ville question and possible coding.’

‘Yes, you, me, and others, have given it a lot of thought.’

The analyst continued, sounding slightly hurt at the sarcastic response.

‘Well,’ he said defiantly, ‘I think when they say Hôtel de Ville, they could be referring to the Palais Bourbon, and the Assemblée Nationale.’

Alain did not interrupt.

‘And when they say Hôtel, it could be the Hôtel de Crillon. From the roof, max 600 metres in a straight line.’

‘You could be right. Well done and Thanks. Now get off the line.’

Alain gave instructions for alert watch to be maintained at the Hotel de Ville, as he raced down the stairs to his car.

Leaping into his vehicle, he also radioed for assistance, both city Police and Air Gendarme with a staccato description of what they might expect.

With his lights flashing and siren wailing, he accelerated up the Rue de Rivoli in the direction of the Place de la Concorde, and the location of the Hôtel de Crillon.

Passing the Tuileries Gardens on his left, he looked up to see a Police Nationale helicopter overtake him flying towards the hotel.

11.00am 8th November 2006

London

On the south side of the river Thames, by Hungerford Bridge, is a public car park, which, from the South East corner one can see, across the river, in a westerly direction, the Houses of Parliament.

A white van, one of the many innocuous unidentifiable vehicles that inhabit London, drove into the car park and located itself on the SE side, with its rear doors facing up river.

Inside, laying on the van floor, was a US made Javelin Anti-tank missile system. The weapons had initially been supplied in quantity to Jordan, but unfortunately poor 'housekeeping' had resulted in the 'loss or misplacement' of a small number.

Amri Behar, sweating slightly, was loading the first rocket and placing the second close at hand, hoping that when the time came he would achieve his Jihad against the West.

Hanif, the trained assistant, could see the nervous actions of Amri and leant across and gripped his wrist.

'My brother, be brave. We have trained and are ready. The Kuffars deserve what Allah (peace be upon him) decides. If we die we have given our lives for the Jihad.

Allahu Akbar.'

Amri nodded his head and echoed, 'Allahu Akbar'.

--

At 11.50am, the House of Commons chamber was already full with MPs debating various issues, and looking forward to Prime Minister's Question Time. Checking his watch Hanif opened the back doors of the van a quarter in order to see out.

From where the van was sitting he could see, in a straight line, past the left side of the London Eye giant Ferris wheel, the Parliament buildings on the North side of the Thames. The distance was about 880 metres.

The location was perfect. What they had researched and planned was correct.
He turned to Amri.
'Now is the time.'
Amri nodded, a thin film of sweat covering his top lip.

1.00pm Wednesday 8th November 2006

Hotel Le Crillon Paris France.
Nabil Selmi lay on the right side of the old lift head, bracing his left side against its wall.
Through the sight of the Saeghe anti-tank weapon he could clearly see the Palais Bourbon, its rich classical external columns and decoration highly visible in the autumn sun.
One rocket as a direct hit to the front, he thought, the second through the roof.
The continuous noise of traffic rose up from the Place de la Concorde and Champs Elycée, partially distracting him from other sounds. Additionally, the lift head structure was blocking sound to the East of him along the Seine, and particularly the Rue de Rivoli.
As he took aim he was not aware, either by sight or sound, of the Police Nationale helicopter proceeding in a westerly direction along the Rue de Rivoli at a height of 150 metres.
It was a clear, sunny day and the pilot and co-pilot were studying the roof tops as they approached the Place de la Concorde.
As the helicopter arrived to the north of the Place de la Concorde, it then turned south towards the Seine and the Pont de la Concorde.

Looking down through the clear plastic nose of the helicopter the co-pilot saw a strong glint of sun reflected off something below him. It was moving slightly.

He indicated to the pilot to fly lower and then saw the outstretched body on the roof of Le Crillon hotel. Simultaneously, Nabil, now fully aware of the chattering helicopter passing above him, looked up to see the aircraft descending towards him.

Panicking, he looked quickly through the RPG sight at the Palais Bourbon and pulled the trigger.

With a huge after flash the rocket was on its way.

11.58am 8th November 2006

Hungerford Bridge Car Park London

Amri positioned himself, kneeling, on the floor of the van.

The first rocket had been inserted and a panel removed from the side of the vehicle to allow the after blast to escape.

Hanif was standing by the rear doors.

'Are you ready?'

Amri nodded nervously.

'Allahu Akbar', Hanif said, his voice rising in pitch.

'Allahu Akbar', replied Amri, pulling the trigger.

The after blast in the confined space was huge.

Although there was no recoil Amri was not properly anchored to the floor, and as the missile was launched he slipped over on his side, whereupon the after blast easily ripped through the floor and the panel that had been removed.

Hitting the petrol tank the after blast created almost instant ignition.

Hanif and Amri, partially stunned by the explosion, tried to escape by the back doors of the van but had already been engulfed by flaming petrol.
Pedestrians, by the entrance to the car park, who had stopped in shock as the rocket had been fired and the subsequent explosion, looked on horrified as two burning bodies fell from the blazing van and collapsed onto the ground.
In the House of Commons the Prime Minister was just entering the chamber as the rocket grenade started its flight.

1.05pm 8th November 2006

Hotel Le Crillon Paris France.
Nabil Selmi scrambled to his feet looking up at the helicopter that was now no more than 30 metres above his head.
He cursed in Arabic, whilst shaking his fist, finally shouting 'Allahu Akbar' at the top of his voice, before turning and walking off the edge of the roof, falling to his death on the Place de la Concorde, in front of frightened and horrified Parisians and tourists.
The rocket's initial blast and roar had alerted pedestrians in the Place de la Concorde who had looked up to see the grenade passing over the square. It was wobbling in its flight, due to the hasty ill-timed launch, which was increasing rapidly in intensity, resulting in a spiral dive into the Seine just east of the Pont de la Concorde.
Combusting immediately, it sent a 30 metre spout of water into the air close to the bridge, luckily with no fatalities, but soaking a number of

pedestrians on the east side, who had flung themselves to the ground.
Meanwhile, the Police Nationale helicopter was given clearance to land in the Place de la Concorde, local gendarmes clearing the locality for the landing, and also cordoning off the area surrounding the body of Nabil Selmi.
Alain Dubois, who was driving down the Rue de Rivoli, siren wailing, was approaching the Place de la Concorde, when he suddenly saw the rocket launch from the top of the hotel, his stomach tightening in dread of what could follow.
As he entered La Place de la Concorde and swung his car towards Le Crillon Hotel, he saw a body falling from the roof, narrowly missing the pedestrians in front.
He skidded to a halt, leaping out of his car and pushing his way through the gawping crowd that was starting to gather around the body.
Waving his DGSE security pass he ordered the small crowd back, and enlisted the help of the police who were arriving on the scene from an adjacent traffic control point.
He took a quick look at the body, without disturbing it.
He recognised Nabil Selmi from previous CCTV and surveillance photographs.
His jihad was now finished.

London

House of Commons Westminster
The rocket sent on its way, but launched from an unstable position, took less than 10 seconds to traverse the Thames, hitting the water about 40 feet

from the terrace of the Commons that looks out onto the river. It was not occupied at that time as all MPs were crowding into the chamber to listen to Prime Minister's Question time.

As the Prime Minister stood up to the Dispatch Box the explosion of the anti-tank rocket was clearly heard, the majority of MPs flinching at the sound and tremor that followed.

A small number standing by the doors of the chamber withdrew, and ran out onto the terrace to see what had happened.

The disturbed water was already settling down.

Apparently the only casualty was the destruction of a small motor boat with two occupants, one of whom was trying to swim to the bank, the other motionless, lying face down in the water.

A Police Patrol launch, normally on duty near the House of Commons, was already making its way across the river to pick up the man swimming, and retrieve the motionless body.

--

Two weeks later 22nd November 2006

THAMES CASUALTY

A minor report, in the Evening Standard on page 4, referred to the casualty, who was apparently killed, when the small motor boat was hit by fragments of the rocket near the House of Commons on the 8th November.

The boatman confirmed he had been chartered by a gentleman, he thought Arab, who said he wanted to see London from the river.

The boat owner, who survived, confirmed that the man who had died was a Mr Omar Najjar.
He was very polite, paid cash, and interested in the history of London and the River Thames, the boatman said.

XXII

Epilogue

Wednesday 22nd November 2006

About 100kms NE of Islamabad

The 4x4 had had an uneventful journey so far. Dai Evans was driving, with Harry sitting alongside. The road was very poor, potholes, ill-defined borders and with unfenced big drops on the mountainside.

They carried no markings on the vehicle. A dirty civilian Toyota. They were dressed like many country Pakistanis. And it was very cold.

They had been heading in a NE direction towards the border of Pakistan controlled Kashmir.

Intelligence gathering had indicated considerable activity in the region, involving a Kashmir militant group, linked to the prescribed organisation Jaish-e-Mohammed. This organisation had had contact with the British Pakistani, Rashid Rauf, living in Pakistan, who had put the UK airline bomb plotters in touch with Al-Qaeda.

Harry, lost in his thoughts, was tired, frustrated, and angry at the inevitable delays that always occurred in this part of the world.

He was edgy, thinking about Anna, wondering where their relationship would go, if it would survive, wondering what was happening to the Deputy, and his continuing fight against the new DG and the increasing politicisation of the Service, which would undoubtedly neutralise its effectiveness.

The situation here in Islamabad was clearly worsening with so many factions struggling to be top dog. As a result the rate of political 'accidents' seemed to be on the increase.

Since he had recruited his 'support' staff from the UK there seemed less of the internal sniping and products of the rumour mill. Perhaps a little more respect had been created, on the other hand perhaps old enmities were being better hidden.

His 'support' staff, namely his driver, Dai Evans, was well versed in the region's idiosyncrasies and corruption. Quiet, but deadly. The face told you a lot. Not the sort of face to mess with, particularly after a few beers, and you thought you might like to take the p**s out of the British Army.

Suddenly the sound of machine gun fire interrupted his thoughts as he saw bullet spurts in the sand, earth, and tarmac, crossing the road about 30 metres in front of them.

Dai had braked, and slewed the 4x4 into the lee of the hill, giving some protection.

Harry and Dai scrambled into the rear of the 4x4, grabbing their SA80A2 weapons, and exiting on the leeward side.

They split immediately, Harry moving to the left round the bluff in the general direction of the hostile fire, Dai Evans meanwhile, laying down some rapid covering and diversionary fire.

Visibility was average, not too bad, but definition of movement would be difficult to pick up.

Firing in both directions stopped. Silence followed, broken only by the mewing of a lofty bird, clearly disturbed.

Harry knew he could trust Dai to the hilt. A man with that sort of SAS experience is just the man you want on your right flank!

He crawled forward to try and give himself some sort of observation point, and found a convenient spot adjacent to rock cover which gave him a view of about 500 metres forward, and slightly more laterally.

From his vantage point he could see Dai moving slowly to the right, well below any sight line from the firing source.

Suddenly the silence was shattered as the LMG opened up again, obviously firing indiscriminately, strafing the road and ground immediately in front of its position.

Fortunately the 4x4 was well hidden behind the bluff, as far as Harry could see looking back.

Suddenly another LMG opened up, this time located about 400 metres away, at 10 o'clock to his position, laying down fire onto the same area as the first.

Harry recognised immediately that the situation was going from bad to worse, and with only small arms and limited ammunition, their options were strictly limited.

To withdraw to the 4x4 would be fatal. They would be picked off immediately.

From his position he could see Dai, and indicated by hand signal for him to skirt round the bluff and join him in his partially protected position.

If push came to shove, then the two of them could lay down some combined, albeit limited, firepower if the opposition advanced.

It took Dai about ten minutes to join him, the two LMGs intermittently firing random bursts.

During one of the short lulls, Harry thought he heard the sound of a helicopter, this being quickly drowned out by the next bursts from the LMGs.

Suddenly the thumping sound of a low flying helicopter drowned out everything, as a Pakistan

Army Aviation Corp (AAC) Bell AH-1 Cobra came flying up the defile from the valley below.

Harry looked up as the aircraft, at low altitude, crossed over his position and that of the opposition in front of him.

Suddenly he saw one of the LMG two man crew stand up, looking skywards, before picking up their weapon and ammunition, and attempting to run. This was replicated about 10 seconds later by the other LMG crew, as both made their retreat as quickly as possible.

The Cobra by now was spinning on its own axis, as its weapon systems were brought to bear on the retreating tribesmen.

Chattering 7.62mm miniguns on the Cobra caught up with them, tossing them in the air like rag dolls, before falling to the ground motionless.

Less than four minutes had covered the action.

The noise of the Cobra was then joined by another helicopter coming into view, an AAC Aerospatiale Puma 330. Having followed the Cobra up the defile the Puma kept low to the ground, one of its side doors open, with a helmeted figure in an orange jump suit kneeling by the opening.

Harry, half kneeling, waved, which was returned by the figure.

Where the hell have they come from, he thought? Anyway who gives a damn, what the hell, grab a ride!

The Puma rapidly descended, landing about 30 metres in front of Harry and Dai.

The figure in the open door gestured to them to get on board quickly, to which they both responded readily!

Dai stumbled once as made his way to the helicopter, Harry grabbing his arm before Dai shook him off.

As they rolled onto the helicopter floor, it took off rapidly, turning quickly to minimise its silhouette in case of other armed groups returning fire.

Harry turned to Dai to see him pulling up his trouser leg, exposing a bullet flesh wound in his calf, apparently having missed the bone, passing straight through. Dai explained it was a ricochet, not a direct shot, therefore not as serious.

It was still bleeding, so the helmeted figure pulled open the medical chest, to get bandages to staunch the flow.

Harry, concerned for Dai, had not noticed two other helmeted occupants in the Puma, one now tapping him on the shoulder.

Harry turned, faintly irritated, as he was concerned and trying to assist in Dai's treatment.

In the half-light he could not initially make out the man's features, who now smiled, and said,

'Bonjour Harry, I have always said I am happy to be of assistance to you!'

'My God, Alain Dubois! What the hell are you doing here, for Christ sake?'

'A long tale Harry! Let's go through that when we are safely back in Islamabad, plus, I can hardly hear you in this noisy machine! Carry on, sort out your colleague.'

'Fine Alain. Who's your colleague?' nodding at the other figure.

'Not mine; yours, I think.'

The other figure came over, hand outstretched.

'Goddam it Harry, when you're around nobody gets any peace!'

Harry, eyes widening as he recognised Jack DeCosta, shook his head in disbelief, whilst taking his hand, saying,

'Christ, if this is a UN party, then nobody told me!

What's with Peace? If you want peace, then scarper back to the US of A!

The problem is Jack, you b*****s get involved in these regional problems, then we Brits have to come and help you sort them out!'

Jack threw a fake punch at Harry's jaw, whilst laughing and nodding his head in agreement.

'Yeah, right! Go on, sort out your buddy.'

Having got Dai Evans properly bandaged up, Harry then turned to Alain and Jack.

'How did you find us, or was that just a bloody great fluke?'

Jack spoke first,

'As you know we, you and the French, have been monitoring everything in this damn country for a long time.

Phones, electronic surveillance of cells and mobiles, satellite observation, drones, men on the ground, our Special Forces, your SAS, etc.

When your friend Inspector Chaudhry filled us in on where you were going, we merely started to track your mobile signal. With one or two minor blips of about 15 seconds each, we knew where you were within about 100 metres.

That's how we tracked you, AND, yes, because of shared Intel between us, the French and Inspector Chaudhry, we decided you might need some backup, particularly bearing in mind where you were heading.'

Harry was silent for a minute.

'I appreciate your assistance, and it wasn't a moment too soon, but our own Intel had indicated that a person of interest was prepared to deal with us. They would provide significant details as to the illicit arms trade carrying on in the NE region, source of weaponry, funding, internal and external to Pakistan, and of particular interest, the clandestine training of UK and European nationals by elements of the Taliban and other terrorist groups, to return and carry out terrorist attacks in the UK, Europe, and the USA, under the banner of a World Jihad. Specific information would cover the recent batch of UK Pakistani airline bombers of August 10th.

I recognise that we were certainly putting ourselves at risk, but the informant was only prepared to meet on his home turf, hence our journey into the North East, and happily your intervention!'

Jack DeCosta started to speak,

'Harry, I appreciate you have to act indep……….'

Harry butted in,

'Yes Jack, before you go on, the last point I was going to make was that I think I'm getting too old for junkets like this. I want to make my pension, if I can!

I think when I get back I'll put in for a home posting. Something dangerous, like looking after records at Vauxhall Cross! I'm sure the old man will find a little backwater for me.'

Jack laughed,

'It won't happen Harry. Admin? Bore you rigid. No, you and I have a few years left. We can't let these sons of bitches win, can we?

Come on buddy, we've got to shake on that.'

They shook hands.

The Puma rattled through the high country towards Islamabad, whilst a man, in a small village near

Masjid, wondered what had happened to his visitors.

London

In London the Deputy was putting the finishing touches to a strategic and operational plan that he was sure, he thought sarcastically, would meet with the DG's complete approval and agreement. Or maybe not!

The game never really changes. New broom, new strategy, new words, new music. By the time the changes are made, another new DG arrives. Strike up the band, here we go again!

However, he was sure of one thing.

He would want Harry Baxter back at Vauxhall Cross to be involved with the Implementation/Change Team, whatever that is, and, if that was the outcome.

Plus, on an operational level, he would like to have a discussion with him about Liaison Officers, and whether that was something the Service ought to consider in the future?

One good thing about Harry were his definite views about Defence of the Realm, plus he told it as it is. Perhaps most importantly he didn't take 'prisoners'!

2007 could possibly, or, more likely probably, be a very eventful year!

Friday 24th November 2006

MI5 Thames House Millbank London

Across the river, in a second floor office, a middle ranking MI5 officer, Peter Connelly, was adding to his case file notes.

It was an unusual surveillance that had been employed over the last six months.
The senior partner, Ladislav Hornik, of one of the UK's top ten accountancy practices, was originally Slovakian, before taking British citizenship, and is married to Asiya, born in Tajikistan. Her professional capacity is as a trade negotiator for a UK Government Department dealing with that region, and bordering countries, including China.
It would appear that one of the major clients of the accountancy practice, an Energy Supply company, is of interest to China. Confidential information concerning the company's strategy, energy relationships, UK and European gas and oil supply lines and pricing, had apparently been passed by the senior partner to his wife, and then onto contacts at the Chinese Embassy in London.
A further complexity had arisen due to the hidden intimate relationship of the partners' wife with a senior figure at the Foreign Office, who has specific responsibility for the China region.
Sensitivities, perhaps shared during 'pillow talk', are the stuff of nightmares for the Government of the day, hence continuing surveillance.
The combination of UK and overseas territories meant that MI5 would need to liaise with MI6 sooner rather than later. However, as yet, Connelly had received no such instruction.
From electronic surveillance and intercepts of telephone, mobile, emails, satellite comms, etc, it was becoming clear that the energy company was a target. For what, was not yet defined. Options could include, among several; acquisition by foreign interests, caused by significant reduction in share price if full financial information and risk areas were made public; or removal of a major

competitor, thereby increasing reliance on the remainder of the energy market, therefore, as a direct result, increasing dependence on fewer suppliers, and, as a consequence, probable significant uplifts in unit pricing of energy.

Chinese Government and related interests play the long game, so clarity at this time was difficult. What was the basic strategy was unknown, but clearly a target had been identified.

Bearing in mind the dependence of Europe on Russian gas supplies, and to a lesser extent oil, there could be some connection therefore between the actions of the Chinese in trying to counter the Russian influence.

At this time purely speculative, but certainly an avenue to be investigated.

Significant concerns were being expressed in Government as to the over-dependence on imported energy into the UK, whether by tankers from the Gulf, or trans-European gas and oil pipelines.

Sabotage and blowing up of pipelines was occurring on a frequent basis in Iraq, the thought of this type of action being transferred into Europe was giving the collective heads of the EU a major headache.

If only one pipeline across Europe was put out of action the consequences could be disastrous for the UK. Its gas storage capacity compared to France, Germany and Holland was measured in days, not weeks.

'When the lights go out' was a nightmare scenario a step too far, and frankly, currently, all too easy to achieve.

Peter Connelly picked up his telephone to seek clearance for contact with MI6.

The level of activity had been increasing in recent weeks. Safe, rather than sorry, crossed his mind. Action this Day.

In Whitehall, in the Foreign Office, a senior civil servant, responsible for the China region, was looking forward to his evening with Asiya.

She, treading a path of her choice, but increasingly unsafe, wondered how long she could continue before her relationships and true loyalties were discovered.

Unknown to them all, events in Russia were unfolding, which could change the order of things, drastically and dramatically.

To the West of Minsk, in the Belarus, the gas pipeline from Russia splits into three.

One goes directly East, to a terminal on the Baltic Sea.

The second goes directly across Poland to Berlin in Germany.

The third goes into Poland, serving Warsaw, before re-joining the pipeline going directly to Germany.

--

That particular night, at about 0200hrs, a reconnaissance party, well camouflaged in black, heads covered in balaclavas, was practicing a dry run to the West of Minsk where the single pipeline splits into three.

They had no idea when the op would go live. They needed to be prepared when ordered.

In Moscow plans were being made. Not by the Government, but by the Bratva, the Russian mafia.

47470843R00221

Made in the USA
Charleston, SC
11 October 2015